GRACIE'S GHOST

THE REVELATION

A testimony of the power behind even the weakest faith

"Compelling characters and a legitimate 'page-turner'"
Paul Bliss – Rosemount, MN

"A wonderful story."
Brian Pavek – Maple Grove, MN

"A surprising and moving conclusion."
Todd Bechausen – Enid, OK

"If Fred Loeb went through half of the stuff he writes about in this book, he is one messed up dude!"
David Blackstone – Burnsville, MN

Novels
by
Frederick Loeb

The Patterson Chronicles
Gracie's Ghost – The Haunting
Gracie's Ghost – The Return
Gracies' Ghost – The Revelation

The Patterson Chronicles

VOLUME 3

Gracie's Ghost

The Revelation

FREDERICK LOEB

Copyright © 2010 by
FREDERICK LOEB

All rights reserved.

SFC Publishing Division

SFC Publishing, Write Right Ink
1210 Lillian Street
Jordan, MN 55352
1.952.239.4238

All rights reserved. No part of this publication may be reproduced, stored in a retrieval system, or transmitted, in any form or by any means, electronic, mechanical, photocopying, recording, or otherwise, without the written prior permission of the author.

ISBN 13: 978-1-456-34283-8
ISBN 10: 1-456-34283-5

Cover Design by Write Right Ink
Interior Set in Garamond, Trebuchet MS, Calisto MT, Calibri, Copperplate Gothic Plate Light and Lynn True Type fonts by Write Right Ink

Printed in the United States of America

Dedication

In every meaningful way this book is a tribute to my wife, Lynn. Two people who are married for a long time owe a large chunk of any success to their ability to draw strength from the other person. In ways beyond description, next to Christ, Lynn has always been and remains my strength.

On a lighter note, this book is also dedicated to my four younger sisters and little brother all of whom have had to put up with me all their natural lives. Only recently, after watching the classic 1979 film "Apocalypse Now," have I begun to understand the terrifying reality with which my siblings have had to contend all these many years.

My oldest sister is absolutely convinced some kind of midlife crisis drove me to write the three volumes of the "Gracie's Ghost" series. I can only imagine she must know a lot of men around my age who just have to put down on paper their memoirs before they croak. Well, time is short so she may have a point. Then again, my oldest sister has always believed deep down she knows everything, I hardly ever know anything and that which I do know isn't worth knowing anyway. There has never been any arguing of this because my oldest sister always, always has the last word in everything.

So, allow this author the opportunity to set the record straight: the original inspiration for the three "Gracie" books was a program on the History Channel.

Late one sleepless night I was watching a documentary about aircraft carrier disasters on the History Channel. The program included a personal interview with an elderly guy (oddly, about my age) who told a story about the terrible 1967 fire aboard the *U.S.S. Enterprise* CVN 65 on station in the Gulf of Tonkin. In this filmed interview, the gentleman described how on the day of this great conflagration he had received a "Dear John" letter from his girlfriend back home. His voice weakened noticeably and his eyes turned wet as he explained how he lost three of his best friends and the only woman he has ever loved the day the *Enterprise* blew up.

Decades after it had happened, this veteran still carried the load of all he had lost that day. At that time I knew there was a very human story there to be had. All I had to do was flesh it out a bit.

Now, I'll admit, even to my oldest sister, I have drawn from more than a small amount of personal experience with similar circumstances from my own life to help write this series. However, that does not make the series my memoirs and I can prove it.

After all, if "Gracie's Ghost" volumes 1, 2, & 3 were actually my memoirs and not fiction, I would not have been as successful in keeping the completely unbelievable back stories offered so readily by my four sisters and little brother out of print as I was. It would have all been too ripe stuff for blackmail for me to resist. So, there.

As Colonel Kurtz in "Apocalypse Now" would say with truly disturbing relish, *"The horror…"* continues.

F.L.

The Patterson Chronicles
Volume 3

Gracie's Ghost
The Revelation

FREDERICK LOEB

SFC

Chapter 1
34 years AG (After Gracie)

0930 hours
11 September 2006
U.S.S. *Hornet* Museum
Hornet Pier
US Naval Air Station
Alameda, California

Steeg Patterson wouldn't admit it, but he almost forgot Carol was on the bus with him. When the fully loaded reunion charter slowed to approach the chain link fence and crept toward the gate at the foot of the pier, as quick as that, his awareness of the 'here and now' left him.

Through the tinted windows the white-on-blue 'U.S.S. Hornet Museum' sign beckoned bathed in the glorious brilliance of morning sunlight. Behind the sign, the Essex Class warship towered tall and proud, gleaming and freshly painted in battleship gray. Thirty-six years earlier Steeg was chipping paint on the same ship and the sight of the massive bow rising high above him now pulled Steeg back through all the years that had passed; back to the ship's decommissioning; back to the dirt and grime of putting the boat into "mothballs;" back to the last time the ship had almost killed him.

He was unprepared for the conflicting rush of anxiety laced with uncontainable excitement. Seated behind him, Paul "Teddy Bear" Muggins, his old shipmate who had contacted him months earlier about the ship's reunion, laughed watching Steeg hurriedly release his seatbelt buckle, jump to his feet, and with a quick darting movement, deftly step past his still seated wife to the center aisle. As soon as the bus driver opened the door, Steeg was the first person to exit the vehicle.

No longer shielded by the tinted glass of the bus windows, the sun's glare was almost painful. Slivers of magnified light bounced violently off the splintered, breeze-stirred surface of San Francisco Bay. From his shirt pocket, Steeg pulled out a pair of sunglasses and slipped them on within two steps into the sunlight. With his shades in place, he turned to see Bear, Bear's wife Sue and Carol step from the bus. They, too, shielded their eyes from the sun with quickly found sunglasses.

Sheepishly, Steeg walked up to take his wife's hand, silently apologizing for his rudeness.

"You almost stepped on my feet, Steeg," Carol scolded mildly.

"I'm sorry, Sweetie," he gave her a quick hug around her waist and steered her toward the gate.

The four of them led the way for the rest of the reunion attendees. Proceeding on the long concrete pier to the forward brow that led to the Officers' Quarterdeck, the magnificence of the *U.S.S. Hornet* CVS-12 took him over. Steeg released Carol's hand to move ahead.

Unlike Steeg, for Paul Muggins this was not the first trip to the restored aircraft carrier. Bear's first visit to the museum occurred two years earlier when he and fellow V-3 Division crew member Karl Klinger attended the 2004 Hornet reunion. This time around, Karl stayed home while Paul brought Sue, his wife of more than thirty years, convincing her to come after he had talked Steeg Patterson into attending the reunion.

Almost four decades had passed since the two comrades in arms had seen each other and the four of them were still younger than most of the other reunion attendees, able to easily outpace the trailing group from the bus. Each anxious step they took increased their lead in front of the older veterans and soon they reached the twin ladders leading to the elevated forward gangway and the ship's Quarterdeck. Bear took pleasure watching Steeg strain in amazed wonder at the immense aircraft carrier's superstructure stretching high above them – a warship upon which both men had served during the worse years of the Vietnam War.

"I can't believe it," Steeg kept repeating, grinning like a Cheshire cat swinging his head far left to far right trying to capture the entire length of the ship in one continuous view. "I really thought they scrapped her!"

A step behind, Carol Patterson swept aside a windblown lock of dark brown hair streaked with hints of gray. A small laugh telegraphed her reply. "We know, Dear. You said the same thing at dinner last night."

"Yeah, yeah, I know," Steeg apologized. "It's just that, well, look at her! She's magnificent! I just can't believe it. I really believed they scrapped her!"

Carol, Sue and Bear shared another laugh.

"I can't believe it!" Steeg repeated yet once more. "I don't remember the darn boat being this big, do you, Bear?"

"She's big, alright." Bear smiled broadly. He knew what Steeg was feeling. It was the same feeling he had two years earlier and still had – a feeling as if some things didn't have to die; a feeling that, despite the years that had passed, there was proof they were part of something that could last forever; something immortal.

Too hurriedly, Steeg took the lead up the ladder two steps at a time and made the sharp turn onto the gangway colorfully trimmed with red-white-blue bunting and an expansive white-on-blue banner that read "*U.S.S. Hornet* CVS-12". Within three steps up the inclined ramp, Carol's shallow complaint from behind pulled his head back around.

Carol stood one step on the ramp with both white-knuckled hands locked onto the rail, her eyes staring hard at the distant water of the bay below her feet. Real fear pulled across her face and Steeg could see she was terrified.

He walked back to her, carefully placing a calming hand over both of hers' still clutching fast to the railing.

"Hey, Sweetie-Petie, how you doin'?"

A small, sideways wince preceded an insecure stutter.

"I'm okay. I'm okay." She trembled as she added, "Really, I'm okay. I just didn't know it was this high up, that's all."

Bear and Sue stood on the landing behind Carol. Sue placed a reassuring hand on Carol's shoulder as she commented how she didn't like heights, either.

"I'm okay," Carol weakly offered once more.

Steeg nodded his apologies to Bear. "Sorry about this, guys. It's her first boat. She'll be fine in a moment."

"No problem," Bear fingered his sunglasses to the top of his nose. "Take your time."

Steeg wrapped an arm around Carol's waist and directed her to look straight ahead. "Just look at the boat. There's no reason to look down, so don't, okay? Just take one step at a time and keep looking up at the boat."

Carol looked up to the superstructure with its forward Admiral's and Navigation bridges blocking out the sky. As she stepped hesitantly following Steeg's lead, her natural curiosity got the best of her. With her initial anxiety still thick in her voice, she uttered a classic Carol-ism: "Who cleans all those windows up there?"

"Probably the curator," Steeg answered. "They haven't the money to contract it out, I'm sure."

"Actually," Bear offered from behind, his arm wrapped around Sue's to help relieve any uncertainty she may be experiencing. "They have volunteers, lots of them. All sorts of people work here for nothing just to help keep the ship looking good."

"That's nice," Carol acknowledge sincerely, keeping her eyes on the ship and making excellent progress up the gangway. "It's just like church, then, isn't it?"

It was the second Carol-ism since they had left the bus and it caused Steeg a sudden blinking spasm as they continued the next few steps.

"Just like church? How do you mean?"

"Well, like in relying on volunteers to help out – churches do that a lot." She concluded, "They have to. Without volunteers, nothing would get done."

Noticeably relaxed, Carol smiled as she completed the trek up the gangway and stepped onto the steel plating of the Officers' Quarterdeck. She stepped away from Steeg, flung her arms open, and with a quick twirl, offered a prideful "Tah-dah!"

"You made it!" Sue said, walking up to her and giving a congratulatory hug.

Bear and Steeg looked at each other in unshielded befuddlement over the fuss.

Carol completed a second pirouette and quickly interpreted the blank expressions of the two men as muted masculine ridicule. Lightly but firmly, she whipped a backhanded slap at Steeg's shoulder.

"Hey!" Steeg protested only mildly, feigning a painful grab for his upper arm. "What was that for?"

"For making fun of me," his wife answered sincerely.

"I didn't say anything!"

"Yeah, but you thought it – both of you did."

Sue turned sideways toward Bear, slapping her husband on the shoulder, too. "Shame on you!"

Bear stepped back from the line of fire. "Shame on me?!"

Sue scolded her husband with a wagging finger. "Just because someone is afraid of heights doesn't mean you're better than that person."

Bear and Steeg shared a confused, panicked glance as together they quickly turned toward the cool, shaded darkness of Hanger Bay One, quickly putting distance between them and the two women.

At the inboard edge of the Quarterdeck on a white pedestal the brilliantly polished and gleaming brass of the ship's bell rested proudly.

"They kept the ship's bell!" Steeg exclaimed with relief, welcoming the opportunity to change the subject toward something appropriate and away from the physical threat of additional female attacks.

"Yes, they did," Bear agreed.

Almost reverently, both men stood before the bell. Neither man touched it. Both women did, though.

"It's so pretty!" Carol remarked, gliding her finger tips gently down the curve of reflective metal.

"And big, too!" Sue's hand followed an almost identical track.

Both men grimaced as their wives finished stroking the bell. The two women turned toward the hanger bay as Steeg quickly pulled a clean handkerchief from his back pocket and rubbed away any telltale streaks or finger prints. What could he say to help the women understand? The ship's bell represented the ship's soul. Men serving their country had died on this ship. No less than Gettysburg, or any other great battlefield, The *U.S.S. Hornet* was sacred ground.

Bear caught up with the women, falling in between the two of them as he explained they were now in Hanger Bay One. He led them to the forward center deck elevator and proceeded to show them one of his personal three favorite locations on the ship: the elevator control panel. His other two favorite places were the elevator control panels at elevators number two and three. During his years of service, Bear was the leading elevator control operator for the V-3 Hanger Deck Division, so it made perfect sense that he would want to show the ladies what he knew best about the ship – the elevators.

Bear began to explain how this particular elevator was used during flight operations, his arm sweeping before them. Steeg brought up the rear where, lagging a good half-dozen paces behind while Bear's words unintelligibly echoed throughout the hanger bay. Nearing the center of the deck, Steeg slowed to a troubling halt as a startlingly real memory unfolded before him.

He stood at the very spot where, in 1969, he was nearly killed. The memory was as fresh as if it were the day before. It was after the Apollo Eleven recovery operations. He remembered the sudden upward roll of the ship at sea; the nose wheel tiller bar slamming into his midsection as it swung brutally to port, lifting him from his feet and catapulting him across the hanger bay. Then the darkness that followed.

Numbly, he turned and walked toward the roller curtains on the port side of the bay. He stopped there and stared at the spot where they had told him he had slammed onto the deck and lain in a bloodied heap, jerking in spasms. Steeg didn't remember any of that. He only remembered waking up in Sickbay three days later, his head wrapped in bandages, his left side heavily bruised from neck to elbow, unable to move and his memory of the previous year and one-half almost completely gone.

Chapter 2
The Tour

The clatter and clash of air operations suddenly filled Steeg's ears just as real and disturbing as it had during the war. He turned toward the startling sounds and the hanger deck was once again crammed with aircraft. It was all there – planes strapped to the deck with tie-down chains; belching yellow tow tractors efficiently pulling helicopters into too-small spaces; aluminum wheel chocks banging onto the deck; Yellow Shirts with whistles blowing, men in blue shirts, others in brown shirts, green shirts, or purple shirts, all scurrying in different directions across the deck. Steeg turned and waved his plane handling crew to follow him into Hanger Bay Two.

He crossed the fire door track dividing bay one from bay two, passed the fuel station on his right where the number two elevator waited at hanger deck level. It was an easy step up and across the short ramp and then out into the stiff morning breeze wrapped in the bright sunlight. Continuing across the elevator platform, Steeg stopped at the low guardrail at the far port side and wire safety net running the length of the elevator platform. He placed a foot on the guardrail to steady himself as he leaned over the side.

Through the safety net the wind-rippled harbor waters about twenty feet below turned from cool blue to a mosaic of black shaded splinters as somehow morning folded away into a stormy night. The elevator platform rocked in heavy heaves first to port and then to starboard. With each dip to port his hanger deck crew was pelted with the warm spray of over-wash from the Gulf of Tonkin. It was December 1968 again, with Steeg under the belly of an SH-3A helicopter straddling a wet, stubby tow bar, seconds away from attempting to swing the tow bar out from under the aircraft to mate with the waiting hook of the tow tractor. Once attached, his crew would pull the aircraft into the hanger bay and secure from flight ops for the night.

He turned to look down the length of the undercarriage toward the front of the helicopter. Through the darkness he could see Karl Klinger squatting below the nose looking back at him. The ship took another severe dip to port and another blast of spray slapped him across his face. He held his whistle tightly between clenched teeth and leveraged the tow bar up and into his chest, his booted toes gripping the deck as he prepared to push the bar out from under the aircraft. It was time to do this.

He blew his whistle hard, paused, and then blew a second whistle blast. Another pause as he braced himself even more firmly against the tow bar, bringing it tighter into his chest. He blew his whistle a third time and leaned his body into the effort.

With the third whistle, his fellow Yellow Shirt Karl Klinger banged on the cockpit window with his hands wide open in a "release brakes" signal. The plane captain behind the controls let go of the brakes at the exact moment the ship took an unexpected surge to starboard. The helicopter rolled forward.

Steeg's grip on the bar slipped. Without warning, the tow bar was under him, jerking him up from the deck as it swung hard aft and then around to the port side, passing over the elevator's low guardrail. The centrifugal force ripped Steeg's whistle soundlessly from his lips and his desperate grabs at the rain-

slick tubular steel tow bar were completely ineffective. In a blink, his body spun free from the bar and he was unceremoniously dumped over the port side of the elevator.

His eyes followed the arc of the tow bar as he relived the frightening moment, turning in a slow, almost trancelike motion toward the safety net running below the outboard length of elevator platform. The net had saved his life that night.

Consciousness returned to him in waves as the blackness slowly cleared to obscured night. His forehead throbbed with a strong, dull pain. Groggy, he could see the sea froth below being split by the prow of the ship. A murky figure emerged from the phosphorous glow rushing beneath him. The apparition took shape below him, rose from the water to float just above the wisps of pale blue-green neon trailing toward the stern. The figure turned to flesh and the woman who appeared looked right through him. A recognizable warm, dull ache filled him. Her deep brown eyes pulled him closer. She had the same familiar impish smile he remembered, the one that always preceded mischief or passion. He felt the familiar agony of unrecoverable loss.

Are you dead? Steeg thought. Her lips parted as if to say something, but he only heard the sea.

You don't feel dead to me... Maybe I'm the one who's dead.

Steeg remembered the odd comfort he had felt at the thought of his own death. He remembered laying face down in the wire cable safety net below the outboard edge of the elevator platform, gripping the netting hard enough to draw blood, pressing his face against the meshing desperately searching for Gracie. She was gone. He remembered the ache for her, a pain quickly followed by the real regret that he had not died that night.

A distant summons echoed out of the darkness. He could hear Bear's voice. The seas calmed, the darkness of the night receded as the sunlight and inconvenient harbor breezes returned. Steeg was pulled back to the present day.

"Here you are!"

His eyes wet with startling awareness, Steeg turned to see his friend cross the elevator platform toward him. His hands trembled as his voice cracked.

"It's so real!"

Bear nodded, placing an understanding hand on his friend's arm. "Yes. It's very real."

They looked at each other, neither man able to say anything more. With a shared nod in understanding the two men turned back toward the hanger bay where their wives patiently waited.

The tours were about to start. There were two tours: the below decks engineering tour and the above decks aviation/bridge tour. Having taken the aviation tour on his two previous visits to the ship, Bear suggested Steeg and Carol follow the above decks guide, while he and Sue would take the below decks engineering tour. Steeg was disappointed that the foursome would be split up, but Bear assured him they'd meet on the hanger deck after 30 to 40 minutes, where they would most certainly drop an embarrassing amount of money at the ship's store, and then explore what they could of the ship itself after that.

With all in agreement, Steeg and Carol collected themselves near the Captain's ladder in Hanger Bay One where the tour guide gave brief introductory remarks, some basic instructions on sticking with the tour, avoiding the temptation of striking out to explore the ship on one's own, and by all means, respecting all passageways chained off and marked with a large white sign with a broad red "X" on it. Under no circumstances would anyone be allowed to open any sealed hatch or door, and anyone who failed to follow these instructions would be removed from the ship.

As the tour guide concluded his prerequisite remarks, the small crowd of maybe a dozen visitors followed him up the ladder to the 02 level.

Carol leaned in close to whisper, "He isn't very nice, is he?"

Steeg shrugged. "Ex-Navy, Sweetie. They don't want people getting hurt, that's all. That and they don't want to get sued."

The ladder was uncomfortably steep, just as Steeg remembered. He also remembered cleaning and polishing the darn thing many times during his assigned duty with V-3 Division. The tour line followed single-file with Carol and Steeg bringing up the rear. At the 01 level on the starboard bulkhead, the ladder made a ninety degree turn to continue upward. Steeg had to pause briefly to catch his breath.

Carol leaned in close to him. "Are you okay?"

Steeg nodded. "You go ahead. I'm right behind you."

Carol tried not to let her concern show as she turned to follow the others to the 02 level and the ridiculously small square landing waiting for them there. Steeg followed only a few steps behind. When they reached the 02 level landing, Carol squeezed into the small space crammed with the tour group, but Steeg remained on the top step to only partially enter the area. From his recessed position at the rear of the crowd he could make out only the top of the tour guide's head. Nevertheless, he immediately recognized the space in which he stood half-in and half-out.

"This first door leads to the Combat Information Center – or C-I-C – the nerve center of the ship during combat operations,"

Steeg heard the guide say. "There is a connecting passageway that leads to CATCC – Carrier Air Traffic Control Center – where air traffic controllers tracked and controlled the launching and recovery of all aircraft. The rooms are small and pretty tight, so watch your step and your heads."

Subdued, the crowd shuffled one person at a time through the doorway leading into CATCC. Steeg cleared the last step on the ladder and followed Carol with a directing hand on her hip. A shivering chill of giddy excitement pulsed through him as he followed his wife into the small, dimly lit room.

Ahead and to the right was the familiar Plexi-glass wall behind which he had, thirty-nine years earlier, learned to write backwards with a grease pencil and kept track of incoming aircraft. Individual panels were exactly as he remembered them, each with its own particular set of chart and status markings. A line of four radar units fronted the clear plastic wall, each with a high-backed, leather padded stool where the air traffic controller would sit. A narrow, rubber inlaid walkway separated the row of stools from a command desk from which the duty officer would monitor activity without getting in the way of things. At the rear of CATCC was an open doorway leading to the much smaller and Spartan-equipped Carrier Controlled Approach room which, when manned, would 'catch' incoming aircraft passed to it by the CATCC controllers. In CCA there was another Plexi-glass status board facing a single metal desk with a lone radio communications box with several rows of buttons and a frequency control dial. The duty CCA controller would work with the pilot in final approach via radio to help him line up with the centerline on the flight deck and "Catch the Ball" on the Fresnel Optical Landing System.

As the tour guide continued his presentation to the group from behind the command desk in CATCC, Steeg took Carol's hand to quietly lead her as he worked his way through the small crowd and toward the door that led to the CCA. He had to stand behind the CCA status board one more time.

"Do you know this place?" Carol whispered softly to not disrupt the tour guide as he continued his explanation of the function of CATCC and some of the salient points of carrier air traffic control operation.

Steeg nodded in response as he carefully side-stepped his way with Carol in tow. The tour guide mention the secure nature of CATCC and CIC and how only designated personnel were allowed in specific parts of the ship generally: snipes were not allowed in certain above deck areas such as CATCC and CIC. Air dales weren't allowed below decks in engine and ordinance spaces. Navigation, the Captain's and Admiral's bridges were separate worlds unto themselves. For ship's company these territorial jurisdictions where made clear early and rigorously adhered to continually. Sailors who went where they didn't belong were dealt with quickly and sometimes severely, including brig time.

Steeg leaned toward Carol's ear. "The OC Division was my first duty station when I reported aboard in '67. OC Division is CATCC."

It was Carol's turn to nod, but she followed Steeg whispered explanation with another whispered question. "What does 'OC' stand for?"

"Operations-Control," he whispered back. "It's part of the Operations Department. There are several divisions in the Operations Department."

Carol nodded again, only to ask another question. "Such as?"

Steeg smiled and suppressed a chuckle. He was about to expound on the various Operations Department divisions for electronics, weather, combat information, air traffic control and photography when he heard the tour guide direct the group toward the CCA, the room he had to get into. So, instead of impressing his wife with his spotty recollections of *U.S.S. Hornet* operational structure, he simply said, "I'll tell you later."

Barely two-thirds of the crowd could fit into CCA. With Steeg and Carol standing nearer to the doorway than most of the others, they were close on the tour guide's heels as he stepped into the small compartment. Inside CCA, Steeg hugged the forward bulkhead and sidestepped his way toward the Plexi status board, leaving Carol with the other attendees. At the board, he couldn't resist sliding behind it to observe the tour guide's presentation through the plastic pane. It was a much tighter fit than he remembered, but then again, he was thirty-nine years older now and he carried just enough of a middle-aged paunch to prove it. Behind the status board in the CCA, Steeg felt as if some kind of temporal tunnel opened up and sucked him back to 1967.

The gathered group turned their attention toward the tour guide. "This is the center for Carrier Controlled Approach. In this room, aircraft status would be tracked on the board behind you," The guide raised a pointed finger in Steeg's direction, pausing before continuing as he noticed Steeg's odd expression from behind the glass. Carol turned to follow the guide's direction and saw her husband with an almost completely blank, trance-like look about him.

The tour guide continued. "And, the controller would be at this simple desk in radio contact working with the incoming pilot on final approach."

The tour guide paused for a moment, quickly looking back with curious concern at Steeg before continuing with his explanation of the responsibilities of the CCA and the people who would staff this phase of air operations. Steeg, staring at nothing, had willingly stepped through the temporal tunnel and hadn't heard a word.

The space behind the status board seemed to expand as the plastic wall moved away several inches and Steeg reached over to scribble the new positioning for aircraft 206, an inbound S-2D Tracker of Squadron VS-35. Gone was his paunch. He could move easily. He was recharged with energy he had forgotten he had. He adjusted his sound-powered telephone headset to fit more comfortably over his Hornet baseball cap and made the necessary corrections on the status entry.

Behind the desk, Second Class Air Traffic Controller William "Hutch" Hutchinson, also with his earphones on, noted the change with a nod and continued his instructions to the pilot.

The door leading to the outside center passageway opened and in walked Third Class Petty Officer Pilar Rodriguez carrying a manageable bundle. "Mail call!"

A collective cheer rose from CATCC, with several sailors hurrying through the doorway to help distribute the fruit of today's most anticipated event. For sailors at sea, mail from home was as vital as chow time.

Wired into the phone jack behind the status board, Steeg was tied to his spot. He anxiously waited for Rodriguez to nod, or offer another regretful shake of his head, to indicate whether he had something for him in today's mail. Maybe today he'd have a letter. Gracie's last letter, several weeks old and wasting away in his wallet, had suffered too much punishment from repeated unfolding and folding. Maybe today there would be a letter.

Rodriguez slipped his arm around the rear of the status board, a single envelope in his hand. Like a man starving for a scrap of food, Steeg grabbed the light blue par avian style envelope. The address was in Gracie's handwriting.

"Thank God!" He mouthed, his fingers seeking out the corner of the envelope flap. He stopped and looked up as the duty officer at the desk barked at him.

"Patterson!" Hutchinson pointed at the board. Steeg had missed the update for incoming aircraft 203.

Embarrassed, Steeg shoved the unopened envelope into his back pocket, scurried to the far corner of the board as he pushed down on the button of his phones' mouthpiece. "Say again status of 203."

He got the update and immediately replaced the previous entry with the new information. Through the glass he could see the petty officer shake his head without further comment.

Steeg stayed focused on the job at hand until all aircraft had been recovered. As soon as the last aircraft was passed from CCA to the Landing Signal Officer (LSO) on the flight deck, Steeg leaned back against the bulkhead behind the status board and retrieved the letter from his back pocket.

At last, a letter. What's been the hold up, anyway?

Her handwriting was beauty itself. He paused at her return address on the corner face of the envelope.

> Grace Ofterdahl
> 302A Gage Hall
> Mankato State College
> Mankato, MN

He ran his thumb across the ink, the loneliness swelling inside him. Carefully, he worked his finger under the flap to open the envelope in as damage-free a way as possible, opened the envelope, removed the single folded sheet of handwritten stationary, opened it and began to read.

April 17, 1967

Dear Steeg,
I'm sorry I haven't written you for so long. I've tried to write this letter at least a dozen times, but I haven't been able to. But now I have to and I still don't know how. So I'm just going to say it and hope you'll understand.

I'm marrying Stewart Smalley in June. We met at school. I fell in love with him. He asked me to marry him and I've said yes.

I know I'm not doing a good job writing this, and I really can't explain it all. I don't want to hurt you, even though I know that's what I am doing. I'm sorry. You're really a great guy. You'll always be very special to me. I'm sorry.

Thank you for loving me. It's meant more to me than you know. Stay safe.

Grace

The room spinning, Steeg's knees gave way to wedge tightly against the back of the status board framing. His slide to the floor came to an abrupt halt, his body dropping only a few inches lower. His lungs tried to work but air seemed in short supply. Something terrifying was gripping the inside of his chest and Steeg was suddenly very afraid. Gracie was leaving him. No, she had left him! She left him alone – completely alone. And now, he couldn't breathe. It was death. No, it was something worse than death.

"You okay?" Concern clouding his face, Hutchinson poked his head around the frame of the status board.

All Steeg could weakly reply was, "Head break."

Hutchinson pulled on Steeg's arm to help him to a full standing, albeit uncertain, footing. The room distorted into a twisted swirl.

The temporal tunnel shrank away in a disconcerting turbulent blur. Steeg found himself behind the CCA status board. Most of the tour had collectively exited CCA for CATCC, ultimately to head into CIC where the tour would continue. Carol, a quizzical expression on her face, patiently waited where he had left her.

Embarrassed, a self conscious smile pulled at the corners of his mouth as he squeezed from behind the Plexi-glass to rejoin her. A step away from reaching for his wife's hand, Steeg glanced at a shadowy movement in the doorway leading to the outside passageway. A sense of hopelessness swallowed him whole, only to be immediately replaced by reluctant acceptance.

Gracie stood at the door looking back at him with her familiar mischievous smile. Steeg was not surprised.

Chapter 3
Reflections

Visiting the refurbished *U.S.S. Hornet* with all the memories it had to offer had been stimulating in surprising ways for Steeg, not the least of which included the frequent and frustrating reappearance of the ghostly specter of Gracie Ofterdahl. While on the old ship, everywhere he turned brought back vivid memories and startling, even revitalizing energy of youth long since lost. But the visit was also frustrating because he had grown hopeful over recent months some resolution had somehow been reached to his decades-long struggle against his self-imposed delusions of Gracie.

Since his discharge from the Navy thirty-six years earlier, whatever sense of normalcy Steeg had secured in his life he owed to Carol. For a long time after their marriage, he had managed with difficulty his Gracie hallucinations. It wasn't easy, and more than a little odd it had taken so many years of marriage before it could happen, but this last year they had finally cleared away the core problem by working through it together. Then, there was this reunion, the visit to the ship and Gracie's ghost returned as real as life itself.

Now, sharing a table in the hotel lounge with Paul Muggins, Steeg hid well the annoying and too familiar dull stab of pain across his upper abdomen. The discomfort lasted only a few moments before, to Steeg's relief, it eased away to nothing. He said a silent prayer of thanks for his new medication.

The 300-room San Mateo hotel was huge, worthy of a central bar-lounge of enormous size, a major consideration for the *Hornet* reunion committee in selecting the hotel for its annual conclave. Draped in the welcoming glow of subdued lighting, overstuffed leather chairs grouped about small round fabric-covered candlelit tables, the lounge wrapped around an expansive semicircular bar. Happy hour was almost over and the lounge was warmly seductive with its relative quiet. Steeg looked forward to the end of a long, tiring day.

Bear sipped his tall iced tea. Steeg slowly nursed a vodka martini appreciating the anesthetic effect beginning to take hold. Short bouts of reflexive finger drumming on the tablecloth punctuated the intervals between sips. Their table was situated midway between the bar and the broad bank of windows that overlooked an outside parking lot quickly falling into the dim light of mid-evening. The men waited more or less patiently for their wives to join them.

"Long day," Bear muttered.

"Yes, invigorating, too." Steeg agreed, taking another quick sip feeling the cold burn of the vodka slide all the way down. "It was a little tiring though, up and down all those ship ladders. I guess I'm not as young as I use to be."

Bear chuckled. "Who is?"

A sideways nod from Steeg: "Better than the alternative. I could be dead."

Steeg's second finger-staccato on the tabletop betrayed him, but Bear mistook it, assuming a shared concern over being late for dinner reservations. For at least the third time in the last five minutes, Bear looked down at his wristwatch. Noticing, Steeg asked his former shipmate how late the girls were. Bear shook his head saying they weren't late yet. Steeg nodded with a relaxed grin and said something about having time to burn.

Another quick, more strident shake of Bear's head accompanied yet another glance at his watch. "I didn't say that."

Steeg smiled, suppressing a chuckle with another short sip from his drink.

It struck Steeg odd that he and Bear, after all these years, were together again, sharing drinks, sharing laughs, feeling not as if they hadn't seen each other for nearly four decades, but more as if virtually nothing had changed. Sure, they were both older, both a little heavier, more gray with faces that held more telltale lines testifying to the reality of passing time. But sitting there now was comfortable, as if only an extended weekend had elapsed. For Steeg there was the additional comfort in the fact that Bear had been there during the time when he had struggled most with the reality of Gracie's ghost.

Bear was talking to him now, asking him if he remembered the Singapore mess with the race riot. Steeg nodded, raised eyebrows confirming he did indeed remember. In fact, he was remembering the last time he and Bear had actually spoken to each other. It had been September, 1973 and Bear could have no idea of the role he played in saving Steeg's life that night.

In 1973, a year had passed since Gracie had left for Boston with her fiancé, Roger Flint. A few weeks after that, Steeg's father died. The year that followed was a tailspin dive into despair for his family and himself as his struggle to hold everything together took its toll. Had it just been his father's death, or only his mother's emotional collapse, it would have been manageable. But Gracie had left him, again. Gracie was gone, again. He needed to mourn, but he could only mourn the loss of Gracie. And the emptiness was all too much to bear.

His despondency almost overtook him the night he stepped over the railing of the Washington Avenue Bridge joining the East and West Banks of the University of Minnesota. He didn't know why he hungered for the dark waters of the Mississippi River silently moving far below him, he only knew he did. He was less than a month returning to the University to resume his education after a year layoff helping his family, but now he could see no reason for the studies, the manic academic paper chase or any of it. The weight of all that had been lost and the darkness of the previous fourteen months were all too unbearable. Something deep and dark within him screamed for him to jump from that bridge. If he did, he would find relief. Holding on with one hand, all he had to do was let go of the railing and it would be done.

He didn't let go. A small voice, familiar and quite clear, told him to go home. Steeg listened to the small voice ask him how his family would feel if he were to do what he so desperately wanted to do. He resisted the answer, but the answer was irresistible – his death would annihilate his family. The loss of his father was still horribly real, and Steeg knew if he stepped off into the blackness the horror would be beyond anything his mother, his sisters and his younger brother could handle now.

Steeg turned toward the railing, holding fast with both hands and stood quiet for a long time. Finally, he swung a leg over and stepped back onto the safety of the concrete walkway. The small voice spoke again, telling him to go home, so he turned and took the long walk back to his shabby, off-campus rooming house where he kept a partially full fifth of Seagram's in the lower left hand drawer of his small, wobbly, old wooden desk.

Steeg was a third way into the bottle when the phone rang. Of all the people who would have called, he was stunned when he immediately recognized Bear's voice. Steeg's mother had given Bear the phone number and his old friend called to simply see how he was doing!

Steeg couldn't help but laugh and Bear, being Bear, laughed along with him. A sense of relief and a special kind of joy swept over him as he slurred his way through the most pleasant and accepting telephone conversation he had ever experienced. For more than an hour, they talked about the Navy, old friends, old enemies and what was happening now. At the end of it, Bear suggested they get together. Steeg agreed. He took down Bear's phone number, and just before hanging up, he promised to get back to him soon to set something up.

But 'soon' fell away as more pressing matters pulled at him. Over the succeeding days the severe emptiness returned. Somewhere along the way, he lost Bear's telephone number. Steeg never called his old Navy buddy to do anything.

Now, 33 years later, looking into the pale glow of a glass encased candle at the middle of the lounge table, Steeg took another sip of a dying martini. The wives were still missing. Bear was still babbling on about Singapore, Hong Kong and the Philippines in no particular order. In the outside parking lot, the evening sky was growing darker.

Steeg signaled the bar for another round, only to turn back when Bear asked if he remembered Harold Henderson. Steeg shook his head. Bear claimed Steeg had to remember Henderson seeing how Henderson, once a V-3 Division hanger deck Blue Shirt, was the guy who was chopped to pieces when he walked into a turning propeller of an S2-D Tracker on the flight deck. Steeg responded to this bit of old news with an acknowledging nod of awareness and a dark comment about how some things in aviation can be rude awakenings.

There was another shared laugh, but Steeg's laugh was subdued by a sudden urge to confess to Bear the role he had played that September night in 1973. It was something important and important things in life shouldn't be ignored. Steeg should just tell his friend, but he didn't know how.

The waitress brought the second round to their table, easily matching her placement of correct drinks with the correct person, and then with equal aplomb, removing the empties in one smooth, continuous movement.

Steeg raised his glass in a toast to old friends, their glasses clinked and Steeg commented on how he would have to cool it after this drink or he'd be sloshed by dinner time. Bear agreed, pointing to his glass and mouthing silently "Iced tea."

"You know, Bear," Steeg began hesitantly. "You, ah, actually saved my life once."

Bear shook his head as he placed his glass back onto the napkin coaster. "No, no, it wasn't me."

His friend's quick denial confused him.

Bear continued. "I told you it was the shipyard workers that went down that hole. I didn't do anything. It was all them."

Bear thought Steeg had meant the mishap on the *Hornet* during the 1970 decommissioning of the ship in Bremerton, Washington. Scraping rust and painting red-lead primer in an unventilated void, Steeg had succumbed to the fumes and passed out. Had Bear not found him in time and gone for help to get him out of that hole, Steeg would have died. The near fatal experience had shaken both men. Steeg remembered coming to lying on the deck with an oxygen mask over his face and hearing Bear's frantic whispered apologies. Perhaps this wasn't the time to bring up the other time Bear had saved his life.

His friend changed the subject. "So, Carol seems very nice."

Steeg agreed with another nod.

"How long you two been married?"

"Quite a while now, since '79. You and Sue?"

"Longer than that, actually - 1975. We dated since high school, though."

They exchanged their mutual congratulations, with Bear asking how two women could be so extraordinarily capable as to put up with two old farts like he and Steeg. Steeg was too embarrassed to answer the question honestly.

"Hard to say, Paul."

"Yeah, but you did good…"

"You, too."

"Now, you didn't know Carol when you were in the Navy, did you?"

Steeg said he hadn't. "I met Carol the first day I started my first real job after college. It took me more than two years to land that job. She was the department stenographer. I was a pretend marketing specialist. The rest is history."

"So, Carol certainly isn't the 'M' something girl you were so serious about."

Steeg blinked even more surprised that Bear remembered Marilyn Johnson. A single mother with an eight year old daughter, Marilyn and Steeg met in 1969 one night in downtown Long Beach, California. Marilyn was handing out religious tracks to passersby on a street corner and Steeg just happened to be one of the passersby. She was alone and Steeg was inebriated just enough to be in full protective mode. He stayed to help her distribute her stack of brochures. When the stack had dwindled to nothing, he offered to walk her back to her place, promising he would not try anything funny and hoping she would believe him. She did. That led to a dinner date later that same week, which led to another date and then every liberty in Long Beach was spent with Marilyn and her daughter.

Then, there followed the Apollo Eleven recovery mission, his battle with Commander Knauts over clean padeyes among other things and the bizarre incident of being thrown across Hanger Bay One by an A-4 jet aircraft. The accident almost killed Steeg. His injuries damaged his brain and he suffered more than a year of memory loss. The amnesia affected everything he knew of Marilyn Johnson and he simply forgot all about her. During that time he developed a deeper dependency on prescribed pain killers and desperate hallucinations of Gracie; both helped make the world go away. Back then, Bear knew Steeg was involved with a person he knew only as the 'M' something girl. Before the Apollo Eleven mission, Steeg had told Bear about her and how special she was. But after Steeg's accident, when *Hornet* was back in Long Beach and Bear asked him about how things were going with the 'M' something girl, Steeg responded that he didn't know what Bear was talking about. At the time, for Bear it was a sad and disturbing revelation.

Now, in the hotel lounge, Steeg took another swig from his drink. "You have a good memory."

Bear agreed, proudly proclaiming with a laugh, "Yes, I do! I remember, too, the parking lot girl!"

His friend's direct reference to Gracie was a second surprise a bit too-brittle and it triggered another memory of his high school sweetheart that caught him off guard. Steeg glanced across the room at the wall of broad windows and the dark reflections of the two of them in the glass. He wasn't surprised as he saw Gracie appear in the reflection to stand between both of them. He wasn't effective in hiding the melancholy that washed over him as he kept his eyes on Gracie.

Bear noted the change in Steeg. He leaned toward him and asked, "What's wrong? You look like you just lost all hope, or your best friend, or something."

Chapter 4
Master of All You Survey

January 28, 1986

The day began as a classic winter day in Minneapolis: solid overcast skies and morning temperatures slightly above zero that frosted your nose hairs. Every hour had slid into serious deepfreeze territory. By 1:30 that afternoon the clouds had smoothed into a solid blanket of gray and a stiff north wind chilled the air to twelve degrees below zero, a temperature easily capable of cutting into any exposed flesh.

With the falling temperatures, intermittent light snowfall morphed into intermittent light ice crystals that pelted streets and sidewalks already covered with gray road slush. It was congealing into a paste-like consistency that made driving and walking more than challenging.

Steeg Patterson's morning business meeting with his newest and now most important client concluded after lunch. Now, he was back downtown cautiously maneuvering his Buick LeSabre among the slow moving, slush-impaired traffic flow to the contract parking ramp on South Ninth Street and LaSalle Avenue adjacent to the Lakewood Building. After an annoyingly prolonged weather induced stop and go delay, Steeg finally reached the parking ramp entrance. With a Zig Ziglar positive motivation tape cassette in glorious full stereo sound loudly filling the car's plush interior, Steeg made his way to the second level and his assigned stall. He carefully eased his Buick LeSabre into the spot, sifted into park and let the engine idle as he continued to listen to Zig.

Ziglar's enthusiastic audio pronouncements died out within a few seconds when the tape reached its end. Steeg shrugged, turned off the engine and immediately felt the cold begin its inevitable conduction into the car. He knew the interior's warmth would be viciously sucked from the car as soon as he pulled on the door handle. Steeg remained behind the steering wheel to collect himself. Still slightly impaired by the three martini lunch, he checked the lay of his tie in the rear view mirror. He then checked his nearly perfect hair; hair literally flash frozen in place when he left the house that morning. Next, he clicked open the two brass latches of his cordovan leather briefcase laying on the passenger's seat, retrieved the signed advertising agreement he had successfully secured over lunch, and smiling, admiringly paged through the document one more time. It was the most beautiful sales proposal he had ever written, another outstanding major sales coup for a sales career already excessively varied beyond reason and the first such accomplishment for Cooper Medical Publishing, his employer of nearly two years.

With reassured pride, Steeg returned the signed agreement to the briefcase, and with a satisfied pat of his hand, snapped the case lid shut. From this one account alone he was going to make a lot of money. January wasn't even over yet and 1986 was already a very good year.

He pulled the briefcase behind him and exited the car, the frigid air slicing brutally through his topcoat and biting bitterly at his face.

Cooper Medical Publishing offices were on the fifth floor of the Lakewood Building. Steeg's private office was located on the middle of the west side and overlooked South Ninth Street. From this closet sized, overly cluttered room with a single double hung window and a single coat hook on the rear of an office door that was almost always open, he managed a fifteen state sales territory for *MEPNews* magazine, an industrial product tabloid serving the medical equipment and product manufacturing industries. Twelve of the fifteen states in his territory were covered by a network of independent sales representatives he managed and supported as Regional Sales Manager. The remaining three states, Minnesota, Wisconsin and Iowa, Steeg handled directly as house accounts. He was pretty good at both selling and managing, although he appreciated the selling side of things much more than managing his small team of independent reps. Total advertising revenues for his house territory matched and often exceeded the big-buck markets of the high powered Northeastern territory. Prior to his arrival at Cooper, this level of performance for the "House" territories had not always been the case. Steeg took pride in the accomplishment for what it was.

The after affects of the martinis at lunch were eased by his brisk walk from the parking ramp. Steeg reached behind his almost always open office door to hang first his topcoat followed by his dark gray pinstripe suit coat on the lone hook almost too small to handle the full load. He released the bottom button of his matching vest as he walked behind his desk, took a seat and punched in Gerry Cooper's intercom number.

A characteristic beep was followed by a grumpy "Yeah, whadda ya want?"

"Hi, Boss, how you doing?" Steeg's visualized Gerry's always frowning scowl as he leaned closer to the speakerphone.

"You tell me," his boss replied, still grumpy. Gerry Cooper was always grumpy. He owned the publishing company, a fact which gave his boss good enough reason to never be satisfied with hardly anything.

Perhaps that would change today.

"Okay, then, I'll tell you," Steeg shot back almost cheerfully. "You're doing pretty good! Or, should I say, 'You're doing pretty well?' Is it 'good' or is it 'well?' I can never keep those two words straight."

"Are you drunk?" Cooper growled, a little tipsy himself from skipping solid food for lunch in favor of a handful of pretzels and two single malt scotches.

"Nope, but I have reason to be."

"Why's that?"

"Because Gorman Packaging has just handed all their medical market advertising to us for the rest of the year, that's why."

"Get in here, now!"

Steeg grabbed the signed contracts from his briefcase and resisted the urge to skip down the long hallway to Cooper's corner office. He entered Gerry's office, closing the door behind him as Cooper, already on another phone call, waved him to a stuffed leather chair in front of the largest office desk in the building. Size mattered to the gray haired sixty-three year old publisher, especially when it came to cars and executive office furniture.

Cooper gruffly informed his called party he expected an update before the end of the day, and then he hung up the phone. He held out his hand. Steeg filled it with the contracts. The publisher pulled a pair of reading glasses from his inside jacket pocket, put them on halfway down the bridge of his nose and proceeded to page through the document. He was done inside thirty seconds.

"Gorman was heavily into McGraw-Hill," Cooper's perpetual frown pulled tightly into furrowed look of doubt as he cast a suspicious eye toward his regional sales manager. "What's happened to McGraw-Hill?"

"The operative term is 'was'," Steeg smiled. "Not any more. As far as their medical promotional budget, Gorman is 100% with us."

"Ha!" Cooper slapped his hand on his desk. His coarse laugh exploded across the room. "It's about frickin' time! That was never the right book for them anyway. Absolutely crazy, a packaging company advertising in a medical journal. We're the only book for them. What the heck took them so long to see it?"

Steeg smiled and smugly shrugged his shoulders. "What can I say? There's a new sheriff in town."

Cooper laughed again. "Yeah, okay, you're a stud, alright. Congratulations. You should feel good about this one, Patterson. This is huge."

"Thank you, Boss. I deserve it."

"Yes, you do," the publisher agreed, adding unrewardingly, "But, in this business, that means you get more on your plate."

Steeg's smile vanished. "Oh. Well, I was thinking maybe leaving a little earlier today…"

"Yeah, sure, to pack," Cooper completed for him.

"Pack?"

"AdCom Sales needs your magic touch tomorrow morning," Cooper roughly cleared his throat. AdCom was their independent representation firm covering Georgia and North Florida. "It seems the only time Amalgamated Medical Devices can meet with our guys, and that means you, is tomorrow morning at 9:00 a.m."

"What's going on with AMD? They like us. They've been long standing advertisers for years."

"Maybe, but their talking about jumping ship," Cooper sounded more than a little concerned and the return of the perpetual frown confirmed it. "That would hurt. You have to get down there and make sure the boys don't screw this up. Sally has your itinerary. Your tickets are at the airport. Beat it, and don't come back if you lose the deal."

Cooper handed the contracts back to Steeg. "By the way: nice looking proposal."

"Gee, thanks," Steeg said suddenly deflated despite the beefy agreement he retrieved from his boss.

He left, hearing Cooper pick up his phone receiver and dial another outside number. Steeg paused only briefly at Sally Raschke's desk as she handed him the all too familiar envelope containing the pertinent information necessary for his trip. He thanked her for her efficiency as he numbly returned to his own office. He dialed his home number.

"Carol, it's me," he began with his perfunctory greeting, knowing this wasn't going to go over real well.

"Hi, Honey!" she returned warmly. "How are you doing? How'd the big meeting go?"

"It went great, actually. I got them to sign on for the whole proposal, extras and everything," he replied. "It was great, really good. It's a whole bunch of money for us; very good meeting, great month, it's going to be an even better later on."

"We should celebrate, then, maybe dinner out tonight?"

She was too bubbly. This was really not going to go over well at all.

"Uh, good idea, but maybe later in the week," his hesitation was more than noticeable.

"What do you mean?" she asked, her voice turning noticeably cooler.

"I, uh, gotta get down to Atlanta tonight. There's a big problem down there and Gerry wants me down there early tomorrow morning."

"Oh, Steeg, you just got back!" She complained firmly.

"Well, not 'just' – I got back last week…"

She interrupted him, suddenly in full offensive mode. "Yeah, last Friday night, no, not Friday, it was really early Saturday morning, wasn't it?! And, when you finally do get home, you go into the office on the weekends to catch up on your paper work. Today is Tuesday, Steeg. What is that, three days home out of the last twelve, and we've seen you maybe a total of three hours in those three days?"

She was right. "Look, Carol, it's my job…"

"Yes, and I'm your wife." Her retort was quick and sharp. "You have a family, you know, two little boys and a little girl. You've had this job for two years, and your own children hardly know their own father…"

"That's not true, Carol, and it's not fair," he objected in mild self defense, trying not to upset her any more than she already was and immediately wishing he hadn't said anything.

"Well, it's not far off the mark, either, Steeg," Carol insisted, trying to control her emotions. He could tell from the strain in her voice she was not succeeding.

"It pays the bills," he defended weakly. "It pays the bills better than anything else I've done since we've been married.

You're at home with the kids. I can't afford not to do this job as best as I can. I'm sorry, but that's the way it is right now. You have to admit, we're doing much better since I signed on here."

Silence on her end of the line. He heard her sigh. Several seconds of more silence followed.

"Okay. You're right, Steeg," she admitted. "I'm sorry. I don't mean to be a nag about this. It's just that it gets really hard, having you gone so much for so long a time, each time, every week it's like this."

"It's not every week."

"It feels like it," she insisted. "I'm home with a six year old, a four year old and the three year old. It's really hard, Steeg. It's important you know you're needed here, too."

"I know. It's tough on you – it would be tough on anyone, heck it would be tough on Atlas. It's 'Mission Impossible' all over again. But if I can make this job work, we can finally get somewhere. I just need time. With time who knows where it can take us."

He heard another sigh. "I know. You're right. I know."

"I'll be home in a little while," he said, opening the envelope and quickly perusing the printed itinerary. "My flight's at 8:30, so we have time for an early dinner out. How's that?"

"I don't think there's enough time to get any of your sisters to baby sit," she said.

"No big deal, we'll take everyone for a family dinner out night," he offered. "They'll love it."

"Okay," she acquiesced. Steeg was going to hang up when she changed the subject. "Wasn't that sad about the astronauts?"

He wasn't certain he had heard her correctly. "What astronauts do you mean?"

"The astronauts on the space shuttle this morning," Carol said, surprised Steeg didn't know. "They all died."

Earlier that morning, the Space Shuttle *Challenger* had exploded 73 seconds after liftoff killing everyone aboard. Steeg knew nothing of it. He had been too preoccupied with martini lunches and Zig Ziglar to have bothered to turn on the car radio.

Chapter 5
Some Guy Wants to Talk

Saturday night April 5, 1986

Steeg was grateful the weather wasn't as cold as in January, but the intermittent swoop-swoop of the windshield wipers testified to the rain and cold as he drove. Spring had come early, riding a crest of several unseasonably warm sunny days the last half of March that had cleaned away winter's remains of mush-slush, dirty gray snow and ice, the dregs of which stubbornly relinquished their bond from streets and sidewalks and resisted the season-ending thaw to the last. Nevertheless, in true Minnesota fashion, the liberating warmth of late March abandoned the state the first weekend of April with a piercing type of wet cold easily penetrating any style of outwear no matter how well insulated it might be.

Steeg slowed to make his turn off 69th Street and direct his Buick into the darkness of the barely lit Southdale Bowl parking lot. He found a vacant spot a distant three rows away from the main entrance to the modern bowling center. He allowed the engine to idle and kept the wipers on as he asked himself once more why he was here. He much preferred the warmth of his house over the frigid globs of muck and moisture falling all around him.

It had been a long week and he was tired. He should have stayed home with Carol and the kids. So, why hadn't he?

After seven years of not hearing so much as a single word from him or any other of his old high school pals from Steeg's past, Matt Cummings called him at his house in Eagan earlier that the week.

Carol answered the phone on the third ring and called Steeg from his comfortable stuffed recliner claiming, "Some guy wants to talk to you."

Steeg grumbled under his breath as he left the network news broadcast on television to trudge from the sparsely furnished living room into the barely adequate kitchen. He tossed a shallow grin of thanks toward Carol and brought the receiver to his ear.

"This is Steeg."

He immediately recognized Matt's distinctive verbal characteristics and almost choked as he asked, "How'd you get my number?!"

"Hey, how you doin'?" Matt ignored Steeg's query with his customary insensitivity. "What's up?"

"What's up? You called me, remember?"

"Oh, yeah, that's right," Matt cleared his throat and started over. "Hey, this is me, Matt."

"So, tell me something I don't know." Steeg was amused. For some inexplicable reason, he missed talking with this guy.

"Like what?" Matt asked.

"Like, how'd you get this number?"

"Your mother."

"Damn that woman!"

Both young men laughed.

"So, you moved to the suburbs, then?"

"New house – just closed on it in December. Still haven't unpacked half the boxes..."

Matt completed the sentence for him. "And, you never will, trust me."

"You're probably right about that," agreed Steeg. "So, to what do I owe the pleasure of this phone call?"

"You mean you're enjoying this?"

"No, that's not what I mean."

"Then, I'll get to the point."

"Please do."

"It's been twenty years, you know."

"Not that long. I distinctly remember you were at my wedding seven years ago."

"And, a magical event it was, but I'm not talking about your wedding, Einstein: I'm talking about our upcoming 20 year high school reunion!"

Steeg hadn't heard about the reunion, when it was or where it would be held. "Oh, geez, no."

"We need to discuss it."

"No, we don't."

"Ace, Wedge, you and me," Matt continued. "Over beers this weekend."

Steeg shuttered again. "Oh, geez, no."

"Oh, geez, yes. There's no backing out of this. Be at the Southdale Bowl, seven o'clock this Saturday."

"I'm busy."

"With what?"

"I don't know yet. Give me a minute or two and I'll come up with something."

It didn't work. Steeg didn't bother using work as an excuse. After several more minutes of inconsequential banter, he ended the call by agreeing to the meeting at the bowling alley.

So, he was there, sitting in the idling Buick in the parking lot watching the sliding wetness of falling snow mixed with freezing rain raked clear from the windshield with each 'gah-thump' swipe of the wipers. He looked at his wristwatch. He was three minutes late.

Carol had encouraged him to go, saying it would be good for him to see his old friends again. After all, at every opportunity she did the same with her tidy select group of high school girl friends, so why shouldn't he? He knew she wouldn't understand and should he try to explain his reservations it could open a line of discussion that could lead into uncomfortable territory. It was safer if he didn't answer her question.

For himself, Steeg didn't deny the real reason why he had come to the bowling alley that night. It wasn't as simple as downing a few beers with old friends sharing in some pleasant "guy time" diversion. That wasn't it, at all.

It was Gracie.

Chapter 6
April's Fool

"I'm thirty-eight years old," Steeg moaned over a half-finished beer as the waitress brought the second round to their table. "That's like middle aged. Why the heck would I want to pay money to spend the evening with a bunch of people I haven't seen since high school?"

"Come on, it'll be fun!" Matt Cummings countered with a too-enthusiastic fist punch to Steeg's shoulder.

Wedge and Ace sat across from the two of them. The years that had passed since their last meeting had begun to take their toll on the men. Wedge had lost at least half his hair, weathered lines gathered at the corners of his eyes, a full beard covered his face and there was a significant increase in his girth. Ace had the first showings of gray at his temples, but his easy smile remained almost youthful with the familiar 'milk and cookies' look still there. As always, Matt needed a shave, but the dark brown of his beard had been replaced by a premature salt and pepper appearance. Unlike the other three, Matt hadn't gained much weight, but he was showing a little paunch across his middle from lack of exercise. Steeg, with a touch of gray at the temples like Ace, had put on more weight than he wanted, but he carried it well enough. Chided by Wedge for the 'love handles', Steeg blamed Carol for being too good a cook.

It was Matt's party, having tracked each of them down to propose the meeting that, somehow, no one had objected to attending. So, there they were, four guys in their late thirties, reminiscing about 'The Good Old Days' as they sipped tap beers in the crowded darkened eatery while bowling pins crashed loudly across the long bank of lanes outside the door. The place was crammed with league bowlers and weekenders out for an evening of fun and healthy recreation.

Matt made a joke of the upcoming festivities. "After all, there's only one twenty-year reunion. You kind of gotta go."

Steeg remained firm with his opposition to the whole idea. "No, I don't. Besides, the only people I knew from high school that mattered, still matter – are sitting around this table. That's good enough for me."

Ace choked back tears that weren't really there. "I think I'm going to cry."

"Me, too," Wedge contributed with a smirk. "It's the nicest thing you ever said to me." He reached for the fresh glass of beer the waitress placed in front of him. He eyed her retreat as he took a good sized gulp. "I think it would be interesting to see some of the old teachers. I gotta wonder how my old English teacher looks now. She was hot – really big hooters."

Steeg rolled his eyes as Ace complained mildly. "Some things never change."

"He has a point," Matt offered. "Seeing people you haven't seen for twenty years can help you compare notes, see where others are in their lives compared to where you're at with yours. It could be therapeutic."

"It could be catastrophic," Steeg moaned again.

Ace's eyebrow shot upward, returned his glass to the table as he recalled something significant and pointed to Steeg. "Hey, it would be nice to see Gracie again."

Steeg shot a cautious glance at his friend. "Gracie?"

"Yeah, Gracie Ondracek," he answered. "I haven't seen her since the Normandale Vets Club days. She was high school homecoming queen, remember? So, you know she's going to be in the middle of this reunion."

Matt's next swig of brew caught in his throat mid-sip. "Wait a minute; Gracie Ondracek was in yours' guys' Vet's Club? How did that work?"

"Very well, actually," Ace said.

Steeg leaned back in his chair with a warm smile. "That's true. She was a breath of fresh, mature womanly air in a bubble-gum infested glorified prep school."

Matt punched Steeg's shoulder again, harder this time. "Well, then, you gotta go to the reunion!"

Ace nodded. "Especially since you and her dated when you were at Normandale."

Steeg met Ace's comment with a classic double-take.

Matt's mouth dropped open. "You telling me you dated the homecoming queen?!"

Steeg shook his head, fingering the moisture coating his half-empty glass. "No. Not really. Maybe we shared a brief time out once or twice, a friendly ride home from school, that sort of thing. Nothing happened. It was nothing. Forget it. We didn't date. We were just friends."

Matt shot a doubting eye at Steeg. "Yeah, right, just like Jockstrap's sister."

Another eye-roll from Steeg came in reply. "Nothing happened with Jockstrap's sister, either."

"Yeah, right."

There was no sense in continuing to deny anything, so Steeg didn't bother.

"Well, I'm going to go to it," Wedge announced. "I just wanted to get together with you guys to find out what you all were going to do."

Ace said he was going to go, too.

Steeg just shook his head as he asked, "When is it?"

"Next month," Wedge answered. "May Tenth. That's a Saturday night."

"They're always on a Saturday night," Ace said.

"Where is it?"

"The Airport Hilton on the Bloomington strip," Matt said.

"I didn't know we had an Airport Hilton." Wedge questioned just before another swallow from his beer.

"Just opened this year," Ace explained.

"How much?" Steeg continued trying not to be irritated with a process growing increasingly more tiring.

"Forty bucks per person," said Ace.

"That means Carol stays home," Steeg groused.

"Geez, you're a cheap bastard," Wedge complained.

"Darn right," Steeg agreed. "Besides, I'm probably too late to register, anyway."

"No, you're not," Matt pulled several sheets of paper from his shirt pocket and unfolded one sheet for each of them. "Fill in the blanks and send in your check to the address on the sheet."

"Ho-ho! You came prepared!" Ace laughed, grabbing the form for a quick perusal.

"He's serious," Wedge took a copy of the form and passed the remaining copy to Steeg. "He really wants us to go."

"If I gotta go, so do you guys," Matt explained.

"Nuts," Steeg resigned as he looked at the sheet of paper. "Too bad I left my pen at home."

Matt pulled a ball point pen from the same pocket that had held the registration forms and handed it to Steeg.

"Gee, thanks," Steeg took the pen and haltingly began to fill in the form. When he was done, he passed the pen back to Matt, who gave it to Ace. Ace completed his form and handed the pen back to Matt. Matt looked concerned as he tapped the pen against the table top.

"Go ahead," Wedge said. "Fill your form in."

"I'd like to," Matt admitted. "But, I don't know…"

"What!?!" Steeg blurted in disbelief. "You don't know?!"

"Look, it would be fun," Matt began. "But, what with all that's going on now, how can I have fun?"

Steeg's eyes narrowed in Matt's direction. "What are you talking about? What's going on?"

Matt shot each man a quick look of incredulity. "You guys living in a vacuum or something? Reagan just bombed Libya this week! I'm telling you, man, this President, if he keeps going the way he's going, is going to end up vaporizing all of us."

Ace leveled an equally incredulous glare back at his friend. "You can't be serious. You're letting U.S. foreign policy keep you from going to a class reunion?"

Steeg shook his head in disgust. "He hates all things Republican. He uses it as just another lame excuse for him to not be bothered."

Matt held a hand out in protest. "It is not. I'm just telling you, Reagan is going to kill us all. He's driving the economy down the toilet…"

Steeg pinched the bridge of his nose in exasperation as he interrupted. "I wasn't aware the economy was in such good shape after Jimmy Carter – double digit inflation, gas prices tripling, unemployment the worst since the Great Depression, my mortgage is at eleven percent and even that's a bargain now. Thank God for the Democrats..."

"I hear ya," Ace contributed.

"It's worse now," Matt rebutted. "Reagan thinks we're going to have a Star Wars missile shield in outer space and he's bombing Arabs in tents in Libya for gad's sake! The guy is certifiable. How can I go to a high school reunion when everything is falling apart all around us?"

With growing impatience Steeg shot back. "How do you want to handle this: fists or guns?"

Chapter 7
Political idiocy

It was as if a cloud had suddenly appeared to hug the ceiling and the small bar seemed to darken considerably.

Matt blinked back nervously at Steeg. "What do you mean?"

Steeg's mouth was tight lipped. "What I mean is you're not getting away with using the President of the United States as an excuse to not go to the reunion. I mean, Matt, I know you're a frickin' bleeding heart liberal, but that only gets you so far. You've practically talked all of us into going to this thing, and now you're backing out!"

"I'm just saying that in good conscience I have a problem celebrating as long as this 'Looney Tunes' is President, that's all," Matt leaned away from Steeg just far enough to keep outside the swing radius.

Wedge moaned as Ace added a point of clarification.

"I think you mean 'Bonzo' – Ronald Reagan was in all the 'Bonzo' movies."

"Whatever," Matt acquiesced. "It's still a problem."

"You have a problem?" Steeg continued with growing irritation. "Ronald Reagan is your problem? Because he's ruined the economy and he's a war monger?"

"That's right."

Stunned, Wedge's face went blank, Ace slapped his forehead with his palm, and Steeg muffled his reply through hands pulled down his face in frustration.

Matt's face held a self-assured smirk. "So? Prove I'm wrong."

"There's not enough time." Steeg grumbled.

Matt dug back. "And you're still a paranoid."

"Thank you," Steeg smiled. "The more things change… And, you're the one too afraid to have some fun because Reagan is President; it's absurd. You're going to the reunion, dumb-shit. Blaming the President of the United States for your not going doesn't make sense."

"Sure it does."

"It defies logic, Matt!" Steeg returned flatly. "You're college educated – that is, I assume you are. Did you ever actually graduate from the 'U'?"

Matt shot Steeg a quick, sour pinched pout. "Now you're playing dirty."

"Hey, I'm giving you the benefit of the doubt!"

Matt turned in his seat to counter Steeg's argument directly. "You know, some kids who have candy should give some of it to other kids who don't. When you spread the wealth, everyone prospers. Reagan is against that."

Wedge took another sip from his beer. "I got a better idea: how about giving kids with no candy a way to earn money so they can get candy on their own?"

Steeg smiled in agreement. "Free enterprise, Matt: tune in and turn on. No other economic system in the history of human endeavor has provided so much for so many for so little. It works if you do."

His retort eluding him, Matt sat tightlipped and said nothing.

Steeg carefully eyed his tablemate as he continued. "Now, this 'Reagan the War Monger' thing of yours: put it into a concept you can grasp. Let's say there's this alley fight and three guys want to beat your face in…"

Matt's face mirrored his sudden concern. "Why would they want to do that?"

Elbows on the table, Ace leaned in toward Matt with an exaggerated glare. "Oh, I don't know, maybe because they don't like you anymore?"

Steeg chuckled at that one. "Anyway, these three guys want to beat your face in. There's no way out of the alley except through them. You have two choices: you can take them on with just your fists, or you can take them on with a 44 AutoMag. Which way are you going to go?"

Matt's dark eyes darted from friend to friend hesitantly. "What's an 'AutoMag'?"

Ace rubbed his brow in growing exasperation. Wedge closed his eyes and moaned. Steeg grabbed the opportunity for a little comic relief, falling into his best Clint Eastwood imitation since his employer's Christmas party the previous year.

"Seeing how it's the most powerful handgun in the world." It was a near-perfect, gritty 'Eastwood-ian' response. "And it can blow your head clean off. So, the question you've gotta ask yourself is, do you feel lucky? … Well, do ya, punk?"

Laughter exploded across the table.

Matt shook his head. "I don't get it."

Ace's laugh took on even louder proportions. "He didn't see that movie! Not artsy-fartsy enough for him!"

"Made in Hollywood, you know?" Wedge contributed. "He only goes to European movies – reading subtitles helps improve his reading!"

"Look, Matt, it's a simple 'Position of Strength' thing with Reagan, that's all. It's the old 'Big Stick' approach – no big deal. It's nothing to get your shorts in a bunch over."

Matt perked up on that note. "You know who came up with the 'Big Stick' foreign policy? Teddy Roosevelt, that's who! He was an environmentalist, you know; A true progressive, not a reactionary like Reagan!"

Steeg raised a pointer finger in agreement. "Yes, a Republican, and then, a Bull Moose. Even a progressive can get some things right."

Silence fell over the table as all four looked at each other for several seconds.

The silence was broken from Ace's corner of the table. "So, you can go to the reunion with a clear conscience after all."

Matt retrieved the pen from the tabletop. "Reagan is just pissing off a lot of other countries. That's what he's doing. The guy is Looney Tunes, that's all I can say."

Ace corrected him again. "'Bonzo'."

"Whatever," Matt grumbled as he started filling in the registration form. "I guess I can go to the reunion, but money's a little tight right now."

"Oh, you poor baby," Wedge pouted from across the table. "Borrow a few bucks from your wife. She makes twice as much as you do, anyway."

Matt shrugged at the comment. "It's closer to four times more than me, but who's counting?"

Ace laughed again as he pointed a crooked finger in Matt's direction. "You ask her, anyway. She'll probably appreciate getting you out of the house for a while."

Steeg was suddenly embarrassed and befuddled. "Wait a minute. You're married? Since when?"

Matt glanced up and then quickly returned to the form as he answered flatly, "A couple of years after you got married."

Steeg blinked. He was stunned. "I didn't know that. I had no idea. I didn't get an invitation to the wedding, did I?"

"Me, neither," Ace chimed in.

"Same here," Wedge acknowledged. "But I knew he got married cuz he told me."

Matt nodded as he finished filling in the form. "Yeah, we stay in touch, Wedge and me."

"I invited you to my wedding," Steeg protested. "You gave us a long, fancy kitchen knife as a wedding present!"

Matt nodded once more. "Yeah, I did. I figured it could come in handy for you."

"Oh, really? I don't cook!"

"No, not cooking; more like self-defense or if things just didn't work out after you find out you married a Democrat, you could use it to slit your wrists."

Ace and Wedge laughed at that one.

Steeg slumped back into his chair and said sourly, "Nice, real nice. Even Wedge invited me to his wedding."

"Which wedding?" Ace asked.

"The first one," Wedge answered.

"Wait, you got married again?" Steeg was incredulous. "After your divorce you told me you'd never do that."

Wedge shrugged. "I shouldn't have. The second one didn't last too long, either. The damn kids drove me crazy."

"Two marriages and you've got kids?!"

"Her kids. She can keep 'em. Good riddance."

Steeg leaned away as he digested this latest revelation and Wedge's obvious lack of concern over it.

Matt broke the sudden silence with a shrugged apology to Steeg. "I'm sorry I didn't invite you to the wedding, but I thought it was best what with your problems and all…"

Steeg's sour expression grew a shade sourer. "What problems are those?"

"You know: the emotional ones."

Steeg sat up more erect, his expression souring even more. "Unfortunately, I regret I'm not aware of the emotional problems to which you refer."

Wedge cleared his throat. "Oh-oh, he's using the good English words now…"

"Grammatically correct English," Ace interrupted.

"Right, grammatically correct," Wedge agreed. "That means he's gettin' pissed."

Matt eased up a bit. "Oh, well, in that case, don't get pissed on my account, Steeg. You're pristine; an emotional 'Rock of Gibraltar'. I didn't mean any of it."

That sounded better to Steeg and he relaxed considerably.

Matt finished his registration form and slid his pen back into his pocket. "Besides, I don't need a reunion to get me out of the house. Elaine does a lot of traveling for her job, so it's not like she's always tripping over me. And anyway, I'm out a lot taking classes at the 'U' you know."

Steeg's mouth dropped open. "Still? You mean you're still going to school?!"

"Yeah. So?"

Spying the waitress across the room, Wedge waved her over to order another round. "You're thirty-eight years old, Matt. You've been going to the University since you graduated from high school. Don't you think it's about time you got a degree or something, and move on with your life?"

"I go for the education, not the credits. Education is my life. I'm always learning. I learn when I work. I learn in the classroom. I learn when I travel to Europe…"

"Ah, yes, Europe: the true Nirvana," Ace smiled.

"Europeans are so far ahead of us, it's embarrassing when I go over there," Matt nodded in Ace's direction.

"Imagine how they feel!" Ace shot back.

Matt continued undeterred. "I choose to experience life, not punch in with a timecard, put in my eight hours and punch out again, day after day, year after year, until I can't get out of bed anymore. And, I have a woman who appreciates my philosophy and the things I consider to be important in life."

"A woman who earns four times as much as you do," Steeg criticized with a humorous smile. "She works. You need a shave. It's a match made in heaven."

Matt frowned. "I work. I just don't choose to be chained to a job, that's all."

Wedge wanted to change the subject. "Well, thank goodness for that…"

Steeg nodded in agreement. "Yes, there's hope for the rest of us."

The brittle ribbing continued for the rest of the evening. Matt put up with the bulk of it, returning what he got with equal skill allowing everyone to appreciate the fun of it without injury to ego or anything else. Steeg appreciated the chance to get caught up with his three friends and the evening went by too quickly. Sooner than anyone wanted, it was past eleven o'clock and time for Steeg to return to wife and kids.

When he excused himself, it gave the others permission to leave, too. They all grabbed their jackets and walked out through the front entry, the overhang shielding them from the steady rain. They grouped outside the front door to continue the lighter conversation for another few minutes before they finally ended the get-together and each man dashed through the raindrops to their own vehicle.

As Steeg exited the parking lot onto 69th Street, the tall blue Southdale water tower was to his right and he remembered what had happened there more than twenty years earlier.

He would go to the reunion. It wouldn't cost much and if Gracie wasn't there he'd simply leave early.

Chapter 8
The Excuse

Unlike the rest of the house, the Patterson kitchen was tidy with freshly brewed coffee poured hot into their cups – Steeg's straight black, Carol's with no sugar and enough cream to make it a silky brown. The morning was bright, cool and wet from the previous night's rain. Church was a little less than two hours away, plenty of time to cover the essential issue from the meeting with the guys.

"So, I get a babysitter, then." asked Carol expectantly. After Steeg filled her in on the details of his upcoming high school reunion, she was clearly excited by the prospect of going.

Steeg took a cautious first sip of coffee. "Why?"

"Well, can you bring children to the reunion?"

"Oh, good God, no. I mean, Carol, I don't want to bring the kids to the reunion!"

Carol nodded her understanding. "Okay then, I'll just line up a babysitter."

Steeg's head bobbed a little sideways in response as he diverted his eyes to the floor. "Yeah, well, maybe not."

"Then, I can't go." Carol was obviously disappointed. "I have to stay here. I can't leave the children alone. Brian's only six and he can't be responsible for the other two."

"You know, Babe, thinking about it, I really don't know if you'd want to go. First, you won't know anyone. Second, you're a good five years younger than the class. Third, you went to Washburn, not Richfield..."

"What are you saying?"

He hid his eyes in his cup again, took a slow sip and lowered the cup to the table. He tried to look at her, but his eyes took inexplicable detours instead. His gaze paused first on the top button of her blouse, followed by the right corner of her collar, then her right ear lobe, her hairline, down to the other ear lobe, then the other collar corner, and finally back to the top button. Then, he gave up, staring at his hands instead.

"I'm saying, Carol, you're probably going to be bored out of your mind. I know I would be if it was your reunion and you dragged me along. I'd end up spending the whole time sitting alone at one of those under-populated, round banquet tables, drumming my fingers on the tablecloth and staring at the four walls as you go off to gab with your old girlfriends. Gad-awful – I wouldn't wish that on anyone, especially you."

Skeptically, Carol crossed her arms and responded not with a question but a flat statement of unbelief. "Really."

"Sure, of course!" Steeg rose to his feet and strolled over to the coffee maker for a refill – a short one because there was still plenty of coffee in his cup. Over his shoulder he continued. "You know, when you think of it, I'm going to the thing just to hang out with a few old high school buddies. Their wives won't be there, either, so who will you talk to? What are you going to do for three, four hours? I don't know. Maybe they'll have some kind of game arcade near the lobby, or something."

"Why do I get the feeling I'm one of your customers and you're trying to sell me something?"

Steeg returned to his kitchen chair with cup in hand, once again fascinated with the top button of Carol's blouse. "I'm sorry, sweetie. I just don't want to subject you to that kind of boring humiliation."

"I don't mind it, really."

"Besides, Carol, I only signed up for me. At forty bucks a person, it would cost us eighty bucks for two. We save money this way."

"Sure, but it's a special thing – a high school reunion doesn't happen every year, you know."

Steeg was about to say something about how the reunion wasn't all that special. After all, it was only Richfield Senior High School, a miniscule public education institution in a shrinking community on the south border of Minneapolis with a dwindling population from decades of 'white flight' to the outer suburban developments surrounding the entire metro area. But before he could say anything in response, his six year old son Brian, still in his pajamas, stomped into the kitchen and headed straight for the refrigerator.

Too roughly, little Brian pulled open the door and made a quick perusal of the family food stores. "We gonna eat?"

His son's rudeness was typical. "Get your head outta the 'frig, Brian!"

"He's hungry, Steeg. It'll be ready soon, honey. Pancakes and bacon! Your favorite – ready in a jiffy."

"But I wanna eat something now!" The boy protested too loudly and Steeg's patience quickly wore thin.

For Steeg, rudeness was one thing, disrespect was something else.

"You don't talk to your mother like that when I'm around!"

"He's just a kid, Steeg. Brian, go keep Nev and Dottie company while I get things going in here, okay? I'll call you when it's time."

Brian, the refrigerator door held open with his foot, crossed his arms with a pout.

"This is not the way to start the day, little man." Steeg warned his son sternly. "Do what your mother tells you."

Brian didn't look at his father as he stomped out of the kitchen more loudly than when he had entered. When the boy turned down the hallway, Steeg came to his feet, walked to the refrigerator and closed the door softly.

Equally softly, he said, "The kid has no respect."

Carol rose from her chair. She reached around him, opened the refrigerator once more and removed a carton of eggs and a bottle of milk. "I think it would be better, Steeg, if you went to your reunion alone."

Chapter 9
Over for Coffee

"He left for the airport before sun up this morning." Carol refreshed the two cups of coffee, one for her, one for her invited guest, Steeg's sister Mary Shulhouse. "He'll be back sometime late Friday night."

She brought the full cups back to the table. Mary thanked her as she took the offered second cup of the morning. Carol lowered herself to a chair. They had covered the prerequisites already – how's everyone doing; what's going on with mom; you're looking so good; the need to lose the winter weight. Mary had then asked about Steeg and that was when Carol offered a warm up on the coffee.

From the open kitchen, the women could see the children playing quietly together in the adjoining living room. Mary's three girls, with Carol's five year old Dorothy and three year old Neville, brought the total count to five children in that room. Oldest brother Brian kept to his bedroom playing with his extensive collection of interconnecting plastic building blocks.

"Your girls are getting so big, Mary!"

"Your kids are catching up. Thanks for having me over. I can use the break."

"Break? You brought the kids with you, how is that a break?"

"Believe me, it's easier this way." Mary took in the new paint and decorating efforts in the kitchen. "You've done a lot so quickly in your new house."

"Not really," Carol shook her head. "We've been here since December, and we only slapped a little paint around. The lower level is a naked shell and a total mess. I can't seem to get the boxes unpacked down there and a lot of what I have unpacked ends up back in other boxes I have no place to store."

The women turned toward the whining complaints coming from the living room. The noise increased as Carol's daughter and Mary's second oldest continue to pull at the same doll.

"Dottie, you need to share with your cousin," Carol instructed from her chair. "No fighting, okay?"

Mary followed suit. "Kim, you have your own toys in the big bag. Behave now, or we go home."

Obviously disgruntled and to the satisfaction of Dorothy, little Kimberly released her grip on the doll and flopped down in a sour pouting squat. Carol lightly laughed and returned to her coffee.

"Neville gets the short end of the stick today – four girls and a big brother twice his age who would rather beat him up than play with him."

"Oh? Gotta break Brian of that bad habit."

"I'm not worried. I'm pretty good at keeping the peace. Brian likes his Lego's, though, and he doesn't like to share. But Nev's going to be a big kid – bigger than Brian. He's got huge hands on him! Brian's six, slender and thin–boned like me; Nev's only three, thick and muscular like his father. In a couple of years it'll be Brian who'll be covering up instead of swinging."

"Bernie and me don't have any boys, at least not yet. You handle it better than I could."

"I don't know about that. I should be handling all my 'boys' a whole lot better than I am."

Mary picked up on the hint of concern in Carol's voice. "So, Steeg is traveling again. He's gone a lot."

Carol nodded in agreement. "It's probably best."

"How's that?" Mary nursed a slow swallow and watched Carol carefully over the rim of her coffee cup.

"He's doing real well at this job. We're bringing in decent money now."

"But?"

"But what?"

"Look, Carol. You don't want to talk about it, that's fine. But you called me over here, so I figure there's something on your mind."

A heavy sigh preceded a prolonged moment of silence as Carol tried to figure out what to say to her sister-in-law, if anything. "Steeg doesn't want me to go with him to his high school reunion."

Compelled by a sudden wariness, Mary waited quietly for whatever would come next.

"I think he's ashamed of me."

"Where do you get that?" Mary asked pointedly.

Carol shrugged. "I don't know. It makes sense, though. I've had three kids. I'm not as small as I was when we got married."

"That's stupid."

Carol wasn't so sure. "Maybe not. Things change. It's been seven years and he sure stacked up the excuses yesterday for me not to be there with him."

Mary vigorously disputed Carol's argument. "Whatever it is, sweetie, it's not you. You're a 'keeper' all the way, and you're the best thing to ever happen to him."

"Tell him that."

"Don't have to; he knows it."

"It still hurts. I don't mind being bored," Carol muttered more to herself than to Mary. "So, I don't know anyone else there, it would be okay anyway. It would be interesting to meet some of his old friends from school, hear some stories about what went on back then. That's what you're supposed to do, isn't it? Learn about the other person? If you care enough, don't you want to do that?"

"Of course you do."

"So, why doesn't he want to take me?"

"Look, Carol, Steeg is my brother and I love him. I would never do anything to hurt him, you know that don't you?"

Carol nodded. "Sure. Okay. But there's some reason why he doesn't want me at his high school reunion."

"Well, things happen, you know? We all do things growing up we're not really proud of. Sometimes you don't have control over everything the way you might like. That's when you get hurt, you know?"

Carol's eyes locked onto Mary's. Something in what she said told Carol the other woman knew something she didn't know. "Something happened to Steeg in high school?"

"Have you talked to him about that time; things that happened to him, maybe even things that happened to you when you were in school?"

Carol shook her head slowly. "No, not really."

"You've been married for seven years and you haven't told him about your first love?"

"He's never asked. Oh, I told him about this one guy I was really serious about, but he acted like it didn't matter and I've never felt it necessary to pursue it with him."

"You mean he didn't push you on it," Mary amended solemnly. "And, of course he's never talked to you about his first date, first kiss, first anything?"

"Well, actually, no, not that I can remember. We're not like that." A little embarrassed, Carol looked away as she added, "We're intimate in other ways, but not so much in others."

Mary cautiously turned her coffee cup in her hands as she wondered how far she should pursue this line of discussion. One thing was obvious to her: there were important things her brother had not shared or been completely open and honest about with Carol.

"This may sound like I'm prying, sticking my nose into something that's none of my business…"

Carol interrupted her. "You're not. I need to know."

Mary nodded with understanding, agreeing silently that Carol was right: she needed to know, and if Steeg wouldn't or couldn't help his own wife be his wife, then Mary's choices were few yet vital.

"Has Steeg ever talked to you about Puerto Rico?"

"Puerto Rico?"

"We lived there for a time when we were children. He's never told you anything about it?"

"No."

Mary hesitated, suddenly not sure how to proceed. "Well, let's just say things happened there. Maybe you should ask him. It would be better and more helpful coming from him."

"Helpful? How do you mean, Mary?"

Mary stopped herself briefly only to start again. "I know some things, but not everything. If I tell you what I know, you have to promise you'll never tell Steeg I told you."

Carol felt a sudden uncertainty swell inside her. Mary knew something about Steeg she did not, and for a moment, Carol preferred to keep it that way. However, the next moment she realized protecting her ignorance wasn't the answer, either. "Okay. I promise. What do I need to know, Mary?"

The other woman's face darkened with an undeniable sadness. She took a heavy breath and continued. "You need to know the main reason behind everything Steeg has done since high school. What has he told you about Gracie Ofterdahl?"

Chapter 10
The Reunion

May 10, 1986

"Carol!" Steeg yelled. "Where's my red tie?"

Dressed only in briefs and his best crisp white dress shirt with its single-stitched, wide spread collar, he found the walk-in bedroom closet annoyingly chilly. The warm tones of the hardwood floors were deceptively cool under his bare feet as he turned the tie carousel, and for at least the third time, thumbed through his extensive collection of neckwear.

From down the hallway he heard Carol's distant reply. "How should I know? It's your tie."

"Crap! I'm gonna be late," Steeg grumbled to himself. "I hate being late!"

Louder so Carol could hear, he yelled back over his shoulder, "I can't find it!"

Carol stood in the bedroom's open doorway leaning against the jam with her arms crossed. "You don't have to scream. I'm right here."

He turned, stepped from the closet to see her standing there and sheepishly replied, "Oh, sorry. But, I need that tie."

"You have lots of ties."

"But I have only one of those. It's my selling tie. It's what I wear at big sales calls. I gotta have it."

"Selling tie?"

"Yeah, you know a 'power' tie."

"Power tie?"

Steeg exhaled an exasperated sigh. "Yeah, my power tie. It's the one I wear to all my sales meetings and presentations. It brings me luck."

"I see," Disdain colored her next statement. "So, what you're saying is you need your red tie, and only your red tie, so you can get 'lucky' tonight?"

Steeg felt the heat of his face flush and quickly stepped back into the closet to the tie carousel. "That's not what I meant. Look, Carol, I just want to wear my red tie, okay. That's all I want, and I can't find it."

Resigned, Carol walked into the closet. The blue three piece suit hung on the closet door. "Is this your 'power' suit, too?"

Steeg did a poor job hiding his annoyance. "What of it? I mean, no, it isn't. It's the middle suit."

Carol fingered the suit's lapel. "Middle suit?"

"Yeah. My black suits are too strong – too 'powerful', okay – the gray suits are too 'business-ie'. That leaves the blue suits."

"Three piece?"

"I like vests, okay?"

"Okay."

More insistently, Steeg urged for her help once more. "Concentrate. My red tie – I need the red tie."

She scanned the section of the closet where his other suits hung. "Your black suits are your power suits?"

Steeg tried to be less annoyed. "Yeah, like I said."

"Did you wear a black suit on the trip this week?"

"Of course. I unpacked it this morning."

Carol walked past Steeg to the most wrinkled black suit on the rack, checked the inside jacket pocket and pulled out the neatly folded red tie. She turned, handed the tie to Steeg and exited the room without another word.

Stunned into embarrassment, all Steeg could do was offer a too late and barely audible, "Thank you."

By the time this meager expression of appreciation had left his mouth, she was well down the hallway a sufficient distance away to justify her non-reply.

More than a half-hour later, with hair perfectly sprayed into place, Steeg hurriedly entered the living room fully dressed in his three-piece, blue-suited, power-tied splendor. His dark, cordovan wingtip shoes gleamed as he did a quick pirouette in the middle of the room for Carol's consideration.

Carol sat on the sofa, looked up briefly from her magazine and then turned another page as she returned to her reading, obviously unimpressed. Six-year old Brian, playing on the floor with his Lego's, glanced at his father only to immediately return to his plastic assembling. Neville, thumb in his mouth and eyes glued to the television, cuddled next to his mother. As far as Steeg could tell, his youngest didn't notice him at all.

Relief came when Dottie bounced up to her father and hugged him around the waist.

"You goin' to work, Daddy?"

He ran his hand across her wavy blond curls. "No, Sweetie. I have a, er, meeting."

"Your daddy is going to his high school reunion, honey."

"You going to school, Daddy?"

"You could say that, Dottie." Steeg check his wristwatch. "Whoa, look at the time. I gotta go!"

His hurried goodbye kiss to Carol was a poor one, hitting only half on the lips and the rest landing on her cheek. As he pulled away he could see she would have been less annoyed had he not offered the kiss at all.

"You kids be good for your mother." Steeg ordered over his shoulder as he moved toward the door.

Before the door closed behind him, he thought he heard Carol's cautious retort as he entered the attached garage.

"You, too."

A second after the door closed, Carol heard the car start. Seconds later, the groan of the lowering garage door signaled Steeg's quick exit from the garage. Nudging past Neville, little Dottie crawled up into her mother's lap.

"Why is Daddy going to school, Mommy?"

Carol wrapped her arm around Dottie and held her close. "When you get a little older, baby girl, you'll understand sometimes straight answers are hard to come by."

Brian let out a burst of anger from his corner of the room. "Because he's stupid, that's why!"

"Don't talk about your father that way, Brian." Carol scolded her eldest child with equal intensity. "It's disrespectful."

Brian's Lego assembly sailed across the room, crashing against the wall and falling to the floor in pieces. The boy stomped down the hall toward the room he shared with his little brother, turned and yelled back, "It's a lot better when he's not here, anyways!"

Chapter 11
Do You Remember When...

The startling slap on his back wasn't painful but it landed with unexpected force.

"Holy shit! Is that you, Patterson!"

Steeg stopped himself from almost stumbling into the person in line ahead of him and then braced himself for another blow as he turned toward the familiar voice. A slightly taller and little less thinner Dave Brunswick beamed a broad grin at him.

"Okay, you're right! Just don't hit me again. How the heck are you, Dave?"

"You're late!" The former classmate scolded. "The others are already inside the ballroom."

"I'm sorry, I just got here; haven't even signed in yet." Steeg fingered Dave's nametag pinned to the lapel of his sports coat. "I see you have."

"Got here an hour ago. They have a pretty good bar set up in the ballroom. You have some catching up to do, so move it!"

"I'll be in shortly. Meet you inside, okay?"

Dave flashed a double thumbs-up as he melted into the throng of people milling about the lobby area. It was a good turnout for the reunion. Steeg shuffled forward patiently waiting for his turn at the registration table. It took a few minutes, but when he finally arrived he found former Class of '66 Homecoming Queen and Normandale College Veteran's Club devotee Gracie Ondracek asking for his name.

"Well, it's Gracie Ondracek!"

"No, that's my name," she looked up from her printed lists with a smile quickly followed by a vague glimmer of recognition when she saw Steeg. She shook her head in apology. "And, I know you, don't I? You look very familiar to me and I'm having such a difficult time remembering names…"

Smiling on the outside but personally miffed on the inside, Steeg silently resented that his first "air ball" of the night should be with Gracie Ondracek. He thought they were closer than for that. Obviously that wasn't the case.

He leaned over to look at her listings, offering pleasantly enough, "I may not be on your list, registered just last month: Patterson, Steeg."

The former Homecoming Queen and all around nice person checked her stapled sheath, turned the pages twice and found the listing. "Oh, yes, here you are!"

To her right, a long, shallow paper box contained a collection of plastic pin-on nametags. As Gracie thumbed quickly down the alphabetically organized tags to find the one for Steeg, Steeg turned her printed list around and quickly scribbled his signature on the line next to his printed name.

When she handed him his name tag, he couldn't let her absent mindedness stand. "I don't mean to embarrass you, Gracie, seeing how you have so much to keep track of at this shindig, but you actually asked me out on a date once."

Her eyes revealed panic as her face went blank. "I did? No, did I?"

He nodded with regret, ashamed of her poor memory as well as his necessity of having to provide the Homecoming Queen a clue to what was at the time for him a momentous event. "It was at Normandale Junior College – actually at a Vet's Club Whappituie party at Phil Denzer's party room?"

"Oh, good God, no – Whappituie?" Her face reddened considerably. "No wonder I don't remember!"

Her sudden admission caused Steeg's hand to jerk as he pinned his nametag onto his suit lapel. The sharp pin punctured his thumb just enough to draw blood and elicit an audible ouch. Quickly sucking on the tiny wound, he realized there was little he could do to gracefully extricate himself from the first major disappointment of the evening.

"Well, it doesn't matter, Gracie. It's still nice to see you again. You look exactly the same: blonde, cute and sexy!"

"Oh, Steeg!" Gracie blushed as she waved him away. "I'm an 'old tire' with sagging sidewalls and thinning tread! But, thank you for the lie, anyway. It's sweet of you."

He appreciated her automotive analogy. "You're very welcome. So, tell me, are any cheerleaders here yet? Besides you, I only remember the cheerleaders."

Immediately he heard a familiar feminine throat clearing come from behind him. Steeg turned to see Gracie Ofterdahl standing behind him, her familiar impish smile slicing into his heart. He promptly lost control, wrapping his arms around her, scooping her up in a long, tight hug and falling into a swirling vortex of powerful memories. Gracie was not immune. He felt her return his embrace warmly, squeeze him closely, her body pressed tightly against his. The electricity of it startled them both but they held fast to each other as everything around them turned into a blur.

After the too-short moment, Steeg pulled back enough to explore the wonder of it all in Gracie's face. Her penetrating brown eyes captured his intimately. His embrace loosened and he took a small step back, her hand in his as he moved apart to look her over.

Her hair was a lighter brown than he remembered, freshly styled into a large bushy afro. There were no gray strands anywhere. She wore a long brown patterned dress, simple with a high collar and long sleeves. The only jewelry she wore hung from her ears: attractive, handcrafted earrings partially hidden by her springy mass of curled hair. She wore light makeup and no rings on her fingers.

"Nice hair!" Steeg smiled as his cupped hands gently cradled her bouncy mass of hirsuteness. The thrill of seeing her was electric. Touching her, the thrill grew more intense as he continued to look at her. However, as surprisingly powerful it was to see her again, he was not blinded. He resisted any comment about how thin she looked.

She barely contained a laugh as she tugged at his red tie. "Nice tie! Wear it often?"

She noticed! Steeg was beside himself. He had to stop himself from blathering forth a lightning explanation of current power wardrobe theory as it related to sales techniques. Instead, he offered half in jest, half seriously, "Well, I got what I came for, so I can leave now!"

His insides melted as she laughed and possessively looped her arm in his. He didn't resist the guilty thrill of her breast pressed firmly against his upper arm.

"Oh, no you don't!" Gracie insisted. "We've got some catching up to do first."

Arm in arm, they left the registration area to head toward the tall double doors leading to the main ballroom. As they walked, he could feel her lean a little more on his arm. He sensed her nervousness as she too-anxiously intertwined her fingers with his and then covered their clasped hands with her other hand. It was an unconfident clinging that surprised him. He couldn't remember a time when Gracie was ever uncertain or insecure about anything.

Skillfully, Gracie steered him toward a small, even more slender woman standing off to the left of the ballroom double doors. Gracie released his arm to smoothly position herself between him and the other woman. As she did so, Steeg's eye caught the movement of Gracie's right earring to spy the badly scarred earlobe partially hidden by the ornate clasp. It was surprise number two of the evening.

"Steeg, I want you to meet my friend, Debra Sperre. Deb, this is Steeg Patterson."

With a toothy smile and an aggressive handshake, Debra said, "Well, at long last I meet you!"

Surprise number three. Steeg less enthusiastically returned the smile and handshake to the somewhat older and thinner woman. "I'm so sorry to have made you wait."

Debra chirped a short, stubby little laugh. "It's just that Grace has told me so much about you and her, and I must say she's right: you are definitely a man."

He wondered what that meant, catching a quick glimpse of Gracie's sheepish smile in the corner of his eye. "Well, yes, at least I was the last time I checked."

Debra released his hand, her thin fingers going up to her mouth as she laughed again, only this time a little louder. "And you're funny! Grace always said you made her laugh."

Steeg wondered what was behind Deb's nervousness.

"I haven't made her laugh in a long time." *Surprise number four.* Speculating briefly on what she had told her friend, Steeg tossed Gracie a quizzical glance.

Perceptively, or perhaps protectively, Gracie quickly looped her arm through his. Again, he felt her breast press anew against her arm. Again, their fingers immediately intertwined. Again, he let it happen.

He was glad to see her. But, this was not going anyway he had expected. How had he expected this to go? He wasn't sure. He had wanted to see her, maybe share a drink and talk about yesterday and today. At least, that was what he thought he had expected. He hadn't thought it through. He hadn't anticipated the emotion of it. Now, all he could do was hold on.

"We have a table already," Gracie nodded toward the double doors. "Should we go in?"

Outwardly smiling, at that moment Steeg was desperate for an excuse to be anywhere but on Gracie's arm. This was an uncomfortable preamble to the rest of the evening and he felt out of control.

"Well, I need to find a couple of friends yet. We kinda agreed to meet around here..."

Gracie's hold on Steeg's hand tightened noticeably as the three of them stepped toward the ballroom doors. "Sure, Steeg, but let's get our seats first. There'll be plenty of time for that other stuff later."

About a third of the chairs surrounding a small inland sea of cloth-covered banquet tables were occupied. Many of the remaining unoccupied chairs were already claimed and titled against tabletops. With Debra on her left, Gracie steered Steeg toward the front of the room to a middle table where three people Steeg didn't recognize were already seated. Of the remaining five chairs, three lean against the table. Gracie claimed the center chair and pointed to the chair on her right.

"This one is yours, Steeg." She pulled his chair out for him.

He paused, looking at the offered chair. It was immediately clear Gracie had planned this little triumvirate seating arrangement. It was as if he was in the middle of some kind of peculiar orchestration and Gracie was the conductor. Why she felt the need to do this, he had no idea. At the same time, he couldn't deny an increasingly uneasy feeling about it.

The problem was he was thrilled with seeing her again. Seeing her again was the reason he came to the reunion in the first place. But the offered chair had been tilted in advance: she had planned on his being there. How she knew he would be at the reunion confounded him. Either she was extremely hopeful he would make it to the reunion, or someone had told her he was coming. While most people had registered months in advance, Steeg and his friends had only filled in the registration forms and mailed checks a few weeks earlier. Prior to April, even he hadn't known he was going to the reunion. It was all curious to him and growing more curious by the moment.

"I'm flattered you thought of me." His smile hid his uncertainty as he took his designated seat.

Across the table, he could read the name tags of the two men and one woman: John Pisarski on the right; Vickie Kemnitz in the middle; Chad Weiblich on the left. None of the names were familiar to him, nor were their faces. Rising from his chair, he reached across to greet each person by their first name, shaking each hand in turn. Each person returned courteous yet vacant smiles. They didn't know Steeg, either.

He returned to his chair. The corner of his eye caught some movement from the opposite side of the large room. At a table tucked deep behind all the others, Dave Brunswick, Wedge Widger, Matt Cummings and Ace Johannson sat laughing. Matt pointed an accusatory finger in his direction, then hooked it into the side of his mouth and tugged mockingly.

Steeg, inwardly relieved he had a workable excuse to excuse himself if only for a moment, audibly cursed under his breath. "Damn it all, anyway."

Gracie leaned in closer, placed her hand over his covering his wedding band in the process. "What's wrong?"

He liked her touch. He was bothered by it, too, but he made no attempt to break the contact – not even a little bit. From her hand on his, he raised his eyes to her face. At first, all he saw was her captivating deep brown eyes and a warm half-smile. Then, he saw it.

She was right: something was wrong, but it wasn't with him. His eyes moved from her disturbingly scarred right earlobe, across her cheek to her comforting smile. Her partially opened mouth revealed perfectly white teeth that were too perfect and too white. He knew her very well. He remembered everything about her, every mole and freckle, every feature and flaw. Her smile was genuine, but her teeth had changed, and changed extensively. It was good dental work, but why had the reconstruction been necessary?

Surprises number five, he thought to himself as his eyes lingered at her mouth. Her lips revealed more to him. Despite her very good job of masking it with a subtle shade of lipstick, he saw a very faint, very thin scar along the top of her upper lip line.

Somehow, someway, Gracie had been injured. Normally, no one would have noticed it, but he did. What he saw told him the injury hadn't been pretty.

He watched the very tip of her tongue take a quick swipe to moisten her lips. Steeg looked up and their eyes met. He wondered if she thought he wanted to kiss her. If she suspected he wanted to, at that moment she very well may have been right.

He pulled back only a little and quickly glanced over his shoulder at his friends at the far corner table. Just as quickly, he returned to Gracie and Debra.

He cleared his throat. "I need to visit some old friends across the room for a few minutes. I apologize, but I promise to be back as soon as possible."

"Can't we come, too?" Gracie objected, increasing the pressure on his hand.

He would have normally assumed she was joking, but now he wasn't sure. "I won't be gone long. Besides, I wouldn't subject you two to these guys. I'm not that cruel. I'll be back. Keep my seat warm."

"You better be back," Debra warned as Steeg came to his feet. "I want to hear your version of the escape from the Southdale Security Police story!"

Three quick, stunned blinks preceded Steeg's shocked look at Gracie. "You told her about the parking lot thing?"

Her short bobbing affirmative nods made her mass of springy curls bounce. With a mildly embarrassed raise of her eyebrows, Gracie admitted, "What can I say? Deb and I have no secrets."

"Yeah, but that was between us; private; our secret." His disappointment was clear and deepened when Gracie weakly shrugged a silent apology.

Resigned to a fate of assured personal revelation and embarrassment, Steeg repeated his promise to return shortly. He then turned to make his way through the many tables obstructing the path to where his buddies sat.

They were all laughing as he walked up and took a chair. Dave was the first to chime in with a "You don't waste any time, do you?" comment. This was immediately followed by Matt's assertion of Gracie having the lobby area staked out just waiting for him. Wedge concurred with a "She looks hot!" observation. Ace simply shook his head and said nothing.

Feigning disgust, Steeg gestured for his friends to calm down. "It's not how it looks, okay?

"Oh yes, it is," Matt countered with a smirk. "She has you hooked before you even walk into the room."

"So, who's that other flat-chested broad she's with?" Wedge queried impolitely.

Steeg glanced back to where he had left Gracie and Deb, but they were both gone. His quick scan of the ballroom came up empty, so he turned back to the guys.

"That was Debra Sperre. She's Gracie's friend."

"Not nearly as hot as Gracie." Wedge judged.

"What kind of friend?" Matt asked.

"A friend. That's what she said."

Matt pushed another question. "Where's her husband?"

A self-conscious shrug from Steeg: "I don't think there is one, now that you mention it."

Dave was confused. "Wait a minute. Is that the same girl you use to date in high school?"

Ace slapped his forehead as Wedge laughed a quick "Try to keep up, Dave."

Dave defended himself with a forlorn, "Well, I didn't know! She looks different."

"She looks hot, that's how she looks!" Wedge insisted.

This was immediately followed by a disharmonious multi-voiced cascade of, "I didn't know – whadda ya think this is all about – good grief – ah, come on! – you need another drink – make mine a double, will ya?"

When things calmed down, Steeg continued.

"Yes, Dave, it's the same girl I use to date in high school. I don't know what kind of friend Debra Sperre is, Matt, but apparently a close one – Gracie told her about the Southdale parking lot thing."

Dave perked up. "What parking lot thing is that?"

Wedge followed. "Yeah, what parking lot thing?"

"A parking lot thing?" Matt scrunched an accusatory glare at Steeg. "You never told me about a parking lot thing."

"You never told any of us." Ace stated flatly.

Steeg looked at each man in turn before he said, "I didn't? Well, of course I didn't. It was a secret."

Draining the remains of his current beer, Matt said, "Not to her it wasn't."

"Well, it was to me." Steeg countered, wishing he had a drink, too. He turned in his chair to scan the room for the bar.

"Let's see if I got this straight," said Ace. "You and her did something in the Southdale parking lot and you never told anyone about it?"

Steeg's bar search was coming up empty. "Well, I almost never told anyone."

Dave leaned in close. "It must have been something good to keep it a secret."

Ace jumped back in. "Wait. You told someone? Who?"

He turned back to the four of them all bending forward in anticipation. Weighing his response carefully, he cautiously admitted, "I may have told the entire V3 Division aboard the U.S.S. *Hornet*. It kinda made me a legend."

Matt exploded. "And, you haven't told us?!"

"What a jerk!" Wedge scolded.

Ace followed with a sarcastic, "Nice guy!"

"A pox on your spawn!" Dave howled with a wave of an accusing finger.

Steeg responded to the last statement with a confused double-take and a furrowed brow. "I'm sorry. What can I do to make it up to you guys?"

"You can buy the next round, that's what!" Wedge affirmed, the others nodding in agreement.

"I would," Steeg readily acceded. "But, I don't know where the bar is!"

"I'll show you," Matt volunteered too willingly, coming to his feet to lead the way. "It's on the opposite side of the room just inside the entry doors."

The two of them left the others for the zigzag trek through the dining tables, many of which held twice as many people as when Steeg, Gracie and Debra had first entered the room. The crowd was picking up.

Only a few steps into their short trek to the disperser of liquid refreshment, they were sufficiently out of ear-shot for Matt to offer what he sincerely believed he had to say.

"I think I know what you're feeling now. You gotta keep your head, Steeg, and realize the truth. This thing with Grace ain't gonna work, you know that, right?"

Steeg shot a crooked grin at his friend. "What thing is that?"

"You know what I mean."

"No, I don't, Matt. Why don't you explain it to me."

Matt exhaled an audible sigh in a rush, remaining silent for the rest of the journey to the bar. They arrived to find the choices were few: beer, light beer, red or white wine and Coca Cola products. No hard stuff.

"Everyone drinking beer, right?" Steeg asked.

"Yeah," Matt confirmed.

Steeg ordered four beers on a tray and a white wine for himself. The bartender was efficient and had it all ready in a jiffy. Steeg pulled the cash from his wallet to pay the man, and then took his glass of wine and motioned for Matt to pick up the tray. The two turned back toward the table across the room where the guys were waiting.

Steeg pushed Matt a little further. "So, you can't explain what you mean, then?"

"I can, but you might not like it."

"I'm a rock. Go ahead."

"Okay, you asked for it. You're fantasizing about a girl you almost married; who dumped you after you joined the service simply so she could have some fun on her own terms; who four years later, goes out of her way to reel you back into her web only to play with your affections and dump you again. Now, after all these years, she shows up again, literally latches onto you as soon as you walk through the door so she can play her little game again, again on her terms, and for what?"

With a somewhat slower pace, they had reached the halfway point of the return trip.

"First, I'm not fantasizing about Gracie. I have no plans to re-ignite anything with her. I simply enjoy seeing her again, that's it. There is no agenda here."

"No agenda on your part," Matt harrumphed. "But, whether you want to admit it or not, she has an agenda. History proves, my friend, she is not happy unless she's pulling your strings."

"You're more protective than my mother," Steeg complained softly, lowering his voice as they neared their destination. "I've got it under control and that includes keeping my 'strings' tucked in and out of reach."

Their arrival to the table was greeted by a small round of applause from the others. Matt distributed the beers and returned to his seat. Steeg remained standing as he turned to glance back at Gracie's table just in time to see her and Debra return, glasses of white wine in hand. He took a contemplative sip of from his glass as he watched Gracie. She found him and made a small wave in his direction as she sat down. He turned back to the guys.

"Anyway, probably should go back to Gracie. They'll be serving dinner soon."

"Why doncha bring her over here?" Dave suggested. "We have room."

Steeg agreed it was a good idea, but declined the opportunity. "I don't know, but she seems to have gone to some trouble to secure that particular table for her friends. I guess I'm included in the group."

"Is that a string I see hanging from the back of your jacket?" Matt asked with a smirk.

Steeg almost looked down for a loose thread before he caught himself. "Cute. No, it isn't a string. I'm just going to have dinner with her and then I'll be back. See you guys a little later."

He moved away to a sarcastic chorus of crude commentary and peculiarly disgusting sounds.

Chapter 12
Food for Thought

"I would have been back sooner," Steeg explained with a smile and an excited rush that betrayed him. He returned to the chair Gracie had pre-assigned to him. "But you guys disappeared."

Gracie was visibly satisfied as Steeg took his seat. "We had to powder our noses."

"Among other things," Debra added with another chirpy, shallow laugh.

From across the table, the stranger named John complained. "Why do women call it that, anyway? 'Powdering your nose' my ass. You're taking a leak!"

Their chosen libations apparently had begun to take effect. The other stranger named Vickie quickly responded with a profound observation.

"You're right," she chortled. "But, 'powdering your nose' sounds so much better."

"It is better," Gracie agreed. The corners of her mouth impishly curled upward. Steeg felt his heart flutter.

Chad felt he had to say something, so he offered a capsulated critique of the general facilities beyond the restrooms.

"Nice place," he grunted. "When do we eat?"

John more impatiently looked at his watch. "Anytime, now."

As if on cue, from the several service doors lining the far wall the white jacketed catering staff emerged wheeling in carts loaded with plated salads.

"You always were in a hurry about things, John," Gracie offered with a too familiar tone. John returned an annoyed glance as Gracie continued. "You hurried often enough in your car, why not be in a hurry to eat, too?"

Her question struck Steeg as stunningly juvenile, carrying a near-accusatory tone he didn't miss. He saw John lean back in his chair with a smirk he directed straight to Gracie.

"I had an early lunch," John explained. "Besides, I don't remember you complaining about my 'eating' habits before. Did I miss something?"

As he turned back toward Gracie, Steeg's furrowed brow shrouded a confused unspoken question successfully stifled by Vickie's second contribution of the evening.

"So, Gracie, I didn't know you and John knew each other in high school."

"Oh, she knew me, alright," confirmed John with another crooked smile. "Just like I 'knew' her."

At that moment, a small squad of white-coated salad bearers descended upon their table. In seconds, each person had their own plated lettuce wedge generously topped with a colorful deep red raspberry cream dressing. There were no other garnishments to the salad. Steeg thanked his server as the salad was placed in front of him. He retrieved the freestanding linen napkin, snapped it fully open and spread it across his lap to protect his neatly pressed navy blue slacks. He then immediately sampled the dressing by poking his finger in the middle of the red stuff and quickly sucking it into his mouth.

"Not bad," he opined.

"It's a wedge of lettuce," Chad complained. "Lettuce and some red shit all over it. We paid for this?"

Steeg chose to ignore Chad's statement of dissatisfaction as Vickie jumped in with yet another question.

"So, Chad, how is it you know Gracie?"

Chad continued to examine the salad as he answered, "We were in the same history class, I think."

"That's true," Gracie added as she began to surgically attack her lettuce wedge. "But, it was more than a class or two, wasn't it Chad?"

Chad glanced over to Gracie only to look quickly away. "I guess you could say that."

Steeg caught Gracie's subtle satisfied smile but said nothing.

Vickie, however, was compelled by her own curiosity. She leaned back in her chair and placed her open hands on the table.

"I'm sorry, but I have to apologize for something."

"No, you don't." Gracie responded flatly.

"Yes, I do," Vickie countered firmly. "Except for Gracie, I don't know any of you. I don't remember meeting any of you in high school or anywhere else. Yet, we're all at this table, and we all seem to know Gracie. Isn't that strange?"

It was a little odd, Steeg thought. He leaned in to whisper to Gracie.

"Where's Cindy?"

Cindy was Gracie's best friend and constant companion in high school.

"She couldn't make it," Gracie whispered back.

Steeg looked over to Debra who met his glance with a strangely self-satisfied expression. *Yes,* he thought, *this is odd.*

"So, if I understand this," Vickie continued. "The one thing we all have in common at this table is the fact we all know Gracie. Am I right?"

The others occupied themselves with their salads as Gracie expanded on the point.

"Well, yes, Vickie, you're right about that. But there's more – another commonality you all share."

Steeg perused the other three across the table. John blushed; Chad seemed to turn a little pale.

Vickie let out a clipped chortle. "Well, what is that?"

Gracie looked up from her salad but didn't answer the question. After a few moments of silence, Vickie's mouth dropped open.

"You gotta be kiddin' me, right? You mean all of us?"

Gracie put her salad fork down on the plate as she nodded toward Steeg. "Except for Steeg."

John's face turned red with growing anger as he leaned toward Gracie. "If that's true, why is he sitting here?"

Everything around Steeg started to spin and change too fast, a sickening feeling rapidly rising in his gut. He recognized the same hollow nausea of betrayal he had first felt years earlier behind the CATCC status board on the U.S.S. *Hornet* when he first read her letter telling him she was marrying Stewart Smalley. Through the same crippling agony, he barely heard what Gracie said in response.

"You all took your turns. But Steeg was the gentlest person I knew and the only one who really cared."

Some kind of invisible force propelled Steeg from the table. Somehow, the room moved away from him as he quickly found himself in the foyer outside the ballroom. He headed for the men's room conveniently tucked behind the corner where the foyer joined the balcony overlooking the entrance lobby. He made the left turn into the first stall just in time to throw up.

More than an hour later, Debra walked up behind Gracie and rested a hand on her friend's shoulder. Gracie stood at the hotel's lobby wall fountain lost in the easy cascade of water flowing into the broad sculpted cistern.

"They had it coming," Debra said softly. "They hurt you. You did right."

Grace's mass of curls swayed slightly with her denial. "Steeg never hurt me. I didn't do right by him. Nothing happened the way I thought it would. And now, I can't find him. One more time, I hurt the only person..."

Gracie's statement hung open for a long second so Debra completed it for her. "... the only person you loved."

Grace quickly wiped away a singular tear slowly sliding down her cheek. She sniffed her request. "If there's anything else I can screw up tonight, let me know, okay?"

Debra patted Gracie's shoulder as she repeated, "The others had it coming."

Matt zipped up, turned from the urinal and moved to the washbasin as Steeg slowly emerged from the stall he had occupied while dinner was being served in the ballroom.

"Well, here you are! Great minds think alike!"

Steeg walked up to the next washbasin, turned on the cold water tap, cupped his hands under the flow and splashed his face. He wiped the loose water away with his hands and looked up at Matt's reflection in the mirror.

"Good gravy, Steeg, you don't look so good. You eat some bad food, or what?"

Steeg almost chuckled at that one. "You have no idea. It's like I've been chewing on the same thing for years and it just came back to bite me."

"Damn hotel food," Matt cursed sympathetically as he reached into his jacket pocket and produced a half-depleted roll of anti-acid tablets. He thumbed out two and handed them to his friend. "Take two of these and call me in the morning."

"Thanks, Matt." Steeg popped the tablets into his mouth and proceeded to chew. "Yum. Kinda pepperminty-chalky. Should help the bad breath anyway."

Matt sniffed the air. "Don't count on it."

Chapter 13
The Chicago Way

With the shallow golden halo of day still hanging tight against the western horizon, the approaching night sky hadn't quite spread enough yet to require the artificial illumination of streetlights barely noticeable on the highway. The dashboard clock read 9:20 and a grunt from Steeg followed a remorseful shake of his head. After the restroom, he had rejoined the guys with Matt leading the way, but he begged off after only a few minutes at the table. s

Leaving the ballroom and following the foyer to the balcony, he stopped at the top step when he looked down at the entrance lobby. He saw Gracie and Debra standing near the fountain. He took several steps back behind a beefy support pillar where he could safely observe the two women without being seen himself.

Grace moved to her left, craning to one side as if looking down the adjoining promenade for something. Debra followed close behind. Too far away to hear, he could see them share a few words and then walk back toward the fountain.

As he watched from his vantage point on the balcony, Steeg struggled poorly with all he had learned that evening. For the moment, all he could take away from everything was the need to talk with Gracie about a great many things too-long left unsaid between them. She owed him at least that much.

Below, the two women turned and walked toward the staircase which would take them directly to where he now stood. He was coolly unconcerned with the pending confrontation. He welcomed it, knowing for the first time as he watched them ascend the steps he also welcomed the chance to hurt her as much as she had hurt him. If he was certain of one thing it was that he owed her that much.

Her dress was ankle-length, so Gracie had to lift the front of it high enough to clear each step she took. She almost reached the top of the staircase before she looked up to see Steeg standing in front of her. She whispered something to Debra who quickly nodded and said nothing to Steeg as she left Gracie for the ballroom.

"I was looking for you," she began haltingly, her eyes unable to hold contact with Steeg's.

He looked away with a squint narrowed by doubt. He couldn't believe anything she would say now.

Gracie tried to continue. "Things I needed to do..."

Steeg interrupted with a voice so heavy and dark he took pleasure in seeing how it startled her.

"We need to talk." It wasn't a request, but a flat, blunt order. From his inside vest pocket, Steeg pulled out a business card and handed it to her. "Here's mine. Where's yours?"

She took the card. "I don't have one. Do you have a pen?"

From his inside jacket pocket he produced a beautiful gold Parker's ballpoint and handed it to her. She flipped his business card over, carefully scribbled her address and telephone number, then handed the pen and the card back to Steeg.

He made sure he could read what she had written. "North Clifton in Chicago?"

"Yes. It's a house mid-block just south of Belmont Avenue. I'm usually at that number after 4:00 in the afternoon."

"Roger there, too?"

Roger Flint was Gracie's 'significant other' fourteen years earlier when Steeg had followed her to the Teens In Crisis phone hotline service and the University of Minnesota.

She looked away with a sigh. "Oh, no. I'm sure Roger is still in Boston. That was over long ago."

He wondered what that story would reveal, but he wouldn't pursue it, not now. There had been enough surprises for one night. He returned his pen to its proper place and slid the card into his shirt pocket.

"I'm in Chicago a lot," he added more coldly than he should. "There are things that need to be said, agreed?"

She simply nodded.

"I'll call you before my next trip."

He moved past her without another word and descended the stairs toward the lobby. She turned to watch him walk away and leave through the hotel's front entrance.

Lost in his memories of the evening, Steeg crossed the Minnesota River on the Cedar Avenue Bridge without realizing it and promptly missed the Sibley Highway turnoff that would have taken him to his house. It didn't matter. He continued south, well past Eagan, into Apple Valley and further into Lakeville. He needed to drive. He needed to think.

* * *

It was almost midnight. Carol was sitting in the rocker-recliner reading another Christian romance novel she had checked out from the library earlier that week. It was a familiar sight for Steeg. It was the hour that was unfamiliar. Carol usually went to bed early.

"How did it go?" She asked looking up from her book. She watched as he walked in, removed his suit coat and released the top two buttons on his vest.

Steeg draped the suit jacket over the arm of the sofa and plopped down. "Well, frankly, it was the pits."

"Oh?"

"Yeah. Be glad you didn't come."

"Why's that?"

"Several spouses were there. You could pick them out easily because they were sitting alone as their partners circulated with the other classmates. Even the 'trophy' wives were alone. Sad. Very sad."

Carol nodded in a silent response and returned to her book.

Several minutes passed with nothing being said before he then asked, "Kids in bed?"

"Of course," Carol responded with unveiled mild annoyance.

"Are you tired?"

Carol shrugged.

"Wanna turn in?"

"After I finish this chapter," she said, turning the page. "Almost done."

He came to his feet and softly strode over to gently rub her shoulders. With a smile he said, "I'll make it worth your while."

"Oh, really?" Carol moved her bookmark into place. "What are you going to do, give me a back rub?"

"Among other things."

Later together in bed, his lovemaking was almost desperate. He needed her. It showed. She welcomed his embraces and held onto him tightly through it all. She was surprised when, only a little later, he reached for her again.

* * *

"Sure, Ronnie, that would be fine," Steeg held the phone receiver between his shoulder and ear as he typed the calendar entry on the computer keyboard. "Wednesday morning anytime after 10:00... You pick it, I don't care. It's your territory, so set it up... No, I'd like to, but I have another commitment that night, and then I have to be in St. Louis the next day... Sounds good, see you when my flight gets in."

He poked his finger on the switch hook to regain dial tone. There was no need to reread the handwritten address and telephone number on the backside of the business card. He had memorized Gracie's phone number as soon as his eyes had first fallen on it. He reread it anyway. More than a week had passed since the reunion. Now, his hunger for the simple sound of Gracie's voice consumed him. His hand trembled as he dialed the number.

It rang several times. No answer. He let the ringing continue. After several seconds, he hung up. His wristwatch told him it was five past ten in the morning. Gracie had said she was usually home after four o'clock in the afternoon.

"Of course," he said to no one there. "After four, then."

Chapter 14
Business First

Outside the kitchen window all was dark. Inside, the coffee was hot and waiting when Steeg walked in fully dressed in his three piece, gray business suit, cordovan wing tips and red power tie. Carol, in her nightgown and bathrobe, sat at the table nursing her first cup of the morning. It was 4:30in the morning.

"I thought you'd appreciate the shorter travel week," Steeg said as he poured a cup for himself. He came to the table and took his usual chair. "I'm back on Friday, early evening."

Carol lowered her cup between sips. She sounded sad when she said, "You travel too much."

"I'm sorry. It's the nature of the business. But, this time it's only three days, not a whole week. And, I promise I won't go into the office this weekend."

Her lowered head revealed her resignation to the way things had been for more than two years. "But then, there's always next week and the week after that."

They said nothing for a while, choosing to sit and drink their coffees in silence. When Steeg's cup was about two-thirds empty, he put it down and rose from his chair.

"I know I have to change some things, Carol. I'll make it work somehow. But, we have a lot of magazines. Each one has a lot of ad space we need to sell. The only way I know how to do that is to be in front of my advertisers every month. I just don't know how else to do it."

She reached for his hand. "I know. It sounds like I don't understand, but I do. I don't want to be difficult."

"You're not," he interrupted. "I'll fix it. I promise."

With that, he leaned down and gave her a warm good-bye kiss. She stroked his face and smiled. There was the familiar, uncomfortable silence when he turned away, exited the kitchen and grabbed his carry-on bag waiting at the stairs. She heard him say "I'll call!" as he closed the connecting door to the garage behind him.

* * *

Harry Smiesrud smoked pungent cigars more or less continuously and wore ill-fitting tweed suits. Easily over three hundred pounds, anything he wore would have been ill-fitting, but the tweed suits were especially so. The thick odor of stale tobacco hung in the man's office, but Ronnie Vanderslip and Steeg Patterson were well-practiced at subduing their natural gag reflexes.

"I don't care all that much about frequency discounts," Harry grunted, shifting the ever present cigar in his mouth. "I'll take 'em when you offer 'em, but I don't need 'em."

Ronnie jumped in with his characteristic youthful enthusiasm. "They can add up a lot, Mr. Smiesrud, especially if you expand your campaign and add our other magazines to the mix."

Harry grumbled some more as he looked down at the media kit folder and casually thumbed through the typewritten pages of Ronnie's proposal. Harry's review didn't take long.

"You know, fellas, cross-frequency advertising discounts don't mean shit when you're in the medical devices industry." Harry flipped the folder back onto his desk's blotter. "I'm the biggest medical devices OEM supplier in the country. What do I care about the pharmaceutical market, or the bio-med industry? I don't sell to those people. I sell to medical device manufacturers. Those other magazines mean nothing to me."

Ronnie's quick, panicked look at Steeg didn't hide his desperateness. Steeg returned a cool squint. From behind his cigar, Harry watched them both for several quiet seconds. Steeg decided to break the silence.

"Harry, you're absolutely right!"

Ronnie's head jerked back in surprise. He and Steeg had talked about the strategy of this meeting. The strategy hadn't included agreeing with a client reluctant to continue his advertising in MEPNews.

"You're damn right I'm right!" Harry's broadening smile forced the cigar deep into the corner of his mouth.

"After all," Steeg continued. "Those other industries, all those other end-users out there making all those different products, providing all those different services, with literally billions of dollars in sales every year – they don't buy from you!"

"Damn right they don't!" Harry's self-satisfied smile remained and the cigar didn't move.

Steeg relaxed back into a chair oddly uncomfortable for all its upholstered luxury and with a more cautious tone added, "They only buy from your customers."

That was when Harry's cigar drooped, his self satisfied smile sagging just a little.

Steeg continued. "Your customers service those other companies continuously; everyday; day in, day out. When product needs repair or replacing, your customers do that, don't they?"

"I guess." Harry halfway agreed as he tongued his cigar to the opposite side of his mouth.

"Harry, when you provide a positive presence in your customers' targeted markets to urge purchase of medical equipment, equipment using your components," Steeg continued coolly. "You produce a flood of customer good will surpassed by only one thing."

Harry's eyes narrowed. "And what one thing is that?"

A single raised eyebrow preceded Steeg's reply. "More customers for your components."

Ronnie nodded in agreement while Harry's face morphed into a "how's that" expression.

"It's simple, really." Steeg explained. "Your customers' competitors find you in print vehicles serving their own target markets. You're not a competitor. You're simply looking out for the better interests of the industry. They come to you. You get more business."

Carefully, Harry removed the cigar and lowered it to the ceramic tray next to the desk blotter. Steeg continued.

"Because of your superior business savvy, you're the only OEM supplier doing this type of end-around market stimulation." Steeg smiled as he added, "Your competitors aren't there... Yet."

Harry threw an arched eyebrow in response. "Yet?"

Steeg returned a half-shrug as he explained, "Well, Harry, you can't expect us to keep this type of energetic, synergistic, wide-view strategy under wraps forever. It has just too much potential. I'm sure you understand."

"I'm sure," Harry said, retrieving Ronnie's proposal once more for a quick re-examination. He fingered his way to the strategy page to review the particulars. He looked back at Steeg. "How long do I got?"

"Ronnie's plan is solid because it helps all our magazines. It's going into all our promos for next year. That means you have from now until the end of the year to make hay while the sun shines. Fair enough?"

Several minutes went by peppered with shallow grunts from Harry as he paged through the proposal once more. With a concluding grunt, Harry pulled a pen from his jacket.

"I'll need a new ad for both of these new audiences – tailored to appeal to each."

"I can help with that," Ronnie offered, thrilled as Harry scratched his signature on the proposal's last page.

Harry handed the signed document to Ronnie and said, "We'll have to move to meet the close date for the next issues."

Chapter 15
True Like

Ronnie pulled his Ford LTD around the drive leading up to the front entrance of the new Des Plaines Marriott.

"Well, Steeg, I can't thank you enough," he said as his car came to a stop across from the hotel entry doors. "Smiesrud's been a tough one to work with and for a minute there, I thought we were dead."

Steeg smiled as he pulled up on the door handle and exited the big Ford sedan from the passenger side. "Just remember one thing, young man."

"What's that, 'Oh, Great Master of the Sale'?"

Steeg opened the back door, retrieved his brief case and carry-on bag from the back seat and then reached over to grab Ronnie by the shoulder. "Remember my son: never let them see you sweat! Go now and multiply your insertion orders!"

With a sincere smile, Ronnie waved as he drove away.

Inside the hotel, Steeg walked up to the long granite topped front desk to confirm his reservation. The neatly groomed dark skinned man behind the desk wore a sharp navy blue blazer, a burnished brass name tag that read Hasim Bhandare, and a friendly smile. Within seconds, the other man had found Steeg's information and handed him the registration card. Steeg, in turn, provided a credit card.

"Room 312. Turn down service tonight, Mr. Patterson?" The other man handed back the credit card along with two of the new plastic card keys.

"Yes, please, that would be very nice, Hasim." Steeg then hastily added, "Hasim, I also need to rent a car. Any ideas how I can do that quickly?"

The clerk nodded. "I'll have our agency ring your room, sir."

"Excellent." Steeg slipped the plastic key cards into his shirt pocket. "Give me twenty minutes to get settled in, though."

The clerk looked at his wristwatch. "Very well, Mr. Patterson, four-thirty it will be."

Steeg thanked the man, grabbed his two bags and crossed the lobby to the elevators.

The third floor no-smoking double still smelled new. The spring-hinged door closed loudly behind him as Steeg tossed the bags on the first bed. He then walked to the window to fully close the drapes. Next, he removed his jacket and tie before he retrieved the television remote to turn on the set. It took a few seconds before the hotel programming information appeared on the screen. Steeg opted for any kind of news channel, pressing the up button on the remote until a local channel appeared. It wasn't news, it was "Jeopardy" but it was noise, so he raised the volume level a step or two and let it play.

Steeg removed his shoes and suit, using one of the wooden hangers with metal clips to protect the crease of his slacks by carefully hanging them from the cuffs. He then stripped down shoving his underwear into the plastic laundry bag he pulled from the closet shelf.

"Let's try 'Books to Move By' for $400." He heard the 'Jeopardy' contestant say.

The show host read the answer from a card pulled from the pedestal: "In 1962, this authoress penned 'Silent Spring' and heralded in the new environmentalist movement."

"Who is Rachel Carson?" Steeg answered before the contestant. Satisfied, he grabbed his shaving kit from the carry-on and walked into the bathroom.

By time the phone rang he was clean shaven, dressed in jeans, a pullover sweater and sneakers. He decided his suit coat would be comfortable enough for the promised pleasant temperatures of the evening.

He answered the phone on the second ring. "This is Patterson... Yes, something clean and comfortable?... A Buick La Saber? That would be fine... With the Concierge?... Very good. Thank you."

He pushed down on the switch hook to end the call and immediately dialed "8" for an outside line. He then dialed Gracie's number. It took four rings before she answered.

"Hi, it's me," he began. He didn't resist the deep thrill when she replied.

"Oh, yes. So, you're in town now?"

He could hear something in her voice he could only interpret as uncertainty.

"Well, I'm in Des Plaines. It's a bit of a drive to get to you, but I should be there before six o'clock. Let's go somewhere to eat, my treat."

Warmth spread through him at the sound of her light laugh. Then he heard her sigh.

"Is that a bad idea?" He asked, concerned.

"No, it's not a bad idea." She reassured him. There was a noticeable pause before she continued. "It's just that... it seems whenever we are together, you always want to feed me."

"Oh, yeah, that. You have to understand, that's because I can't sing or dance, remember?"

"I remember."

"It's your neighborhood, so you pick the spot," he suggested, reluctant to hang up. "See you in a bit."

Pulling the receiver away from his good ear, he heard her say, "Be careful."

Be careful, he thought as he lowered the receiver to its cradle. *What did she mean by that?*

He turned and his eyes fell to the double bed closest to the window. Hasim had scheduled turn-down service for the night. Steeg assumed they would provide a couple of those foil wrapped mint chocolates on the pillow. He wondered if he shouldn't call down to have them leave fresh roses, instead. The bed's plush comforter moved, the top edge peeled back to reveal Gracie's smiling face. He quickly blinked the vision away. Should she be there with him that night? Hell, no! But, would she be there, anyway?

He should have felt different; he should have felt some kind of severe apprehension, or a convicting, punishing sense of guilt for even considering bringing Gracie back to the hotel. But he didn't feel any of those things. He could never break his marriage vows; vows made to Carol and to God. It was out of the question. He had never cheated on Carol. But when it came to Gracie, somehow none of what he felt violated the vows he had made, the promises he kept true, or the honor he supposed. Intellectually, he knew better. He also knew the one person he could not resist was Gracie.

Taking I90, aka the Kennedy Expressway, into town was an idea that at first blush contradicted common sense. The traffic was rush hour thick but the substantial flow of vehicles into town was a great deal less than the endless massive multi-lane river of headlights heading in the opposite direction. The Buick La Saber, a beautiful car with power in a blink and an interior so luxurious he felt underdressed, handled like a dream. Once on the toll way, he found a large collection of vehicles moving at a sane speed he effortlessly copied and maneuvered the sedan smoothly into the flow.

An overly large Chicago street map he had strategically folded down to a manageable size rested under his hand on the center armrest. He only needed to find the Addison exit. It seemed to take longer than it actually did.

Steeg knew the side streets would be slow and interminable with bumper-to-bumper, stop and go traffic all the way in. When the exit for Addison appeared in the distance, he was reluctant but resigned to take it. Off the expressway, Addison stretched forever. Short sprints with massive numbers of cars insufferably followed prolonged pauses at too many light-controlled intersections. Time crawled like the traffic and he frequently checked his street map for an alternative route to free him from the crush of slow moving vehicles. The Lincoln intersection offered him an out.

At Lincoln, he turned right. For excruciating miles, he followed a waving river of brake lights until he reached Belmont. At Belmont, he followed an illuminated crimson branch of the tail light river to the left to join with another endless stream of tail lights. At every slowdown or full stop, the same thought kept returning to him: how do people live in a place like this?

He knew he was anxious. The drive was taking on frustrating proportions and yet the dashboard clock showed it wasn't even 5:30. Time was standing still and it didn't feel right. Continuing east on Belmont, had he not known Lake Michigan was somewhere ahead of him, he was certain he had driven clear out of the state of Illinois. Chicago was an annoyingly huge town.

Finally, he approached Clifton Avenue and, with relief, he slowed to take the right turn and ease the Buick onto the quiet street. The house was where Gracie had told him: on the west side, the middle of the block – a small, weathered two-story squeezed between two other narrow two-story dwellings in a tight row of similarly squeezed residential abodes for as far as the eye could see. He wasn't surprised to see both sides of the street lined bumper-to-bumper with parked cars. He quietly rolled the car farther down the block. One block later, a usable space presented itself. Steeg eased the rental tight against the curb, exited the car, making sure the doors were locked before he hoofed it back to Gracie's house. He took the front stoop in two steps and rang the front doorbell.

A few seconds went by before he heard footsteps on the opposite side of the door. This was followed by a number clicks as the door locks were released. He took a breath and held it as the heavy wood entry door swung open.

Debra smiled broadly at him. He was struck by how much older she looked than when he first saw her at the reunion; not objectionably so, just older. Maybe it was her hair. She wore it differently at the reunion. Or, was it the floor length frock she was wearing? He didn't know.

"You're early!" She said pleasantly enough. "Grace's still with her five o'clock, but she should be up in a few minutes. Come in, come in."

With a smiling "Thank you" he obeyed as she waved him into the front foyer of the old house.

A carved wooden L-shaped staircase darkened with age led upstairs to his right. To his left a simple wood framed arch revealed a warmly welcoming living room, neat as a pin with near perfect and absolutely spotless furnishings.

Debra led the way into the room, the stylish sterility of which struck Steeg as a pleasant departure from what he was used to with his own house. Had these two been husband and wife, with as few as one child, no way would the orderly decorum of this room be possible.

"Just have a seat and make yourself at home," Debra offered, gesturing toward a perfectly sized stuffed sofa behind a dark oak coffee table. "I'll let her know you're here."

He thanked her and she moved through the adjacent dining room to disappeared down a hallway leading to the rear of the house. Steeg gave the room another quick appreciative perusal of the aged woodwork as he picked up the lone magazine from the coffee table. It was some kind of academic publication – no ads – but the cover had an intriguing photo of a Middle Eastern adobe style dwelling with two matching dome-like structures protruding from the roof. It took a few seconds for Steeg to realize the reason why the photo intrigued him: in his mind the pergola topped adobe mounds in the photo became nipples and the domes became the naked breasts of a reclining woman. He shook his head to snap out of whatever funk he was in the process of falling into, relieved as the breasts in the photo became adobe domes again.

The evening hadn't started yet and he was already in trouble.

"Would you like some tea?" Debra's voice traveled lightly from the kitchen.

He left the sofa and the magazine to move cautiously in the direction of her voice. "That would be nice, but I'll pass for now." He added more truthfully than he knew, "I'm not sure exactly what's going to happen tonight."

He entered the kitchen to find Debra placing the tea kettle on the stove's burner.

"Does she often conduct her counseling sessions this late in the day?"

"Actually, most of her sessions aren't during normal working hours," Deb explained, turning to the cupboard to retrieve a colorful ceramic canister labeled "Tea". She loaded the loose material into a single perforated metal tea ball. "Most of her patients work during the day and psychotherapy isn't often covered by employee health insurance plans. Her sessions are usually in the evening hours after people get home from their own jobs."

She's telling me Gracie gave up prime income producing hours, Steeg was suddenly concerned and oddly relieved.

He saw an opportunity for a safe, respectful exit. "That would make my visit this evening more than an intrusion. Perhaps now is not a good time."

The water was nowhere near ready but Deb checked the tea kettle anyway. Rendering undue attention to a pot not boiling, she didn't look at him as she said, "You underestimate yourself. She's been looking forward to seeing you."

As she said it, her voice turned noticeably hollow. Steeg sensed that, beyond his being in that house at that moment, something else was amiss.

Abruptly, she excused herself and he watched her leave the kitchen by a rear hallway. He turned at the sound of people talking coming from outside the lone kitchen window. Through the gray film of a window in need of cleaning, he saw a Latino-looking couple and a young boy with bushy black hair emerge from a lower level doorway and walk toward the sidewalk fronting the house. His wristwatch read 5:55.

The sound of quick, light footfalls echoed from the stairwell hidden by the wall behind the stove. A door opened and Gracie stuck her head around the corner.

She smiled when she saw him. "I need to change. It'll take only a few minutes, I promise!"

"Take your time, Gracie." It please him she seemed excited. "I'm not going anywhere."

She quickly disappeared down the same hallway Deb had just used. He leaned against the countertop near the sink and waited in the kitchen, his own words echoing back to him: *"I'm not going anywhere... not going anywhere... going nowhere."*

The minutes passed and his doubts, or was it guilt, grew. He immersed himself in trying to invent a good excuse to back out of this whole deal, admonishing himself for making the date in the first place. *I'm married, for Christ's sake!*

With the growing whistle of the tea kettle Debra returned to the kitchen.

"She'll be down soon," she said as she removed the kettle from the burner. Steam rose from the spout as Debra poured water into her prepared cup, so carefully attentive in the effort it bothered him. It was obvious she was uncomfortable.

Before his intrusion apology found breath, from around the corner Gracie appeared dressed in a multi-colored pantsuit thing that looked like a strange combination between old fashioned pantaloons and a cowl-less Middle Eastern styled berka. The material flowed and billowed with each step Gracie took.

Debra immediately walked up to smooth Gracie's afro style locks over her right ear, hiding the scarred earlobe already partially hidden by a dangling earring. Deb's hand then moved to straighten the matching scarf around Gracie's collar. In a subtly self conscious movement, she stopped short of caressing Gracie's cheek. Instead, almost as if she was suddenly burned, Debra pulled her hand back with a noticeable blush.

At that moment Steeg knew with startling certainty the two women were lovers.

Chapter 16
The Final Good Bye

It was the sudden realization of how much a coward he truly was that was most stunning. Failing to come up with an excuse good enough to allow for a graceful, if not stumbling, exit from the evening, a convicting truth slapped him across his bruised psyche: even if he had an excuse to get out of there, Steeg wouldn't have used it.

Gracie had bounced into the kitchen with an almost ebullient aura that caught him off guard. When he realized the truth of the relationship the two women shared, he froze. Why had she agreed to this meeting? What did she really think of him? What did it matter, anyway? She was a lesbian and going out to dinner with him! It didn't make any sense! Oddly, at that moment, the lack of sense was the one thing that seemed right about the whole charade. She was gay. He wasn't. Of course they should have dinner together. It was completely safe and harmless. It made all the sense in the world.

His growing panic ebbed, replaced by a growing strength as one thing became certain: whatever came from the rest of this evening, he was confident he would at last have some honest answers from Gracie.

Since leaving Debra at the front stoop of the house, Gracie's exuberance over their "date" was punctuated by a more or less non-stop babbling recap of her busy day. Steeg silently wondered if she was more nervous than he was. She continued her self-centered litany for the entire block and one-half walk to the car. That was when she abruptly stopped. The sudden silence drove home the fact he was too distracted to have heard a word she had said during the entire trek from her house.

He opened the curb-side door and guided her by the hand as she slid into the passenger side bucket bench seat. When he got in behind the wheel, she ran a hand across the upholstery and said something about it being a nice car.

"It's a rental," he replied, turning the key. The engine immediately came to life. "I got it just for you."

Maneuvering the Buick from the tight parking space required a couple of back-and-forth contortions of the steering wheel. He soon squeezed the sedan down the canyon of curb parked autos, silently grateful for the lack of oncoming traffic. Gracie instructed him to turn left on Barry and head to Sheffield Avenue. There he turned left again, shortly passing the Vic Theatre on the right as they continued to the Clark Street intersection where Gracie knew of a modest diner specializing in Mexican cuisine. Nosing into a parking spot of ample size two doors down from her chosen place would prove to be his easiest maneuver of the evening.

The building was old, the floor-to-ceiling street side windows were dirty, and the floor needed a good stripping and waxing. The half-occupied tables were vinyl covered, the dim lighting fluttered annoyingly from ceiling mounted fluorescents, and the aroma of refried beans and tortillas permeated the place.

"Interesting establishment," Steeg dryly commented as he nudged Gracie's chair gently from behind before taking his own seat across from her. "Is this normal for mid-week dinner traffic?"

She didn't say anything, only smiled and shrugged her shoulders. An unshaven younger man dressed in a dirty white T-shirt and an apron appeared, placed a simple, single page typewritten menu in front of both of them, and with a heavy accent that definitely was not Mexican, asked if they'd like something to drink.

Resisting the urge to ask for the wine list, Steeg was humorously encouraged: the evening, he was now convinced, could only improve from that point on.

He followed Gracie's lead and ordered exactly what she did. The two of them tried to get comfortable and settled in to a discussion of she chose as well: a stimulating and non-threatening exchange of "Do You Remember?"

She asked him if he remembered Mary Handerhousin from TIC – "You do, don't you? You know she and I have stayed in touch. She's really doing well, has a position in the state government, you know…" She followed this by asking him if he remembered some other guy, a name he had never heard before – "You don't? Well, of course not, he wasn't there when you were…" So, she moved on to Mike Swenson also from TIC – "He was on your shift? That's right! I had forgotten. You'll never guess what he did. He married Mary! That's right, they got married! They got two kids! Isn't that wild?"

Every word tumbling from her mouth avoided everything that needed to be said. He took it for what it was: testimony to the insecurity she felt with him. When he reached across the table and covered her hand with his, her eyes met his and she immediately fell silent.

"Tell me about Roger," he asked, referring to Roger Flint, her 'significant other' when he knew her at the University and after her divorce from Stewart Smalley.

Her eyes fell, but her hand stayed motionless under his. "Nothing much to tell, really."

"I doubt that. What happened?"

Her wry chuckle preceded what he assumed was a lie. "Nothing. Really, nothing."

If she had ever given a fully honest answer to any question he had ever asked, he didn't know. If she did so now, he doubted he had the ability to either recognize or trust it. He saw an abused woman sitting before him and he knew she'd say whatever she needed to keep herself safe. But, he needed to hear her say something, anything.

"The last time I saw you," he commented softly, easing deeper yet cautiously into the Flint topic. "Before the reunion, I mean, – at the University – you and he were driving out of town in an old, yellow Volkswagen Beetle. You had told me you were going to Boston with him. You seemed quite certain about it at the time."

Carefully, he moved his hand from hers to tuck her hair behind her right ear. She didn't stop him, but quietly reached up to adjust the locks back over the scarred lobe.

He repeated his question. "What happened?"

Her response was long in coming. She wouldn't look at him as she searched for a simple answer his simple question. There wasn't one.

She took a difficult breath. "The thing with Roger was over a long time ago. It didn't work out."

"Why not?"

Another breath. "I guess you could say we had our disagreements."

The only thing Steeg was certain of was Gracie's willingness to let him think the worst of Roger Flint. Years earlier he had been willing the kill the man, but now it was Gracie he didn't trust, not after the revelations at the reunion. Looking at her avoid eye contact, he doubted he'd ever be able to believe anything she said.

The arrival of their meals provided a short respite and an opportunity for Steeg to steer the conversation along a less disturbing course.

The food was excellent. He said so.

"That's why I like this place," Gracie smiled, pleased that he was pleased.

As they ate, he decided to play the next line of inquiry as the brick head she must think he was. Steeg offered a non-threatening commentary. "So, Debra seems very nice."

"She's a good friend."

"What does she do?"

"She's beginning a new career in social work, actually."

"How long have you two known each other?"

"Since '81."

"Well, it's always nice to be able to split the rent." He pulled a paper napkin across his mouth. "Anyone special in your life, now? Anyone you're serious about, that is?"

Her mouth tensed noticeably into a pinched little smile and she carefully weighed her words as she once more looked directly at him. "Well, yes, there is."

His steady gaze braced him for something Gracie evidently had trouble with: the simple truth. "Oh. Who's that?"

She waited for a two-count before answering. "An aspiring social worker who I split the rent with."

He sighed as he sat back in his chair. At last: the truth.

He wasn't happy to hear it. In fact, he considered it a tragic waste: a waste of the incredible value she held for any man who could truly protect, provide and love her; a waste of all he had ever held for her, all he had struggled for years to regain, and although he wouldn't tell her, a waste of all he still carried deep in his soul. The only thing he had ever wanted for her was her happiness. Now, it ended for him with a profoundly disturbing sense of personal loss.

She reached across the table, covered his hand with hers and asked with concern, "You okay?"

He twitched a slight smile. "I'm not sure. Give me a clue, here. How do others react to this?"

Gently, she squeezed his hands. "The people I knew before, I still know. The things we shared before, I still treasure. I'm still the same person, just different. My friends respect my choices for a new life."

He wanted to understand what had driven those new life choices of hers, but at the moment it felt just too exhausting. A disturbing thought truly frightened him: had there been something he may have done, or not done, years ago that had somehow contributed to those life choices? He turned his hands to enclose hers.

"Gracie, what's passed is past. Whatever happened before, whatever half-truths or downright lies there were, none of that matters. You and I, somehow, we've gone our separate ways and yet here we are, in Chicago eating spiced pork, tortillas and rice and beans together."

She returned a light, ironic titter.

He continued. "None of that makes any sense at all, I know. But, this does: my promise to you remains. If you are ever in trouble, if you ever need anything, all you have to do is ask and I'm there for you."

It was as anti-climatic a statement as he could make and it laid there between them for the rest of the meal. As they ate, he tried to clear it away with casual redirections asking her how she liked living in Chicago, how her psychotherapy business was doing, her pursuits for a PhD, and whether she and Debra hung out at the night spots along Rush Street. Gracie evidently respected him enough to keep within the less threatening, less committal parameters of a discussion they had redefined by unspoken consensus.

As they continued to eat and talk, he mentally sifted through the high school years they had shared; her lack of honesty in their relationship at that time; her betrayal after he joined the Navy; the confusion of their meeting again at the University of Minnesota where he really screwed everything up. It was all a God awful mess. He mentally pummeled himself for not being stronger for her.

With the meal finished and the check paid, he matter-of-factly stated, "I have to fly to St. Louis first thing tomorrow…"

"That's okay." Too quickly, she resigned with an understanding smile and ignored his scrunched expression of displeasure as she adjusted her scarf to prepare for leaving. "You may not believe it, Steeg, but I've enjoyed the evening. It's really good to see you again, I can't tell you how much."

"You know, one of the things I really don't like about you," Steeg complaint caused her to pause in her leave-taking. "You always think you know what I'm going to say or do before I say or do it."

She leaned forward with a self-assured manner and stated, "That's because I know what you're going to say or do before you say or do it."

"And, that's another thing: you're redundant," he concluded flatly as he rose from his chair to lead her from the restaurant. Outside, he offered her his arm. "And, you're probably not going to believe this, either, but I've enjoyed the pleasure of your company so much, I need to digest it all. Let's go for a stroll around the neighborhood, whadda ya say?"

She looped her arm with his and hugged him close as they stepped off the curb to cross the diagonal Clark Street and headed to Sheffield Avenue. The evening temperature was perfect, the air was still and they took their time saying little, but when either spoke it made the other feel glad for it. Only a few blocks later, a huge building loomed tall ahead of them.

"What the heck is that?" Steeg marveled.

"That is Wrigley Field," she answered.

"You're kidding. You mean you live in the same neighborhood as Wrigley Field?"

"Well, yes, I guess I do."

He grabbed her by the hand and ran across the street for a closer look. The park itself was dark, but closer to the main entry gates, a well lit open lower level side service ramp beckoned. Still grasping her hand, Steeg led Gracie down the ramp where they were promptly stopped by huge black man wearing a black windbreaker with an embroidered rent-a-cop badge on the front and a silk-screen printed "Park Security" across the back.

The guard held up a beefy hand. "Hold on, folks. No one admitted here."

"No problem, officer," Steeg enthusiastically responded, hands raised chest high. "I just wanted to ask if it would be okay if I could go upstairs and maybe, you know, go out onto the field just to, you know, look around?"

Steeg's enquiring smile was greeted by the other man's sullen frown.

"What are you, some kind of idiot?"

Steeg stuttered his stunned denial.

In his defense, Gracie offered, "No, he's from Minnesota."

"Big deal," the guard dismissed. "Ain't never met no one from Minnesota worth spit. It's too cold in Minnesota. Their brains get all freezed up. You just proved it. People from Minnesota are stupid."

"No argument there," Steeg recouped soberly. "Does that mean I can't go out onto the field?"

The guard folded arms with biceps thicker than Steeg's thighs. "What do you think?"

Steeg ignored Gracie's subtle tug at his sleeve and gave it one more try. "How about this: I don't go out onto the field. I just stay in the stands…"

"Leave." With a flick of his wrist, the guard shooed them back the way they had come.

Halfway up the ramp, Steeg wondered aloud, "I bet he would have taken a small bribe."

Gracie laughed. "Maybe, but he could have folded you up like a lawn chair. Welcome to Chicago."

Steeg slumped his shoulders slightly. "Thanks for the vote of confidence, woman. You really know how to flatter a guy."

The pace back to the parked car was considerably quicker. Soon they were settled into the welcoming softness of supple upholstery inside a body by Fischer. The engine started with an easy turn of the ignition key. For only a moment, his waiting hotel room and the vision of Gracie smiling at him from under the bed comforter flashed across his mind. He mentally willed the scene away. It didn't work.

So, he tried a more direct management technique. "I guess I should take you home and get back to the hotel for some sleep."

"I understand," she said simply.

"Yes, I know you understand." He echoed with intentional sarcasm, but inside he continued to poorly resist his baser nature screaming for him to act. Replacing the sarcasm with something several shades warmer, he added, "So, knock it off, okay?"

"Okay."

"As I was saying, I'm taking you back, but we're going the long way around. We're in Chicago and I've never driven Lakeshore Drive. Tonight's the night."

Checking carefully for oncoming traffic fore and aft, he moved away from the curb as he asked, "How the heck do I find Lakeshore Drive from here, anyway?"

Gracie directed him to head south on Sheffield, and then turn left on Belmont. Within blocks the highway 41 entrance lay before him.

From the North Shore at twilight, the Chicago skyline was spectacular. The traffic lanes were relatively clear and Steeg eased the machine a comfortable five miles above the posted limit. They sped down the expressway with him asking questions about what was this, that, and the other thing.

"Look at all the boats!" He marveled at a packed marina in an inlet on his right. "How do they get in there? It looks landlocked to me."

"I'm not sure." She was enjoying his excited reaction. "There's an entrance from the lake somewhere, but I think we passed it already."

He pointed to the tall buildings towering in a seemingly endless line fronting the great city like sentinels. "What are all those high rises?"

"Mostly condos," she answered. "This is some of the most expensive real estate in the state."

"And the flat land between?"

"It's a park; Lincoln Park, I think. Yes, it is. Chicago is famous for its parks, you know; parks and Picasso sculptures."

He drove on, past another huge marina at the lakeside, past Grant Park with the brilliantly lit Buckingham Fountain, and Soldiers Field where the hated Chicago Bears played professional football. When he saw the turn off for the McCormick Place exhibition center and Interstate 55, better known as the Stevenson Expressway, Steeg slowed to take it.

It was decision time. The Stevenson linked up easily with I-90 and would take him to Des Plaines and the hotel. He glanced over to see Gracie smiling. She had caught his eyes as if she knew he would look at her at that exact moment. The tingling he felt was undeniably electric, yet eerily foreboding.

His attention returned to the road as he took the easy turn onto the Stevenson, keeping his less than honorable thoughts to himself. Something was wrong. Instead of excitement, Steeg felt the weighted return of a familiar sadness. After all that had happened, or perhaps better said not happened, between them, he was certain now of something he could never accept before: Gracie most probably had never loved him. To her he was one of a chosen variety, like a chocolate candy from a box. Only, her box of chocolates apparently had plenty of other choices he never knew about. Had she ever said she loved him? He couldn't remember a time when she had actually uttered the words.

He could feel her eyes on him.

She must be enjoying this, he thought. How could he have been this big of a fool; her fool for years, coming along whenever she tugged at the leash? That Wrigley Park security guard was right: he was an idiot.

He took the next available interchange to double back on the Stevenson and return to Lakeshore Drive.

"Time to head back," was all he said as he settled to a less hurried pace than the rest of the sparse traffic.

He accepted she had made some choices, although he didn't agree with the choices she had made. But what did it matter? She couldn't have ever really loved him. He had tricked himself into believing she had. The trick justified his pining for her. It justified his wasted effort to get back into her life. And he did all that for what? She was a lesbian!

A lez-bo! A frickin' dyke!

He didn't want to be angry with her. For as long as he had known Gracie, he had supported her any way he could, as best as he could, as the situation would permit. After high school, while he was preparing to go into the Navy, he supported her efforts to go to college, even helping her move into her dormitory. Years later at the University of Minnesota, his concern about not disturbing her academic pursuits most probably played a major role in his anemic milk-toast efforts to win her back.

But this development, this was different in a way he could not have anticipated. Gracie had rejected him before, several times in several different ways, and his devotion for her allowed him to rise above her insensitivities. But this time was different. This was the ultimate rejection. This was a purposeful insult designed to do as much damage as possible to everything he had ever felt for her.

Steeg drove on, struggling to push his growing anger down deep as everything in him wanted to slap some sense into her.

The dumb bitch! Does she even care I still love her, care about what happens to her? Does she care I still need her?

Educated, trained, certified and now a professional psychotherapist, in Steeg's eyes Gracie had fallen badly. His anger, now hot enough to explode, began to cool with the unwelcomed thought he may have contributed to her present life style choice. His short, quick breathing slowed. He mentally constructed a string of consequences resulting from how he had failed her. He wasn't responsible for Gracie's choices, but it was easier, oddly more comforting to accept the blame. He should have been more of a man, the type of man she wanted him to be. Everything would have been different if he had been different. She had fallen to this because he had failed her years earlier.

An audible sigh was followed by a regretful shake of his head he should have concealed but didn't.

Noticing, Gracie asked, "What are you thinking?"

"Nothing," he answered too quickly, and then he added more slowly, "Everything."

She turned toward her window and looked out at the blackness of Lake Michigan and said, "I know."

By the time he exited from Lakeshore Drive to Belmont, he was heartsick for all the truth about Gracie he could no longer ignore. The drive down Belmont was a quiet one. He turned on Clifton. Parking was again out of the question. There were no spots to be had, so he slowed to a stop across from the front of her house, shifted into park and let the engine idle.

"I can walk you up."

"Don't be silly."

"You're right. I guess I've been silly enough already." He half-smiled no longer caring if the pain showed. Whatever they had shared was over now and it hurt like hell. "Well, Gracie, after everything that's gone by, I'm at a loss for words. I don't know what to say."

"I appreciate you taking me out tonight," she offered reaching around his neck for a good bye hug.

"Thanks for saving me from that felon at the ballpark," he lightly joked as he kissed her forehead.

They hugged cheek-to-cheek, holding tightly to each other. Then Gracie moved ever so slightly and brought her lips to meet his. He fell into the swirling vortex of the softest, deepest, warmest kiss only she could give him.

Her faint moan was too intimate and too real. The kiss lingered but was too short. He reluctantly pulled back when Gracie reached behind her to tug up on her door handle.

Her familiar, impish smile, blushed by an undertone of embarrassment, preceded her exit. "I have a reputation around here I need to protect."

It was Gracie's way of apologizing. She left the car, firmly shutting the door behind her.

He watched her hurry between the parked cars and across the front sidewalk. He waited until she entered the darkened house. The door closed behind her. When the drawn curtains in the front window glowed with pale yellow light, with a trembling hand he reached for the gear shift. That was when, with tears suddenly pooling in his eyes, he was blinded and everything around him melted into an indistinguishable blur.

Chapter 17
Darkness and Light

December 16, 1993

"He said I was an answer to his prayer, so I had to say, 'yes'." Carol smiled, entering the living room from the kitchen carrying two full cups of coffee on a tray complemented with a small crystal cream pitcher and matching sugar bowl.

Having willingly responded to Carol's morning invitation, Mary sat in the stuffed chair facing the matching sofa. She carefully removed the offered cup from the tray.

"How romantic, and so, you two got married and it's been wedded bliss ever since."

Carol responded with a curious sideways nod as she stirred a modest amount of cream into her coffee. "Well, blissful sometimes. It hasn't been easy. In many ways, it's harder. Don't get me wrong, I love Steeg. He saved me from a life of living with my mother, so I have to love him!"

Both women laughed before Carol continued. "No, seriously, I knew early on we were going to get married."

"How early?"

"After our second date, I think."

Mary was skeptical. "Yeah, sure."

Carol carefully placed her cup on its saucer. "No, really: I was a mess. He showed up for our date on time, but I was sicker than a dog. I wanted to be with him so badly but I couldn't. I cried like a baby. My mother met him at the door and told him I was ill. I was wrapped in blankets trying to keep warm and I walked up to him to tell him I was sorry. I probably thought he'd run away in terror, but he didn't. Instead, He takes one look at me, wraps his arm around me, feels my forehead and says, 'You're sick! You should be in bed.'

"Then he takes me to the couch and we sit together with him holding me close. He asks me if I've taken anything for the fever – I might have told him I had some cold medicine or Tylenol. I do remember curling up against him – he's so warm, you know – and we sit there for a couple of hours. Do you believe my stupid mother sat in the same room the entire time? But he stayed with me the whole afternoon. It was the nicest thing, really."

Mary cast a doubtful look to her sister-in-law. "You sure we're talking about my brother, the insensitive, bumbling clod?"

Carol smiled and continued. "That's when I knew. On the outside, he's a little hard, demanding sometimes. But, on the inside he has a good heart. You see it with the kids, although I was a little concerned this last time, with Roberta."

"Your brand new 'surprise' baby? She's such a cutie. How old is she now?"

"Six months, two weeks already. You would have laughed if you'd seen Steeg's reaction when I told him he was going to be a father again."

"I can imagine."

Carol quietly chuckled. "He could barely breathe! It was before Thanksgiving last year. I told him he was going to be a daddy again and he just sank into the same chair you're sitting in right now, blowing out these big, heavy puffs of air so his cheeks bulged out. I was worried he was going to go into shock."

"It's his own fault." Mary claimed with a squint and a self-satisfied nod.

"Well, you know, Neville had just turned nine, Brian was twelve, Dottie eleven. I'm sure he thought he was done with having babies."

"It serves him right," Mary took another sip of her coffee and commented on how much better it tasted than her own. Then, she added, "Kids are important assets. They keep a man focused on the straight and narrow."

"Steeg's good with the kids," Carol beamed. "Did he ever tell you what Brian did as a newborn? Steeg is in bed playing 'Roll-off' with Brain – that's where Steeg lays in the bed with baby Brian on his chest, and with Brian's big bug-eyed look at his daddy, Steeg lets the baby roll off to one side or the other, catching him in the crook of his arm. Each time, Brian would giggle so loudly you could hear it all over that little south Minneapolis house we lived in then. It was so sweet.

"Anyway, after a while, everything is quiet, right? So, I walk into the bedroom and there's Steeg asleep with Brian lying quietly on his chest. Then, Little Brian looks up, spies Steeg's nose in front of him, pulls up closer and starts sucking on it!"

Carol joined Mary in a shared scream of delight; the giggling continued as Carol concluded the story.

"Steeg's eyes pop wide open and they cross when he looks down at his new son trying to get a free snack! It was so funny!"

The shared laughter lasted for several minutes with both women multiplying the comedy with their own cross-eyed expressions and puckered lips to mimic baby sucking sounds.

Mary leaned forward to accept the offer of more coffee as Carol continued on a more serious vein. "And then, there are the other times."

"Other times?"

"Well, we're not perfect, you know," Carol expanded with a self-conscious shrug. "we're far from it. I think something's off or there's something I'm not doing right. More now than early on in our marriage, Steeg falls into these periods that can last for days, even weeks. Sometimes he can be so violent, it truly frightens me."

Mary placed her cup onto the saucer, her brow furrowed with concern. "Violence? Steeg? Against you or the kids?"

"He's never hit me," Carol backed up noticeably. "It's just that, out of nowhere, he sometimes goes into these rages that can come from the smallest thing – from nothing really. He won't tolerate sass or talk-back from the kids, especially if they sass me. I've seen him literally throw Brian against the wall and threaten real harm if Brian says or does anything disrespectful toward me. It scares me because I believe he means it. I think he does it to scare the kids into behaving, but I don't go along with it at all. The kids have problems with it, too. It's as if they have two different daddies, you know? It confuses them."

Mary was suddenly worried and it showed. She fumbled with her napkin, folding it this way and that, only to lay it flat again on her lap. Carol could see her sister-in-law was upset so she tried to put her at ease.

"I'm sorry, Mary. I shouldn't have said that. It's not a real concern, and it certainly isn't anything I can't handle."

"Don't mind me," Mary apologized, dismissing herself with a brief wave. "It's just that it reminds me of things. Steeg may have mentioned something, but you know when we were kids, our dad was a little like that with us."

"I don't know about that. Steeg's said things about his father, but he's never used his experiences growing up as an excuse. I think it has more to do with his losing the publishing job. That was hard on both of us, but really hard on him. His boss just walked into the office one day and told everyone he was closing the doors at the end of the month. Forty-two people let go," Carol snapped her fingers for emphasis. "Just like that, our only source of income was gone. He couldn't find a job. We couldn't keep up payments on the new house. We ended up moving to Wisconsin when one of his former advertising clients hired him for a sales manager job. He didn't like the job, but he took it anyway. Two years later, the job disappears. Two years after that, we move back here, live in this rental as he jumps from one sales job to the next. He's not happy, I know. We're always scraping for money, the kids need things we can't give them, and of course there was no medical insurance to cover the bills for the new baby."

"You know, Carol, I can help with some cash if you need it. Bernie makes good money."

A flush of embarrassment crossed Carol's face. "That's good of you, Mary, but it's not the money. It's Steeg. He's not happy. I can tell. I'm the one who's supposed to take care of that, and Mary, it's hard because I don't know what to do."

Mary moved from her chair to take a seat next to Carol on the couch. "Can you cover the rent? Do you need food? What can I do to help?"

A rattled sigh escaped from deep within her. "I'm thinking I need to go back to office work, but I've been a mom so long my skills are out of date. They don't advertise for stenographers anymore. I don't know what kind of work I can do."

"You can't go back to work," Mary denied. "You have Roberta, now. She's too little to leave alone. You need to let Steeg take care of the financial side for now."

Carol's accepting nod contradicted her honest evaluation. "He's not doing so good."

"Your stepping in won't help as much as you think. In fact, it could do more harm."

"I need to do something, Mary. I don't know if Steeg can work his way through whatever he's going through."

"Whatever that is, he can do it. You have to let him do what he has to do."

"I'm not so sure," Carol's faraway look revealed her feeling of helplessness. "I guess this is why I called you over today. This morning, he and I are sitting in the kitchen having coffee and he turns to me and says he thinks this 'stuff' as he called it can't go on much longer. I asked him what he meant and he blows up at me. He yelled 'What do you mean 'whadda ya mean?'! You can't tell me you're happy living this way, can you?' It broke my heart, Mary."

Mary reached over and covered Carol's hands. "Of course it did, but how did he explain what he meant?"

"He didn't explain it. He threw his coffee mug into the sink – pieces of it are still hiding from me in there – and he went into a rant about the crappy house, the crappy car, the crappy things we have. If that's what he's feeling when he gets up in the morning, what is he feeling the night before?"

Mary cautiously mouthed the words. "Are you having, you know, bedroom problems?"

With a patient smile and a calming pat of Mary's hands, Carol tried to explain. "You know how I said the children think they have two different daddies? It's like I have two different husbands. Sometimes, he's marvelous: the most sensitive lover, I can't tell you."

"And, other times?"

"Withdrawn. It's like I don't know that man. He doesn't touch me. He disappears for days, even weeks at a time. And then, he's back, he says he knows he was wrong to say the things he said, or do the things he did, and it's wonderful again… only a little less wonderful because you're bracing yourself for the next time."

Mary nodded slowly with understanding. "Jeckle and Hyde. You're not unique, you know. Men are like that sometimes, especially when there are money problems."

"Yeah, I guess. Anyway, it looks like I'm in for another round of the withdrawn Steeg. It's getting harder. I'm open to suggestions. Got any?"

"I'm not sure," Mary said, knowing full well she had plenty of things in mind. "Any coffee left?"

Chapter 18
Pedestrian Concerns

It wasn't much of a sale job, not really. Then again, since the publishing company folded six years earlier, none of the jobs he had held were much of anything. He now sold business telecommunication equipment and services for a small independent company out of an office located in a northwest suburb of Minneapolis. It was a long commute from the Bloomington house they rented, but the extended drive time had helped him recoup from that morning's inexplicable explosion all over Carol. At least in the office, he could pretend he was worth something.

At ten o'clock, he paged through his address book and, almost by accident, found Matt's long ignored home number. On a good day, he used lunch as a convenient excuse to spend time with a valued client or a sales prospect of above average potential. This was not a good day.

Matt answered on the fourth ring.

"Surprised you're not at class at the 'U' or some place."

Matt recognized Steeg's voice immediately. "I'm surprised your wife lets you out during the daytime."

"Free for lunch?"

"You buying?"
"Who else?"
"Then I'm there!"

They agreed to meet at the Perkins Restaurant on France Avenue and Interstate 494. Less than a minute after he arrived, Matt walked through the doors. They greeted each other with genuine gladness and a warm handshake.

Despite more than seven years passing since he had last seen the man, Matt had hardly aged. Dressed in a parka, typical corduroy trousers and a pullover knit shirt, only the slight salt and pepper graying of perpetually unshaven facial hair gave evidence of time marching on.

Steeg, on the other hand, was a considerable contrast with his neatly trimmed hair sprayed into motionlessness styled perfection, dress shoes gleaming, dark blue 'mid-power' suit with matching vest and red tie. After the hostess directed the men to their booth, Steeg slipped off his camelhair topcoat and hung it from a hook on the booth stanchion. Settling in, and before the waitress arrived with the complimentary glasses of ice water, Matt opened the conversation.

"I think it was Ace who told me you moved to Wisconsin. You move back, or are you just visiting?"

Steeg half-smiled and shook his head. He looked around for the person bringing the ice water. "No, I moved back. Got a house in Bloomington. You and Elaine still married?"

"Of course, she won't let me leave. Go figure. You?"

"Oh yeah. Four kids now, too. World's worse father, guaranteed. It's amazing. I don't know how all of it happens, really…"

Matt leaned forward his hands cupped as if holding a great truth. "Well, it involves a fertilization process: the sperm swims up the fallopian tube to unite with the ovum, causing the splitting of chromosomes. Cells multiply..."

"That's not what I meant."

The waitress suddenly appeared with glasses of ice water and two menus in hand. Placing the menus and glasses in front of each man, she asked, "Anything to drink?"

"Serve beer here?" Matt asked.

The waitress apologized. "Sorry, not now but maybe later this year. They applied for a license for beer and wine, but Edina hasn't approved it yet."

Matt stuck with the offered water, carefully extricating the wedge of lemon from the rim and placing it on his paper napkin. He then nonchalantly tucked the napkin and lemon slice behind the condiment rack.

Steeg noticed, but ignored Matt's little subterfuge as he smiled at the waitress. "I'll have some coffee, black, please, along with a couple more napkins."

With an understanding nod, the waitress retrieved Matt's napkin-wrapped lemon slice from behind the condiment rack and quickly disappeared. Steeg looked across the table to Matt who looked a little irritated.

"How is it you moved, anyway?" Matt questioned abruptly. "You just kind of dropped off the map. The last time I saw you, God it was a long time ago, now..."

"Class reunion, '86, the Airport Hilton."

"That's right. Man, that was seven years ago!"

"Closer to eight," Steeg corrected. "Next year is only a couple of weeks away. We're old. When my youngest graduates from high school I'll be sixty-three. Soon after that, I'll be dead.

By the way, I want you to know you are under no obligation to invite me to your Christmas party this year."

"Wouldn't think of it," obliged Matt. "Besides, we celebrate Kwanzaa now and your obvious cheery disposition would spoil the festivities."

"My cheery disposition? Okay, I apologies for the curmudgeonly behavior. Personally, I'm relieved to hear you haven't fallen victim to the one true faith."

"It's better than being molested by a priest. So, anyway, was it something we said, something we did? You're at the reunion on day and the next thing anyone knows, you're gone. Where did you go?"

"A small town called Whitewater." Steeg fingered the condensation on his water glass. "I got a sales manager job with a manufacturer there. It didn't work out. I'm back."

"Why didn't it work out?"

Steeg's hesitated as he weighed the possible consequences of opening this line of conversation. After a moment of reflective consideration, he decided Matt was probably the one person with whom he could safely share almost anything.

"One night, Carol and I are invited out to dinner with my boss and his wife. There's a local Chinese place that serves wine, lots of wine. My boss got a little too friendly with Carol, made some suggestions to me as he paws at her while his own wife looks on. This was about a year and eight months after my previous employer sold his magazines' publishing rights to his chief competitor and the next day everyone in the company is on the street. It was a deeply educational experience in commerce and catastrophe, so I didn't have a whole lot of patience in Whitewater with silliness, you know? I pulled my new boss' hand off my wife, rearranged some of his front teeth and resigned the next Monday. For the next two years, I try to sell telephones, real estate and want ad space. Nothing works. All in all, it proved to be an expensive real-life exercise."

Matt leaned back in his seat and whistled. "I've always liked that about you: you're always looking for the bright side of things, just spreading joy where ever you go. Sounds to me the guy had it coming. Good job."

"Maybe, but it doesn't feel like it. We've been in a financial tailspin ever since. I had to sell the house because I was going to lose it to property taxes. The last couple of years in Wisconsin we lived off food stamps. To tell you the truth, if mom hadn't got sick, we'd still be there."

"Your mom's sick?"

"It's terminal. She's slowly wasting away. The doctors figure she has less than five years, but she's getting so weak so quickly, I don't think it will be that long. She asked me to move back so she could be closer to her grandchildren. What could I say, no? It wasn't as if there was a whole lot of anything holding me in Wisconsin."

The waitress reappeared to take their order. They both ordered a Supreme Burger with fries and the waitress once more quickly disappeared.

"So, what did Whitewater hold for you in the first place?" Matt asked. "The Twin Cities certainly has a larger job market to pick from than that place."

Steeg shrugged. "I had other reasons to move to Chicago."

"You mean Whitewater." Matt corrected.

"That's what I said."

"You said Chicago."

"No, I didn't. I said Whitewater."

Matt nodded with a dismissed frown. "Okay, Whitewater, whatever. Is it close to Chicago or something?"

"It's an hour and one-half, maybe two hours, by car depending on the route."

"So, you guys went to Chicago often then?"

"Occasionally, why?"

It was Matt's turn to shrug. "Nothing, I was just trying to understand how the two places were connected."

"Oh, I see. I wouldn't say they're connected though. I'd say they're in relative close proximity to each other."

"Relative to what?"

"Well, you know, it's relative to some other place, like the Twin Cities."

"I see. There must not be a whole lot of things to do in Whitewater, then."

"Why do you say that?"

"Well, because you said you went into Chicago a lot, that's why. I assume it was out of boredom."

Steeg shook his head. "That's not true. I said I went to Chicago occasionally. That's not a lot, it's occasional. There's a difference. Besides, Whitewater is a perfectly nice little town. There's a college there with a very good Division III football team. And, there's a great little restaurant, actually a supper club that has the best steaks you'll ever eat and a turtle style cheesecake no one else can match."

Matt held up his hands in surrender. "Whoa, you convinced me. I'll talk to Eileen tonight about moving. So, tell me this: if Whitewater was so great, why did you spend all that time in Chicago... Occasionally, that is."

Steeg caught his response in time for a brief moment of reflection. This was a sudden opportunity for a serious, truthful interchange, something unique, nay foreign, to their decades-long friendship. He proceeded cautiously.

"I'll answer that, if you answer a question for me first."

Matt returned glibly, "Okay, shoot."

"Okay, here it is: is it possible – and I mean really possible – to love two women at the same time?"

"Oh, God, this is either an ultimate fantasy, or you're into something I've only dreamed about!"

"I'm serious."

Matt nodded his understanding. "Well, if you're serious, then the answer is, yes, but not in the same ways. Men are naturally attuned to polygamy, so it's more than workable."

"It's not as great as you think," Steeg scowled as he looked away. "The other woman lives in Chicago."

Chapter 19
Management Strategies

What had started as a light, mildly abusive conversation of rebuke and ridicule was suddenly a serious interchange. The food arrived and both men quickly exchanged the bottle condiments to personalize their individual platters. Raising his burger for the first bite, Matt looked at his friend with growing concern. He could tell something was on Steeg's mind.

"As much as I might enjoy listening to all the sordid details," Matt spoke through the first chomp he chewed. "And, I'm sure there are some, I don't think that's what you need right now."

"I don't need anything," Steeg slid a ketchup dipped fry into his mouth. "I'm fine."

"Yeah, sure, that's why you're in such good shape right now, because you're fine."

"I'm fine." Steeg repeated more firmly.

"Does... what's your wife's name, again?"

"Carol."

"Right, Carol: does Carol know about Chicago?"

Steeg half-nodded and half-shook his head in short, quick jerks. "I'd never hurt her with that."

"How do you know you haven't hurt her already?"

"Because, Matt, I'd just know if she knew, that's how." Steeg was certain.

Matt was not as sure. "Would she tell you?"

"Probably not."

Matt shook his head. "Sounds like a great relationship: you don't talk to her and she doesn't talk to you. You guys are obviously made for each other."

Steeg framed his response with a frown. "We talk. There's a lot of talking. With four kids, there're all kinds of talking all the time, along with a whole lot of other noise that can drive a person stark raving mad, okay?! It gets to you sometimes, you know? It sure got to me this morning. Not that anything's ended, you know, but I can't figure out how I ended up this way. It's more like a water park ride that never ends; it just turns this way and that, going on forever. You have no control over anything. You just try to keep your nose above water."

"I don't know what you mean," Matt countered. "What's that got to do with Chicago?"

"Everything and nothing at all." Steeg's pace of consuming his cheeseburger had slowed significantly behind Matt. He hadn't yet touched it. "It doesn't matter, anyway. Chicago is dead. It died seven years ago, even years before that. For some reason she didn't think worth mentioning, Gracie made some life choices for herself that somehow made things better for her and left me hanging out to dry even more than I knew. I should have been angry being insulted that way, but all I could feel was... I don't know what I felt. Whatever it is, it's still there and sometimes it pulls me under. I just need to get my nose above the waterline, that's all."

"Ah, allegory," Matt bemoaned, feigning disgust. It was Steeg's old girlfriend again and Matt was wondering how he could turn this to his advantage, maybe even get Steeg to pay for the check. "Give me a minute to decipher this: waterline; drowning; no control. Okay, I think I have it: you're married and you still have the 'hots' for Gracie 'Off-her-rocker', and you've been getting it on with her on the side, am I right?"

Matt was surprised by the firmness of Steeg's snapped reply.

"Don't call her that! Her name is Ofterdahl. I've never 'got it on' with Gracie, especially since I've been married."

"Okay, I apologize. You're pure as the driven snow. But, Steeg, it's been like forever since high school. What are you, nuts? If you felt like this for Gracie, why'd you marry Carol?"

Steeg looked straight at the other man. "God wanted me to. Who am I to deny what God tells me to do?"

"You're certifiable," Matt bluntly criticized, shaking his head as he returned appropriate attention to his lunch. "You really believe God told you to marry her?"

Steeg nodded, used his knife and fork to cut a wedge of burger and slide it into his mouth. "I really believe He wanted us to be together, yes. I know this is a difficult concept for intellectual elites to grasp, but God works in all our lives whether we want Him to or not. Some of us are just more sensitive to His leadings, that's all."

"I'd rather be an elite intellectual than a religious snob," Matt countered calmly. "Do you love your wife?"

"Yes, actually, I do. I always have. She's the glue that holds me together no matter how bad everything else becomes. She's the mother of my children. She's the companion and helper no other person could be. She keeps me level."

"Great. Why isn't that enough? What's lacking? Why do you need Gracie?"

Still chewing on another wedge of burger, Steeg brought a finger to the side of his mouth and started to nervously nip at an uneven nail as he tried to explain. "It's what you'd feel for someone you'd walk across burning coals for, or sacrifice your own life just to keep the other person safe. I feel some kind of desperate need to guard this woman from harm, protect and provide for her in any way she would let me. When we lived in Wisconsin, maybe two or even three times a year I'd drive to Chicago and stake out Gracie's house…"

Matt's expression turned to worry. "Oh, shit, no you didn't!"

Steeg stopped his nervous fingernail chewing long enough to make a pointed accusation. "You going to be a judge or a friend, now? Decide. I can cut this short if you'd be more comfortable."

"Okay, sorry," Matt apologized, pointing to Steeg's knife cutting another slice from his plated burger. "Go on. Maybe I'll learn why you eat hamburgers with a fork!"

A displeasured scrunch crossed Steeg's face. "I don't want to get any on the suit, okay?"

"Okay, good enough. Now, tell me what you got out of spying on your old girlfriend."

With an accepting nod Steeg continued. "Nothing much. I never knocked on her door. I just watched her house hoping to catch a glimpse of her to know she was okay. That woman works like a dog. She's going for her doctorate, she conducts group therapy sessions in her house, private counseling; she's heavy into the Gay-Lesbian-Transgender community…"

A loud snort of laughter emerged from across the table. Too late, Matt covered his mouth.

"Don't laugh," Steeg pointed the nail bitten finger in warning. "I imagine it's a goldmine for her. I can't think of a bigger group of psychologically confused people from whom to draw clientele. Besides, she's gay, too."

"Are you kiddin' me?" Matt laughed louder. "She's a lesbian?!"

"I didn't mention that? Yes, she's lives with Debra, her significant other. It's obviously my fault. Somehow, it's an effect I have on women I care for."

"Name one woman, I dare ya."

"Gracie."

"One woman who isn't Gracie," Matt challenged.

"Maybe my first year journalism instructor at the 'U' but I'm not positive. Look, I'm not making light of it, Matt. I think it's a tragedy. Gracie's a remarkable person who has been hurt, I mean physically. I think she's been abused, certainly after college, if not earlier."

"Not by you."

"No, of course not. But there are scars you can see if you know what to look for. I asked her about it, but she skirted around it. I think I know who did it, but she didn't confirm or deny it. She's like that. She leads you along a certain path, and then, leaves you there to draw your own conclusions."

They continued eating their meals for several minutes appreciating the chance to digest more than just the food.

When they were both close to finishing up, Matt reinitiated the discussion. "My conclusion is simple: you've got it bad and it's screwing you up inside big time. You need to stop this. Life is too short to waste energy and time this way."

"I can appreciate that, Matt. There might be better ways for me to waste my life, who knows? Any suggestions?"

"She's a lesbian, Steeg, a frickin' lesbian! She's not worth this kind of devotion, or obsession, or whatever you want to call it."

"She's chosen to be a lesbian, Matt. You don't know her. You don't know how she thinks. She needs to be in control. Her choice of lesbianism was a decision that reinforced that need."

Matt sat back and crossed his arms. "You have no idea how wrong you are, do you? What are you, living in a tube somewhere, or what? Don't you ever read 'Hustler' magazine?"

"It's porn." Steeg editorialized sourly.

"That doesn't make you better than me, okay!" Matt defended robustly. "In case you haven't noticed, Mr. Know-it-all, lesbians are hot, man. They know things. They're so much better in the sack than you could ever be there's no way a woman who was a lesbian would ever find a man who satisfies her as well as another woman does."

His unexpected chortle surprised even Steeg. "Praise the Lord! The scales are dropping from me eyes and what do I see? My best friend suffers from perfectly understandable, deep feelings of his own sexual inadequacy."

"Oh, no I don't!" Matt protested animatedly. Looking cautiously about the restaurant, he leaned closer and with a lowered voice added, "But, don't tell anyone, okay?"

Steeg marveled how they could always joke about anything no matter how serious. "Look, Matt, lesbians aren't hot, they're confused, scared people driven by influences and experiences they don't understand and over which they have no control. As with all same sex life styles, sexual behavior isn't constructive. In every way, it's destructive and they intuitively know it. They can't figure out why they do what they do, they only know they have to do it. They selfishly continue only to hate themselves for failing to suppress their own destructive behavior. It's a 'lose-lose' situation. Professionals tell them they are normal and everyone else has a problem. Preachers, teachers and wannabe social saviors tell these confused people to simply accept the way they are and everything will be fine. Nothing is further from the truth."

Very seriously now, Matt cut him short with a brittle interruption. "You don't know what the fuck you're talking about. I have friends who are gay…"

Defensively, Steeg countered, "So, love them enough to help them. All the experts gave up on them. The American Psychiatric Association declared homosexuality was not a mental illness and the entire medical establishment turned its collective back on the most vulnerable of our society. Instead of helping people overcome damage caused by this addictive behavior, the professionals cover it up with a false cloak of normalcy. Homosexuals are cut loose to sink or swim on their own. They're abandoned by those who could help. Their demand for acceptance is something society can never give and survive. As a result, they're forced into a sexually deviant underground sub-culture that reinforces the very thing destroying them. It's like a cancer in society. It can only go on for so long before it kills the host."

More irritated, Matt spat back, "They're people, just like you and me. Why can't you just let them live the way they want?"

"Because self-destructive behavior isn't healthy for anyone and because there're bigger things going on here than how people get their rocks off."

Visibly upset, Matt crumpled his napkin and threw it on his plate. "And, you're homophobic! And, you're a hypocrite! And, you piss me off! You actually think stalking Gracie from the bushes is somehow a good thing, like you're going to save her somehow? You're more screwed up than you know."

"I'm afraid I'm more aware than you might think." With cool detachment Steeg took a cleansing sip from his water glass. "Of course you don't understand. Why should you? Matt, I don't stalk Gracie. I'm not the stalker, I'm the stalk-ee! I'm stalked by Gracie's ghost."

Chapter 20
More Coffee

For lunch Carol had made shrimp salad sandwiches. She had taken care to trim the bread crust, hand cutting each sandwich diagonally into two equal pieces and arranging them neatly on a colorfully patterned metal tray lined with a pressed white paper doily. The tray was large enough to also hold a small dish of Green Goddess dressing and a plate of grouped raw broccoli, cauliflower, sliced red and yellow peppers. She brought it all into the living room and placed it on the coffee table, handing Mary a plate and napkin and then refreshing their cups with freshly brewed coffee.

"This is so very nice, Carol," Mary said sincerely as she selected a sandwich and some of the veggies for dipping. "You went to too much trouble. I didn't bring anything."

"It's no trouble and don't you worry about it. I don't do enough of this sort of thing."

The two women quickly adjusted their seating to safely accommodate their lunch plates within easy reach on the coffee table, and then they settled back into the flow of the morning's earlier discussion.

"I just pinned all his difficulties on his losing the sales manager job with the magazine," Carol continued roughly where she had left off. "It was such a stressful thing. Not that it hasn't happened before – you know it has – but that's when it seemed to all unravel somehow."

"Unravel? Do you mean it was Steeg who unraveled, or just things in general?"

Carol shrugged between bites. "Kind of like everything, you know? He worked really hard at the magazine. He got a promotion, managed sales for all the magazines the company published – like three of them – and that helped the money situation quite a bit. Then, he changed. Not a lot, just a little. His traveling increased, but when he was home, sometimes he'd sit on the sofa with the TV on…"

Mary laughed. "Like that's unusual for a guy? When Bernie's home, all he does is sit in front of the television."

"Well, yeah, you're right, but with Steeg he'd be sitting there with the set on and you could tell he wasn't actually watching television. He just stares at nothing at all for the longest time. After a while, sometimes hours later, he'd get up and go down stairs, or go into the garage, or drive away in the car all by himself. That was different. Sometimes I'd ask him what was on his mind and he'd say something like 'Oh, nothing, just thinking about stuff, that's all.' Then, he'd make a comment about how we might need to fix the deck, or paint a room, or do something or other. Of course, whatever it was he wanted to fix, paint or whatever, it never got done."

"Of course: S-M-O-P." Mary could see Carol was confused. "That's short for 'Standard Male Operating Procedure'."

"Oh. Well, then the publishing company closed down, we didn't have any money coming in; we fell behind in our house payments and some bills. When the only decent job he could find was three hundred miles away in southern Wisconsin, he jumped at it. I didn't want to move, but he couldn't find anything better. So, we sold our new house, moved and inside two years, the big job was gone. It's been a real struggle since then, so when he has these explosive emotional episodes of his, I give him all the space he needs."

"Wise move on your part, girl. I worry about you, though, if he gets violent."

"He's never really hit. His threats to hit can be a little terrifying, but when they occur his physical reactions are directed to objects not people. Like the shattered coffee cup this morning. Once, in Wisconsin, he put his fist through a bathroom door – right through it! No one said anything about it. Two weeks later, he replaced the door. That was it."

"I don't like the sound of that, Carol. What if the bathroom door wasn't there? What if it was you, or one of the kids? Have you considered counseling?"

Carol laughed at the suggestion. "Well, maybe, but I'd think long and hard before bringing it up. Steeg would never intentionally hurt any of us. He can be very stern and strict about things that's for sure, but he'll protect his family. One time in Wisconsin, we were having problems with Brian and his little friend from school. Brian's friend came from a bad home. The boy lived with his father and had many problems with getting into trouble at school. So, when Brian wanted to sleep over at his friend's father's house, we said he couldn't. Brian had a fit, started throwing a tantrum along with every toy in reach. Steeg grabbed him by the front of his shirt, lifted him off the floor and slammed him against the wall. As Brian hung there, Steeg's voice dropped down into something that sounded like Darth

Vader and tells Brian the next time he talks back to his mother or shows disrespect, Brian will lose a couple of teeth."

At Carol's telling of the story, Mary looked sad. "I'm trying to find the good in all this."

"Well, the next week at school, Brian apparently decided he'd get even for not being allowed to sleep over at his friend's house. He reports his father to the school principal claiming child abuse. The principal reports this to county social services. That Saturday, a social services officer comes to the house to speak to Steeg. I'm seriously concerned, Mary, sitting there watching the county official explain to Steeg the nature of the complaint against him, certain that within the next few minutes the officer may not be able to leave the house under his own power. Anyway, Steeg stares right through the guy, listening to every word. Finally, he asks him, 'Are you finished, now?' I know things are going to get bad because he uses that Darth Vader voice of his. The officer said Steeg needed to be aware this was very serious and it would go very bad if the man had to come back on this matter again.

"Steeg leans in toward the man, tells him to his face that he's a fool and he's been duped by an eight year old smart enough to run rings around county social services simply because mommy and daddy didn't let him have a sleepover with a budding juvenile delinquent. Steeg takes the officer by his arm, in the fleshy part above the elbow, you know? – I could tell he's really hurting the poor guy – and walks him to the door and out of the house. There's another exchange of words and I hear Steeg say, 'You're right it'll be very bad. Next time bring some friends to help. See ya!'."

"Oh, good Lord! Carol, what did you do?"

"Of course, I was concerned for Brian," Carol admitted. "I held him close to me on the sofa, but when Steeg came back in he told Brian to sit next to him instead. The brave little guy got up and went to his father. The two just looked at each other for a while. Then, Steeg told Brian he had been very clever, but he had also insulted and betrayed his own family. Steeg told him he was ashamed because of the lies Brian had told and said he hadn't raised him to be a liar. You could tell he was very disappointed in the boy. He grounded Brian from any outside activities separate from school for two weeks and then sent him to his room for the rest of the day. The next day, he gave Brian a handwritten list of chores to complete every day for the rest of the school year."

"And, that was it?"

"That was it. And, you know what, as headstrong as Brian still is in a lot of different ways, we haven't had any kicking and screaming tantrums since then. That's five years, Mary. I appreciate your concern, but Brian's a handful and somehow what Steeg did made things better. He's a good man."

Mary daintily washed down the last bite of her sandwich with a quick sip of coffee. After taking another moment to consider her sister-in-law's situation, she offered what she believed Carol needed to know.

"Steeg's my brother, and I love him. But, be careful, Carol. There were things that happened when we were kids that may have contributed to his temper problems."

Carol crossed her hands on her lap. "Steeg's told me how his father regularly made him dig ditches during the summer months and how hard that work was for him."

"But he hasn't told you about when he was thirteen and our dad whipped his bare legs with a wire hanger until he had bleeding welts down to his ankles, did he?"

Carol blinked several times, stunned by the sudden slap of what Mary had just said.

"It's not surprising, really. My brother would never tell anyone about those things. For Steeg, everyone had to know his dad was the greatest dad and he'd absolutely fight anyone who said otherwise."

Carol clasped her suddenly shaking hands. "He told you."

"No." Mary denied sadly. "He didn't have to tell me. I knew because I washed the blood from his wounds after it happened. These kinds of things continued off and on until Steeg left home to join the service."

The two women sat silently for several uncomfortable minutes. Carol could understand how it all fit. That kind of abuse could condition Steeg to believe he should be the same way with his own children. She silently prayed and gave thanks to God he wasn't that way at all. He only acted the part, going through the motions of being violent. She didn't know Mary was aware of other things that had happened, things that could push Steeg's anger beyond his control.

"I asked you once to talk to Steeg about Puerto Rico," Mary finally said. "Did you ever do that?"

Carol shook her head. "No. He never mentioned Puerto Rico. I couldn't bring it up out of the clear blue – he'd know if I did, you or someone else would have told me about it beforehand and I didn't want that to cause any trouble."

Mary understood and wondered if she should confront Steeg directly and urge him to talk with Carol about what had happened while they had lived on the Caribbean island.

Intuitively she knew it would not be a good idea. Mary returned her plate to the tray.

"I appreciate you being careful, Carol. Thank you. But, he needs to tell you about Puerto Rico. It's important for him to tell you everything about our father, Puerto Rico, other things, honestly with no secrets. It may help you. It would definitely help him. But, it has to come from him."

Carol searched Mary's face for an answer before she asked, "Can't you tell me?"

Mary shook her head. "It has to come from him."

Chapter 21
A Grand Plan

Matt noticed Steeg's resumption of nervous fingernail chewing as the disappearing waitress suddenly reappeared. Clearing away their plates, she asked if Matt and Steeg wanted anything for desert. Both men declined her kind offer. Without comment she left the single check on the table between them, turned, and as quickly as she had arrived, disappeared again.

With elbows on the table, Matt leaned forward. "Gracie's ghost? Are you serious? You're not the one hiding in the bushes, Gracie's ghost is?"

Pensively, Steeg spoke through clinched teeth busy trimming the fingernail. "Nobody knows this, okay, Matt? You gotta keep this to yourself."

"Why would I tell anybody?" Matt shrugged. "No one would believe me anyway. You're delusional. People would believe that, alright, but your old girlfriend hiding in the bushes spying on you? That's something else."

"No, Gracie's not spying on me. Gracie doesn't give a flying fig about me. She's a 'lesbo' now, remember hot women-on-women sex? I know you can relate."

Matt was not amused. "No more joking around. I'm serious about this."

"Me, too," Steeg agreed, pulling his finger from his mouth to nervously gesture while making his point, only to resume more nail chewing. "Look, Matt, I'm not explaining this good enough to help you understand…"

"I understand alright: you're approaching felonious indictment territory because you're still hung up about never getting it on with your high school girlfriend."

Steeg waved the finger in denial and released a long, frustrated sigh. "That's not it, not even close…"

"Bullshit!" Matt barked more than loud enough for others nearby to hear. He caught himself and lowered his voice back down to a more private level. "You're as old as me, Steeg, forty-five. What's wrong with you, man? How long have you been married?"

"Longer than you," Steeg countered self assuredly. "Unlike some people who get married, at least I was thoughtful enough to invite you to my wedding."

In response, Matt returned an eye-roll of significant proportions. "Forget about that, okay? The point is you've been married longer than me and you should be proud of it. Your wedding was a public spectacle of your commitment, for cryin' out loud! But, if you were still hung up on Gracie, why in God's name did you ever marry Carol? What, did you really think she'd provide everything you needed from Gracie?"

"Maybe," Steeg admitted, returning the fingernail to his teeth. "It sounds a little crazy, I suppose…"

"Nah, it doesn't sound crazy," Matt's voice ticked up another level. "It's nuts! Don't you think you should've cleaned out the old closet before you started shoving the new stuff in? Especially the Gracie closet – that thing is crammed solid with crap that goes way too far back and you know it. You knew it then, you know it now, and you know it's time to just end it. You don't take care of this business, Steeg, your marriage is over. No woman puts up with this and you know that, too. Hell, if I were you, Elaine would have castrated me by now! That's why you haven't told Carol anything about Gracie, isn't it?"

Ashamed by yet another uncomfortable truth, Steeg looked away from his friend. "Not really, no."

"Yeah, right. What do you think she's going to do when she finds out?"

"She's not going to find out."

A disgusted laugh came from Matt. "Wanna bet? If you guys haven't at least talked about Gracie, you don't know what Carol knows. She could already know everything and she's building a portfolio for her divorce lawyer already."

"Carol's not like that."

Matt directed another condemning eye-roll in Steeg's direction. "I wonder if you know anything about women at all. Security, Steeg, that's what it's all about. You take a vow to cherish and love another person, forsake all others 'til death do you part, blah, blah, blah. For you, all of that means a bunch of things, but to them it means one thing: security. And, by the way, somewhere in those vows is the implied promise to be honest with the other person, you know?"

"I haven't lied to Carol."

"You haven't told her the truth!" Matt caught his raised volume once more and immediately turned it down. "Withholding evidence is a 'sin of omission'. You're still just as guilty as if you actually committed the crime. You need to air out the closet, man. The least you should do is tell Carol what happened between you and Gracie and that means everything that didn't happen as well."

Without the slightest consideration, Steeg immediately dismissed the idea. "I wouldn't hurt her that way."

"Well, one way or another, you're going to hurt her because, when she finds out, your toast."

"I'm toast already," Steeg admitted. "I'm having a harder time hanging on. This morning was another sign of it. These fits of frustration, anger, rage, whatever you want to call it, are increasing. Intense waves come over me so strong now and they last longer every time. Instead of holding onto Carol when I need her most, I can't stand being around her when all I can feel, or think of, or see is Gracie…"

That brought a raised eyebrow from Matt. "See? You actually see Gracie?"

Steeg's shoulders sagged as he nodded. "That's what I meant – Gracie's ghost. She's always with me. You're going to think I'm really crazy, but I see her anywhere."

Without moving, Matt eyes traced the space around the booth. "Is she here now?"

Steeg shook his head. "I feel her presence, but she's not here. She could be. She could walk right up to us and sit down, real as life. I'd see her, but you wouldn't."

Matt drummed his fingers on the table top. "You're hallucinating; you know that, don't you?"

Steeg could only nod, accepting of the obvious. "Yeah, I know. I've been hallucinating for decades, long before I met Carol. It's my problem, not hers."

"Oh, shit. This is serious," Matt exhaled with a rush of real concern for his friend. "This is like schizophrenia or something.

Steeg, really man, you might need professional help, maybe some kind of counseling or drug therapy or something."

"Maybe," Steeg's fingernail returned to the side of his mouth. "I've never cared all that much for doctors and stuff like that. It would be easier and more effective if I simply come up with a way to kill the ghost. I get rid of the ghost, I get rid of Gracie, things should be fine, right?"

Matt's veiled concern grew noticeably more apprehensive. "Talk like that is crazy, you know that, don't you? How do you kill a ghost? Seriously, you might need help. Don't fool around with this, okay?"

Continuing his fingernail chewing, Steeg's rush of sudden mental machinations revealed a distracted agitation, preventing him from fully hearing what Matt said. He nodded with shallow bobs as a plan took shape in his mind.

"Right, killing the ghost would work, or I could figure out a way to transfer Gracie into Carol. I put Gracie into Carol, focus on both at the same time, I could manage things better."

Matt cleared his throat with an uneasy, doubt filled laugh. "You mean like a fantasy thing? I guess that could help. Lord knows fantasizing helps me from time to time; comes in handy with those few times when the 'old ball and chain' is actually in the mood, if you know what I mean."

Steeg pinched the bridge of his nose in annoyance. "Gee, no, Matt, I don't know what you mean. Paint me a picture, will ya? I don't mean just in bed, Matt. I mean all the time. Think about this, Matt: I make Gracie meld with Carol. Presto-change-o! No more ghost, no more guilt, no more internal conflict. Every time I see Carol, I see Gracie, too! I can be with Carol and Gracie at the same time!"

Matt was skeptical and more concerned about Steeg's grasp on the key issue: his hallucinations and what caused them. "I don't think so. You're going to direct a hallucination to produce another hallucination? You're not really serious about any of this, are you?"

"If I can think myself into seeing Gracie when she's not there," Steeg persisted. "I can think Gracie into Carol. Carol becomes the vessel for everything I feel and need. It could work. If I can do this, it's a way to handle things."

The conversation had taken a darker turn and Matt knew he was definitely out of his depth. He softly offered the one piece of advice he hoped would register with Steeg.

"If you love Carol, really love her, you should talk to her about all the stuff you've been carrying."

"I do love Carol," Steeg tossed off too casually. "Always and forever, but I'm not stupid. If I can do this without hurting her, that's what I should do."

"You can see this is faulty reasoning can't you, Steeg?" Matt's serious tone surprised even him. "Normally, you'd be able to see that. And, if you keep chewing on your fingernails that way, you're going to draw blood."

Steeg pulled his finger away from his mouth and looked at the gnarled remains of yet another fingernail chewed to the quick. He shrugged. "If you had seen 'Taras Bulba' –Yul Brynner and Tony Curtis, 1962 – you'd know blood is the only thing that counts."

Chapter 22
A Dry Run

A significant advantage working for a telephone company in 1993 was the prestige in having a company provided Motorola MicroTAC cellular telephone. Compact with its dark gray plastic shell, the phone's microphone transmitter was a flip down cover behind which was hidden a full 12-button key pad with an additional two rows for function buttons at the bottom. It was state of the art communication technology and Steeg's model had the beefier, extra thick extended life battery attached to boot! Folded up the phone was as bulky as a hand grenade. Flipped open, it looked like something out of 'Star Trek' and he often drove with the open phone pressed against his ear pretending to talk to absolutely no one at all. He enjoyed seeing other drivers notice he had the latest in cell phone mega-power.

Merging into the bumper-to-bumper cram of peak evening rush hour traffic, Steeg had the phone pressed against his ear again, only this time he was actually talking to a real live person: his wife.

"I owe you a dinner out," he explained, carefully feathering the brake pedal to keep sufficient maneuvering room between his front bumper and the pickup truck belching exhaust ahead of him. "I was a jerk this morning. I'm sorry for yelling at you and acting like that. You don't deserve it. You deserve dinner. Maybe my niece Kelly can babysit. Can you call Mary?

"Just you and me... Tonight, that's right... Yes, I guess it is short notice... Well, then, we can take everyone. The point is to give you a break from the kitchen and a little assuagement for my guilty conscience. I can achieve both whether we bring the kids along or not... The way traffic is right now, maybe forty minutes... You pick it, whatever you like... I love you, too... 'Bye."

He folded the phone back up, and with a satisfied sigh, tossed it onto the seat next to him. Even on the phone, he could tell: he was better, significantly more sincere visualizing the other end of the call with Carol and Gracie together as one.

He got off cheaper than he thought. The buffet restaurant charged the kids based on their ages – a bargain he'd have to take more advantage of now that they were back in Minnesota – and baby Roberta got in for free. Heck of a deal! After he covered the tab with a credit card, he relieved Carol of the baby and followed the highchair-carrying hostess to the larger six-place table. The older kids were in single file behind him with Carol bringing up the rear, the strap of the diaper bag draped across her shoulder. A few steps into the short trek, baby Roberta reached up, grabbed Steeg's nose and giggled as she squeezed tight.

Not missing a step, his response was a heavy muffled nasal drone. "You like daddy's nose? Ouch! Why you like daddy's nose? Ouch!"

With every 'ouch' the child giggled more in delight. She complained with a shallow wine when they arrived at the table and he strapped her into the high chair. Like magic, Carol produced a prepared baby bottle of apple juice from the diaper bag.

Steeg turned to his eldest son. "Brian, go over to where the soup counter is and see if you can bring back a packet of crackers, okay? They'll keep Bobbie occupied."

Unfairly put upon, the thirteen year old scowled, muttered an 'ah, gee' and turned to follow the direction indicated by his father's pointed finger. Steeg offered to stay with the baby while Carol led the other kids to the serving counters to make their selections. Steeg took a seat next to his broadly smiling youngest daughter who was suddenly very busy repeatedly slapping her hands onto the table top. A few seconds later, Brian returned empty handed.

"No crackers?" Steeg asked, disappointed.

Brian shrugged and slid into the seat across from his father. "Nope. They don't have any. I looked everywhere."

"I see," Steeg said, not believing a word. "Go over to the serving counters and scoop up whatever you want – no desserts, no cookies, okay? Real food, meat, veggies, stuff you're supposed to eat, got it?"

"Got it," Brian replied flatly, left his seat and followed the same path his mother and siblings had already taken.

When Carol, Dottie and Neville came back, it was Steeg's turn. At the array of culinary alternatives neatly grouped and displayed, he loaded up on roasted chicken, green beans, boiled cabbage and buttered carrots. He returned to the table with his full plate along with a packet of saltines for Bobbie. He'd share some buttered carrots with her a little later. Settling into the corner seat across from Carol, he spied Brian eating from a sparsely populated plate of French fries, red jell-o and chocolate pudding.

"Brian, that's not exactly what I meant by 'real food' is it?"

Brian shrugged. "Well, it's not dessert or cookies, either."

Steeg successfully resisted the sudden urge to swat the kid across the back of the head. Instead, he offered a more constructive alternative for the boy.

"Tell you what, son: when you're done with that truly remarkable selection of non-desserts, I'll get your second plate for you, okay?"

Brian didn't respond directly. At that moment, he was laughing along with his ten year old brother while Dottie looked on braced for whatever came next.

"Let me do it," Carol offered. "He'll do better if I do it."

As if I'm incapable! Steeg thought angrily, grimacing as the hair on the back of his neck bristled in irritation.

He caught himself before saying anything. Carol's face held an unspoken question as she waited for his approval of her suggestion. It was a while in coming. With a firm bite to his upper lip, Steeg mentally willed his vision of Gracie to meld with Carol. It took him several more seconds before he could see the joining, but then it happened. When he spoke, it was to Carol, but it was also directed to Gracie as well.

"You don't have to, Sweetheart, I'll be fair. I promise."

"I want Mom to do it!" Brian insisted.

Firmly, Carol told Brian to be nice as, to Steeg's own amazement, he acceded to both of them at the same time.

"Okay, Brian, Mom can do it. As long as you have something reasonably balanced for dinner, okay?"

Brian looked a little surprised at his easy victory and he was silently grateful things had not ballooned into yet another conflict. Carol simply smiled at her boy with a knowing wink. Sitting wide-eyed, Dottie and Neville didn't know what to make of it. The most surprised of the group was Steeg: the kids were fine; there was no anger with anything. Whatever irritation he had initially felt was suddenly, remarkably gone. He looked back at Carol, feeling the same warm glow he always felt with Gracie being near.

A refreshing release of tension flowed over him as muscles he didn't know he had relaxed. He marveled. Assimilating Gracie Ofterdahl into Carol Patterson had been stunningly, almost eerily, easier than he had expected.

Chapter 23
Friends, Indeed

April 17, 1995

The Monday morning sales meeting had gone longer than normal, almost to noon. It was yet another irritation for him. The restructuring of sales objectives, reallocation of assigned accounts and revised compensation plans had been the agenda items for the meeting, but the last item, revised compensation, had monopolized the discussion well past the allotted time.

The meeting ended, Steeg returned to his office cubical, slapped his well-scribbled note tablet onto his desktop in disgust, loosened his tie, released the top two buttons on his vest and slumped into the chair. The chair had a non-functioning caster that acted as a break against the others. This made the chair not roll but only pivot. It was another thing about the place that aggravated him.

He tried to rub the tension from his eyes, and then looked up to the ceiling to mouth a quiet prayer.

"Save me from this, please."

There was no immediate answer.

His frustration grew. That morning's sales meeting had revealed the new reality: his employer's new sales operation and revised objectives had become untenable. Beyond frustration, Steeg knew there was nothing he could do about it. He leaned forward fingering the note pad with its pages of freshly handwritten notes. To his right he saw the blinking red button of his office phone message light and his irritation increased.

"Well, whadda ya think?" The sandy haired Mike Cassidy was tall enough for his chin to easily clear the top of the cubical partition. He looked down at Steeg with a shared skepticism.

"I think we're screwed." Steeg pointed to his blinking message light. "The morning's shot and I've got customer messages piled up on the phone because I wasn't here to answer when they called. How's that for customer service? Given this new compensation plan, why should I care, anyway? There's nothing in it for me."

Cassidy reluctantly agreed. "I tried to work the numbers, but they keep coming up short…"

"Across the board, Michael," Steeg interrupted. "Monthly, quarterly, annually, no matter how you look at it, even if we hit our numbers, it's still nearly a sixty percent cut in pay. I'm at a lost. I have no idea what to do."

Cassidy moved around the partition to enter the cube. In a lowered voice, he said, "I can't figure out what the boss is doing. He certainly can't believe this new structure provides incentive to sell more stuff."

"He's not stupid," Steeg cautioned. He had experienced a feeling like this before, a similar occurrence he couldn't put his finger on. "He's up to something. Something else is going on here and he's not telling us."

The right corner of Steeg's vision suddenly disintegrated into a small patch of glittering splintered light. He rubbed his right eye to ineffectually relieve what he knew was a preamble to an approaching migraine. These brutal headaches were becoming more frequent for some reason: something else he couldn't quite put his finger on.

Cassidy shook his head sadly. Turning to leave for his own cubical he said, "Well, when you figure out what he's up to, let me know, will ya?"

Within a minute, a patchwork quilt of slivered sparkles had virtually covered his vision, effectively blinding him. He could see only very narrowly things at which he could look only indirectly. The annoying blinking of the red light message button on his phone was one of those indirect things.

He picked up the receiver and pressed the blinking message light button which connected him to his voice mail. There were seven messages. Grateful for the raised bump of the center '5' key on the dial pad to advance to each message in turn, Steeg mentally noted who had called before going on to the next. He was surprised the last message was from Matt Cummings. It had been a year, no – almost two years now – since he had last heard from the guy.

Matt's total message consisted of, "It's Matt. Call me."

Matt would have to wait until Steeg could see the dial pad. He knew when his vision cleared the pain would come in a rush. He opened the top right hand desk drawer and felt for his almost empty bottle of extra strength Excedrin. Finding it, he moved haltingly from his cubical to the restroom down the hall. He'd take three tablets. Maybe they'd help this time.

It was passed three o'clock that afternoon when he dialed Matt's number. After ringing four times, to Steeg's mild surprise, Matt answered the phone.

"Ah, you're home," Steeg began. "Your message was the only good thing…"

Matt interrupted. "I'm just going out the door, so you gotta do something for me."

"What's that?"

"What's the best night for you to meet me for dinner?"

"With wives, or without?"

"What, are you crazy? Without, of course."

"Probably Carol's choir night – Wednesday. What's up?"

"Sounds good. Call the other guys and set it up. I'll meet you wherever and whenever."

"The other guys? How am I supposed to call? I don't even know everyone's phone number!"

"And, I do?" Matt countered in a rush. "Get real. You need to call them."

Steeg disagreed. "Matt, this 'guys night out' is your idea."

"What's that got to do with anything?" Matt came back. "Look, we haven't all been together for anything in years, maybe decades. There's some kind of worm hole-time tunnel thing and pretty soon we'll all be dead. Now's the time, call them and set it up. You gotta. You're much better at that sort of thing than I am. I'd screw it up. You can talk them into coming, I can't."

"So, you call me, you tell me we should meet with the rest of the old gang for a guy's night out, and you want me, not you, to call the old gang to set it all up. Is that it?"

"Pretty much, yeah. After all, I called you first, now it's your turn. And, make sure it's some place that has some decent food to eat."

Grabbing his pen and note pad from the desk to scribble a few quick notes, Steeg switched the receiver to his left ear, wedging it tight into his shoulder. "Why?"

"Because I have to eat it."

This was followed by an eye roll he knew Matt couldn't see on the other end of the line but wished he could. "That's not what I mean, Matt. I don't want to be the one who calls everyone to set this up. It's your idea."

"Yeah, well, you're better at it than me!" Matt repeated impatiently. "Don't be such a baby. Call me when you got it nailed down, okay? Gotta go. Talk with you later!"

The line went dead.

Beaver's Bar and Grill was the new name of an old establishment in an older building in downtown Buffalo, Minnesota. It was long, skinny, and with a curious mezzanine level running the length of the place, darkly cavernous. It was also packed that Wednesday night. The surrounding conversational din was overpowering. Fortunately, Steeg had called ahead for reservations.

A very cute, freckled faced red-headed hostess in form fitting black slacks and white long sleeve dress shirt led Ace, Wedge, Matt and Steeg to a cloth covered four-place table tight against the brick wall, dead-center across from the longest continuous wooden bar in Minnesota.

"Busy place," Ace commented taking an inside seat.

Matt settled in the outside chair. "Very busy for mid-week."

Steeg took the remaining inside chair and Wedge sat next to him opposite from Matt. The hostess handed each man oversized leather bound menus and asked for their drink order. Ace and Wedge ordered tap beers; Matt ordered a Black & Tan; Steeg followed with a double vodka martini on the rocks with three large olives. The other three were duly impressed.

"Vodka martini," Wedge wowed. "You must like them because James Bond drinks those."

"Shaken, not stirred," Ace contributed.

Nonplussed, Steeg explained his beverage choice simply, "What's the problem? It's a bigger buzz without the volume. I spend half the time in the restroom than you suds sipping saps, so sue me."

Matt didn't care what Steeg drank. "When you told me we'd be at a place called 'Beaver's' I was expecting something a little more salacious."

Ace chuckled.

"That's because you're morally decrepit," Steeg said as he unwrapped his place setting from a large white cloth napkin. He carefully placed the napkin across his lap before he held up his steak knife with open admiration. "I've seen meat cleavers smaller than this steak knife."

"Man tools," Ace offered in a deeper voice. "It's called 'Beaver's' but it is definitely a man's place. I like it."

"You haven't eaten anything yet," Matt cautioned.

"Doesn't matter," Ace answered firmly. "I like this place."

"It's in Buffalo," Matt continued sourly. "I practically had to camp out overnight to get here on time."

"I picked it!" Wedge bragged with a broad grin.

Steeg nodded in agreement. "That's true. I called Wedge, asked him to name his favorite steak place, and he said,

'Beaver's' in Buffalo. I said, 'Well, that's where we're going to meet, then!' And, look, here we are!"

"I like it," Ace repeated with a smile.

"Me, too," Steeg nodded across the table in Ace's direction. "Too bad Brunswick doesn't return calls. He missed out."

The others all nodded in agreement.

"Well, this whole thing was Matt's idea," Steeg continued, turning to Matt. "Now is your big chance to explain yourself. What's up?"

The drinks arrived in the middle of Matt's explanation for the meeting. It turned out, after a prolonged verbal work-around, Matt admitted he simply appreciated the times in the past when they would get together and he thought enough time had passed to justify another meeting.

He was right. Enough time had passed. They were all older, a little grayer, heavier in spots than before, and in Wedge's case, follicly challenged with a broad swath of bald scalp expanding from his brow to the back of his head.

Before anyone could respond directly to Matt's confessed need for company, the waitress returned and asked if they were ready to order. Each man quickly opened their menus to scan the comprehensive list of entrées. In record time, Ace led the way, selecting a medium rare 'Beaver's Bourbon Rib Eye' – a mammoth sixteen ounce slab of prime beef. Each of the remaining three men echoed their own 'Me, too' to expedite things, handing their menus to the waitress as they did so.

The waitress disappeared and Wedge leaned forward. "So, Matt, what you're saying is the reason for this little thing here tonight is because you are lonely?"

Matt's headshake was a denial Ace interrupted.

"Children," Ace nodded knowingly. "You don't have any children, do you?"

Steeg added another denying headshake.

"Ace is right. As long as you have children, you'll never be lonely, Matt."

Even Wedge agreed. "Take my second wife's kids..."

"Please!" Ace quickly threw in ala Hennie Youngman and everyone blurted out laughing. It took a few moments to recover before Wedge continued.

"Take my second wife's kids, for example. They were her kids and I gotta tell ya, there were times I wished I was lonely! Thank God, she got custody!"

"Dogs." There was an obvious combativeness in Matt's retort. "Elaine and I have two dogs, okay? I'm not lonely..."

"No, you're not," Steeg budged in. "You're watching where you step! The tough thing about dogs: you can't train them to use a toilet. Kids are better. Eventually, kids learn to do things for themselves. When I get to that point, I'll let you know."

This was an opening for Matt to be smugly satisfied with himself. "Yeah, Mr. 'Newborn-kid-at-forty-five' – how old is your youngest, now, still in diapers? Hey, you'll be able to share! And how old are you going to be when she graduates from high school – a hundred and what?"

"I'm not apologizing for my virility."

"Well, you should apologize for something," Matt came back. "I see you're still biting your fingernails."

Steeg looked down at his chewed fingertips, each nail gnarled to the quick. "Well, so, I have a bad habit."

"Kids do that to you?" Matt chided. Smiling, he waved fanned fingers showing his perfectly trimmed fingernails for all to see. He quickly regrouped for another verbal thrust. "And, you know what else? At least I don't have an inferiority complex so thick I gotta wear a three piece suit to a dinner night out with my friends!"

Self consciously, Steeg adjusted his tie and smoothed the lay of his vest with a tug. "I worked late. I didn't have time to change, and besides, the office is closer to Buffalo than the house in Bloomington. I saved half the travel time."

The four of them continued the cross-deprecating discussion throughout the evening meal, each guy taking their fair share of abuse from the other three, with the exception of Ace who defended whoever was the focus of the ridicule at any given moment. Wedge and Matt were especially primed for sniping put downs directed toward Steeg: more criticism of his suit, his polished shoes, his fathering of children after senility had set in. The verbal jabs were made in fun. For his part, Steeg lobbed volleys of a more personal nature: Wedge's baldness as an inadvertent diverting risk for approaching aircraft; Matt still suffering the effects of getting clap from a girl in high school. He couldn't match the others' number of insults, but he enjoyed the dark pleasure of stinging back with more intimate truths.

The steaks were great; the brick and wood ambiance was warmly masculine, and Steeg was grateful for a fresh double martini for dessert. Wedge and Ace each ordered another beer, and Matt switched to a Manhattan. Steeg was feeling the drain from a long day. The others did not miss his quick glance at his wristwatch preceding another slow sip from his martini, the ice tinkling as he returned the glass to the napkin coaster.

Steeg bit one of the three speared olives into his mouth. "Well, gentlemen, it's a work night and…"

"And, you're past your bedtime," Wedge chided, wiping his beard as he lowered his beer mug.

"No, wait, you can't go yet," Matt insisted. "You need to finish your drink, and then, you need to wait for at least an hour before you get behind the wheel."

"I'm not impaired in any way."

"Yes, you are," Matt disagreed. "You just don't know it. Besides, I wanted to ask you if you've heard how Gracie's been doing lately."

Wedge slapped the tabletop. "Ah, yes, your old girlfriend; what would tonight be without an update?"

It might have been the alcohol, Steeg didn't know, but the vindictive string of words flew from his mouth with a viciousness that stunned everyone except himself.

"What the fuck do I care about that fucking dyke? The little shit! Who the hell needs to bring her up – I sure as hell don't!"

The other three blinked wide-eyed in surprise.

"Where'd that come from?" Ace asked.

Behind a nervous laugh, Matt's concern was revealed in a directed frown. "I'm not sure."

Wedge was suddenly intrigued. "Dyke? Who's a dyke?"

"Gracie," Matt answered warily. "It's a long story."

"I've got time," said Wedge. Ace added a 'Me, too' from his side of the table.

"Forget about it, okay?" Steeg brought his glass to his lips and drained it in gulps. He returned the glass to the coaster with a firm finality. "Gracie doesn't mean shit to me."

"Since when?" Wedge pushed back. "So, what's the story? If she's available, I need to know."

Steeg shot Wedge a warning glare as Matt succinctly capsulated what he knew of Gracie.

"It's a sad story, really. It turns out Gracie is a lesbian."

Ace looked askance. Wedge exploded in laughter easily exceeding the general noise level of the establishment.

"Gracie's queer!" Wedge roared too loudly. "What did you do to her? Spoil her for other men?"

Steeg's irritation grew. Saying nothing, he looked back over his shoulder and noticed the exit sign near the short hallway leading to the restrooms.

"Good point, Wedge. Apparently, he did," Matt agreed with a chuckle "Because she's playing house with her girlfriend in Chicago, isn't that right, Steeg?"

Steeg didn't answer, so Wedge did.

"So, your old girlfriend likes girls! Don't that beat all?" Wedge was irritatingly too loud. "You gotta admit, though, it just kind of figures, don't you think? You know, Steeg, I ain't never seen no one with such lousy luck with women as you."

Steeg stared at his hands, nodded silently, biting his lip as Wedge laid on another layer of his point of view of Gracie, Steeg and the dynamics of human relationships.

"Here's this one woman you wanted all your life, the one woman who ain't never put out for you and now we know why! She's a queer!"

Wedge's too loud laughter was met by Ace's growing uncomfortable concern. "That's enough, Wedge. Cool it."

Steeg's eyes met Ace's, and then he quickly looked down and away as Wedge continued.

"No, really, think about it: he's got to be responsible for some of this. He's madly in love with her for years – this ain't a teenage crush kinda thing, it's a undying 'I'll love you forever' kinda thing – she returns, keeps him on a short leash while she's playing around with another guy right in front of him; he almost gets killed – remember that night we were all in his old Mustang watching him tryin' to spy on Gracie at the 'U'? He's so lovesick he almost gets run over crossing the street!"

Steeg kept 'eyes-front' as Ace and Matt both nodded at Wedge's recollection of the event.

"Maybe if he were a real man, maybe if he showed Gracie something of what a real man is, she wouldn't have turned queer!"

Ace raised a calming hand. "Alright, alright, that's enough. No more joking around, Wedge."

With a chuckle delivered with a smirk, Wedge nudged Steeg with his shoulder. "Come on, I'm just kiddin' you."

Steeg nodded acceptance without looking at the other man.

Then Wedge added, "But with the way you affect women, if I were you, I'd hide video cameras in the bedroom! You might catch some girl-on-girl action at home with the neighbor ladies and Carol!"

For Wedge, it was as if time had suddenly stopped. His laugh had only just started to leave his mouth when the fist slammed across the front of his face. The floor between the tables soared upward and smashed into his back pushing the air from his lungs. Unable to breathe, Wedge lost what air remained as Steeg landed hard on top of him, punishing punches pummeling his face. Wedge tried and failed to shield himself from the blows as his arms oddly became too heavy to lift and an eerie silence filled his head. He could hear nothing but Steeg's fists pounding against his face.

Screams filled the restaurant as people scrambled to clear away from the fight.

"Jesus!" Matt sprang from his chair, tackling Steeg and pulling him off Wedge.

Ace hurried from around his side of the table, sliding on his knees to help Wedge. When he got there he saw the damage. "Holy shit!"

Wedge's eyes were clouded and his mind was trying to comprehend what had happened. His nose was bleeding badly and obviously broken. Blood streaked across his face to join more blood from a split lower lip and a swelling gash on his left cheekbone.

"Wedge," Ace leaned over and whispered. "Can you hear me, Wedge?"

Through a sudden reality of agonizing pain, Wedge could barely mumble, "God, for a little guy he hits hard."

Ace patted the other man's shoulder. "Just lay still. Don't move, okay?"

More than groggy, Wedge nodded.

The commotion from the crowd had died down considerably. That made what came next even more disturbing. From across the floor, Steeg struggled against the press of Matt's weight holding him down as a frightening howl filled the air.

"Hey!" Matt yelled as Steeg heaved unsuccessfully to buck him off. "Hey! It's me, Matt, okay?"

Steeg's eyes started to clear, focusing on Matt's face inches away from his own. His struggling lost a noticeable measure of vigor. He gulped in huge volumes of air trying to recoup strength quickly draining from his body.

Matt could feel Steeg's muscles relax, but he held tight to the man's shoulders just the same. He looked behind him to where Wedge lay on the floor. Wedge's face was a bloody mess.

"Jesus Christ, Steeg," Matt groaned. "What the hell is wrong with you, anyway?"

Steeg tried to rise up on an elbow to crane his neck around Matt. That's when he saw what he had done to Wedge and his stomach turned sick.

"He shouldn't say things like that about Carol."

"No, I guess not," Matt agreed. "Can I let you up? You goin' to try to kill him some more, or what?"

Steeg shook his head, adding with a quiet animosity, "No. Just let me get to my feet."

When the two men stood up, a large man wearing a sincere frown, a "Beaver's" black T-shirt and weighing at least three hundred pounds was there to greet them.

"I don't like disturbances in my place," said T-shirt man sternly, looking directly at Steeg. "It gives me a bad reputation. You know how hard it is for someone like me to have a good reputation? It's downright impossible, that's how hard it is. Now, I gotta call the cops about all this."

"No, you don't." Steeg ignored the pain stinging his bloodied knuckles as he pulled his wallet from his inside jacket pocket and removed all the bills he had. From his vest pocket he added a business card to the pile. "Two hundred for the damages. Call me. I'll cover whatever else there is."

T-Shirt man took Steeg's business card and returned the cash. "If I don't call the police, I can't put in an insurance claim for damages. Do you have any idea how much stuff needs to be fixed in this place?"

Steeg looked back at Wedge who, with Ace's help, was carefully lowering himself into a chair. Wedge held a blood stained cloth napkin to his nose and mouth. For a brief moment Steeg's eyes met his friend's. The guilt flooded over him. Steeg removed a credit card and handed it to T-shirt man.

"Put all our tabs on that card."

Wedge's muffled objection was loud enough. "I pay my own gaddam tab!"

"We'll all pay our own tabs," Ace concurred, handing Wedge a clean napkin.

T-shirt man directed Steeg and Matt away from the tables and over to the bar, signaling the waitress as he went. Within a few minutes, the necessary transaction was completed. As Steeg's credit card was returned, Ace walked Wedge toward the entrance doors, leaning close in to Matt as he passed to quickly explained he was taking Wedge to the local hospital emergency room for treatment.

"Okay," Matt nodded. "I'll follow after we take care of things and settle up here."

Ace then went to T-shirt man now standing behind the bar, his credit card in hand.

"It's on the house," said the man as he waved Ace off. Steeg had covered all of everything on the credit card. "Don't worry about it. Take care of your friend."

Matt watched Ace lead Wedge toward the door as he rejoined Steeg at the bar.

T-shirt man stepped over to them. "Well, I can't say it hasn't been fun, but you guys have five minutes before I make the call."

Matt tugged at Steeg's sleeve and together they exited the front doors for Division Street and the front sidewalk. The evening twilight had turned to a cooler night. Still confused and upset, Steeg looked down the length of the street leading to Buffalo Lake. On the opposite side of the street, he saw Ace maneuver his car from the curb, Wedge sitting in the passenger seat next to him. He watched as the car moved down the street and made a right turn at the corner.

"Where's the parking lot. I didn't park here."

"Around the back," Matt explained, motioning to steer him to the left. It was a short walk to Lake Boulevard.

Steeg shoved his hands deep into his pants pockets. "I really screwed up in there, didn't I?"

Matt nodded. "Yeah, you did. Where the heck did that come from, Steeg? I've never seen you do anything like that before."

"I don't know." Steeg felt the weight of his shame pull at his gut. "Something just snapped. I don't know why. I do know one thing for sure, though."

"What's that?" Matt asked as they reached the corner and made the turn toward the back parking lot.

"I know if you hadn't pulled me off when you did, I would have killed him."

Chapter 24
Going Crazy

"What happened to your jacket?" Carol sat in her stuffed living room chair, an open library book on her lap and the lamp on the side table set low. The kids were in bed and the rest of the house was dark and quiet.

Holding his lapels open, Steeg looked down at his suit coat. Nothing seemed wrong.

"There's a tear," she said, returning to her book and turning a page. "The back of your shoulder."

He reached across to feel behind the left shoulder.

"The other side," Carol commented without looking up.

He removed the jacket and held it out to examine what he had missed after the fight. The seam of the rear right shoulder was separated to the armpit. "Ah, gees, look at that. Crap! It's ruined!"

Again, without looking up, Carol corrected him. "It's not ruined. It's on a seam. Take it to the dry cleaners. They'll fix it good as new."

Steeg carefully draped the wounded jacket over the back of the sofa, careful to avoid straining the damaged seam before he took a seat across from his wife. He was tired and it showed.

"You didn't have to stay up for me."

Carol shrugged. "So, how are the guys doing? Have fun?"

His response was accentuated with a clipped snort. "Oh, yeah, they're just ginger peachy keen; an evening none of us will ever forget. We'll have to do it again sometime, I'm sure. Great steakhouse in Buffalo, though. You'd like it."

"Sounds nice." She kept her eyes in her book. "Maybe we can go there sometime."

"There's an idea. It's a little pricey. I'm going to have to do something to bring in some extra money if we're going to hang out at places like that."

Her eyes left the book. She threw him a questioning look. "I wanted to talk to you about that. You know, with your company cutting your paycheck the way they are, now might be a good time to consider making a change."

He rubbed his eyes, the ache of tiredness increased. "I know. But, Carol, I don't know if I have another job change in me. It's really getting hard to do."

"I don't mean you. I mean me."

Steeg felt himself grow limp. An exhausting night was turning into something truly arduous. "I don't like that idea. You're needed here with Bobbie and the other kids. I sure as hell don't want you working in a fast food place flippin' burgers and hauling bags of trash to the dumpster like you did in Wisconsin when I couldn't find work."

"It helped. It brought in enough money to pay some bills and keep our house."

He was too worn-out to fight. "I know."

"Besides, I'm not talking about that kind of work. My clerical skills are almost gone. I've been away from an office job for so long, I can't even take dictation anymore…"

"No worry. They use machines for that now."

"What about computers?"

"What about them?"

"When we got married, all I ever used were IBM Selectric typewriters. Now, everywhere you go there're only computers. I don't know how to use a computer. I've never had the training."

"So, does that mean you want to go back to school to learn about computers?"

Carol put her book on the side table, opened the small drawer underneath and pulled out several small brochures. "I've looked into it and there are several places that offer training on some new Microsoft software. The classes are day time or night time, very flexible and only a couple of hundred dollars."

Great, he thought. He had already dropped a couple of hundred dollars a few hours earlier in Buffalo. He watched his wife open each brochure, fan them out and reach across to hand them over. Each brochure had several courses marked with surrounding inked circles. Carol had spent more than a little time checking this out. It was admirable, but he also knew there were larger issues involved.

"You know, Carol, just because you complete a skills course doesn't necessarily mean you get a job."

"They all offer job placement services, too." She leaned forward and pointed to one of the brochures he held. "I like the 'School of Business' course offerings. Not the most expensive, but courses on everything: word processing, spreadsheets, something about databases, I don't know. From what I can tell, they're computer versions of all the things I did manually before. I think I can do it."

"I know you can do it." Steeg scanned the 'School of Business' brochure more closely. "It's only that I don't know how you can do it. Night classes? Okay. Three months later, you have a certificate. I can get you that far. After that, you get a job somewhere what do we do? What do we do with the kids? Brian's maybe old enough to be responsible for himself, but he's not going to babysit his younger siblings. Dottie's more responsible than Brian and she's almost two years younger! Nev's not even twelve yet and needs steady parental supervision. And, Roberta? Well, enough said. If I'm working full time, who's minding the store?"

Disappointed, Carol slowly sat back into her chair. She looked at him but did not speak.

After a long moment, Steeg broke the silence. "I'm sorry, Carol, but we need to answer that question. Who's minding the store? It's important."

"I know that," she snapped back too defensively. "Don't you think I know that?"

"I didn't say you didn't."

With surprising aggression, Carol leaned forward. "Well, I know something you don't. I know if I don't do something outside of this house, I'll go crazy. It may be a shock for you to hear this, but cleaning house all day is not my idea of a meaningful career!"

"I'm sure it's not…"

"Well, it isn't! I've been doing it for years and it's time for a change. You can criticize my fast food job all you want, but I'll tell you what: during that time when things were really hard I felt like I was doing something worthwhile. And, I was!"

"I didn't mean…"

"I know, okay? I just think you should support me on this, that's all." Carol sat back again into her chair, caught her breath and added, "Besides, we can't make it on forty percent of what you used to be paid and you know it."

Steeg fingered a gathering headache behind his brow. "But, I'm the one who's supposed to support."

Carol turned toward the blackness of the night outside the front window. "I don't think that's all that true anymore, Steeg. From what I see, more married people are both working full time jobs. They have to just to make ends meet and pay taxes. Single wage earner households are a vanishing species."

She was right and he knew it. He felt alone. He was highly skilled at willing the warmth of Gracie into his consciousness and he needed that comfort now. With very little effort, he visualized the melding of the two women he loved taking place in front of him.

"You gotta understand," he said quietly now to both women in one body. "If they weren't cutting my pay, we wouldn't be having this conversation."

Carol disagreed, but she responded sympathetically. "Steeg, you gotta understand two things: one, I need to do this; two, your company is cutting payroll because, for some reason, they really need to look good on paper right now. The question you have to ask is, why? I think the answer is obvious. They're either financing some kind of major move or they have an interested outside buyer for the company."

Immediately, Steeg knew Carol's second supposition had nailed the entire situation with his employer. It was that familiar sinking feeling he couldn't put his finger on after the sales meeting. He mentally kicked himself for not seeing what he should have intuitively known. His boss was selling out, just like Gerry Cooper had done with the publishing company.

He didn't want to believe it. "Not again."

"Yes, again," Carol said sadly. "It's in the works and we haven't much time. I need to get this training now so I can get back into the workforce."

This time it was Carol, not Gracie, he saw and he took renewed comfort in what she was saying. He always knew Carol was a strong woman, but now he felt the power of her strength rising to meet a threat she saw coming, but for which he was too close to see at all.

"You're right," Steeg nodded slowly. "We need to make some changes. You should get your application in as soon as you can."

With a nod, Carol left her chair and turned toward the hallway leading to their bedroom. Leaving the room, she got Steeg up to date with an over-the-shoulder, "I already have. Classes start in June."

Chapter 25
Taking Care of Business

It was 7:30 the next morning when Steeg arrived at the office, his energy level sustained slightly above average with the confidence he looked pretty good in his gray three piece suit. The only clue he had been up all night was the dark circles under his eyes.

His early arrival time was not unique. Steeg liked to get in before the rest of the company showed up so he could grab a good parking spot and then get ready for the day. The 'readying' process included checking voice mail, powering up his computer, reaffirming the organizational integrity of his workspace by making sure everything in his tight cubical was in its proper place, sometimes depositing nonessential clutter into either the trash container, or if appropriate, the top desk drawer. Then, he'd check his 'In' basket for any surprises left from the day before. Most important in his normal morning office routine was his securing the first hot cup of coffee from the lunch room coffeemaker. Of course, this would rarely be his first cup of the day; it was closer to his fourth or fifth.

Coffee cup in hand, Steeg returned to his cube to check his calendar, a thick, stubby, spiral bound affair with multi-colored tabs denoting the months by sections, another section for expense tracking, another section for automobile expenses, and a back section for notes or journal purposes. Steeg flipped the book open at the 'April' tab and quickly paged to the Thursday, April 20th page.

It was a sin for a salesperson to have a completely clear business day free of all appointments. In sales, if you weren't seeing people, you weren't selling. That was why Steeg always had at least one two-hour block of time penciled in for an appointment even if he didn't have an appointment! Every weekend, he would take the time to 'advance book' the coming week. On even numbered days, if no actual appointment was scheduled, Steeg would routinely assign the 1:30 to 3:30 block to some company he knew. On odd numbered days, the 9:30 to 11:30 block would be similarly assigned. This way, should some nosey person of recognized or supposed authority pull a surprise calendar inspection on him, his week would always appear half-booked. It wasn't as sneaky as it may seem. In fact, the penciling in of sales calls before the companies were actually contacted performed a valuable proactive 'To Do List' function. More than once he had found himself calling on a company for a meeting that was written down in the calendar but not actually scheduled, apologized for the confusion only to be ushered into the person's office for a perfectly satisfactory result.

Steeg's Thursday, April 20th calendar page showed his morning free and only one appointment: penciled in across the 1:30 to 3:30 block was Harvey Hellman of FPI. Steeg rhythmically tapped an index finger on the desktop as he considered the potential positive consequences of actually keeping that date. Harvey was a good customer. Better yet, Harvey was a no nonsense company owner who would shoot straight with him on just about any discussion topic. Steeg made a mental note to make sure he and Harvey spent some quality time together that afternoon.

But, first things first: he needed a warm up on his coffee. It was passed 8:00 a.m. and the place was quickly filling with sales department devotees increasing the noise level to a comparatively annoying cacophonous level. There was a short, three person line at the coffee urn in the lunchroom. Fortunately, someone had conscientiously anticipated the need to prepare the second pot in advance and Steeg quickly secured his second, or fifth or sixth, cup of the morning.

With a refreshed cup in his hand, Steeg returned to his desk and punched Matt's home number into the dial pad of his phone. He pressed the outside call button and monitored the call over the speakerphone as the number was dialed. Matt answered after two rings and Steeg immediately lifted the receiver to his ear, deactivating the speakerphone in the process.

"Hey, it's me."

"Ah, yes, the psychopath!" Matt was joking, or so Steeg hoped. "How'd you sleep?"

"I didn't sleep at all; stayed up all night sipping tea, looking out the windows and thinking a lot. There's a lot of stuff going on right now, you know how it is. And then, there's what happened last night. I feel bad about Wedge. I don't know why I lost it like that."

"Well, if it's any comfort for you, Wedge probably slept better than you did," Matt supposed. "By the time I got to the hospital emergency room, he was obviously shot up with pain killers and his face was stitched up like a baseball."

Steeg released a moan of real pain. "Oh, great. I'm goin' to get sued."

"Maybe not," Matt countered without the levity. "I'm overstating things a bit. Most of the damage is covered up by all his facial hair, anyway. You'd think they'd shave him first or something, but they didn't."

"Just the same, he can't be a happy camper. I won't be surprised when I hear from his lawyer."

Matt disagreed. "Seriously, I don't know about that. Last night after he got patched up, the three of us are hanging out in the lobby just talking. Maybe it was the pain killers he was on, but Wedge didn't seem all that upset. He's sitting there, stitches in his lip, his nose braced and bandaged, looking like he got run over. But, he wasn't angry. Instead, he was kinda, you know, sad. Ace and me, we're putting you down big time, calling you a son of a bitch for sucker punching him and going all crazy on him like you did…"

Steeg moaned again. "Gee, thanks."

"Don't mention it. Anyway, the next thing I hear Wedge is blaming himself saying how it was his own damn fault! I thought it was the drugs talkin', you know? Then he says he knew as soon as he said that stuff about Carol being a lesbian he had crossed the line. He only regretted he wasn't fast enough to get out of the way of your fist. It's crazy, but I think he thinks he had it coming."

Steeg, modestly relieved to hear this, nevertheless couldn't deny his regret. "Just the same, Matt, it will be a while before we have our next 'guys' night out'."

"I guess you're right about that," agreed Matt. "We need some time, I think."

The conversation went on for a few more minutes before Steeg signed off with a promise to call Wedge, talk about what had happened and apologize. Matt agreed it was a good idea and asked for a call back to let him know how the conversation goes. Steeg promised to do that, too.

After the phone call with Matt, Steeg left his cubicle for another visit to the lunch room for a coffee cup refill. The office manager, Rita Sanchez, walked in as he topped off his cup.

"Happy Thursday, Rita." Steeg's 'happy day-of-the-week' greeting was a standard in the office. "How are you doing this fine, clear, chilly morning?"

In her typical mood, the more-than-thirty-something short, plump and extremely hierarchical Rita was having none of it. "Fine. Whadda ya want?"

For a moment, Steeg feint an expression of hurt feelings, but Rita's well known lack of humor made him drop his phony attempt to be friendly.

"Well, now that you mention it, I could use your help on something I'm working on. You know the revised sales objectives for the department?"

"Yeah. What of it?"

Steeg marveled at the remarkable consistency of her attitude, wondering how she could maintain such an extraordinary unpleasant demeanor and still hold the same job for the same company for more than ten years.

"Well, I'm mapping out a new marketing promotion campaign for the company to help us reach those numbers, and I need a copy of our complete existing customer list. Could you get me that on disk?"

"Forget it!" Rita turned to the cabinet where the Styrofoam cups were and grabbed one.

"Please?" Steeg asked with a small laugh trimmed with a hint of nervousness. "Pretty please, with sugar on top? With whipped cream and a cherry?"

"Oh, good God, grow up!" Rita finished pouring her coffee, reached for three packets of sugar and proceeded to empty each into her cup.

"But, Rita, I really need…"

"Look, Patterson, that's confidential company data." She reached for the non-dairy creamer, dumped a healthy portion of the powder into her sugar-rich concoction and stirred it vigorously with a plastic stir stick. "No one gets it. We start letting that kind of stuff get out, pretty soon all our competitors know who we do business with. That's not going to happen. Not on my watch, got it?"

At first, he wanted to remind the woman the company's competitors already knew which companies did business with any other competing company, but he thought better of it when Rita cut off his unspoken objection with a scary glare.

"You want that database, sweetie, you're going to have to go over my head. See how far that gets you."

And, with that, Rita left the lunchroom stirring the stuff she considered coffee.

The entire exchange with Rita had been unpleasant from the start. It wasn't as if Steeg had forgotten he really didn't like the woman, but the encounter helped remind him why. When he returned to his desk, his red message light was blinking. Carol had called. He dialed the home number.

"The School of Business called to let me know my application has been accepted." She sounded very excited about it. "I need to get down there this week to register for classes."

"You mean today or tomorrow?"

"Yes. They are closing registrations for the summer classes next week already. The thing is they want me to sign up for a full curriculum on office management. That's a whole lot more money than just the Microsoft classes."

"Sure, if you go for the full certificate, a business college will want you to take additional related courses as well as the subject areas you want. That's how they make their money. Can you take just the courses on the Microsoft software we talked about, go for the education and not the 'sheepskin'?"

Carol hesitated. "I don't know. I didn't think to ask them that. It sounded like I had to take the whole load of subjects. I'm not sure I want to do that."

"You probably don't need to – it's like riding a bike: you know most of the stuff all already." Steeg contributed a word or two about the value of real life experience over 'book learning', adding, "Can you test out of pre-requisite courses?"

"I didn't ask that, either. I wish we would have talked about these things before you left this morning."

Great, he thought. *Now it's my fault!*

He caught his sourness before he took a breath. His mind visualized Gracie on the other end of the phone and immediately he mellowed.

"My bad," he confessed. "I didn't think of it. You talking with them again today?"

"I can, if I know what I want to talk to them about."

Steeg understood her concern. Steeg prompted her with a short list of questions Carol wrote down.

"There, have those in front of you when you call," he said.

"Okay, I can do that. Do you think you can go with me tomorrow when I register for classes?"

Steeg flipped the page of his calendar to Friday. It was another morning with a penciled in non-appointment. "No problem, as long as I can be back in the office by noon."

"Thank you," Carol sounded truly relieved. "Anything else you can think of?"

"Yes. Do they take plastic?"

"A credit card? Yeah, I think so. There's a Visa logo on this information pamphlet."

"Good." Now it was Steeg's turn to sound relieved. "We'll finance it. It will be the first of a whole lot of plastic financing we'll have to do."

BizTelCom was owned and operated by Clarence Peyton, a partially bald married thirty-eight year old with a four year old son who was, through no fault of his own, spoiled mercilessly by his father. Clarence was also three years late in reaching his personal goal of being a millionaire by his thirty-fifth birthday. It was a tardiness that each year since his thirty-fifth birthday contributed to a surliness that diminished his normally good humor considerably, mutating him into a less agreeable and a great deal more aggressive person; in other words, he was a typical 'Type A' pain in the ass. His father, Robert Peyton, was a true telecommunications pioneer and trailblazer heeding the government call when legal actions against the monopoly that was A.T. & T. in the '60's and '70's helped open the door to greater competition in the industry. As a consequence, Clarence was raised in the telecommunication industry and knew little of anything else.

Steeg knocked on the open office door. Peyton raised his eyes from the latest printout of the company expense report, saw Steeg standing there and waved him inside.

"Clarence, Rita says I need your permission for a copy of the client database."

Clarence's brow furrowed with sudden concern. "Why do you need the client database?"

A half-smile and a shrug indicated a lack of concern Steeg didn't feel. "I only need it if you want me and Cassidy to sell stuff. If we're going to hit the numbers you outlined at the meeting, we need to orchestrate a multi-pronged market stimulation effort to be in their faces continuously. This will help steer sales into the company and every salesperson's numbers will benefit. Other than that, I don't need the database."

"What sort of 'multi-prongs' are we talking about?" Clarence sat back with his furrowed brow intact. "I don't want to spend a whole lot of money on advertising now."

Yeah, I bet you don't, Steeg thought. Instead, he replied with a knowing nod, followed by a string of empty sales gibberish he knew always impressed Clarence.

"Understandable. I'm talking about 'piggyback' things to go along with stuff you're already doing. You send out an invoice, there's a promotion in it. When you hold a seminar on voicemail technology, you include low cost incentives for the prospects to remember you by. Your sales guy makes a call, there's a functional 'leave behind' – a calendar, maybe one of those clear plastic encased digital clocks with the BizTelCom name on it, whatever – and a follow up note with a discount offer for long distance service. We 'piggyback' all that stuff on top of things you are already doing. It's personal: no mass media buys, none of that stuff. Costs are kept low while positive sales results are pushed high. Your margins will be fat and happy."

Clarence's furrow dissolved into a single raised eyebrow. "You're sure?"

"Well, yes, I'm sure. You'll be a lot more fat and happy than if you did nothing."

Clarence leaned back again, interlaced his fingers to twiddle his thumbs while he thought of possible consequences this marketing business might have on his plans. Steeg, mindful of the sales adage 'He who speaks first loses', waited in silence.

Clarence lost. He leaned forward and punched a speed dial button on his phone. "Rita, get Steeg a copy on disk of our customer database, will you?"

Rita's response came across the speaker loud and clear. "Are you sure?"

Clarence grimaced. "Yes, Rita, I'm sure. Today, okay?"

"Ooookay." Rita sounded cold as ice.

"Thanks." Clarence disconnected the intercom call.

"She doesn't sound convinced," offered Steeg.

"She's a pushy, know-it-all bitch," Clarence griped. "If she wasn't the best office manager I've ever had, I'd fire her ass."

"The price of the indispensable employee?"

"Maybe," Clarence acknowledged, returning to his report only to put it back down and point to Steeg. "Once this is set up, I want a complete financial report on everything, with updates every week, understood?"

"Of course," Steeg agreed with a curt nod. "I wouldn't do it any other way."

Rita Sanchez was nothing if not prompt. When Steeg returned to his cubicle, a 5.25 inch floppy disk was laying on his desk blotter. Steeg craned his neck to scan over the partition, but saw no evidence of Rita anywhere.

"Like a ghost," Steeg said to no one there. "A slightly aged, chubby ghost."

Making sure the notch on the disk was in the proper position, he slid the thing into his computer disk drive and proceeded to download the database. It didn't take long.

He used his resident DBIII program to open the file. The total number of accounts was smaller than he had assumed, disappointing considering BizTelCom was a second generation telecommunication company. Steeg rhythmically pressed the 'page down' key as he scanned the alphabetically organized list. When FPI popped up, he paused and remembered what he had to do. From memory, he dialed Harvey Hellman's number and picked up the receiver on the first ring. The receptionist answered, and with Steeg's request to speak with Harvey, transferred the call accordingly.

"Harvey, Steeg Patterson calling. How you doin?"

Harvey Hellman was a rolled up shirt sleeve kind of guy. His company was of his own making, employed a total of 22 people and he was proud of it. "My phones are great, you already sold me every service you have on the books, so whatever it is you're selling, I don't need it and I don't want it!"

Steeg laughed. "I'm not selling, I promise! I just wanted to ask you a totally unrelated question about something you might have some insight on."

"You're too old for my daughter," Harvey grumbled. "So, leave her alone!"

Steeg laughed again as he wedged the receiver between his ear and shoulder to free up his hands for no reason at all. Immediately he felt a familiar pinch of pain at the base of his neck and took the phone receiver in hand as he replied, "I'm married, anyway. You know that."

"What, my daughter not good enough for you? I'm insulted."

"No, seriously, can you help me out on something not related to telephones? I'd really appreciate it."

"Is it going to cost me anything?"

"Not really, no."

"Okay, shoot."

Steeg leaned forward, cupping his hand over the mouthpiece and lowering his voice. "Thanks. Now, your company makes processing and packaging equipment…"

"That's right," Harvey acknowledged. "For the food industry mostly; a lot of our stuff goes into making other manufacturers larger systems that our stuff fits into, for the really big producers, you know?"

"Right. I got it." Conscious of the office full of people outside the confines of his own meager cubicle, Steeg's voice lowered another volume level. "Here's the question: when it comes to promoting and advertising your products to this industry, what irks you the most?"

"Advertising products, what irks me the most?" Harvey repeated thoughtfully. "That's easy: stupid ad agencies and ridiculous ad costs."

Steeg nodded to himself. "Let's take the first one first: advertising agencies. Why are they stupid?"

"They don't know my company, my markets or my equipment. They don't take the time to really learn it, you know? I suppose that's asking a lot, seeing how there's not enough to choose from out there."

"Not enough? How's that?"

He could hear Harvey take a breath of what sounded a lot like frustration. "Two reasons, I suppose. First, we're not that big of an account for the good ad agency around here to even bother with. Let's face it, when you have a total advertising budget of a hundred grand a year, the good agencies can't afford to take that kind of business. The Twin Cities are agency-rich and there are bigger fish for them to fry. We're using an agency now that makes more money subbing themselves out to bigger agencies than what we pay them. Where do you think they're going to spend their time?"

Once more, Steeg nodded his understanding. "Wherever the money is, I suppose."

Harvey's snorted reply was loud enough for Steeg to pull the receiver away from his ear. "You got that right! And then, there're the production costs for everything. You know the agency is marking up everything big time. I know I'm getting hosed with every project. But, what can I do? You need an ad, whose going to do it? I haven't the time to find that kind of help. That's why I'm stuck with the agency and their three thousand a month retainer."

"Ouch! Harvey, that's more than a third of your total ad budget right there!"

"Tell me about it. Now you know why I'm 'irked'."

Steeg was pleased. Everything the man was telling him fit almost perfectly in the plan he had spent all night working on in his head.

"Harvey, I may have an answer for you: someone who is highly skilled and experienced in the trade publication business, looking for an opportunity to write and produce high quality business-to-business communication projects. He's not an agency per se, but he is good."

"Good is okay," Harvey sounded mildly encouraged. "Cheaper is better."

Steeg responded with another short laugh. "I hear you. Suppose this person cut your current retainer in half and any production work that was subbed out would be billed directly to you without any pass-thru markup? Would you be interested in giving him a shot?"

Anything that got things done at a lower cost intrigued Harvey Hellman. "Yes, I believe I would. What do we need to set up a meeting?"

There was only one thing more Steeg needed to put the plan into motion. Harvey needed to help him get it.

"I need the contact information of every company owner you know who feels the same way you do."

Chapter 26
Pro-activity

The afternoon of April 20, 1995 would prove almost prophetic for Steeg. That was when Harvey Hellman and FPI gave birth to an independent business communications fulfillment specialist. The delivery was surprisingly easy. Steeg met Harvey in the somewhat drab surroundings of the FPI Eden Prairie offices, specifically in the main (and only) conference room. The lone window overlooked the meager expanse of a too-small parking lot bordered by humpback mounds of sod-covered earth segregating the many single level structures of the business park. The view was a peculiar mix of asphalt and greenery: suburban functionality trimmed with a subdued landscaped homage to the growing environmental sensitivities of the times to the satisfaction of city ordinances concerned with the general esthetics of commercial development.

Steeg's spoken proposal was presented in three parts: a summation of Harvey's promotion predicament; a simple description of the services Steeg would provide to solve Harvey's problem; a detailing of the compensation necessary for these services, including a provision for direct sub-contractor billing to FPI for those project elements requiring outside assistance. Steeg handed Harvey the two page contract for services, a document he had drafted the night before and printed on BizTelCom's sales department printer, pointing out the salient sections where services and prices were detailed.

Harvey examined the document carefully as he commented, "I had no idea you had such a varied background: industrial advertising, public relations, collateral design and production, sales, sales management. I thought you were a telephone guy?"

"Started there," Steeg smiled leaning over Harvey's shoulder to respond to any question even before Harvey asked. "The old Northwestern Bell Telephone Company back in '77. I handled hundreds of small business accounts and I love it. Met my wife there, too! A win-win situation if ever there was one. Made a jump into multi-media and industrial ad sales in the mid-'80's; went into sales management for a Wisconsin company after that, handling their ad work for free at the same time. I'm with BizTelCom now and setting up my own business as well. You are the very first client for my new enterprise."

"Honored," Harvey said, taking a pen in hand and signing the signature line on the bottom of the second page of the agreement. "Your secret is safe with me, but if Peyton gets wind of your little side business, he'll fire your ass."

Harvey's observation brought an ironic sideways grin to Steeg's face as he retrieved the contract from Harvey and scribbled his own signature on the companion line. "In a way, he already has, I'm just being a little more proactive with things. You should know if things go right and I can get to the business level I need, BizTelCom and I will part ways inside the next two years. I'll make sure Cassidy gets your account. He's the best they've got."

"Next to you?"

Reaffirming the point, Steeg returned a curt nod in Harvey's direction. "Next to me."

* * *

Wedge lived in a 100-year old two-story brownstone three blocks north of Main Street in downtown Princeton, Minnesota. Steeg had visited once before years earlier when Wedge first moved in and began restoring the place one room at a time. The restoration was a work in progress with the progress still 'in progress.'

With the meeting at Harvey's over earlier than expected, Steeg had jumped on the northbound side of U.S. Highway 169 to pay a quick visit to Wedge and eat whatever amount of humble pie was required. To help make things a little more palatable for his old friend, he made a short stop at a liquor warehouse just south of the Interstate 694 interchange, picked up his peace offering of choice and stuck the case of 24 Pabst Blue Ribbon 12-ounce bottles in the trunk of the Buick. Traffic being the way it usually is, it was almost an hour later before Steeg steered his car down the crunchy gravel of Wedge's driveway, the afternoon overcast filtering through a canopy of mostly bare tree limbs waiting for spring budding.

The house was weather tight and showed its age. The front porch was in need of paint, railings and balusters. With no doorbell, Steeg balanced the case of beer on a raised thigh to free his right hand for three quick knocks. The muffled response came through the door.

"Go away," Wedge's heavy growl could be heard through the door plainly enough. "No rematch until I heal!"

Steeg took a heavy breath of regret. "I've brought beer!"

The sound of shuffling feet preceded the quick, squeaky opening of the door. Wedge stood on his own, small bandages covering stitches above his left eyebrow and along his upper lip. There was a larger bandage across the bridge of his nose. His left eye was blackened and blue-red bruising blotched across the man's face. As Wedge looked at the case of beer Steeg held out with both hands, Steeg's shame forced his own gaze to fall down and away.

Wedge reached out, grabbed the case by the hand-holes, pulled it from Steeg's grasp, and with a kick of his foot, slammed the front door shut. Steeg stood alone on the porch in silence, his mouth agape. After a moment, Steeg found his voice.

"I wanted to apologize," he said loudly through the door.

Wedge's voice came back slightly muffled. "The beer is a good start."

"Thank you," Steeg responded, groping for whatever else he could say.

"It's cold!" Wedge added with surprise. "A full case of beer, already cold!"

"Yeah, I got it right out of the cooler at the store," Steeg admitted. "I figured you'd appreciate that."

Several seconds of silence followed. He thought he heard the hiss of a twist-off bottle cap, but he wasn't sure. Several more seconds of silence, and then, the doorknob turned. Wedge stood in the doorway, an open bottle in his right hand and his left hand extending an unopened bottle toward Steeg.

"Apology accepted," Wedge said through a painful wince that in healthier times would have been a smile.

Steeg took the offered bottle, twisted off the cap and clinked bottles with Wedge before taking a sip. Wedge motioned the other man inside and the two sat across from each other in a sparsely furnished front room with windows trimmed in roller shades browned and cracked with age. The sepia-esque quality mingled with the mustiness of the old place; an oddly warm and comfortable setting as the two men continued their respective fence mending.

"I'm not too sure I know why I did what I did," Steeg began.

"My big mouth, that's why," Wedge tossed back with a regretful shake of his head. "I was out of line…"

"No you weren't. You were poking fun. I should be able to take a little kidding without trying to beat the hell out of you. Normally, I would let it roll off. For some reason, I lost it. I don't know why."

Wedge pointed the neck of his bottle in Steeg's direction. "The 'why' is as plain as the beer in your hand: some jerk was insulting your wife and you defended her honor. There's some kind of a noble thing about that, I think."

"You're letting me off the hook and I don't deserve it."

"That's what you're trying to do for me," Wedge stopped him. "I ain't worth it. Look, Steeg, I know I'm an idiot. I say things before I think. I do stupid stuff. Like last night when I got pissed off with another round of your Gracie Ofterdahl hang-up. My mouth didn't stop running and I tied it all to your wife. There was no reason for me to do that."

Steeg nodded, Wedge's words about his Gracie Ofterdahl hang-up echoing in his ears. "So, it's that obvious? The hang-up thing, that is – obvious and annoying?"

Wedge shrugged. "Look, we all have our little things; things we keep to ourselves; things we don't want other people to know about us. It's just that you were sitting there cussin' Gracie out for being a dyke and I got really pissed you were still hung-up over her. I mean, after all this time, and after all you and your wife have built together, your kids and all, you know? And here you're still beating yourself up over a broad who isn't worth even a fraction of what you've put yourself through. It seemed to me you were trying to blame yourself for the mess Gracie made of her life, so I added your wife to your self-blame list. It was wrong. I shouldn't have said it."

Carefully, Wedge pressed the back of his hand along the side of his jaw. "If I had known how hard you hit, I would have kept my mouth shut."

Steeg hung his head. "I sucker punched you when you weren't looking..."

Wedge chuckled through another pained grimace. "Oh, I was looking, alright. Believe me when I tell you I saw it comin'. I just couldn't get out of the way."

"I'd feel better if you'd slug me."

"I'll keep that in mind for later," Wedge offered as he came to his feet. "How about another beer?"

Steeg was half-done, so he declined. "I have to get down to that new computer store near Southdale, but thanks anyway."

Wedge swapped his empty for a second full bottle from the case and returned to the sofa. "You're buying your own computers now?"

"Yeah," Steeg drained half of what was left from his bottle. "Going in a new direction with things, and I have to gear up to do it right."

Wedge narrowed squint was tinted with suspicious hope. "A new direction that doesn't include Gracie?"

Steeg used the remains of his beer to buy time before he answered. He didn't know how he could explain to his friend that Gracie was always with him. How could he make anyone understand how important Gracie was, especially when he knew he didn't know the answer himself?

"Let's just say," Steeg began as he moved to return his empty bottle to the case. "It's time to I put my family first in everything I do."

"Now you're talking," Wedge winced with another painful smile. "Sounds like a plan."

* * *

"Fifteen hundred a month?" Next to the side table with the reading lamp Carol sat in her preferred stuffed living room chair, incredulous as she scanned the two page document. "For what?"

Seated in the sofa across from his wife, Steeg's face almost radiated with pride. "It's in the contract. See paragraph '2.A – Services to be Provided'."

Carol flipped back to the lead page, eyes falling to the designated paragraph two-thirds down. "Well, you certainly have the experience for these things…"

Still beaming, Steeg felt the irritating pricks of doubt in the insecure uneasiness of Carol's reaction. Cautiously, he added, "Thank you."

Steeg watched Carol reread the remains of the first page. She then flipped to the second page a second time. He could see she lingered at the compensation paragraph.

The minutes of silence were insufferable. Carol flipped back to the first page again to briefly reread something, only to flip again to the second page. Steeg annoyingly wondered if she was committing the thing to memory.

Almost holding his breath, he asked her cautiously, "Well, What do you think?"

Carol took too long to say nothing.

Growing more exasperated, Steeg said, "Surely you have some opinion about this; a reaction either pro or con; something to say?"

She looked away. "Yes, well, I guess I'm concerned. We didn't really talk about any of this. You get home late, after the rest of us have had dinner; then after the kids are in bed, out of the clear blue you lay this on me. I'm a little stunned, I guess. You should have talked to me first, I think."

His slow nod conveyed a stubborn understanding. "I'm sorry. You're right. We should have discussed this first."

She glanced at him only to shake her head and look away again. "When did you come up with all this, anyway?"

"Last night," Steeg leaned forward in concern. "While you were sleeping, I stayed up trying to come up with a way to get you what you want."

"What I want?"

He could feel the irritation underneath her words.

"Yeah. You want to go back to work. This is how we can make it happen."

Carol's shoulders sagged in disbelief. "How's that?"

Steeg pinched his mouth to keep himself from speaking too quickly as he struggled to find a way to help her understand.

Surely she sees the wisdom in all this, he thought.

"Carol, the way I see it is we are parents first, wage earners second. Whatever we do, we do first to provide for the children. So, when you said you needed to go back to work or you were going to go crazy, I had to come up with a way you could do that while we still provide for the kids. This is that way."

"But, Steeg," she complained too loudly, her hands outstretched in desperation. "Fifteen hundred a month? You were at seventy thousand a year, now the company's cut you back to twenty-eight thousand. How's fifteen hundred a month going to help us? I just don't get it!"

Steeg came to his feet and quickly left for the small adjacent dining room where he had left his briefcase on the table. In seconds, he returned and handed Carol a stapled quarter-inch thick sheath of papers.

She took the papers from him. "What's this?"

"A list of two hundred and thirty-two executives in the food processing industry, complete with business summaries and contact information," Steeg explained, remaining standing in the middle of the living room. "Or, it's a goldmine. Take your pick."

She thumbed the edges of the stapled stack and shook her head. "I still don't get it."

Frustrated, Steeg pulled the fingers of both hands through his hair. "Okay, let me put it this way: you're right when you say we're not goin' to make it on fifteen hundred a month. That's why I keep my day job with BizTelCom, probably for two years. During that time, I add clients like FPI, each one bringing in fifteen hundred a month. All I need is three more of those clients and I'm grossing over seven-two thousand a year. When I get to five clients, I cut the BizTelCom string. From that time on, I go full time on my own.

"In the meantime, you get the computer training you need. In two years, I'll be on my own and you'll have whatever certification you need. Then, you land a full time job outside the house while I work here and take care of the kids. I know it's a two years from now. I know there are risks. But this plan gives us a chance and a heck of a lot more control over our income situation than what we have now. Multiple clients provide security not possible if I'm employed by a single company alone. This can work, Carol. I can make it work."

Her face reflected a growing understanding of everything Steeg had said. "And, you came up with all this last night?"

He replied with a single raised eyebrow and a slight shrug. "Yeah, kind of. It's not as if I've had a decent night's sleep in the last two years, anyway. You know that. I've been thinking about this for a while. Everything hinged on FPI and Harvey. Now, with him in the fold, I can move to the next step. If we're lucky, it will mean two more years of sleepless nights, who knows?"

"But, where are you going to work?"

Steeg threw a thumb in the direction of the dining room. "In there. We never use the room, anyway. We eat in the kitchen all the time. I've got the phone company coming in next week with another telephone line for voice and fax double-duty."

"What about equipment?"

"In the car," Steeg said sheepishly. "Computer, printer, scanner, fax machine, printer ink, toner, five reams of paper, envelopes – three different kinds – over five thousand dollars of stuff all boxed up in the trunk. That's why I was late getting home. I put it all on the Visa card."

Carol came to her feet with a knowing smile. "A computer? With software?"

The first glimmer of hope as Steeg thought, *Got her*.

"Yep, Microsoft Word, spreadsheet and database programs, too. Also, I have state of the art publishing layout and photography editing software. I don't know how it all works, but I can pick it up."

"We can learn together," Carol said hugging her husband close.

Chapter 27
Gracie Always Understands

July 30, 1997

Fifteen year old Dottie, her light brown curls framing a face too quickly maturing into something terrifying – womanhood – stood pouting at the corner of the small computer desk Steeg purchased for fifteen bucks months earlier at a neighborhood garage sale. For several minutes, he successfully ignored his daughter standing there while he concentrated on his computer screen and the masterpiece that was his brochure layout for Amalgamated Dryers, Incorporated. With his mouse, he rolled the curser across the layout, clicked on a dryer photograph, dragged it to the opposite side of the column in the layout and adjusted the text wrap accordingly. Then, he leaned back in the creaky armless office chair to evaluate his change at a distance. His gaze darted in Dottie's direction only to quickly return to his computer screen.

"We need a puppy," Dottie said flatly.

"Bad idea," Steeg's eyes stayed glued to his computer monitor screen. "I can't keep up with all of you kids as it is. A puppy would complicate things."

Dottie was insistent. "You need a puppy, too."

"I don't like dogs, never have."

"You need a puppy because you're always talking to yourself when you work."

"I don't talk to myself." Steeg denied. He leaned forward to make yet another minor adjustment on the layout. "Where's your little sister?"

"She's outside playing in the back yard with Amelia." Dottie answered, her irritation showing.

"Amelia? Which one is Amelia, again?"

Dottie exhaled in a rush of exasperated frustration. "The little girl next door? She's three? Bobbie and her play together all the time, remember?"

"Oh, yeah, that Amelia," Steeg nodded, made another minor correction in the layout and leaned back somewhat more satisfied with what he saw. "I suppose you're getting hungry. It's almost lunch time."

Dottie folded her arms across her chest. "You need a puppy more than the rest of us, Dad. You spend too much time alone."

"Alone?" Steeg punctuated with a short laugh. "Alone is not a problem here. Three budding juvenile delinquents and a pre-schooler! Trust me, I don't need company."

She wouldn't let up. "You do, Dad. Sometimes, really, it's like you have another person in here. You carry on complete conversations for a whole day. But there's no one in here except you. It's kinda scary sometimes, you know?"

Steeg pulled his eyes from the computer screen to see Dottie looking at him with honest and undeniable concern. She was right. He had become sloppy in managing Gracie. She was with him every day. With Carol at work, Gracie infused him with a special energy he needed. Everything he did he discussed with Gracie, and in the process, like a sponge he absorbed a strange power from her. How could he explain to his daughter what drove him, what made him positively joyous for the start of every day, what made him feel great and pain free? He couldn't explain it to himself. If someone heard him talking to himself from time to time, what of it? Gracie was the best drug ever. Gracie was anesthesia.

He massaged his brow with his fingertips as a growing heaviness behind his eyes warned of another approaching headache. The rubbing had no effect. When he pulled his hand away Dottie was looking even closer at him.

"You, young lady, are wise beyond your years." Steeg came slowly to his feet. "Keep an eye on your sister."

He walked toward the hallway bathroom where the medicine cabinet held his bottle of migraine tablets. He'd take two now, and this time, he'd remember to refill his pocket tablet holder.

Dinner was a large, hand tossed 'everything-on-it' monstrosity of a pizza. Delivered pizza was becoming a familiar banquet for the family since Carol had started working at a sales office for a local insurance company. Outside, the too hot and humid day had mellowed slightly with the approaching evening. Heavy overcast skies, a light and steady rain with rolling thunder in the distance, dictated the family ate in the kitchen and not at the backyard patio table.

Using the pizza cutter, Carol trimmed a second slice by half and hoisted it from the box to her plate. "What happened in the boys' room today?"

Across the table, Brian and Neville shot warning glances at each other without comment. Dottie lowered her head while four year old Roberta, elevated in her child seat and happily unaware, fingered another cut cube from her pizza slice into her mouth. Steeg directed his stern attention to his eldest son.

Not getting an answer to her question from anyone, Carol continued. "It's just that when I got home I looked into the room to see if they made their beds like they're suppose to and there's a pile of books, toys and other stuff laying in the corner on the floor. That stuff should be in the bookcase, but the bookcase is gone. What happened to it?"

Steeg's steady stare at Brian met the boy's eyes for only a moment before his son looked away.

"Well, the bookcase is in the process of being replaced, Sweetie." Steeg offered plainly while keeping his stare fixed on his eldest son.

Carol's eyes followed Steeg's line of sight directly to Brian, to whom she repeated, "Replaced?"

Brian sprang to his own defense with a too loud, "It's not my fault! Nev did it!"

"I did not!" Neville shot back angrily.

"He stole my Lego's!"

Steeg calmly and firmly put an end to the accelerating shouting match. "No yelling at the table, you two."

The two boys immediately fell quiet. Steeg turned to explain things to Carol.

"They got into a fight this morning. Apparently it started when Brian caught Nev playing with Brian's Lego collection. Brian started pounding on his little brother and Nev didn't like it. So, the little brother threw the big brother against the wall, crashing him into the bookcase. The thing disintegrated under the onslaught."

To Steeg's surprise, his wife directed her disgust at him.

"I see. That explains the tear in the window shade then, too." Her mouth was pinched tight in disapproval she directed only at Steeg. "And, you just let this happen?"

"I, uh, well..." Steeg needed a few seconds to figure out how any of this was his fault. After due consideration, he concluded none of it was his fault and his response revealed his resentment of Carol's implication. "Look, 'Sweetie', I was working on a project. The boys were in their room. When the quiet of the morning was shattered by their little disagreement, I went to the room right away. When I got there, the damage was already done and Brian was on top of Nev trying to kill him. I put a stop to it. End of story."

"He tried to kill me!" Brian exploded, pointing to his father. "He choked me!"

"I did not," Steeg fired back in disgust. "Brian, you're seventeen and you're beating up your little brother for playing with your Lego's, for Christ's sake! What's wrong with you, anyway? Haven't you outgrown Lego's by now?"

"They're my Lego's, not his!" Brian spat angrily.

Carol leaned toward her oldest son, fingered his shirt collar down to reveal faint discoloration on the boy's neck just above the shoulder. When she turned back to Steeg, the hurt and fear was plain in her face.

"You choked our son." It was a statement of tragic disbelief, not a question.

Steeg shook his head. "I held him down, that's all. I had to get him off of Nev, Carol. Hell, he's taller than I am! I held him down on the floor so Nev could get free."

Her face revealed real fear as she said, "You held him down by his throat?"

Steeg let out an exasperated sigh. "No, not really…"

Tears swelled in her eyes. She cupped her mouth with her hands, her chair tumbling backwards to the floor as she jerked to her feet and ran from the kitchen.

Steeg watched her go and then rubbed his face in regret. He then looked down at his plate and the slice of pizza he wasn't going to finish. When he raised his head, Brian met his father's gaze with a typical self-satisfied smirk. Immediately, Steeg felt the hot rage surge from deep inside; a real hatred so powerful the urge to smash his son's face in almost overwhelmed him. It was the same rage that had taken him over earlier that morning. It was the same rage he had felt the night two years earlier when he almost killed Wedge.

Struggling, he lowered his face to his hands, his breathing coming in deep, quick gasps. Steeg didn't know where this incredibly horrifying anger came from and it took everything he had to resist it.

The anger gripped him like a vice. He sprang to his feet, kicking his chair to the wall and glared at his first born who was already braced for the attack that was surely coming.

But the attack didn't come. Steeg needed to get away. With more strength then he knew he had, Steeg left the kids at the table and exited the house through the backdoor. Outside, he took the path leading to the garage. He pulled open the double garage door, climbed into the car and slammed the door loudly behind him. He sat there long enough to calm down before starting the car and pulling cautiously down the driveway for the street. He drove to the nearest interstate entrance where there would be no stoplights or intersections to slow him down.

"It's not that I don't love them," Steeg said as Gracie pulled her seatbelt across her lap, fastening it with a loud click. "I don't know why I get so angry with them, especially with Brian. The kid's got a real attitude problem, you know? He pushes his weight around, really beats up on his younger brother and sister – not Bobbie, thank goodness. He's very cruel and selfish. He doesn't share anything with anyone. Can you believe he beat his brother up over Lego's? He's seventeen! Lego's at seventeen? There's got to be something really wrong with that picture, don't you think?"

Gracie listened intently and nodded. She didn't say anything. She didn't have to.

Gracie always understood.

Chapter 28
The Wicked Witch

11:23 p.m.
November 23, 2005

"I would imagine Debra and you are still together, then?" Steeg stated carefully, bringing the rim of the coffee cup to his lips for a cautious sip of the still too hot liquid. It was late and the extra caffeine of the all-night diner's overcooked black brew would provide him a needed boost.

Gracie sat across from him, her own coffee cup in hand as she first nodded and then, with her warm little laugh, shook her head in response to his question. "Yes, we are. It's the one relationship I've had that has actually lasted."

Almost twenty years had passed since he had last seen her. She was older, but still beautiful in his eyes. Her hair was shorter, closer cropped with only the most subtle hints of gray and barely long enough to partially hide her scarred ear lobe. She wore an open top coat over an eclectically stylish outfit that smacked of academia. She had changed, perhaps matured, or maybe she was trying to project an image different from what she suspected he expected.

She would do that just to keep me off balance? He wondered. *She's developed accessorizing into an art form and that's explanation enough for me.*

He knew change was important for her. Good, bad or indifferent, for as long as he had known her, Gracie Ofterdahl was perpetual change. The one thing that hadn't changed, her relationship with Debra Sperre, was an interesting contradiction.

"You sound proud that you two have lasted this long."

A sideways nod preceded her, "Sure, why not?"

Interesting, he thought. *Nonverbally, she implies the relationship is not all that important, but her words are defensive, protecting what – her relationship or herself?*

"No reason." He changed the subject. "I appreciate your call. It took guts. Carol could have answered."

Another sideways nod. "In town for a conference, it seemed like a good idea to see you before I head back to Chicago. Besides, I'm sure she already knows all about me."

Steeg's eyes firmly narrowed. "I've never told her anything about you, not even your name."

Something resembling disappointment crossed Gracie's face as she repeated, "Never?"

"Never."

"Oh. I see. I guess I wasn't that important to you after all."

"It's not that."

"Then, why haven't you…"

"I'd have to explain why I married her, that's why."

She lowered her eyes from his and took a few moments before responding. "Because you love her, that's why."

"Something like that." He watched her look away, imagining she was checking for the nearest exit.

She avoided his gaze. "After how long, twenty-five years…"

"Twenty-seven years this coming January."

"That's a long time, Steeg. You can't tell me you don't love her. I won't believe you."

His firm demeanor broke as a grin cracked across his face. "Yes, it's a conundrum, isn't it?"

The tension relaxed a bit and they shared a cleansing laugh quietly, sipping their coffees in silence for a short time. Outside the diner, the air was cold, almost frigid. Inside, they both enjoyed the warmth of each other – old friends with old secrets – so it wasn't necessary to fill every moment with talk.

Gracie lowered her almost empty cup to the table and leaned forward to gently lay her hand across his. "You know, Steeg, sometimes we make mistakes that change the direction of our whole lives. But, even so, we have this capacity to just go on, make the best of it. And, that's how we become what we are. It's an evolving process of change and in the end it works out, doesn't it?"

"How 'Polyanna-esque' of you," he smiled, taking note of her hand remaining on top of his. "Surprised to hear it coming from you. But then, you always were good at avoiding responsibility for your actions."

She warily pulled away to the refuge of her side of the table.

He continued. "I'm sorry. I don't mean to offend. It's just that you're threatening my marriage. You don't mean to, I know, but you are. You have been for years. I'm glad you're still with Deb. At least you're not alone and that's a good thing. But, know this: your relationship with her is little more than two little girls playing house. My marriage with Carol and all we've built together, the kids, how hard we have worked, scraped for everything we have, is so much more than anything you and

Deb have pretended doing it isn't worth the energy to compare the two."

Her anger shook the tears from her eyes. "What do you know about it? You're way out of line, here! Why are you saying these things to me? You promised me! Damn you, you promised me!"

From the far end of the diner, a head turn in their direction. The mostly bald gray haired old man was the only other patron in the place. With a lowered voice, Steeg leaned toward Gracie. She backed away.

"Gracie, I don't know what we have, you and me, together; probably nothing; maybe everything. Maybe once, had we made the right decisions at the time, we could have had it all…"

If the seat would have allowed it, she would have curled into a fetal position. "If you only had a set of balls, we would have. You didn't do anything. You just stood there with that stupid puppy dog look on your face."

Disappointed, Steeg sagged back into his chair. Without deflecting her accusation, he said, "You left me, Grace, twice, if you remember."

She shook her head in firm denial. "No. You did it. You came home. New Years Eve, you dumped me. You hurt me. You know you did. How could I trust you after you did that?"

"Gracie, you're not being fair. You know you were already seeing Stewart Smalley behind my back by then. I only wanted to do the right thing."

She looked away. "The right thing, sure. Good for you. For months, Stewart was on me like white on rice, so what did you expect me to do? I wanted you to save me from him so badly, but what did you do? You break up with me. My hero."

"It wasn't like that," Steeg denied quietly. "I didn't know. You should have told me. I would have done the right thing if I had known."

"I couldn't tell you." She crossed her arms, partially covering her mouth with her hand as a sob rose from deep within her. "If I had, I would have broken your heart. I couldn't do that."

She quickly wiped away the tears before they fell. He sat there having trouble breathing. Together, they shared in the silence, he looking at her, she trying hard not to look at him. After a long while, her chuckle preceded his.

"God, we're idiots."

Steeg nodded. "Comedy of errors, the whole thing."

She took a deep breath. "I love you so much."

"And therein is my conundrum. How can I love two women at the same time? One holds my sacred vow. The other holds my whole heart. I gave my word to God and it is a promise I will never break."

"You made a promise to me, too."

A promise? What promise? He searched her face for a clue. All she returned was her knowing look.

"You promised if I ever needed your help you'd be there for me. You promised you'd love me forever, no matter what."

He remembered and then knew her visit was more than courtesy call.

"You need my help? What do you need me to do?"

"Something I don't think you can do," she began slowly. "I'm not a home wrecker. I won't ask you to break your vows for me."

"What are you saying, Grace?"

Gently but nervously, she drummed the fingers of both hands on the tabletop before answering him. "You see, Steeg, I'm older now. I see things differently. Things have changed…"

"They usually do with you," he interrupted with a smile.

"Yes, you're right about that. But when you realize you may have a window, an opportunity to make things right, but only if you act quickly because, if you don't, the window will close and your chance to turn it all around will be lost, then you know you have to do something."

"What are you saying, exactly? What is it you feel a need to change, Grace?"

She held his gaze for a long time before she spoke. This wasn't like her, compelled by forces she fully understood yet could no longer control, but she knew the one person she could depend on now was Steeg. It was true when they were kids in high school when his simple yet overwhelming devotion scared her so much she had to run away. It was true in college when he returned from the service and she stopped breathing for two years until she had to run away again. And then, again after the 1986 high school reunion when he visited her in Chicago: her knees were so weak she had to hold onto his arm for support. Then there was that kiss. Almost twenty years had passed and Grace could still feel the joy of his lips against hers.

"Deb and I are good friends," Gracie began slowly. "We've been together a long time. But, I know now I need more. You're right, you know. We're playing house. We've been playing house for decades. We go through the motions; we have our friends, our little social circles, groups made up of similar people with similar interests, similar shortcomings. We have more than enough opportunity to commiserate with others about our failings, so many failings. Deb and I, we're great pals: not all the time. We're not joined at the hip, if you know what I mean."

A small titter accompanied a sad, lost hollow stare Steeg had never before seen from her. There was a time when he would have moved to hold her. This time, he sat quietly, kept his distance and listened sympathetically.

"You know, Grace, they say you can never go home again."

She revealed the warmth of a perceptive grin, an agreeing raised eyebrow and then the hollow stare disappeared. "All of it is so vapid, Steeg, I can't tell you. It's shallow beyond sense or meaning. I don't know how to explain it, but I need more. I need depth, real significance to my life…"

"You have your work," Steeg gently suggested.

She grabbed his soul with her eyes and continued as if he had said nothing. "The kind of depth I once wanted to have with you. We were so close, Steeg, and I remember. And, I'm a little, what, older now?"

He returned a warm smile. "You still look like that cute little seventeen year-old I met in the gym at school."

She softly deflected the compliment. "Thanks, liar. The truth is, I guess, I'm – I'm worried. I have to do something to get control before it's too late…"

"Whatever 'late' means."

"Yes, whatever 'late' means," she agreed, gathering her courage with a deep breath, and then, stepping into the void. "You see, Steeg, I wouldn't leave Deb just to leave her, but I'd leave if I knew you'd be there for me like you promised."

He said nothing, allowing his gaze to be locked into the deepness of her dark brown eyes; the same captivating obsession which had burned so deeply inside him for his entire adult life was grabbing him again; the same curse he would carry for eternity, a curse he for which he truly resented her; she was asking him to save her from the abyss. Everything in him screamed to walk away and leave her to the consequences of her own decisions. It would be a type of justice. It would be retribution at last.

He couldn't do it. He still loved her too much. He also wished with everything in him that he didn't.

His lips barely moved as he mouthed his proviso. "No matter what I feel for you, I can't leave Carol. I'm sorry."

She clutched at her midsection as her voice cracked with a desperate plea. "I'm not asking you to leave her. I'm not asking you to do that. You don't have to do that. Just be there... like you promised. Can you do that for me?"

As I had promised, he thought. *Have I the honor to keep my promises, or am I truly godless?*

Almost regretfully he said, "I'll always be there for you, Gracie. You know that."

Relief flooded over her and she could breathe again. "Thank you. It means so much, Steeg. You've always been strong and, well, I'm so grateful."

Her hands reached across the table for his. His hands remained folded in his lap and he returned only a smile. She immediately pulled back to rearrange the flatware on top of the table napkin.

"I don't know when, exactly," she said in a flutter. "But I'll get back to you as things progress..."

Humorlessly, he responded, "Thank God for progress."

Hastily, she noted the time. "It's really late. I gotta get back to the hotel, and I'm sure you've got things to take care of with tomorrow being Thanksgiving."

"Yeah," he agreed with a sad smile. "Football watching takes a lot of prep time: comparing line-ups, checking the standings, making sure you have enough chips and dip…"

With an almost little girl giggle, she gathered her purse, stood to adjust her coat slightly and bent down to give him a quick peck on the cheek. She thanked him for meeting her and then quickly exited the diner. Through the windows, he saw her enter her car, pop on the headlights, drive out onto the street and into the night. He exhaled heavily, left the table, and on wobbly legs, headed toward the men's room to throw up.

* * *

With hair in her eyes Carol Patterson awoke as she often did: the digital dial of the bedside alarm clock reading 2:43 and Steeg's side of the bed empty. She ran her hand across his half of the mattress and felt the residue of warmth still there. At least he had been in bed this time. Maybe he actually got some sleep. She curled back on her side, closed her eyes and begged for the return of the blissful dark shroud that had left her.

It didn't work. It rarely did for her. Once Steeg left the bed, she'd wake up no matter what. This time, she stayed in bed for a whole twelve minutes before giving up. Dressed in her nightgown, she left the bedroom and barefooted it down the hall to the vaulted ceiling spaciousness of the front room.

He stood off to the left at the double glass patio doors looking out across the already frozen beginnings of winter. There was enough moonlight for her to see he was naked, not an unusual occurrence because that was his preferred way of sleeping. Nevertheless, it was a cold night and she immediately returned to the bedroom to retrieve his bathrobe. He turned when she came up behind him and helped him slip on the robe.

"You'll catch cold," Carol said, reaching from behind to tie the sash around his waist.

"That's an 'Old Wives' tale'," he denied as he turned and gave her grateful kiss on the lips. "But, thanks anyway. I was getting a little chilled."

She smiled. "I could tell."

"I didn't mean to wake you."

"You didn't. Rough night?"

"No, not really. I just don't sleep all that much anymore. Getting old, I guess. Time marches on, you know. Perpetual awakeness is the price we pay for longevity."

His arm wrapped around her and she yawned as she rested her head against his shoulder.

"You hardly ever sleep through the night, Steeg. Maybe you could take something to help. Maybe you should see a doctor and get checked out. You need your rest."

"You know I don't trust doctors. Never have. They're too expensive and I just never understood the logic in believing anything anyone tells me who has a vested interest in my being ill. I mean, really, why would you believe someone who loses money as soon as you're well? It defies reason."

"Yes, dear, I know," she said with forced patience. "On the other hand, you're not sleeping, you haven't had a decent night sleep in years, and if you don't get your rest, you'll probably die way before your time."

"Probably," he agreed, smiling as he hugged her across her shoulders. "Then, you'll be able to retire on my life insurance. See, it all works out in the end."

"That's not funny."

He winced at the sharp jab of her thumb in his ribs. "You're so physical sometimes. You know, now that we have the house pretty much to ourselves, we could take advantage of your physicality right here in the sunroom."

Carol cautioned him. "Bobbie is still here, fast asleep in her room right down the hall."

"Ah, yes, the youngest," he moaned regretfully. "You'd think she'd be married by now."

"She's twelve, Steeg."

"And I feel like I'm eighty."

"You're fifty-seven."

"I feel older."

"You're not. You're tired. You work very hard…"

"Not hard enough," he interrupted, giving her a little squeeze to hold her tighter to him. "We're teetering on the brink of personal bankruptcy in the land of plenty. Go figure."

She continued. "You do everything yourself. You even designed this house the way you wanted it…"

"I had to. I needed a real office. That dining room in Bloomington was smothering me. And, look who's talking about working hard! You've been home two days just preparing for Thanksgiving dinner! What have we got now, four pies, sweet potatoes, green jell-o salad no one is going to eat…"

She interrupted with a correction. "Orange jell-o salad, sugarless for my Dad."

"Orange, green, what's the difference? It's still jell-o."

"And I had to take the time off from work to clean. I don't want my guests to eat Thanksgiving dinner in a dirty house."

"Ah, yes, the guests: your mother is coming, too. Praise the Lord, I can hardly wait."

"My mother is the reason I had to take time off. This house has to be perfect or she's going to say something. You certainly can't clean…"

"Can, too."

"Cannot, not to her standards, believe me, I know." She forced him to adhere to a more serious vein. "Anyway, I'm not talking about me, I'm talking about you and how hard things seem to be for you. You work and work, but we just seem to keep struggling all the time. It would get anyone down. You're depressed, I think. Not in a mopie kind of way, but sometimes you seem so unhappy I cry. I love you. I pray whatever it is that makes you so sad I haven't been the cause of it."

His grip around her shoulders relaxed and his eyes fell low. Across all the years they had been together, he had kept her safe from Gracie, but to no avail. His near-uncontrollable bouts of rage, days of forced silence while he wrestled with his inner demons and more recently the physical consequences of all he carried – the headaches; the increasing frequency of stabbing abdominal distress; the sleepless nights – all of it had become her burden, a weight she had carried with strength he didn't have and with grace at which, when his mind was clear, he could only marvel. For several absolutely quiet moments, they said nothing. Then, he leaned in close, kissed her head and whispered.

"You must know you are my salvation," Steeg said barely above a whisper. "You have given sense to my life. You have provided me purpose, substance, truth and the only real peace I have ever known. I could have none of it without you. You have given me the blessings of children. You provided spiritual strength raising these children in a Christ-centered home that would not have existed without you. You even got me back into church after years of me trying to avoid churches…"

"You still don't trust them, though, do you?"

"True enough," he agreed with a cheerless nod, adding with a chuckle, "It defies logic to trust another person who has a vested interest in your spiritual salvation."

Another sharp poke in the ribs before Steeg continued.

"But, seriously, Carol, you must never blame yourself for me or what you may perceive to be my unhappiness. Whatever happens, no matter what, you must know you are God's answer to my prayer. You are the joy of my life."

* * *

Eloise James was less than one month past of her eightieth birthday. She was wife to Herbert James, who was slightly more than one month away from his eightieth birthday, and mother of Carol James. She was also Steeg Patterson's mother-in-law. She held inexplicable disdain for almost everyone who cared or held concern for her, disdain she justified with her sincerely held belief that no one liked her or wanted anything to do with her. Eloise was not far wrong. For the twenty-six years Steeg and Carol had been married, Steeg could honestly say Eloise was the most unpleasant person he had ever met.

He managed his difficult relationship with his mother-in-law by self-assessing her problem as mostly mental illness.

"She's not a well person," he would often say to Carol, usually when trying to comfort his wife after another episode of painful rejection and ridicule from her mother.

Carol had suffered her whole life with her mother's open dismissal of everything Carol had ever tried to do or held important: school work; ballet; music; business school, the list included many things. Steeg didn't realize how defeated Carol was until two weeks after they married in 1979. While he was at work, Eloise dropped in for a visit at their circa 1920's two-bedroom starter home in south Minneapolis. The newlyweds were still living out of boxes, only half of which were partially unpacked, so although Carol wasn't rude to her mother, she was also not pleased with the unannounced stopover.

"Just thought I'd see if I can help," Eloise explained as she walked from the front entry directly into the postage stamp of a living room filled with pillars of cardboard boxes. "Still haven't unpacked yet, I see."

Her dark brown hair pulled into a ponytail and a kitchen apron tied around her waist, a cleaning rag in her hand testified to her work. Carol tried not to show her irritation with her mother's two-edged offer to help.

"No, Mom," she sighed. "Haven't unpacked yet; trying to clean the place up before we start shoving stuff into closets, drawers and places."

Eloise nodded as she took in the small cluttered confines. "Good idea. Not a very big house, is it?"

Her mother's implied affront slapped across Carol's psyche as painfully as an open hand across the mouth. She could feel the tears begin to gather in the corners of her eyes as her mother continued.

"He isn't very successful, is he?" Eloise stepped around a stack of cardboard boxes and moved from the main room to the center hallway that joined the front and back bedrooms. After visually checking out the lay of the space, she turned back to her daughter. "I suppose you knew what you were doing, but I think Jeffrey Ellenson really liked you. I don't know why you two didn't hit it off better than you did. Now look where you're at. You deserve better."

Carol turned away, the air punched from her lungs. "Mother, don't, please. Steeg is my husband."

"Yes, well, he is now, isn't he?" Next to the wall Eloise found a small chair clear of clutter and took a seat with an exasperated exhale. "And, that name: Steeg. What kind of man has a name like that, anyway?"

The shaking came before the tears. Carol hurriedly left her mother for her bedroom, closing the door behind her.

Later that evening, when he returned from the office, Steeg found Carol alone in the bedroom, sitting curled in the corner on the floor, rocking back and forth. He didn't know what was wrong; he only knew she was in pain. He joined her on the floor, wrapped her close in his arms and simply held her as she quietly wept. After a long while, she simply said she was sorry.

He stroked her hair gently from her face and told her she did nothing wrong. Carol didn't agree.

"She's so mean, Steeg. I don't know why. I don't know what I ever did to deserve…"

He shushed her quietly, repeating once more she had done nothing wrong.

"You don't understand," she said. "If you hadn't come along when you did, saving me like you did, I don't know what I would have done."

Mostly due to the necessity for stabilizing the predicament he found himself in shortly after he and Carol married, Steeg rationalized his mother-in-law was emotionally damaged in ways not worth his effort to understand. His rationalization was necessary because whatever Eloise's problem was, he couldn't allow it to stand in the way of what he needed. He needed his marriage. He needed Carol. For at least once in his life, he needed a normal relationship with a woman who wasn't Gracie:

a real woman, not a ghost of his own making. He accepted Eloise's mental illness as a fact. He had to. It was the best way for him to stay true to his vows and keep his marriage intact.

Eldest son Brian, now twenty-five years of age and a freewheeling bachelor with his own house in the South St. Paul suburbs, was the last to arrive. He still wore his casino worker's uniform from which he changed into more comfortable jeans and a sweater he carried in a grocery bag pre-packed before going to work earlier that morning. His sister Dottie had preceded both her brothers by hours, leaving her apartment before 9:00 a.m. to lend the hand she had promised her mother. By noon, the whole house was thick with the rich aromas of Thanksgiving. Middle son Neville appropriately arrived just in time for kick-off of the Atlanta-Detroit football game. With diet soda in hand, he joined his father in the family room to watch the game.

"You need a new TV, Dad." Neville commented flatly, claiming his corner of the sofa and setting his drink on the end table there.

With eyes remaining glued to the TV screen, Steeg said, "Use a coaster, Nev."

His son sighed an acknowledging "Right," reached for the insulated flat disk near the base of the table lamp and relocated his soda can accordingly. "A new TV is a must, Dad, one of those new flat screen jobs. Watching football on this dinky thing gives me a headache."

"Complain, complain, complain. It's a Trinitron screen, a little small maybe, but a great picture. I wonder if Detroit can win this one?"

"Not likely," Neville answered assuredly.

From the kitchen, Dottie loudly announced, "Gramma and Grampa's here!"

Neville almost choked on his soda. "Oh, joy."

Carol followed with, "Steeg, could you help them? Mom's bringing the salad and a bean dish!"

Less than enthusiastically, Steeg came to his feet and pointed a warning finger at his youngest son. "Be nice, Nev. Remember, it's Thanksgiving."

"I'm always nice, Dad," his son replied, leaving his corner of the sofa to follow his father to the front door. "It's Gramma who's the problem."

Eloise and Herbert were already on the front stoop, Eloise holding a large something or other wrapped in multiple layers of newspaper, Herbert holding a ceramic bowl topped with aluminum foil.

"A little slow today, Steeg?" Eloise criticized in her typically unpleasant manner as Steeg opened the door. In the true football spirit of the holiday, she pushed her wrapped food offering firmly into his gut, making sure he had it before letting it go. "Be careful with that, it's the bean hot dish."

She turned, grabbed the salad bowl from Herbert, turned and, with a warm smile filled with love for her grandson, handed the bowl to Neville.

"Thank you, Gramma," Neville replied politely.

She patted his arm gently. "Be a good boy and take the salad up to your mother, Sweetie, would you please?"

Steeg and his son shared a veiled "here-we-go-again" glance as Neville quickly escaped in the direction of the kitchen. Still holding the door as his in-laws stepped across the threshold, Steeg offered a "Happy Thanksgiving" with the sincere hope it would be one.

"Yeah, sure," Eloise groused. "Do you think you could have moved any farther out of town, Steeg? The drive takes forever to get out here."

Steeg twitched a regretful smile and turned toward his father-in-law. "Got the game on for you, Dad: Atlanta and Detroit. Then, there's the second game."

Herbert nodded and smiled. "Sounds good to me, Steeg. I like baseball."

Steeg blinked, not fully comprehending exactly why his father-in-law said that. He shut the door firmly to seal out the cold. "Let me take your coats."

His mother-in-law gripped her coat collar snug against her throat and passed Steeg to leave the short entry foyer in favor of the kitchen. ""Not mine, it's cold in this house."

Herbert removed his coat with slow, obvious effort. Steeg reached for it at the collar and helped his father-in-law shed the garment, flipping it over one arm as he pointed Herbert in the direction of the family room. "The TV is that way, Dad."

"Thanks," Herbert said with a nod as he moved toward the route Steeg indicated.

Steeg walked to the hall closet, skirting behind and past Eloise in the process. He almost dropped the bean hot dish as, with one hand, he worked Herbert's coat onto one of the few vacant hangers suspended from the closet rod.

"Well, we finally made it," he heard Eloise announce as she entered the kitchen. "Carol, I don't know why you let yourself move way out here. This place is just what I knew it would be – Steeg's revenge!"

Steeg let out an exasperated sigh loud enough to be heard as he stared at the crammed clutter of the closet. His head fell and he silently wished he could step into the closet, close the door, bury himself in the mess of it all and simply disappear. The weight of the package he held pulled at his arms, so he thought better of it and turned toward the kitchen. The rest of the day would only be worse.

Chapter 29
Doctor's Orders

The examination room was clean, earth toned, and sterile with overhead fluorescent lighting that was too harsh and a pathetic cheap framed print of green-on-green foliage hanging on the wall adjacent to the sink. The whole clinic smelled of disinfectant and it made Steeg slightly nauseous.

"Take a deep breath and hold it."

Steeg didn't know Dr. Wilbur Fong, a lab-coated clinic staffer disturbingly younger than he was. As uncomfortable as he felt, he still did as he was told.

"Let it out."

Steeg emptied his lungs in a rush. Dr. Wilbur Fong moved the now slightly less chilled disc of his stethoscope to the opposite side of his back.

"Again."

Steeg took another deep breath and held it.

"Let it out."

Another heavy exhale followed as Steeg's concern grew. The matters at hand were not being adequately addressed by the good doctor.

"It's indigestion, Doc, not my lungs."

Dr. Fong smiled politely. "Yes, so you said. Lay back on the table please and unfasten your belt and pants."

Skeptically, Steeg eased back onto the examination table and followed the doctor's instructions. *So typical,* he thought. *Anything to drive up the bill.*

Fong could feel Steeg's reluctance as he pulled up his patient's shirt. Starting on the left side, he proceeded to probe expertly with his fingers along Steeg's upper abdomen.

The doctor firmly and steadily pushed with his fingers at several places, each time asking, "Does that hurt?"

"No."

One more time, Fong pushed a few inches on the far right side. "Does this hurt?"

Steeg twitched only slightly. "Well, it's not comfortable."

"Sharp or dull?"

"Dull, I guess."

Fong moved over another few inches. "This?"

Steeg winced noticeably. "Yeah, sharper there."

The doctor muttered a non-committal "uh-huh" before he moved down to Steeg's lower abdomen to continue his finger pressing around there.

"Any pain here?"

"No."

Fong moved below the waist band of Steeg's shorts and poked around some more. "Here?"

"No, not really," Steeg replied, his annoyance growing more evident. "Look, Doc, it's indigestion. I need something for indigestion, that's all."

Old men, Fong thought. *They make the worst patients.*

"Okay, Mr. Patterson, let me explain things as you lower your shorts to your ankles, please."

More skeptical, Steeg stayed flat on his back, raised his butt and pulled his shorts and pants down to his calves.

"You come in here today complaining of indigestion you say you have had since Thanksgiving. That's interesting. Today is Monday. Thanksgiving was last Thursday."

What an idiot! Steeg replied, "The clinic was closed over the weekend, Doc."

Fong reached between Steeg's open legs and began the uncomfortable fondling.

"What are you doing down there?!" Steeg objected, rising up on his elbows.

"Relax, just a testicular exam. You do give yourself regular testicular exams, don't you? After all, you're almost sixty."

"Fifty-seven," Steeg corrected firmly.

Fong chuckled. "Yes, please excuse my error. You're fifty-seven – nowhere near sixty. The point is, Mr. Patterson, indigestion that lasts for five days most probably isn't indigestion. According to your records, you haven't been in here for anything medical for over a half-decade. That's longer than I've been at the clinic! Dr. Schmidt noted back then you had slightly elevated blood pressure. It's higher now…"

"Ah, Dr. Schmidt – I liked him. How is the old guy doing?"

"He died of old age and freed up a spot for me on staff," Fong's sardonic demeanor coolly colored his factual statement. "You've never had so much as a physical examination here…"

"I'm healthy, so what?"

"So, what is it? You have a hang up and don't like doctors or are you Superman?"

Staring at the ceiling's filtered fluorescent light fixture, Steeg answered honestly. "It's doctors. I'm not real crazy about doctors."

Fong nodded, switching to the second testicle. "Makes sense. I'll take your blood pressure a second time before we're done. It'll probably be lower."

Fong concluded his examination of Steeg's balls, removed his latex gloves, took a seat on the stool next to the small corner desk and reopened Steeg's file for another look. Steeg sat up and pulled his pants back on.

"If it isn't indigestion, what is it?"

"Not sure, yet," Fong replied honestly. "What did you do for the indigestion over the weekend, anything?"

"Tried two different anti-acids, chewables and drinkables."

"Did they help?"

"Obviously not or I wouldn't be here, would I?"

"Good point," Fong admitted, tapping a finger on Steeg's open file. "It says here you had an MRI for a neck injury?"

"Yes, that was the last time I was in."

Fong checked the record entry again before coming to his feet and walking over to Steeg still seated on the examination table. "It says you have fractured vertebrae, C6 and C7, with a ruptured disc and floating bone chips. Did you have surgery to correct that?"

"Of course not," Steeg answered as Fong placed his probing fingers near the base on the left side of Steeg's neck.

"How did the injury happen?"

"Long time ago – in the Navy. No big deal."

"Any discomfort, numbness, tingling, that kind of thing in your left arm or hand?"

Fong's fingers found the exact spot, pressed slightly with his fingers. Steeg noticeably flinched.

"Depends on how you define discomfort, I guess," Steeg confessed. "When something is all the time, you get use to it."

"Really?" Fong pressed his fingers more firmly on the spot.

Steeg couldn't prevent the audible yelp. Fong released the pressure immediately and folded his arms across his chest.

"I suspect, Mr. Patterson, your constant discomfort is occasionally much worse. So much so, there are times when the pain in your left arm is so severe you can't stand it. Floating bone chips can have that effect. That was why you came in last time. Am I wrong?"

Steeg looked at the man and said nothing.

Fong nodded. "I see. Your hypertension and a body mass index of twenty-nine, combined with your longstanding physical problems make for a less than desirable combination."

Frustration showing, Steeg steered the conversation back on track. "I just want my gut to ease up. Can we concentrate on the issue at hand?"

Another nod from the doctor. "Okay, let's talk about your gut. How long have you had these 'indigestion' episodes?"

"I told you, since Thanksgiving."

With a shake of his head, Fong rejected the dodge. "No, I mean when was the first time you first experienced this type of 'indigestion' problem? How far back?"

Steeg exhaled heavily, pausing to search his memory. *When was it these things started? The better question is: how far back was it when I didn't have these attacks?*

"I don't know, a long time ago, several years."

"Good. Well, not good, but good that you know you've had this condition for longer than just the last five days. What is it you do, Mr. Patterson?"

"Do? For a living, you mean?"

"Yes."

"I'm a freelance business communication consultant."

"And, what sort of activities do you do?"

"I consult." Steeg was growing more tired of the 'twenty-questions' routine.

"I'm sorry. I meant leisure time activities, recreation, that sort of thing."

This was the very thing he didn't like about doctors. It was none of Fong's business what he did. More deliberately, he mouthed the words more slowly.

"I – con - sult."

The doctor nodded in understanding, closed Steeg's folder and tucked it under his arm. "I see. Well, coincidentally, I 'doctor.' You're obviously over stressed and there are still things we need to know about your 'gut' problem. To learn those things, I need to run more tests. I'll have the nurse come in to draw blood. It'll be several vials because we're going to check everything, agreed?"

Oh, goodie! Bloodletting! Steeg thought. He said, "If it helps the gut, I agree."

Three hours later, Steeg was returned to the same examination room by a very young thing in a ponytail dressed in surgical scrubs. He lowered himself wearily into the side chair next to the dinky corner desk. The nurse informed him politely the doctor would be in to discuss things in a few minutes. Steeg nodded his thanks and the young lady closed the door behind her as she left.

He checked his wristwatch.

Eighteen minutes later, a soft knock on the door preceded Dr. Fong's entry. He carried Steeg's open file with him as he took his stool and rolled toward the desk.

"Well, this is interesting," the doctor commented. "You don't have a bladder infection, your PSA is fine, and you don't have any STDs."

"'Sexually transmitted disease'? You tested me for the clap?"

"Among other things, yes."

"Ah, well, what a relief," Steeg mocked what he considered to be a colossal waste of time. "Don't you have to send all my 'samples' out to a lab for analysis?"

"Yes, for some tests, but we have quite a bit of new technology that allows us to do most of it right here," Fong decided to throw in a personal jab to even the tally between them. "Not being a regular visitor to our clinic, you may not know of some of our more recent advances."

"It's so nice to hear progress is still being made in the medical profession," Steeg tossed back, the chip on his shoulder showing even more. "It's so comforting. Can I go, now?"

"Actually, after we talk a bit, yes." Fong pulled the new chest x-ray from its envelope, slipping the gray-black sheet of film under a clip on the wall mounted view screen and flipping the light switch to 'on'. The screen quickly flickered to a frosted white glow. Fong pointed to the x-ray in instruction. "These are your lungs and rib cage, down here your spleen, pancreas, stomach; over here, liver; here small and large intestines."

"Got it," From his chair, Steeg acknowledged unimpressed.

Fong's finger ran the length of indistinct shading just under the rib cage. "See that area, there?"

Steeg leaned over the desk to take a look. "Yeah. What is it?"

"I'm not sure, yet, but it's something between your lungs and abdomen, maybe breaching your abdomen, and it shouldn't be there." Fong switched the screen off and returned to his notes in Steeg's file. "Have you had any problems breathing?"

"Such as?"

"Hard breathing after minimal exertion?"

Steeg preferred a chuckle to any uncomfortable confessions. "I consult. I don't exert."

Fong smiled. "When you do 'exert' do you find yourself breathing very hard very quickly?"

Steeg could feel his humor abandoning him. *This may be serious.* "I suppose so."

Fong glanced again at his notes. "Frequent fevers, either slight or severe?"

Suddenly very tired, Steeg shrugged, leaned back in the chair and folded his hands in his lap. "That's difficult to say. I'm not the kind of guy who often takes his own temperature."

Dr. Fong threw a hand up impatiently and barked back, "No, of course you're not. You're the kind of guy who nearly breaks his own neck but doesn't bother to get it fixed. You're the kind of guy whose gut pain has lasted for so long you can't tell me when it first started, pain so severe it almost doubles you over, and you're the kind of guy who thinks it's all just indigestion! I know what kind of guy you are, Mr. Patterson: you're an idiot."

Regretting it even as the words were leaving his mouth, Fong drew his hands down his face, taking the necessary moment to bring his frustration with this patient under better control.

Steeg smiled and a little laugh brought the doctor's eyes up to meet his. "Well, what do you know – an honest doctor; who knew?"

A flush of embarrassment rose in the honest doctor's cheeks. "I'm sorry. I shouldn't have said that. It was really not called for. Please accept my apology."

"Never," Steeg denied with another chuckle. "It was too refreshing and I'm keeping it."

The two men looked at each other in silence for several seconds before Dr. Fong continued.

"Okay, then, how about this: do you often find yourself sweating all of a sudden, even in air conditioned rooms?"

Yes, a lot. Not as honest as the doctor, Steeg said, "I suppose that's true, too, if you put it that way. Carol always says she can't understand how she can be so cold all the time while I'm always so warm."

Fong added a quick handwritten note to the file, flipped to the previous page to check something he had written earlier, and then looked up with awareness of a new possibility.

"You said your neck injury happened in the Navy."

Steeg nodded. "Yeah. So?"

"What did you do in the Navy?"

"I pushed airplanes on an aircraft carrier and developed a sincere appreciation for the taste of beer."

"What aircraft carrier?"

"The *U.S.S. Hornet*, CVS-12, a conventionally powered Essex Class carrier World War II vintage, retro-fitted and updated for anti-submarine warfare."

Fong nodded. "How long were you on the ship?"

"Nearly four years. We decommissioned her in 1970. The Navy gave me an early release."

"Decommissioned? That's what they call putting a ship in 'mothballs' isn't it?"

"Yeah."

Fong made another note. "Dirty work, isn't it? There's a lot of dirt and dust."

Steeg laughed as he remembered how filthy he and his crew would get every day working on that old boat in the massive Bremerton, Washington naval shipyard. The fine black particles were in his ears, nose, even his underwear.

"Covered with it," Steeg admitted. "You ever want to get really grimy, Doc, spend four months chipping paint and non-skid on a hanger deck."

"What's 'non-skid'?"

Steeg shrugged. "It's a coating they put on the decks so you don't slip and slide when the deck gets oily or wet. It's kinda thick, I guess, with something in it that makes it, you know, grippy. It probably had some kind of sand or granulate mixed in because when it dried it was rough to the touch. Your flight deck boots really grabbed it when you walked on it."

"Was it fire resistant?"

"Oh, sure. Fire was always a huge concern on the ship. Non-skid was on all exposed deck surfaces. I'm sure it had some kind of fire retardant properties."

Fong made another note in Steeg's file and then closed the folder. When he looked over at his patient, he did not hide his suspicions well.

"We need to schedule more tests, Mr. Patterson," the doctor said, adding, "This time downtown at a hospital."

Chapter 30
Travel Plans

Wednesday, December 7, 2005

So far, a good twenty minutes had gone by and the two men had shared maybe two or three sentences between them, tops. Matt Cummings lowered his frosted beer mug to the booth tabletop and complained almost loud enough for other nearby bar patrons to hear.

"What's wrong with you, anyway?" Matt grumbled impatiently. "You depressed or something? You're like Mr. Sad Sack. What's going on?"

From across the table Steep shot his old high school pal an overplayed frown. "Well, thanks a bunch, Mr. Nosey, Merry Christmas to you, too."

Matt wouldn't be put off. "No, really, I'm serious. You call me up, tell me to meet you here for a beer and you're like zoned out or something; like you're in some other place. You got something on your mind you want to talk about, or what?"

Steeg shrugged. "I don't know: it's the holiday season; I don't buy Christmas cards but I do buy Christmas beers for my friends; I thought you'd appreciate it; I gave you a call; you came; whalla! We're here! What else do you want me to say but Merry Christmas?"

Matt raised his beer for another sip. "Yeah, okay, then: Merry Christmas."

"To you, too," Steeg raised his mug in turn and joined Matt in the toast. He returned the mug to its coaster. "It's been a while, that's all. We haven't had a gathering of the gang for a long time."

"You got that right," Matt agreed. "Not since you beat the bat snot out of Wedge at that steakhouse in Buffalo."

"Really? That long ago?"

"Really."

Steeg brought a hand up and pinched his mouth in concern. "That was back when I decided to go into my own business – years ago. Crap. How's Wedge been, do you know?"

Matt shook his head. "Beats me. He's older, I know that, probably more ornery. I think Ace told me he got married again. What would that be, number three or four? I don't remember."

Steeg didn't know how many times Wedge had been married. "At least he made honest women out of them and that's something. We should have another group get-together just to see how things are now."

"God help us," Matt rejected. "What for? We could barely stand each other as it was and now you want another chance to pummel Wedge?"

They both laughed.

"Come on, it'll be fun. Let's set it up before Christmas, whadda ya say?"

Matt waved a cautious hand. "You do the calling. I'm not going to do it."

"I always did the calling, anyway," Steeg complained. "It's your turn."

The two of them shared a few more "Do you remember when" memories that lasted until their beer mugs were empty. As if on cue, the waitress walked up and asked if they wanted another round. Matt turned the question over to Steeg and Steeg said, "Sure, why not." In short order, two more beers replaced the empty mugs.

Steeg took a sip and noticed over the mug's rim Matt looking at his watch in a classic leave-taking cue.

"Need to go somewhere?"

Matt shrugged. "Not right away. I got time. So, anything new and exciting happen lately?"

A sideways smile crossed Steeg's face. "You could say that, but you wouldn't believe it."

Matt cringed. "Oh, good God, don't tell me: your wife is pregnant again."

Steeg laughed. "Hardly, no, nothing like that. Someone came for a visit."

Matt asked who and waited for Steeg's one word answer. It stopped him cold.

"Gracie."

"You're shittin' me."

"No, I'm not."

"When?"

"The day before Thanksgiving. I was working in my office at home, the phone rang, I answered and it was Gracie. She asked if I had time to meet her that evening for coffee."

"I don't believe it," Matt leaned back, doubt and skepticism pulling the corners of his eyes into a penetrating squint. "Gracie Ofterdahl? Miss In-Contol; Miss Manipulator par excellence; the dyke from Chicago wanted to meet you for coffee the day before Thanksgiving. Why?"

"That was the same question I had, why? I was curious, so naturally I didn't ask it. Instead, I said yes."

"Naturally," Matt said with regret.

"She was in town for some kind of psychotherapists' conference and had to head back to Chicago the next morning," Steeg explained. "So, I agreed to meet her at the old Hiawatha diner – you know the one near the Minnehaha Falls – around 9:00 that night."

Matt nodded, waiting for Steeg to continue. When he didn't, Matt asked a simple question. "Did you bring Carol with you?"

"Of course not, don't be stupid."

"What, Carol just let you take off in the middle of the night without explanation? This whole thing sounds like BS."

"I'm not making it up, Matt," Steeg came back, while inside he felt a sudden uneasiness. He couldn't remember exactly how he explained to Carol his little sojourn into the city that night. He shrugged it off. "Carol trusts me."

"Okay, so what did you two talk about at the Hiawatha Diner the night before Thanksgiving?"

Steeg leaned forward and in a lowered voice confessed, "She wants my help when she leaves her, you know, friend; her partner, roommate, or whatever it is you call your lesbian lover in polite company."

Matt's doubt-creased expression turned to wide-eyed open laughter. "Now I know you're BS-in' me! There's no way in hell any gay woman is going to give up hot girl-on-girl sex! No way, José and you can take that to the bank."

"I'm serious, Matt. She wants my help."

"I'm serious, too, Steeg. Either you're a fulltime resident of Never Land, or she's playing you for something. Have you seen the stuff on the internet?! Lesbos are hot, man. She ain't leaving that, no matter what, and she certainly isn't leaving her girlfriend for you. She may very well be leaving her girlfriend for another girlfriend she likes better; after all, from what I've seen those relationships are pretty much open-ended anyway..."

"Open-ended?"

"Yeah, pardon the pun."

Steeg rubbed his eyes, feeling very tired all of a sudden. He thought Matt would understand. Evidently, he was mistaken. He had to help Gracie. He had promised.

"You know, Matt, people can change. Gracie said her life was shallow. She said she needed more depth, more meaning. She's tired of playing house. If someone you cared about came to you and said those things and then asked for your help, what would you do?"

Matt took two stiff gulps from his beer and lowered the mug back down onto the coaster with a heavy thump. "I'd see a shrink, that's what I would do! Because you gotta be crazy to even think of doing anything for someone who would actually say those things to you. Did it ever occur to you it might be Gracie who is really screwed up in the head? It's not uncommon, you know, for psychologists and psychiatrists to be deranged, hopped up on prescription drugs, sexual deviates, serial killers... My God, Steeg, the list is endless! They're all psycho! That's why they go into that profession to begin with! They're nuts! You're nuts, too! Gracie comes to Minneapolis, calls you up, meets you and lays this in your lap, begging you to help her go 'straight' and you say, 'Of course, Gracie, I'll do anything to help.' Do you know how crazy that sounds? Stay away from her! If she calls you again, hang up! Wear a crucifix and a string of garlic cloves around your neck just in case she comes knocking at your door, because if ever there was a Vampira, it's Gracie Ofterdahl!"

Steeg sat back stunned as he watched Matt collect himself. It took several moments for his friend to bring his heavy breathing back down to something resembling normal.

"Gee, Matt, why don't you tell me how you really feel?" Steeg asked with a wide grin. "And, just for future reference, garlic cloves only work on werewolves, not vampires."

Matt threw Steeg a disgusted look.

Steeg shrugged, took a deep breath and made his resigning confession. "I'm thinking of going to Chicago to see her."

With an audible moan, Matt buried his face in his hands shaking his head in disbelief.

"I know, Matt, but you have to understand she asked me to be there for her. I can't turn my back on that."

Matt looked up through fingers drawn down his face. "So, your marriage means nothing, then?"

"My marriage means everything to me," Steeg replied gently. "But Gracie and me, we go way back. Matt, she knows now. She knows she took a wrong turn for reasons that, at the time, compelled her down a wrong path. She gave it everything she could and now she knows. Now she needs to set things right. She's asked me to help her, Matt. She's an important person in my life. I'd do anything to help her."

"Even leave Carol?" Matt accused.

The full weight of his friend's question pressed uncomfortably against all he felt for Gracie. Could it be his devotion to Gracie was so strong she was the one person for whom he would walk away from his marriage and everything

Carol and he had shared and built together? Walk away even after all the time that had passed? He honestly didn't know and that singular fact disturbed him.

"Gracie's not asking me to leave Carol," Steeg countered quietly. "But, I see God at work here…"

"God? You're kidding, right?"

"I'm serious, Matt. You may not believe it, but God may be showing her a way back. She probably doesn't even know it herself, living like she has, spiritually isolated, morally upside down. Try and see it from God's point of view. She's His child and He wants her back. I'm not going to say 'No' to God if He wants to use me as a tool to get that done."

With growing disgust, Matt shot back, "You're a tool, alright. You give a whole new definition to 'Looney' and that's a fact. You're using God as an excuse to cheat on your wife! If you've made up your mind to cheat, then cheat. You don't need to justify your indiscretions by bringing God into it."

Matt laughed out loud as he added, "I mean, if this God-angle actually works, let me know! Like that crying evangelist guy on TV – Fallburn, Ballfern, whatever his name was – doing God's work could be a heck of a racket – all the debauchery and none of the guilt!"

Steeg shook his head, regretting he had brought any of this up. "He had a lot of guilt, Matt, so much guilt he had to confess his sins on national television."

"Yeah, because people stopped sending him money, that's why!"

"God works in all of our lives, Matt, even yours. There was a reason why Gracie and I met when we did, fell away from each other when we did, got together when we did, and parted again when we did. Maybe all of it was something we both had to go through, I don't know. Maybe there's something much greater going on here than just us, I certainly hope so. I leave those things to God."

"If you're so convinced God is behind these latest developments," Matt interrupted. "I got an idea: you and Carol pray together on what God wants you to do about Gracie. Go ahead, put your god where your mouth is and find out how much God is at work in all this. I dare ya. See how much Carol supports your efforts for saving Grace."

Matt's words, brittle with truth, sliced deeply into Steeg's consciousness with a frightening exactness. He sat there in numbed silence unable to toss a clever, pithy comeback, stunned by an awareness Matt's words may not have come from Matt at all. The words may actually have come from God.

"'Saving Grace'," Matt repeated with a chuckle. "Sounds like a song, doesn't it? That's pretty good."

Chapter 31
The Common Thread

Steeg scooped up the large cardboard box off the laundry room floor and angrily flung it over his shoulder. In flight, the huge container annihilated the lone lighting fixture on the low ceiling. To the sound of tinkling glass, the room fell into a gray pallor of dim late afternoon light falling through the small basement window. The box smashed against the furnace so hard the exhaust stack snapped from its moorings with a loud bang. A loud echo exploded through the ventilation ducts as the box fell to the concrete floor, spilling out all it had contained.

He didn't hear Carol's "What was that?!" yell from upstairs. With mounting rage, he blindly threw more boxes and other debris pulled from the mess on the floor. He barraged the small room with missiles heaved in every direction, cursing more vehemently with every launch. He didn't hear his wife running down the stairs.

When Carol reached the laundry room door, she froze with fear. Steeg raved obscenities as he continued to destroy everything he could grab, his face contorted in hateful wrath. On the far side of the room, she saw the shelving assembly in a heap along with what was left of that which the shelves had once held. Across the rest of the room laid pieces of everything else. With tears in her eyes she saw her husband raise a cocked arm ready throw a vase.

"Stop it!" Carol screamed as she stumbled through the clutter to grab his hand. "Stop it! Stop it!"

He glared back, pure hatred in his eyes and shoved her away. She staggered back a few steps as he pointed the held vase at her. "It's your fault this happened! You keep so much crap on these shelves it's amazing they lasted this long! Their vinyl-coated wire shelves, Carol, not damn steel girders! When in hell are you going to throw something away?"

She trembled as more tears fell and she pleaded in desperation. "Why do you always do this? Why do you hate me so? What did I do?! I try, Steeg, I really try, but you do this and do this! Why?"

"I don't collect all this stuff, you do!" Steeg bellowed back shaking the vase at her.

"I'm not talking about that," Carol yelled in return.

"I am!" He growled vehemently. "For the love of Christ will you throw something away?!"

He held the vase out and released his hold on it. Carol sobbed as it fell and shattered to pieces on the concrete floor.

Her question came in short, sob-punctuated gasps. "Why do you hate us so? You're like two different people and when you're like this, I don't know what to do. Our kids don't know what to do. You make us fear you when you do this. Is that what you want? You want us to leave? Because that's why the older kids moved out, you know. You do so much, you work so hard, and then, you do this and I don't know who you are. I don't know what you want me to do."

Steeg stood immobile, scowling. He had heard all this from her before, many times. Yes, he was the good daddy, the good provider, the good Christian husband; perhaps not so much lately. Sure, they all loved him when things were going well, no hiccups, no cash flow problems. But let the cash dry up, let the bills go unpaid, and then listen to their tune change. He was sick of it. He was sick of everything.

In a low ominous voice Carol didn't know and which frightened her more than anything he had said, he threw the question back at her. "You want to know what to do?"

She sobbed as she quietly nodded. "Yes."

Steeg waded through the rubble, his foot punching pieces aside in disgust. His threatening tone didn't change as he passed her to exit the room.

"Throw something out."

* * *

Steeg pulled the credit card from his wallet and presented it to the bartender who looked disturbing like someone Steeg felt he should know. *I'm so terrible remembering names,* he mentally chastised himself. "Have I met you before? You look really familiar to me."

The thirty-something year old man behind the bar smiled as he leaned in for a closer look at the card Steeg held, affording Steeg the opportunity to more closely scrutinize the pleasant, comforting features of the younger dark haired man with an olive complexion and pleasant smile.

"You look too young to be a bartender," offered Steeg.

"I'm over thirty. I've always looked younger than my age, though." He pointed to Steeg's credit card. "Sure, we take those cards. You want to set up a tab, I take it?"

"Please," Steeg acknowledged. He glanced about the heavy oak-trimmed establishment bathed in the warm glow of candle table lamps and hanging brass lighting over the perimeter booths. "Slow night, tonight. Just a few people."

The younger man wiped the bar area in front of Steeg with a bar towel. "Yeah, you know: the New Year's thing is over now. It was great while it lasted."

"Okay if I eat at the bar? Tables and booths are a little too conspicuous."

"Sure," the bartender said, producing a small plastic bound menu from behind the bar and placing it in front his lone bar patron. "What are you drinking tonight?"

Steeg order a locally brewed beer which the younger man produced from the tap, placed the perfectly filled glass on a cork coaster, and then left for the back kitchen as Steeg perused the menu alone.

He read the menu poorly, all the while the echoes of Carol's pleas repeating in his head. After leaving the house, he drove aimlessly into the winter evening, following a meandering route that took him toward downtown Minneapolis with its stoplights at every intersection. While waiting at one corner for the light to change, on the opposite corner across the street he noticed the dark paneled entrance of a bar-supper club he recognized from years earlier. Steeg immediately felt his stomach issue a discontented rumble. A quick glance at his wristwatch told him it was already passed 8:00 o'clock, freezing outside temperatures were falling even lower and he hadn't eaten anything since lunch at the house. It was as good an excuse as any to add more to the charge account bill, so he parked the car at a vacant meter just a couple of doors down and briskly walked the frigid distance back to the place on the corner.

When the young man returned, Steeg handed him the menu and quickly sent him back to the kitchen with a simple order of burger and fries. Shortly, the young bartender returned, walked to the far end of the bar to quickly handle a waitress's drink order, and then quietly cleaned a few glasses. With each rinsed glass placed on a folded bar towel, the man would glance at his customer seated down the bar. The last glass washed and rinse, the young man offered Steeg an observation.

"You have a peculiar expression, if you don't mind my saying so."

Curious and slightly annoyed at the same time, Steeg looked over at the man. "How do you mean, 'peculiar'?"

"Oh, I don't know. You look like you're bothered, I think. No, that's not it, not bothered, more reflective? No, not reflective... Maybe, maybe..."

"Maybe pissed off?" Steeg suggested with a light chuckle.

"No, you're not angry. Working here, I see a lot of angry and you're not that. No, you're... regretful. Something happened and whatever it was, you regret it."

Steeg used a less than enthusiastic quip to poorly hide whatever the other man saw. "Yeah, I regret having to charge this meal instead of paying cash. Much more of this sort of thing and I'll max-out the card. Then, I'll really be regretful."

The bartender dismissed Steeg's concern with a small wave as he dried his hands on clean bar towel. "Ah, money's tight all over. Use what you can. Everyone else is in the same boat."

Steeg shook his head and confessed, "My 'boat' is full of holes, my friend. Business is in the toilet, has been for a few years now. My wife works, thank God, but it's not enough. I started by financing the business on the card, now I'm financing the house payment the same way. It's only a matter of time until the whole house of cards comes crashing down."

Steeg tried to hide the flush rising in his face as he looked sheepishly at the other man. "I probably shouldn't be telling you this until after the food gets here, should I?"

The bartender shrugged with a knowing smile. "Your plastic is good here. Don't worry."

Steeg's bobbed his head in appreciation. "Well, thanks for letting me be honest. The card's good, I promise. God help me if it ever turns bad. And that, my familiar looking but unknown friend, is an expression of frustration, not regret."

"True enough," the other man nodded. "But, there's something else going on, isn't there?"

Before Steeg could answer, a small bell rang from the kitchen. The bartender excused himself to retrieve Steeg's burger and fries which was accompanied by ketchup, mustard and a place setting of stainless flatware wrapped in a large linen napkin. Quickly preparing the burger with the offered condiments, Steeg took a hasty bite from the oversized sandwich and moaned with pleasure.

"This is so good, I can't tell you."

The younger man smiled with satisfaction. "Thank you. We make good sandwiches here. I'll let you be so you can eat. We can talk more after, if you want."

Halfway through the burger, fries and beer, Steeg still hadn't placed a name with the young man's face. He watched the bartender prepare another drink order and place it on a waiting tray for the waitress who, as Steeg looked closer, was significantly older than her black chinos and high-collared pressed white shirt led him to first believe. She caught Steeg looking at her, smiled pleasantly enough, picked up the tray and returned to the dining area.

"She's been here a while, hasn't she?" Steeg motioned with his eyes.

"Doris? Oh, yes." The younger man replied as he washed more glasses one at a time, placing them on the folded towel to drain dry. "She's an institution here, started more than thirty years ago, I think, as a cocktail waitress. Of course, she's older now, only works weeknights, but she still has it."

Steeg felt increasingly annoyed not being able to place this young man. "I'm sorry, but you really remind me of someone I use to know. But, that was years ago…"

There was an odd, comforting ease in the other man's simple reply. "Who was that?"

"That's the problem – I don't know!" Steeg admitted, a little embarrassed by his poor memory. "I'm thinking maybe when I was in the service, Vietnam, that time frame. Did you have a father or an older sibling in the Navy back in the '60's?"

"In the Navy? No. But my father was in Vietnam. I take after my father a lot. Maybe you ran into him when you were there."

Steeg nodded. "Maybe, although I was never in Vietnam, itself. I was on an aircraft carrier in the Gulf of Tonkin. I don't know, maybe in Hong Kong, Singapore, the Philippines…"

The bartended stepped closer to where Steeg sat and leaned his hip against the bar. "So, we were talking about your business going down the toilet and something else happening that bothered you. What happened?"

His hunger completely gone, Steeg nibbled at a fry, his eyes hooded in shame he wished he didn't feel. "Big blowout with my wife; one of many – too many."

"Who blew, you or her?"

"Me. It's always me. Carol's practically a saint; I'm the boneheaded jerk," Steeg shook his head, dropping the barely eaten French fry onto his plate. "Sometimes something inside me just snaps. I go crazy. I don't know why."

The younger man offered a non-judgmental shrug. "Could be drugs, maybe alcohol."

A light, ironic laugh came from Steeg. "I wish. At least then I'd have an excuse. At least then I'd know what to do."

The bartender turned, crossed his arms and leaned in closer. "Well, if it isn't a chemical problem, maybe it's a 'heart and soul' problem. Maybe it's something from a long time ago, before the two of you got together, what do you think?"

Turning toward the younger man, their eyes met. At that very moment, Steeg's mind flashed on a horrible and frightening recollection from long ago, something he almost could see, but then, just as quickly, it disappeared. Visibly upset, Steeg blinked several times to clear away the sudden unwelcomed moisture from his eyes.

"I'm sorry," the bartended said with real concern. "Did I say something wrong?"

Hurriedly collecting himself, Steeg stammered as he cleared his throat. "No, I just thought I… I mean, actually, I guess I'd feel funny boring you with the details…"

The young man looked about the almost empty establishment and chuckled. "It's not as if I've got a whole lot else to do tonight. Besides, it might help you figure things out. Go ahead, let it roll out easy. Just concentrate on the things in your heart and soul. Don't worry about the business stuff."

Normally, Steeg wouldn't have bothered, but this was someone he didn't know and most probably would never see again: someone safe. After all, it wasn't as if he was going to give him his social security number or anything.

And so, with a deep breath, Steeg began.

"To show you how screwed up I can be, do you know I was jealous of Jesus Christ?"

Both of the bartender's eyebrows bounced up in surprise. "How's that?"

"My wife loves Jesus more than she loves me," Steeg admitted sheepishly. "Every morning, without fail, she's in her Bible and praying. I mean it: every morning, for as long as we've been married, without fail. If I joined her during those times, she'd let me know I wasn't welcome. Same thing at night: in the evening, I like to watch TV and unwind. She doesn't like TV, so she sits alone in the living room reading. When I come in to sit with her, mostly because I feel guilty watching television all the time, she closes her book and just looks at me. Her silence is deafening. It's like I'm intruding on her private time. I never last more than a few minutes before I retreat to the TV room."

"Well, everyone needs some alone time, even married people – maybe, especially married people."

Steeg shrugged. "Yeah, you're probably right about that. I'm making too big of a deal about it, I know."

"So, what is the big deal you're not talking about? What's the thing that pulls at you so you blow up like you say you do?"

Steeg ran a hand across his brow and rubbed the pressure from behind his eyes. "It's probably Gracie. Yeah, I have to admit, even now, it's still Gracie."

Steeg had heard of things like this, where a guy goes into a bar, has a couple of drinks and spills his guts to the kindly, seasoned old bartender too long in the tooth to be surprised by anything, too much in need of a good tip to not lend a non-judgmental ear. It was all just so much melodramatic pabulum, he knew. Yet, now, for some reason he couldn't make clear, it was Steeg's turn. *What the hell,* he thought. *It's not as if we're best buddies, or anything.*

He began anew with a comical aside. "Being the way you are, with those Hollywood matinee idol good looks of yours, you won't be able to relate to any of this."

"Try me," the young man said sincerely.

"Well, it's like this: have you ever met someone who, when you first see her you know she's the most important person in your life? Well, Gracie was that person for me."

"What made her that important so quickly, do you think?"

"I wish I knew," Steeg admitted almost sadly. "We were just kids in high school, no way was I ready for anything that real or intense. But, for some reason, I needed her more than air, and when I wasn't with her, I felt as if I couldn't breathe. Frightening to need someone like that, no matter how old you are..."

Steeg continued, encapsulating his relationship with Gracie through his high school years, even sharing the parking lot and the big, blue water tower story. When he got to the part when the Edina police patrol car pulled up behind with red lights flashing, both Steeg and the bartender shared a long, emotionally cleansing laugh.

With an embarrassed shake of his head, Steeg continued his story of his Navy years and all that had happened there. When he mentioned the hanger deck accident and his prolonged physical problems from the injuries, the bartender nodded with honest concern and an understanding smile.

Time sped by as Steeg openly confessed everything, including his hallucinations, his misdirected attempts to find solace with other women, and how things changed when he met Carol. He talked at length about how he clung to his belief that Carol had to be the answer he was looking for. After all, since college he had prayed, really prayed, God would bring someone to him to break the curse that was Gracie's ghost. Why couldn't Carol be the answer to that prayer?

But instead of the relief he needed, when he and Carol married and started their family together, Steeg admitted things turned darker. Gracie became an addiction for him. He couldn't let go of the comfort that was the self-imposed obsession for Gracie. The obsession became a strategy. To make his marriage work, he needed Carol to be more like Gracie. His effort to make that happen had succeeded only partially.

It was all too familiar for Steeg, but he covered the major aspects and various plot twists in remarkable detail, surprising himself with his open candor, especially concerning his own failings in effectively managing his Gracie fixation.

All the while the bartender listened intently, frequently injecting a well-placed query concerning Steeg's reason for doing one thing or another, or how Gracie responded to something Steeg said or did, or something else that helped keep Steeg focused and on-track. Steeg knew he was babbling through a completely one-sided conversation that was, nevertheless, purifying, eye-opening and too short to be comprehended to anyone other than himself.

Only half of the long-ignored beer remained. The bar was clean and the plated remains of his meal had been long since removed during Steeg's soliloquy.

"So, I left the house, got into my car and somehow drove down here," Steeg concluded with an exhausted sigh. "A twenty-four carat, solid gold jerk at a dead end with no answers and no clue about how to fix this."

The young bartender, still leaning with elbows on the bar, his chin resting in his cupped hand, asked in a matter-of-fact manner a simple question.

"But, you do see it, don't you? The common thread?"

An expression of complete, helpless ignorance preceded Steeg's response. "The common thread? What common thread? You mean me? Yeah, I'm to blame. I'm the one who has screwed my life up, I admit that. I'll admit to anything if it means I can work my way out of this mess."

The younger man smiled. "No, it's not you. You're not the common thread, at all. Gracie is. Gracie is why you exploded today and why you exploded all those other times. She's why you're frustrated, why you have these episodes, migraine attacks and abdominal problems. By the way, how was the food? Your stomach better?"

Steeg smiled. "The stomach is fine. The food was great."

The bartender nodded appreciatively. "Good to hear it. At least that's a positive, isn't it? All the stuff you can't control, or control as poorly as you do; it's not the kids, it's not your wife, it isn't even the storage shelves collapsing this afternoon. All of that is just poor proximity, clumsy coincidence and wrong-place, wrong-time stuff. It's Gracie. She's the one person you needed the most who never gave you anything of any consequence – not of herself, nothing of any permanence, with the possible exception of prolonged agony and rejection; just the temporary pleasure of her company.

"You don't see the common thread because you blame yourself for all of this. You completely absolve Gracie of all responsibility. You confess you have been blessed with children and a wife who loves you, but you won't accept their love because you're convinced you don't deserve it. After all, the one woman you had to love, even love now and will always love, Gracie, rejected you as unworthy how many times? Gracie has to be right, doesn't she? Gracie being always right proves you don't deserve love from anyone else, doesn't it? You know what some people call it when a person takes on the burden of other people's sins? They call that a 'Messiah Complex'."

Steeg's mouth hung open in dumb silence at the outspoken bluntness of the man. After an uncomfortable period of silence, he caught himself. "I don't consider myself a messiah."

"Of course you don't," the bartender acknowledged. "But you have to admit you've hoisted yourself on some kind of cross as a sacrificial lamb for something, haven't you?"

"No," Steeg denied uncertainly.

The younger man responded with a light laugh. "I see. Well, then, let me ask you this: you have tried to protect your wife and children from all of this by splitting your life in two – one part the life you have; the other part the life you believe you should have had – and now, after years of living in two directions at the same time, is it any wonder you have so much trouble keeping all of this together?"

Steeg slumped back on his barstool stunned again by the man's clarity of thought. He realized in a blink, *It's an impossible way to live.*

His bartending friend nodded with a smile, saying as if he had read Steeg's thoughts, "Yeah, it is, isn't it?"

Steeg's words tumbled forth. "How do I fix this?"

The other man leaned closer. "You have protected Carol from the truth she deserves to know and has to have if she is to fully love you. You're not protecting her. Without the truth, you are denying her love for you, a love you believe you don't deserve because you still need Gracie as desperately as you do. Truth is the only way, Steeg."

As if too ashamed to look at the man, Steeg turned away. "I don't know if I can do that. Carol wouldn't be able to handle it."

"She's stronger than you think."

"Not that strong. No one can be that strong. Besides, what good would it do if Gracie is still there, the common thread as you say, to all of this? I need to remove the common thread; I need to remove Gracie first."

The other man nodded. "Yes, you're need for Gracie is deeper; a primal threat you need to confront, and in doing so, a threat you can overcome. It's something that happened long ago, you've only forgotten. When you remember, you'll know what to do and you'll be victorious."

The metallic tap on his driver's side window startled him from his trance. Deep in recall of the events of the evening, Steeg was irritated as he turned his head to the left. Through the fogged window the shadowy figure of a police officer stood outside. He turned the ignition key to the accessories setting and pressed the button to lower the window.

"Yes, officer?" Steeg asked slightly irked and more confused.

The policeman's aged features were dimly lit behind the glare of the flashlight shining into Steeg's face. "May I see your driver's license and registration, please?"

"Did I do something wrong?" Steeg asked as he fished his license from his wallet and retrieved the registration info from the glove compartment. "I'm sorry, aren't the parking meters free after 6:00 anymore?"

The officer thoroughly examined the documents Steeg handed him. "The meters aren't the question. You've been sitting in this car for some time now. Are you having car trouble?"

Steeg shook his head trying to lower the irksome factor. "Car trouble? No, no car trouble. I just got done with dinner and was sitting here thinking about stuff, that's all."

The flashlight beam burned again into Steeg's eyes. "You had dinner? Where?"

With a hooked thumb, Steeg gestured over his shoulder. "At the bar-lounge place on the corner."

The officer turned in the direction Steeg had indicated, paused, and then returned to Steeg. With a noticeably more firm tone he said, "Step out of the vehicle, please."

Showing a touch too much exasperation, Steeg pulled the collar of his jacket closed against the frigid night air, opened the door and stepped from the car. His jacket fell chillingly open as he followed the officer's instruction to hold his arms out and touch his nose first with his left hand, then with his right.

"I'm not drunk, officer," Steeg complained as he did what he was told. "I didn't even drink all of the single beer I had."

The office pulled a small square black box from his jacket, adjusted the plastic tube and brought it toward Steeg's mouth. "Then, you shouldn't mind blowing into this. Take a deep breath and blow hard until your lungs are empty."

Steeg did as the officer instructed. As the policeman pulled the little box away, Steeg continued his complaint.

"Look, I came out of that place over there..." His pointed finger hung motionless when he turned toward the corner where the bar-lounge was and saw only a vacant parking lot. His head jerked around, darting in the direction of all four corners. The bar-lounge wasn't there.

"There?" The officer queried. "There, where? I've got cause right now to throw you into the tank, Mr. Patterson, and I would, too, but according to this readout, you're stone cold sober. You're obviously disoriented. Are you on something, maybe prescribed medication of some kind?"

Steeg's pointing hand dropped slowly to his side as he struggled to make sense of the disappearance of the place he had only moments before left."A diuretic; a little pill once a day for blood pressure. I take it in the morning."

Flashlight up and trained on him, the officer moved in for a closer look, moving the light from eye to eye. "You slip on some ice, or something, hit your head maybe?"

"No, nothing like that," Steeg said, realizing he needed to get away from there as soon as possible. "You know, I'm not downtown often. I think I just got turned around here somehow. I'm fine, really."

"Yeah, well, it's just that you seemed to be in your car for a long time," the officer explained, his eyes continuing to scan Steeg's face for evidence of whatever the problem may have been. "I drove by a couple of times. You just sat there, so I thought you needed some help."

"No, really, I'm okay."

With no reason to contradict Steeg, and no desire for unnecessary paperwork back at the station, the officer handed back the license and registration. "Okay, then, here you go. You have a safe evening, now, Mr. Patterson. Sorry to bother you."

"I appreciate the concern," Steeg said, uneasily returning to the chilled interior of the car. He shut the door and reached for the keys still in the ignition. He didn't know why his hands were trembling, but it was difficult to turn the keys to start the engine.

Chapter 32
Truth and Other Elusive Qualities

It was almost 2:30 in the morning when Steeg slowly drove the Buick up the snow packed driveway crunching all the way into the garage. He turned off the engine, pressed the remote button on his visor, and then grimaced when the garage door too loudly growled its frozen complaint as it lowered to seal out the January cold. He left the car, squeezed his door shut as quietly as he could until he heard the click, and then moved toward the door leading into the house. He tried the doorknob. It was not locked; a good sign.

Inside, the house was dark. He removed his jacket, leaving it draped across the short bench in the hallway and made his way through the shadows to the basement stairs. At the lower level, he switched on the overhead light and turned down the adjoining hallway that led to the laundry room. He reached around the corner of the door, found the light switch and flicked it to the 'on' position.

Nothing happened. The room remained absolutely black.

You broke the light, you idiot!

He quickly made his way back down the hall to his office where he kept a flashlight and spare light bulbs in a double-door storage cabinet. He then pulled a small step ladder from the corner of the closet before he returned to the laundry room.

Steeg made sure the light switch was in the 'off' position before expertly removing the remnants of the broken light bulb from the ceiling fixture and screwed in a new 100 watt Soft White. He tried the switch again and the room was bathed in clear white light.

A violent sob rose hard to catch in his throat when he turned to see a completely ordered room. The floor was cleaned swept; nothing remained of all he had been broken or shattered earlier that afternoon. Many of the boxes and single items the shelves once held were neatly arranged and stacked against the corner wall; the wire shelves that had collapsed were now stacked and leaning against the adjacent wall where the shelving assembly once stood. In his absence Carol had cleaned it all.

He took it all in, able to feel only shame. He turned to the furnace where the first box he had thrown in anger had landed. The exhaust vent his tirade had damaged was repositioned, the top of the furnace box neatly clean and dust-free. Steeg surveyed the room again, shaking his head with regret.

Well, dumb ass, before you do anything, make this right first.

In the darkened bedroom, Carol's deep sleep dissolved to a more shallow state when the annoying buzzing of what she thought was a fly began to awaken her. Through the haze of her ebbing slumber, Carol thought it odd. A flying insect buzzing around the bedroom in the middle of January in Minnesota didn't make a whole lot of sense. She pulled against her fading sleep, more tightly closed her eyes and tucked the bed covers more snuggly under her chin. The buzzing noise became more distinct. Eyes still closed shut, Carol knew whatever the sound was, it wasn't a bug. It was something electric, running somewhere in another part of the house.

Suddenly the annoying buzzing sound stopped. The silence of it forced Carol's eyes wide open. She continued to lay there straining to hear the next sound – any sound.

She heard it: a faint, barely audible rhythmic, repetitive mechanical clicking sound coming from somewhere on the lower level. She rose up on one elbow and continued to listen to more clicking noises for almost a minute. Then, the clicking suddenly stopped. Her breath caught in her throat. She turned toward the opposite side of the bed. Steeg was not there. The bedside alarm clock read 4:47.

With a start, she jerked upright to a full seated position in the bed. The buzzing noise returned. Carol shot out from under the covers, instinctively retreating to the far corner of the bedroom.

"Steeg, you're supposed to be here!" She whispered angrily to no one there. Immediately, she felt foolish. She took a deep breath, gathered her resolve and accepted her responsibility to protect her daughter and her home.

The buzzing stopped again. In the darkness, she felt her way along the dresser to the closet, opened the closet door and reached around the corner. Deep in the back behind boxes stacked tight into the narrow space, her hand felt for the cold metal of the muzzle of Steeg's shotgun. She grasped it tightly and carefully pulled the weapon from its hiding space.

She jerked her head toward the distant repetitive mechanical clicking sound, every nerve in her body alerting her to danger.

The one thing she did know was that the gun wasn't loaded. She wouldn't allow Steeg to keep a loaded gun in the house. But she didn't know where the shotgun shells were – she thought they may be in a storage cabinet in the garage, but she wasn't certain. It didn't matter. Carol didn't have a clue as to how to load the gun, anyway.

She knew something else, too. Raising the weapon to bring the butt under her armpit, Carol knew she had to confront the intruder. Barely able to breathe, she quietly padded her way out of the bedroom and down the hall in the direction of the noise.

In the laundry room, Steeg tightened the last lag bolt to complete the anchoring of the two-by-four wood top plate onto the overhead joist. Satisfied, he stepped down from the small ladder, grabbed the near edge of the second 'H' frame he had assembled from lumber he had retrieved from the garage rafters and gave it a good solid tug. The assembly didn't move, not even a little bit.

I could park the car on this shelving and it would hold.

The top of the 'H' frame members were lag bolted into the overhead joists on both sides of the wire shelving. Each wire shelf was secured with brackets and screws to the vertical 'H' frames on either side. The reinforced shelving assembly would never again collapse no matter how many boxes Carol could load onto it.

Steeg stepped back to admire his work. From behind he heard the creak of the laundry room door slowly opening. He turned and saw Carol standing in the doorway, pointing his shotgun directly at him.

"Oh, Steeg!" Carol's arms went limp and the shotgun suddenly was too heavy for her to hold. The butt of the gunstock hit the floor. Weak with relief, she dragged the weapon behind her and fell into his arms. "I thought… I was so afraid…"

He held her close and comforted her as she buried her face in his shoulder. He took the shotgun from her hand and leaned it against the shelving behind him.

"You're okay, Sweetie," he said softly, calming her gently. "My fault. You did good. I didn't want to wake you. I'm sorry."

For a long time he simply held her close. Between sobs she told him how worried she was, how she didn't know what was wrong, or where he had gone, or when, or even if, he would return home. Her words, terrible and horrifying for him to hear, exposed the true consequences of the abuse he had put her through; years of abuse during which time he believed he was protecting her by keeping secret his struggles with personal demons of his own making.

I'm so sorry, Lord, he prayed silently. He raised her chin and their eyes met. He needed to explain things, he knew. "I need your forgiveness, Carol, if you can give it. If you can't, I'll understand. I know now that I was wrong in so many things. Somehow, I will make it right; I'll make it up to you. And I promise, with God's help, all of this will be over soon."

She buried her face into this shoulder again. "I don't know what I did wrong…"

He gently shushed her. "You never did anything wrong. It was me. It was all me not taking care of something I should have taken care of long ago. Everything I've put you and kids through, all the times I screwed up, lost a job, exploded, walked away, or hurt you; all those times you said I was like a completely different person you didn't know, there was a reason for all of it, a common thread tying together everything every time. I know what that common thread is now, and I know now how I must remove it."

She looked up at him, searching his face for an answer. "I don't know what you mean."

He softly kissed the top of her head. "You will soon. I'll explain it all. It will take a while, but when I'm done, I'll explain everything. But first I have some things I have to do."

"What things do you have to do?"

He smiled to put her concerns at ease. Inwardly, he was not confident he succeeded. "First, I need to figure out the best way to take care of old business. Second, I need to take care of the old business, a lot of old business. After that, I'll be done and you'll understand."

Chapter 33
Taking Care of Business

"I can't feel my toes anymore."

Each hurried step validated Matt Cummings' complaint. By half a step he followed as Steeg led the way until together they halted at the corner coming to a stop of their third circuitous route around yet another downtown block, this time from the southeast block kitty-corner from where Steeg had parked two nights earlier.

"Look," Steeg said, anxiously surveying the intersection one more time, his impatient retort puffing from his mouth in clouds of frozen breath. "It's only what, ten – maybe twelve degrees below zero? What's your problem? I brought you along to help me find this place and ever since we got down here all I get from you is complaint."

He shoved his gloved hands deeper into his jacket pockets in a failing attempt to retain what remained of his body heat as he continued. "'Complain, complain and complain' is all I get from you. Here it is, a beautiful sunlit Minnesota Saturday morning in Downtown Minneapolis, quiet, clean and crisp, and all you can do is complain about how cold it is. You were born in Minnesota, weren't you? What's wrong with you, anyway?"

Matt's answer almost preceded Steeg's question. "I can't feel my frickin' toes, that's what's wrong with me! And, as far as finding this place you say you were at, you promised me breakfast when you called last night. Hot food, you know? When is that going to happen, eh?"

"Soon enough." In vain Steeg continued his visual search of the intersection desperate for an answer different from the only answer that made sense to him. "I was thinking of going through a drive-thru somewhere."

"Oh, no," Matt shivered. "None of that kind of crap: real food prepared from fresh stuff, where we sit down at a table in someplace filled with breakfast aromas, hot coffee and warm enough to thaw my toes!"

"Picky, picky, picky; complain, complain, complain." Steeg's voice fell away as he accepted the confusing fact the place in which he had dinner two nights earlier was nowhere near the intersection where he had parked his car. "Well, one thing's for sure: we aren't going to have breakfast at the bar-lounge place I was at. There's no way I have the right location here."

Steeg pointed to the parking lot at the opposite corner. "I could have sworn it was there."

"I told you, Steeg, there is no bar or supper club anywhere around here. The way you described it, I thought you meant Nye's across the river."

Steeg shook his head. "It wasn't Nye's. I know Nye's and that wasn't it."

"Well, the only other place I know of anywhere near here is the Rosewood Room in the Northstar Center and that place is on the umpteenth floor, nowhere near street level."

"The Northstar center is at least two, maybe three, blocks over, so that wasn't it, either."

Matt's shivering was becoming chronic. "Okay, look, you got disoriented; you had a few too many drinks and kinda blacked out. It happens."

"I had half a beer, Matt, I swear."

"Maybe you just remember having half a beer. It happens, you know."

"I wasn't drunk. The cop gave me a breath-alizer test and it registered zero. I was sober. You know downtown better than anyone else I know. Think: do you remember there ever being a bar or supper club at this intersection?"

Matt, exasperated but willing, shivered against the cold as he perused the surroundings in earnest. "Well, not recently. But, you know, I do remember the old Haag place."

"What hag place was that? Is that a place where old hags hang out, or what?"

"Not 'hags', Haag's. It was almost an institution, lasted for decades, maybe all the way back to the prohibition days." Matt pointed to the parking lot across the intersection. "It used to be right over there. But, they tore it down during the urban renewal boon back when they needed more office space and they started building all these new high-rise office towers."

"How long ago was that?"

"Twenty, maybe twenty-five years ago; maybe it was longer, I'm not sure. Funny how that corner survived as a simple parking lot. Valuable real estate now, I wonder why they never built anything on it?"

Steeg's brow scrunched in deep thought as he tried to make sense of what he had experienced two nights earlier. He couldn't, not easily. "They didn't build on the lot, Matt, because they stopped building when the glut of excess commercial office space made it financially undesirable to build: no tenants, no money, no building: simple enough. It's comforting to know once upon a time there was some kind of bar or lounge or something there. Now the question I need an answer to is do you believe in parallel universes?"

"You wanna know what I believe in? I believe in breakfast, that's what!"

Steeg nodded, stepped from the curb on the light just then changing to green, with Matt quickly following.

"Sounds good to me, Matt; you pick it."

In predictable fashion, Matt chose the Mother Earth Emporium for breakfast, a near-windowless black hole refuge for '60's radicals, trimmed in weathered barn wood with an eclectic collection of tables and chairs in various stages of ill-repair, sparsely populated with a handful of patrons, all tables were positioned in a single row that stretched the entire length along one wall of the cavernous establishment. The concrete floor was dirty, and to Steeg, the place smelled funny.

"Nice place," Steeg mocked, testing the stability of a vinyl-covered chair with pitted chrome legs of irregular lengths before he sat down. "Are these the breakfast aromas you told me about that I smell or did something die in here recently?"

"They got good food here," Matt countered defensively, slipping his jacket off and hanging it on the back of his chair before taking a seat. "It's healthy. You'll like it."

"Oh, yum! I can hardly wait!"

"I come here a lot. It's not that far from the 'U' so that makes it a good place to stop in for something to eat."

Steeg's mouth dropped open. "My God, man, are you still going to the University?"

Matt pointed a warning finger in Steeg's direction. "The pursuit of education is no vice."

"No, it's only pathetic."

"I'm enriching myself."

"You're a little kid on the shore afraid of the water."

"I admire an intellectual mind."

"'Birds of a feather…'"

"What does that mean?"

Steeg leaned forward to stress his point. "It means, Matt, institutions of higher learning in this country have become asylums for Marxists, Communists, Socialists, and all manner of extreme leftists, especially those who have turned blowing up government buildings into an accredited art form. Hang around enough with those people and eventually you become one."

Matt scowled back, "Yeah, well, at least they have real answers to real problems. They know what the real truth is, they know what really works for economic and social justice and they don't have their heads stuck in the mind-numbing clouds of capitalism, which is the real source of everything that's wrong with this country! They solve real problems for real people!"

Steeg grinned. "And, all the rest of us are artificial people? I think you just proved my point."

"Hell if I did," Matt shot back. "It's the collective power of the people that will change things for the better!"

"Maybe," Steeg bobbed his head once. "I prefer to believe in the rights of the individual over the 'collective' – it's safer and less vulnerable to tyranny."

With unveiled repugnance, Matt threw up his hands. "There you go, again, with the anti-government drivel! What is it with you? You see black helicopters in your sleep, or what?"

A tall, underfed man in need of a shave, haircut, clean T-shirt and apron, interrupted Steeg before he could answer.

"You two goin' to order something, or just argue?"

They both looked up to the man standing next to their table, with Matt the first to reply.

"Yeah, since you put it that way. I'll have your huevos rancheros and coffee, please."

Steeg did a double-take in Matt's direction, and then placed his order.

"I'll have some bacon and eggs, coffee, too."

The cook/waiter scratched his unshaven chin as he gave Steeg a disgusted look. "We don't have bacon."

Undeterred, Steeg amended his order. "Oh. Okay, then, sausage. Links, please."

The cook/waiter rolled his eyes. "We don't have sausage, either. We don't have meat products here. It's a vegetarian restaurant, or didn't you see the sign on the door when you came in?"

Steeg exchanged a knowing glance with Matt. "Nice place. Breakfast but no bacon, no sausage…"

The cook/waiter interrupted. "I can fry you up a veggie patty. It's very good."

Not entirely comfortable taking the cook/waiter at his word, Steeg asked, "What's in the veggie patty."

The cook/waiter replied, "Vegetables, sprouts, grains, very low fat, high fiber and very nutritious. We fry in virgin olive oil. How would you like your eggs?"

"Over easy?" Steeg carefully queried.

"Of course," the cook/waiter acknowledged shaking his head. "We have excellent organic multi-whole grain toast. I assume it will be satisfactory."

"I'm breathless with anticipation." Steeg's smile belied his trepidation. The cook/waiter left for the small, mostly hidden kitchen on the opposite side of the barn wood walled cavern. Steeg leaned toward Matt. "You could have told me this place was vegetarian. I would have brought a snack."

Matt literally beamed with pleasure at Steeg's discomfort. "I thought you knew. Just like I thought you knew what you were looking for downtown. Why the heck is it so important for you to find that bar, anyway?"

Steeg looked away buying time to carefully structure his reply. "It's like when you've been to a certain place once, and you remember every detail of it, and you go back to where it was and it isn't there. It's very unsettling, spooky, you know?"

"You remember being there? But, you said a cop stopped you and gave you a drunk test right on the street."

"He didn't stop me, I was parked at the curb, sitting in the car. He walked up, tapped on my window and had me get out for the test."

"And, he said you weren't drunk."

"That's right."

Matt leaned back in his chair and chewed on a thought or two as he pieced things together in his mind. "Do you remember leaving the bar and getting back into the car?"

"Yeah," Steeg answered uncertainly. "I think so. Sure, I paid the tab on my credit card, as usual, thanked the guy for listening, got up and left. It wasn't that far to where I parked the car. I got in, put the key in the ignition, then this cop is tapping on my window."

"Just like that, that quickly, he's at your door?"

"Well, maybe not that quickly," Steeg half-shrugged. "I may have sat there for a few minutes just thinking about stuff."

"What stuff?"

"Things we talked about at the bar, mostly stuff about me: stuff that had happened in my life; the kind of person I am and how my personal strengths could lead me to make mistakes; mistakes I had to rectify." Steeg took pause, wondering if it was worth opening up to Matt on what had happened at the bar. Despite his friend's undeniable socio-political shortsightedness, Steeg knew Matt had always been a dependable and reliable confidante and certainly someone he trusted. "The bartender told me I had tried to protect Carol from the truth, but I wasn't protecting her at all, I was denying her because Gracie had proven to me long before I met Carol that I didn't deserve her, or Carol, or anyone. The bartender said Gracie was the common thread linking together all the frustration, anger and just plain rage I have been wrestling with for so long. That guy cut through all the crap so easily... I wanted to find that bar so I could go back and talk with him again."

Matt listened carefully, taking his time before speaking.

"Well, speaking for both myself and Wedge, I'm sure we'd all appreciate you getting a better handle on the anger and rage thing. What was his name, this bartender?"

Steeg admitted he didn't know. "But, he looked real familiar, like I knew him from some place before. He told me he looked a lot like his father and his father had been in the service in Vietnam around the same time I was there, so maybe I met his father, you know? Anyway, that's why I need to find the darn place. I really want to talk to this guy again."

Matt indicated his understanding with a quick nod. "Well, I think it's fairly obvious what happened. I think you were at a bar and then you left the bar, got into your car and drove away. You were so lost in thought over all that heavy stuff you were talking about with 'Billy the Barkeep' you don't remember pulling over to the curb and parking the car. The cop comes over and checks you out because it's late and he thinks you're probably drunk. But, you're not drunk. You're confused because the bar you think you just left isn't there. Your confusion doesn't help your case with the cop, but you test sober, so, there's nothing he can hold you on. He lets you go. No harm, no foul."

Steeg took in all of Matt's explanation, his head moving in short, acknowledging bobs. "Okay, I guess that could have happened. That would mean the bar is somewhere else in or near the downtown area. That makes more sense than the alternative: conjoining parallel dimensions causing a rift in the time-space continuum."

"Praise the Lord," Matt blurted cavalierly. "So, where does that leave you? What do you need to do?"

"More things than I can count." Contriteness colored his response. Resolutely Steeg added, "But first, and most importantly, I need to remove the common thread. Gracie coming back from the 'Dark Side' is a clear and present threat to my marriage. I can't allow Gracie's need for a soft landing in her personal conversion cross over into my marriage in any way. The 'common thread' has to be cut out."

Matt had his doubts. "That sounds ominous. How do you intend to do that?"

Steeg's eyes locked onto Matt's. "She came to me last time, told me how she needed my help to succeed in returning to a normal life. Right now, she thinks I'll be there for her because I've always been there for her; I promised her that. This time, I'll go to her and end this."

"Again, how will you do that?"

Steeg leaned back in his chair to make way for the suddenly returning cook/waiter gliding up to the table with their food orders. Each man quickly had a plated breakfast and a steaming mug of coffee in front of them. Matt immediately dug into his mound of salsa covered mess. Steeg took his time, examining his meal thoughtfully.

"So, that's a veggie patty, then?"

Speaking poorly through a mouth already full of huevos rancheros, Matt repeated once more, "How will you do that?"

Steeg took a bite from a wedge of multi-whole grain toast. It was dry. "Gees, there's no butter on this!"

"They don't use butter – animal fat, you know. Answer my question: how will you end this thing with Gracie?"

"Well, I suppose it will be a lot like surgery," Steeg began as he carefully maneuvered his over-easy eggs onto the dry multi-whole grain toast, after which he poked open the yolks with his fork and prepared the breakfast as best he could with salt and pepper. "Like cancer surgery: you cut out the bad tissue and throw it away."

"Yeah, well, I hope you use anesthetic."

"I'll bring my Smith & Wesson 357 Magnum."

Matt stopped in mid-chew, his eyes widening and his face falling a shade paler. "You're kiddin', right?"

"Of course not, I always conceal and carry when I'm in Chicago. It's Chicago, for Pete's sake!" Steeg stated in a matter-of-fact way, loading a forkful of fried egg and dry toast into his mouth; each chew was accompanied by an audible crunching noise. He lied as he said, "Oh, this is just wonderful. Yum! So glad we're here, I can't tell you."

Matt dismissed the criticism. "You wouldn't know good food if it bit you in the ass."

"There's something to look forward to," Steeg answered back, his hard swallow accompanied by a quick sip of coffee to aid the esophageal matters along. "Still, I need to find that bar. I'd really want to talk to that guy again before I drive down there to take care of things."

Chapter 34
Road Trip

For reasons Steeg didn't understand, searching for the mysteriously vanished bar became a fixation even more urgent than his obsession for Gracie. For more than two months, he looked for the eating establishment as time and circumstances allowed. Being a self-employed consultant, he was able to find the allowable time very easily and with great frequency. Weaving his way back and forth across the maze of downtown intersecting streets until he had exhausted the possibilities, Steeg would only return the next week to the same locales and resume the search in ever widening circles.

Finally, on a rainy Saturday afternoon in mid-March, Steeg's efforts to find the place and the bartender he needed so desperately to talk to ended disappointingly in a small roadside parking lot off the West River Road under the Franklin Avenue Bridge. Outside his car, here and there small crusted gray-black mounds of snow dotted a brown/green landscape slowly emerging from a long Minnesota winter.

Inside his car, Steeg sat alone, his head bowed. The steady patter of rain pelting the windshield seemed appropriate accompaniment to his failure. He prayed a simple prayer.

"Lord, help me find this man. Let it be Your will, Lord that I find this man… Your will be done. Amen."

Through the rain splattered windshield he saw the hospitals and other University of Minnesota buildings on the eastside bluff on the opposite side of the river. In his mind he could see a young Gracie walking across the Washington Avenue Bridge with him at her side, the sun in her face and smiling that certain smile that always melted his heart. Through the windshield, everything turned to mist. In his soul he felt the old, familiar ache of longing spread throughout his body. How he needed to feel the warmth of her smile again.

"Damn," he cursed himself, turning the ignition key and bringing his car back to life with a powerful V8 roar. He slapped the gearshift into reverse and emphatically said to no one there. "It's time to end this!"

Steeg's first client, Harvey Hellman, inadvertently provided the way he needed to put an end to Gracie's ghost. It happened when Harvey called Steeg's office line the following Monday.

"You going to be there, aren't you?" Harvey was concerned. He didn't much care for what he was hearing in Steeg's voice: a foreboding tone of resignation, or defeat, or something else that obviously wasn't helpful for Harvey's plans.

The "there" Harvey referred to was the annual Food Equipment Manufacturer's Conference and Exhibition, aka the FEMExpo, in Chicago.

Steeg leaned back in his well-worn and too creaky leather desk chair, the phone receiver tucked hard between his left ear and shoulder as he tried unsuccessfully to ignore the familiar and still uncomfortable reminders of his neck injury pulsing shooting pain down his left arm.

"I don't like going to those things, Harv," Steeg explained, returning the receiver to his hand and sitting more upright. "The exhibiting companies are there to sell, not to be sold and I always think they resent me showing up. I can't afford to irritate people that way."

Harvey persisted. "So, irritate them some other way. Show up. We've got things to discuss."

"Such as?"

"Business, what else?" Harvey parried. "Look, I'm coming off a good year. This coming year looks even better. It's time to make some hay while the sun shines."

"You mean, before a Democrat is elected."

"You got that right. So, be there, will you? There's a lot of work we need to do."

Steeg wasn't as anxious as his old friend and for good reason. "I thought your daughter handled your marketing promotions now that she's out of school. What happened to that?"

"Yeah, well, she's doing pretty good on some things. She's learning that special code for websites, TMH? MHT? XYZ? Whatever you call it…"

"HTML."

"Right, HTML. Well, she's getting that stuff down, but I gotta admit she doesn't have the style you have. She hasn't the same grasp on marketing stuff," Harvey added a little too enthusiastically, "You two would make a good team!"

Ah, the truth, Steeg thought. *The kid is cheaper but inept and it's costing him business.* "I don't know, Harv. I've been thinking about hanging it up, maybe joining a full-fledged agency downtown: less work with more money, you know?"

"Steeg, you don't want to do that. People respect you for the 'Lone Ranger' you are, riding in to rescue the day when things have to get done right…"

Steeg interrupted. "… When things have to get done below market costs, you mean."

"Okay, good point. But that's part of your aura, Steeg."

"An 'aura' with an inconsistent cash flow," Steeg amended, not hiding the despair. "My family needs to get out of debt, Harv. My self-employment has been financed through an overly generous bank credit line which is close to being maxed out. Now, with more expenses coming soon, I need to make money, real money. So, this 'work' you say we have to do needs to be substantial, Harv, or I just can't do it."

Harvey assured Steeg the 'work' was substantial and he could guarantee it.

"I'll tell you what you can guarantee, Harv: you can guarantee me a two thousand dollar advance against expenses to be at the tradeshow. Think of it as a good faith gesture that the 'work to be done' will justify the expense."

Steeg was surprised when Harvey didn't hesitate. "Done. The check is in the mail today."

More seasoned now with more than a decade of experience behind him, Steeg made a preemptive move to seal the deal. "I'll drive over and pick up the check after lunch, not that I don't trust you…"

"Of course."

Well, he's serious, then. Before ending the call, Steeg added an appropriate question. "Now then, you need to tell me when this tradeshow is, okay?"

* * *

He returned from the bank that afternoon with two hundred dollars cash in his wallet along with a checking account deposit receipt for $1,800 dollars. Steeg stood at his desk and dialed the only telephone number he had for Gracie. The phone rang four times before an answering machine clicked on and the sudden shock of Gracie's familiar voice filled his ear.

"Hell-o, this is Dr. Grace Ofterdahl. You have reached my private voicemail. I am not able to take your call right now, but if you leave your name, a return telephone number and a short message, I'll return your call as soon as possible. I look forward to speaking with you soon."

There was a moment of silence followed by a harsh, metallic tone. Steeg froze, absolutely unable to think of anything to say. It felt like an eternity before he was able to slowly return his phone receiver to its cradle without having said a thing.

He looked at his wristwatch. It was 2:17.

Doctor Grace Ofterdahl? She didn't say anything last fall about getting her doctorate. That's huge! Almost twenty years go by, we meet and she doesn't say a thing about an accomplishment that significant. Why didn't she tell me?

He casually reasoned he didn't want to leave a message on a machine anyway; he wanted to talk directly to Gracie.

Once again, he looked at his wristwatch. It was 2:18. Barely more than a minute had passed since he had heard her voicemail greeting. His face flushed remembering the surge of pleasure he had felt just hearing her voice.

You idiot. You're not a schoolboy anymore.

"You promised," Gracie's voice echoed in his head. "You promised you'd be there for me."

He wouldn't be there. He knew now he couldn't be there for her and the promise he had made to her years ago was a promise he wouldn't keep. Desperate to leave the smothering confines of the Chicago GLBT community, Gracie needed to turn her life around. And now, when she needed him the most, he wasn't going to be there to help.

"You said you'd always love me." Her voice in his head was so real he looked up fully expecting to see her standing across the desk from him.

To no one there, he replied, "I always will. But, this has to end, Gracie. I have to end it."

Receiver in hand, Steeg pressed the 'redial' button on the phone. After several rings, Gracie's voicemail greeting repeated, thrilling him more than the recording had the first time. Then there was the beep.

Lightly, he cleared his throat before proceeding.

"Hell-o, Gracie, this is, ah, Steeg Patterson. I, ah, ..." Steeg silently steeled himself against his own insecurities, gathered a deep breath and forged ahead. "Well, look, I'm going to be in Chicago on April 25th through the 27th at a trade conference and it, um, could be a good opportunity for you and I to, you know, get together over lunch to get caught up on things..."

Too many 'ums' and 'ahs' – you're way too old to sound this silly and childish.

He persevered. "I'm thinking Wednesday, the 26th would be good. If you're open to that and can make the time, give me a call back on my office number..."

He left his number, concluded with a hurried, "...Talk to you soon" and immediately pressed the '#' key and waited for the voicemail prompt that would allow him to rerecord the message. Nothing happened. He pressed the '#' key again. Only silence.

She's got a simple answering machine. I can't delete the message, I can't rerecord. Good God, I'm stuck with it!

His finger silently pressed down on the switch hook to disconnect from the call. A sudden queasiness rose in his gut as the doubts took hold. Would he ever have the courage to end anything involving Gracie?

Steeg jumped, startled beyond reason when the phone rang. Before the first ring died, his hand shot out to harpoon the receiver and bring it to his ear.

"Hell-o?"

"Yeah," a man's voice said. "DPI Printing. Harry says you wanted to see the bench proof on this job?"

Bench proof? Bench proof? Oh, the bench proof for the Andecco Company brochure!

"Yes, I do. When can I come in?"

"You're supposed to be here, already. We're waiting. Didn't anyone call you?"

"No, I don't think so…"

"Well, gaddam it, it's a bench proof. That means it's on the bench and the press is set, ready to run. Get your ass down here because we want to finish this job now."

"On my way," Steeg hung up the phone, grabbed his jacket hanging on the office door knob and ran to his car.

Steeg returned to his office before 4:00 to find his twelve year old daughter, Bobbie, home from school, curled up on the sofa with an aromatic bowl of Raman Noodles on her lap and another exciting episode of "SpongeBob Square Pants" blaring from the television.

He momentarily blocked her view as he walked over to press the down arrow volume button several times. "How was school, Sweet Pea?"

"Daaaaaad!" Roberta complained as she scrambled for the remote control. "Now I can't hear it."

He turned to head toward his office. "You're going deaf, then. And, you're going to spoil your dinner with that mass of worms you're eating."

"Duh, they're healthy for you, Dad." His daughter's sarcasm was palpable. "Besides, I'm out of lunch money. I didn't have breakfast and I'm starving..."

He paused briefly at his office door. "You skip breakfast all the time, Bobbie. I'm not going to force feed you. And when you need lunch money, all you have to do is ask... Which you didn't, did you?"

With obvious annoyance Bobbie thumped her head backward against the couch, ignoring her father as she continued to slurp noodles with her eyes glued to the TV screen.

He entered his office closing the door behind him and immediately spied the blinking red message light on his phone. For privacy, he brought the receiver to his ear and felt the lump in his throat form even before pressing the message button. It was Gracie's voice and he silently cursed his weakness as the message began.

"Steeg, this is Grace returning your call. It was so nice to hear from you again and yes, I'd very much like to have lunch with you when you're in town. I have it marked down for noon, April 26. I know of a couple of places nearby we could go, but we can talk about that later. If you need to make any changes, call me... And Steeg, I really appreciate your call. We have so much to discuss. Thank you. Talk to you soon. Take care."

A brief but annoying dial tone followed the message, then dead air. When Steeg wiped a trace of sudden perspiration from his brow, his hand trembled. Then, after a few seconds, he pressed the button to replay the message just to hear the warmth of her voice once more.

Less than two minutes later he busied himself reorganizing small groups of paper on his desk before he weakened once more and picked up the phone receiver. Listening to the message a third time, he painfully accepted the fact he didn't have the strength he needed to overcome his addiction for Gracie.

Chapter 35
"Hell-o, I love you, won't you tell me your name..."

April 26, 2006

What am I doing here?

Steeg looked at his wristwatch for at least the third time since he had parked under the huge oak a half block east of Gracie's house. Less than five minutes had passed and their scheduled noon lunch was still a solid two hours away.

Idiot.

It was a chilly, on-again, off-again rainy morning. The old oak trees towered overhead along the boulevard on both sides of the narrow street, their spring greenery already full and growing. Cars parked bumper to bumper along both curbs, making the narrow street literally impassable for any two-way traffic.

Through his rain streaked windshield, Steeg had an unencumbered view of the attractive wrought iron gate and the front steps leading up to Gracie's classic old brownstone. He knew he was lucky to find a spot this close and he wasn't about to give it up unless an opening even closer became available, or unless his bladder demanded relief. If that were necessary, he knew where he had to go. Earlier he had used a restroom in a McDonald's off Clark Street two blocks west.

It had been a week of weak excuses. First, there had been the excuses with Carol. *"It's a trade conference, Carol. I need to go to these things if I want to keep any business coming in."*

He hadn't lied, he simply didn't tell the whole truth. His omissions ate away at his gut. *So, what was I suppose to say? "Carol, Sweetie, I have to go to Chicago so I can see my old high school girlfriend, maybe help her realize the terrible mistakes she made, maybe have sex with her, and maybe, just maybe, have her confessions of undying love for me convince both of us to turn our backs on our respective domestic situations so we can live the rest of our lives together in wanton carnal debauchery!" Right, Steeg, that would have gone over real well.*

He tried to remember his marriage vows, wondering if there was ever anything in them about always telling the truth, the whole truth, and nothing but the truth. If not, it would be of some comfort. Knowing the "whole truth" statement was not included in the vows – implied, perhaps, but not specifically stated – was something he had convinced himself of during the long drive from the Twin Cities.

Then there were the weak excuses to Harvey the first day of the tradeshow. The opening day show traffic was heavy and welcomed. After everyone returned from lunch in good spirits, Steeg figured it was the best opportunity for announcing he had an appointment the next day and wouldn't be at the show.

Harvey's good mood sustained him. "Well, if you have to, you have to. We could use you here, though."

Harvey's too plump daughter, the budding company marketing communications specialist, was less secure. "But, if you're not here and Daddy gets tied up with people, I don't know what to do! Daddy, he has to be here!"

Before Harvey could comfort his offspring, Marty Scetchmeister, the company's too long-in-tooth sales engineer, offered his input. "No, he doesn't. He's an ad guy. What does he know, anyway? No offense, Steeg."

"None taken," Steeg smiled, knowing full well Marty didn't care for him enough to be concerned about offending him.

"You go on your little appointment," the sales engineer said. "We got it covered here."

Tradeshow; appointment; lies, all lies.

Gracie and Debra had moved near North Chicago's Roger's Park area in late 1989. Back then, from his relatively close proximity of Whitewater, Wisconsin, Steeg had followed their progress from the old rental house on Clifton Avenue to their purchase of a century-old duplex brownstone within walking distance of the Loyola University campus. Since that time, the two women had made slow, laborious progress on a major remodeling of the place, contracting out the heavier projects to convert the building from a duplex to a single housing unit. The remodel required first the completion of the lower level offices for Gracie's psychotherapy practice where she would conduct her patient and group therapy sessions. The rest of the remodel of the living spaces was so extensive the two women had to vacate the place for several months, renting an apartment on nearby North Broadway Avenue for a short time.

He thought back to those days of two-hour road trips between Whitewater and Chicago; casual drive-bys to see if Gracie was there; hours of empty, binocular-assisted surveillance from the shadows; the too few moments when he actually saw her come home, or leave in the evening too late for him to wait for her return. Thinking about it now, he cursed himself.

God, she screwed me up so much. What an idiot!

Suddenly, real exhaustion overcame him. He leaned forward, his head resting on the rim of the steering wheel, feeling something akin to his life-force draining from his body.

This is not a good idea. This whole lunch thing, getting together, seeing each other again; the most that could come from it is complete desolation of my family. What in hell am I doing?

"You promised." Gracie's voice triggered his well-tuned obligatory reflex.

Yes, I promised. I promised. I promised, but you're asking me to do something I can't do. You expect me to catch you so you don't fall when you leave your lesbian lover. What does that require of me? Once you're safe, what do I have left? I can't do this, Gracie. It will destroy Carol in the process. I just can't.

Her words echoed in his head. "You promised me... promised me... promised..."

Steeg looked at his wristwatch once more: only an hour and forty-five minutes to go.

Still heavily overcast, the rain had stopped a full half hour before Steeg walked through the front gate, up the short flagstone walk to the concrete steps of the front stoop. He could hear the three-toned chimes from inside as he pressed the doorbell button. Next, he heard the hurried bounce of many feminine footfalls coming down a staircase. He couldn't keep his mind from remembering the same sound years ago when he was young, waiting in her parents' house for Gracie to come down from her upstairs bedroom. He was pulled back to the present when the deadbolt lock of the heavy paneled oak door was thrown and the door swung open.

Her face beamed with the funny, impish smile he remembered too well. Seventeen year-old Gracie Ofterdahl stood before him and he scooped her up in his arms in a tight, desperate hug.

"Thank God," he whispered sincerely as he held her close and buried his face tightly between her shoulder and the base of her neck.

She hugged him back with appreciation and then released her hold to step back, a broad smile showing how pleased she was to see him again.

Before his eyes the seventeen year-old was replaced by a much older Gracie; still slender, even athletic in the way she moved, with the same smile that had always captivated him so. Surprisingly, her hair, still brown but much shorter now with gray streaks, was an explosion of bushy spikes, much different from when they had met the previous fall. She wore an ensemble of black boots, black denim jeans, matching denim jacket over a deep purple button-down collar dress shirt unbuttoned at the throat. For Steeg, it was a startling transformation. He hoped his shock didn't show.

"You want to come in?" She asked still smiling.

He was momentarily concerned as he noticed the fine wrinkles at the corners of her mouth and eyes.

So what? He dismissed immediately. *I've got wrinkles, too, and I'm fifty pounds heavier than when I was in school.*

He stepped into the foyer. To his right an arched entry led to a front room with bare, plaster-less wood lathe where walls should have been, a dusty floor of cluttered and exposed subfloor slats, and several piles of building materials stacked in the corners. To his left a wide staircase led to the second floor.

"You're still remodeling, I see," he said, too late to stop himself. He caught her eye fearing he may have tipped her to his spying of seventeen years earlier.

"Afraid so," she admitted with a light laugh, oblivious to Steeg's slip. "Finally getting around to the main level."

"Well, that's good," he said, inwardly relieved she hadn't picked up on his gaff and amazed she and Debra had apparently lived for so many years in a house constantly under reconstruction. "You got time to show me around, or should we go eat?"

"Let's try to beat the rush," Gracie suggested, moving quickly to his side and steering him by the elbow through the front door.

At the top of the stoop, her hand fell easily into his, just as it had so many times when they were younger and in love. He couldn't deny the thrill of her touch, in fact, he welcomed it. The pleasure flooded over him as he intertwined his fingers with hers. Gracie returned a quick, smiling glance, equally returning the pressure of his touch. But as they took the first step down, something about the too-intimate moment made him release the hold. He immediately moved his hand to the small of her back in an empty chivalrous gesture of protection as they continued down to the walkway.

Gracie hadn't missed his hand pulling away from hers. In the moment it happened, her fingers reflexively reached for his, but she caught herself. Instead, she gently grasped the sleeve of his jacket for support she didn't need until they reached the boulevard sidewalk.

Steeg scolded himself. *Good God, what's wrong with me?* To Gracie he said, "You know, there's a diner just a few blocks away on Clark Street. You want to go there?"

"Yes, that's fine," Gracie said, reinforcing her smile just a little. "Good food and I've got a 1:30 I have to be back for anyway; the closer the better."

Silently resenting the limited time he had, Steeg led the way across the street to his parked car, dodging a light sprinkling of raindrops just then resuming after a short respite.

The diner was three-quarters full and they easily grabbed a comfortable booth at a street-facing window. The waitress was younger then both of them by several decades, with curiously styled hair colored in blue, black and platinum blonde streaks, a disturbing metal stud through one corner of her upper lip, two more smaller studs at the end of her left eyebrow and a rather large tattoo of something female with flowing tendrils covering her left arm from elbow to wrist. She placed plastic covered menus in front of them.

"How are you guys doing today?" The waitress asked pleasantly enough but with some obstructed difficulty due to the metal stud in her tongue.

"We're terrific," Steeg replied honestly. He smiled back and wondered what had compelled the young woman to mutilate herself so thoroughly. "And, how are you?"

The waitress returned a humorous smirk and a casual shrug. "What can I say, it's a job. In real life, I'm an actress."

"Ah, 'The world is but a stage, and we are all but players,'" Steeg offered in pleasant homage, confident the actress would appreciate it.

The waitress missed it. "Huh?"

With a half-nod, Steeg apologized as he explained, "It's from Shakespeare. No big deal."

Grace casually interrupted.

"What's your special today?"

The waitress shrugged. "The whole front sheet of the menu, I guess; the soup is chicken noodle and we have chili, of course."

Steeg raised an eyebrow in interest. "Chili? Does that come with cornbread?"

"No."

"Breadsticks?" Steeg followed up.

"No."

Steeg was running out of appropriate chili accompaniments. "Saltines?"

"No, but we do have crackers."

Gracie's hand quickly found her mouth as she tried unsuccessfully to stifle a giggle.

"Ah, crackers," Steeg was relieved. "I'll take the chili, then, with two packets of crackers, please."

The waitress dutifully wrote down Steeg's order on her pad and then turned to Gracie.

"I'll have your pulled pork sandwich with chips, please."

The waitress nodded, turned, caught herself and then turned back. "What about drinks?"

Gracie ordered a coffee and Steeg did the same, adding two glasses of water.

When the waitress was well out of earshot, they leaned toward each other, breaking into subdued laughter they could no longer contain.

"She didn't know you were quoting Shakespeare!" Gracie giggled. "An actress who doesn't know Shakespeare?"

"Bless her heart," Steeg felt sorry for the young woman. "She doesn't know Saltines are crackers. It's so painful you have to laugh or you'd cry."

Her giggling subsiding, Gracie asked sincerely, "Why do these things seem to happen only when I'm with you?"

"I don't know, but it's pretty obvious why you live in Chicago. The whole city is a goldmine of whacky people ripe for your psychotherapy practice."

Gracie agreed. "Yeah, well, you may have a point. But she reminds me of the time you and I were at a restaurant and you made me laugh, I think, or something happened that was funny, or something…"

"It's hard to remember what with so many restaurants to wade through. All I ever did was feed you."

She looked away briefly, her face reflecting for only a moment an expression he preferred to interpret as regret. Her eyes returned, but not directly to meet his.

"So, why did you want to see me?"

Her open question caught him off guard. He silently chastised himself for not expecting it.

"What do you mean?"

"Well, you said you wanted to meet to get caught up on things: what things?"

Steeg hadn't heard her question. He had fallen suddenly deft to everything around them when his eyes locked onto her damaged earlobe. He was struck speechless by the fact her earlobe wasn't damaged. The lobe wasn't torn, it was whole again. Her earlobe had been surgically repaired; completely normal with only the smallest single, pale scar as evidence she had ever had an injury there. Real fear began to build in his gut as his mind raced trying to recall if her earlobe had been that way when they met in November. He mentally pictured her in the Hiawatha Diner, distinctly remembering seeing her ear still scared and damaged. That couldn't be. It didn't fit.

Aware his silence had lasted too long, Steeg's voice was cheerless. "So, tell me, when did you have your ear fixed?"

Self consciously, Gracie reached up to lightly run her fingers along the edge of her ear. She quickly relaxed. "Oh, yes, that. I had to have the work done. It's silly, really, but it was affecting my business. My patients would become so distracted by it, the sessions would suffer."

He still needed an answer. "I see, yes, but, when did you have the work done?"

Her eyes narrowed with an unspoken question. "Well, several years ago…"

As if falling through a long tunnel, Gracie was pulled far to the opposite side of the diner. Steeg fell into a cascading vortex of spinning confusions. He could see her talking, her lips moved but he heard nothing as his mind struggled to make sense of a sudden new reality; the true reality: he knew at that moment the late night meeting at the Hiawatha Diner on Thanksgiving eve had never taken place. It had all been a hallucination.

Looking down to the far end of the tunnel, he could see Gracie still talking, her voice now an indiscernible jumble of echo against echo. All the while, real fear moved up from his gut to tighten its grip across his throat.

If it never happened, she isn't leaving Deb. She doesn't need my help for anything. She doesn't need me at all.

The echo took on improved definition as the tunnel grew smaller and Gracie moved closer.

"… But, I can't remember where we were at the time, can you?"

His blank expression in response to her question told her he was thinking of something else and most probably hadn't heard a thing she had said. Gracie shook her head and apologized.

"I'm sorry, Steeg, for all my small-talk. I'm avoiding you. What did you want to talk to me about?"

Help me, Lord. Steeg blinked to clear his head, leaned forward just a bit and opened his mouth: his words fell forth with very little effort.

"Carol and I have been married for more than twenty-seven years. We have four kids, all brought up to be strong, Christian people, self-reliant and hard working – that's probably why they're all screwed up..."

Gracie chuckled. "I doubt that."

"No, really, it's a factor, I'm sure. You never really know if you've been a good influence or a bad one when it comes to kids. It's very scary, being a parent..."

The actress/waitress returned at that moment placing their lunches and coffees in front of them and then walked away without asking if they wanted anything else. Straightaway, Gracie went for her sandwich. Steeg sampled the chili, wincing slightly at another sudden abdominal flare that in a blink put him off the dish completely. He opened one of the Saltine packets, shoved a single cracker into his mouth and hoped it would quell the distress before it got too bad.

As Gracie chewed, she waved her hand in a tight loop to urge Steeg to continue.

Steeg picked up on her signal. "So, anyway, there's another very scary thing about marriage: it's very scary when you reach a point where you realize, because of the reasons why you did what you did way back in the beginning, your entire marriage is false. You realize getting married was quite possibly the biggest single mistake of your life."

Gracie swallowed hard, sat back and looked at him, her expression a peculiar mix of clinical detachment and sadness. She said nothing.

"You see, Gracie, when you marry someone, you're supposed to give your whole heart to the other person. If you don't, you lose so much, I can't tell you."

A shallow nod of acceptance came from Grace, her clinical detachment growing.

"Let me tell you a story – a true story," he continued. "Long ago, when I was a high school student, I met a cute little brunette with the deepest brown eyes I had ever seen. As soon as I saw her and fell into those incredible eyes, I lost my heart to that young girl and I never got it back.

"We were together for a while. Then, I went to war and she went to college. She got married. She divorced. I came home and we met again. I behaved badly…"

Painful recollections brought a quick wince to her face as Gracie interrupted. "No, you shouldn't think…"

"No, not badly," he corrected, raising his hand to silence her. "Very badly. I hurt her, again. She left, again. I must be a slow learner because it took me several years after that to realize I had to find someone to be with if I was to ever have a normal relationship with a woman. I prayed to find that woman. I met Carol and I was convinced she was God's answer to my prayer. Maybe she was, but the truth is, with my hidden agenda, my marriage to her and all we have shared, was false. I didn't marry her because I loved her; I married her to get over you. When that didn't work, I allowed my Gracie fantasies to convince me I could manage well enough and continue our lives together without consequence or harm. But I'm a poor manager. The migraines became worse; more sleepless nights; blind rages would take me over, uncontrollable fits of anger coming from some place I didn't know; years of this, over and over again, each time more severe than the last. It wasn't until recently I found out why all this crap was happening. Like I said, I'm a slow learner. The common thread to all of it was you..."

A shadow of hurt and disappointment crossed her face, but Gracie quickly recovered. Steeg noticed and just as quickly relieved her of any responsibility.

"Not 'you' but my version of you; the ghost of you; the 'you' I constructed from memory; the 'you' I depend on so completely. It is that 'you' that has caused me so much disappointment only a few alternatives are left for my trampled psyche to handle the consequences of it all. I either get rid of you, or I get rid of Carol. The way I see it, either way I lose."

The silence between them forced Gracie to look down at her hands clasped together on the table. She flexed her fingers open and closed several times as she considered what to say in response to all that Steeg had just shared. She could talk with him as Gracie, a woman he needed to see now. Or, she could be the cool, collected clinician she was, a well-practiced persona she used with every one of her patients. Inside, she felt something stir, a feeling she had not allowed herself to feel for a long time; a feeling she couldn't allow now.

She looked up from her hands and their eyes met. "I'm not saying you should leave your wife, Steeg. I am also not saying you shouldn't..."

Steeg stopped her. "I'm not looking for your instruction, Grace. I'm intelligent enough to figure out that if the shoe was on the other foot, if things were reversed and it was Carol going through all this instead of me and I found out about it, I'd leave her like that." His fingers snapped harshly startling Gracie. "I'd turn around, walk out and never look back. If it were you, wouldn't you leave?"

"Like I said, Steeg, I'm not saying you should or shouldn't leave your wife," Gracie took a cleansing breath before continuing. "But, what I do think would help you, and I really hope you consider it, is therapy. Do you have a therapist?"

Steeg blinked several times before a small laugh followed a shallow shake of his head. "No, Grace, I'd be too embarrassed to talk to a therapist about any of this."

"You're talking to a therapist now."

His laugh eased to a steady chuckle. "Are you saying you want to be my therapist? Wouldn't that be a conflict of interest, or something like that?"

Gracie looked away as she shook her head. "No, I can't be your therapist. We're too, too…"

"Close?"

"Entangled," she corrected.

"Good word," he agreed, his chuckle fading to a serious, tight-lipped smile. "It wouldn't work, anyway. I'd let you do it just to be close to you. I'd have designs on you; I'd want to take you away from Debra so you and I could be together. I'd use you to feed my delusions."

Grace sat back, growing too uncomfortable not to let the cool, detached clinician facade cover her like a shroud. Safely assimilated, she uttered a disconnected observation. "I'm trying to help you, Steeg. You need help. I can make some calls; find some people closer to where you live."

"Maybe," he accepted with regret. "I appreciate the concern, but you see living without a heart is like living without an arm, or without a leg. After enough time goes by, you get used to it. I lost my heart to that little brown haired girl in the high school gym. I'd have to get it back before I could possibly care enough to accept your kind offer."

Steeg reached out, held his open hand toward her and waited. Gracie looked at it, then back at him, the clinician in her calmly in control saying nothing.

Steeg withdrew his hand, retrieved his coffee cup and took a short sip. "You've barely finished half your sandwich."

Coolly, she nodded in his direction. "You haven't touched your chili, either."

Steeg gently moved the bowl away. "I'll ask the actress to put it in a 'doggie bag' for me."

"Not hungry?"

"Stomach problems," he admitted with a slight frown. "One of the newer things, I guess."

He saw Grace quickly glance at her wristwatch.

"You said you had to be back by 1:30," he reminded her. "We've plenty of time yet to get caught up on 'stuff'."

She fidgeted a bit with her napkin only to elect to take another bite of her sandwich. A potato chip followed the bite. A sip of coffee followed the chip. She could see him watch her as she ate and it made her more uncomfortable.

"Well, you may not be hungry," Gracie explained defensively. "But, I didn't have much of a breakfast."

"Perfectly understandable," he smiled, motioning her to continue. He knew whatever Gracie had expected from this little get-together, the course of the conversation had changed into something she hadn't counted on. He, on the other hand, had looked forward to the meeting convinced he was going to help her start a new life as a straight person!

Fool!

His sudden bursts of laughter made her look up from her lunch, wondering if she should be offended. "What's so funny?"

"Motives," he answered, poorly collecting his composure. He brought himself under control. He had questions that needed answers. "Gracie, I have to ask you something, and I really need you to be honest with me. Please, can you do that for me?"

"Of course!" She shoved what was left of her sandwich into her mouth and chewed it down with some assistance from her water glass. "Shoot!"

Another burst of laughter as he felt the familiar bulge nestled in the small of his back reminding him he was indeed 'armed and dangerous'.

"Why are you laughing like that?" Gracie asked uneasily, obviously perturbed.

"Motives," Steeg repeated once more. "I'm sorry. I'll try to be serious now, because this is serious: Gracie, in all the time we have known each other, did you ever really love me?"

The reality in his question made her more uncomfortable. Suddenly she knew she didn't want to help him. She looked at him, feeling the threat of his emotions and said nothing.

Steeg continued. "I mean, I know how I felt about you: when I was with you, it was like I couldn't breathe. When I was away from you, I couldn't think of anyone or anything else. It felt as if you were always with me. Did you ever feel anything like that for me?"

Mentally, she wrapped the clinician demeanor around her more tightly, resisting the part of her that wanted to answer him, knowing the best thing she could do at that moment for both of them was to simply let him talk.

He didn't wait for a response. "In sales, there's a saying: 'Silence is acceptance.' In my experience, however, silence usually comes from someone who doesn't want to hurt your feelings by saying 'no'. So I'll take your silence as a 'no.'"

Her lips parted as if she wanted to say something. Instead, she stopped herself and pressed her lips tightly together.

He followed with another question. "But, that doesn't explain things very well, does it? That doesn't explain what happened when I came back after the Service and we met; then we worked together at the 'Teens-In-Crisis' hotline. It doesn't explain the night I spent with you in your bedroom. Why did that happen? You were already involved with Roger Flint and yet, there I was in your bed. Why?"

Around her eyes, with the smallest of flutter, Steeg saw the clinician's shroud fracture just a bit.

"And long before you left for Boston, the afternoon we were walking across the Washington Avenue Bridge toward the West Bank of the campus when, like a complete buffoon, I blurt out that thing about Kelly Nulf and me. You tried to hide it, Grace, but I saw the tears; I saw the pain in your face. It hurt you, deeply, didn't it? It wouldn't have hurt you if I didn't mean something to you."

"We were younger then," Gracie coldly replied looking past and not at him.

"Okay, then, let's look at something when we were older: Chicago, twenty years ago; remember? We have a nice night with dinner, a little automobile tour of the Chicago lakefront area. I was respectful, concerned for you and how your life was going. Oh, I may have had a few tempting thoughts, but I didn't act on any of them; not me; not good old dependable Steeg. Of course, there was that little bombshell about how you were cultivating a new lifestyle with Debra, but I believe I handled it reasonably well at the time. At the end of the evening when I dropped you off, you laid a kiss on me like I've never had before or since. I can still feel your tongue halfway down my throat! If you didn't love me, where did that come from? What was behind that kiss, Grace? Tell me, cuz I gotta tell you, I took it for another solid gold confirmation you still loved me as much as I still love you. It's important for me to know. Am I wrong?"

Gracie pushed against the tabletop with both hands, steeling herself against the clinician shroud ebbing away. "I don't know what you want from me, Steeg. I really don't know how I can help you, but you obviously do need help."

Steeg repeated more firmly. "Am I wrong, Grace?"

She looked at him only long enough to shift her gaze to the wall behind him, then to the window, and then to people walking passed outside.

More quietly, Steeg leaned forward and asked once more, "Am I wrong?"

Now she looked down; her fingers casually swept a few scattered crumbs off the tabletop and onto the diner floor. She looked up to him once more, but she couldn't hold it. When she answered it was again the clinician he heard.

"At the time, both of us crossed over some moral boundaries we probably shouldn't have. If that caused you some discomfort, problems of one sort or another, I'm sorry, but living in the past isn't an answer either, Steeg."

He persisted for an answer. "Am I wrong, Gracie?"

The corners of her mouth turned down as she bristled at the question he refused to let go. "I stay in touch with many people I used to know from high school and college. You're not unique, you know. My other friends, my true friends, love me for real, not pretend. They love me for the person I am now; for the person I have become, not a made-up version of someone they want me to be."

He was going to ask the question one more time, but he stopped himself. There was nothing he could do to force her to honestly answer him if she didn't want to. Nor could he force her for an answer she couldn't give even if she wanted to.

He half-reached across the table and pointed to direct her attention to her wristwatch. "It's almost twenty after, Grace. It's time to get you back."

Chapter 36
The Revelation

Steeg could feel Gracie's body stiffen as he gently gave her a parting hug at her door.

She really resents me, he thought, an odd sense of desolation beginning to hollow him out on the inside. Strangely for him, at that moment humor mixed with the melancholy of his final acceptance the two of them could never salvage anything good from their relationship, not even a relationship. The thought tripped a silent laughed inside as he released the hug and looked with all the love he still held for her. *Let's see if she'll let me kiss her.*

She didn't. His small move toward her was immediately met with a cool turned cheek, to which he softly delivered a small peck he would have given his mother had she been alive. He pulled away to look at her, her hand limp in his, returning nothing. Somewhere, somehow, during their brief lunch, he had said something that had hit a nerve. If so, it was curious he couldn't recall it. All he had wanted to know was what she really felt for him. She wouldn't, or couldn't, answer even that one simple question.

He smiled as he gave her hand a small squeeze. "Thanks for taking the time."

Her face was a mask of calm neutrality. "Of course."

Steeg turned and walked down the steps. Over his shoulder, he offered, "I'll be upset if you visit the Twin Cities and don't at least call."

She almost allowed a smile. "You take care."

She was in the house before he reached his car.

It was just after 4:00 when Steeg met Harvey and his daughter at the show floor reception. A double vodka martini in hand because he felt he needed something to untie the knots from that afternoon's gloomy festivities, Steeg elbowed his way through the throng surrounding the bar to a bare patch of carpet where the two Hellmans stood.

"So, how was your meeting?" Harvey asked in greeting.

Steeg took a second quick sip before answering. "It was surprisingly non-eventful in a disturbing kind of way. How was the show?"

"Better than yesterday, wouldn't you say so, JoAnn?"

The young Ms. Hellman nodded wide-eyed and speechless.

"So, you didn't miss me, then?"

"Not at all, did we, JoAnn?"

Harvey's daughter shook her head, her eyes wide and unblinking, again saying nothing.

Steeg leaned in closer to Harvey. "Cat got her tongue? Or, was she that overwhelmed?"

"Both," Harvey whispered mildly irritated.

Steeg smiled as he steered Harvey a few steps away for a private word.

"Harv, unfortunately, something has come up that requires my attention and I have to go home. I'm sorry, but I can't stay for the final day."

Harvey frowned. "Is it serious?"

"Yes, and personal. I'm sorry."

Harvey didn't like the idea of Steeg cutting out on him like this, but things had gone well enough that day with Scetchmeister and him handling things so there wasn't much necessity for Steeg to stay.

"Well, if you have to go, Steeg, you have to go," Harvey acceded. "We have more to discuss, though. Let's meet again at the office on Monday, okay?"

Steeg agreed without reservation as he took two gulps to down half of his drink. He placed what remained on a bus tray, waved his goodbye and headed toward the door.

Debra Sperre, several years older than her life partner, Grace, was looking forward to her Social Security kicking in within the next few years. She dearly loved Grace for many reasons, not the least of which was Grace's ability to earn a consistent income. For as long as Deb had known her, Grace had worked hard, first to earn her PhD, aggressively plugging into the matrix of social service groups catering to the Gay-Lesbian-Bisexual-Transgender community of greater Chicago in the process; then, with her degree in hand and with awe inspiring determination, Grace willed life into her fledgling private psychotherapy practice. All the while, Grace had worked to pay her own way while supporting the domestic situation the two of them shared. It wasn't until they decided to purchase the brownstone near Roger's Park that Deb knew she had to secure regular, gainful employment if they were to qualify for financing. And so, through contacts Grace provided, she landed a job with the county welfare department. She was over qualified for a position of menial responsibilities, long daily hours filled with tedious and repetitive paper pushing duties, but the extra money made the brownstone possible. Now, almost two decades later, they were still only two-thirds completed with the remodeling of the place. She had grown to hate two things about the never ending remodeling: the pervasive dust coating everything everywhere and all her beautiful artwork stacked in piles against the walls of the spare upstairs bedroom.

It was 5:45 when Debra came in through the backdoor and leaned toward the stairs leading down to the lower level where Grace's office and the small kitchen were.

"Grace, you down there?" Debra asked with a raised, mousy voice that barely carried.

"Making some tea," she heard Grace say pleasantly enough. "I'll make some for you if you want."

Tired, Deb accepted the offer. She shouldered her satchel and trod heavy-footed downstairs. A few minutes later, the two of them were seated in the polished honey oak warmth of Grace's office, sharing some kind of liquid herbal concoction purchased from a local food co-op.

"So, fill me in," Debra began expectantly, taking a seat in a facing chair. "How did today go?"

"It's not over yet," Grace said, easing back in the softness of her padded vinyl covered desk chair, wishing the stress away with a slow sip of freshly brewed tea. "My 8:00 o'clock group is tonight, remember?"

Debra frowned. "I'm not talking about your clientele. How did it go with your old boyfriend?"

Grace resisted the irritation as she felt the sadness return. She softly place her cup on a cork coaster near the corner of her desk. "What can I say? He's older. He's changed… He's the same."

"Did you sleep with him?"

Debra's blunt question brought Grace's eyes up. Without malice or defense, she answered. "Of course not, he's a married man. I do have some boundaries."

"Yes, you do; some."

"What can I say? He's a man. Worse than that, he's a spiritual man; a man who believes God actually answers prayers. Men like that are too dangerous. They take chances they shouldn't."

"That's interesting," Debra observed coolly. "He must have pushed some buttons, then."

Reflexively, Grace's hand wiped away a small gathering of moisture from the corner of one eye. "We talked about the two of us. Actually, he talked about me mostly. In many ways, he's quite insightful."

"Insightful for a man, you mean," Deb mused. "Did he like your new outfit and haircut?"

A sad smile revealed much as Grace ran her fingers through her short sheared locks. "He didn't comment one way or the other, a little disappointing considering how much effort I put into it for him."

"Do you think it worked? Do you think he 'bought' it?"

A pall of sadness came over her as Grace recalled their parting on the front stoop. After a long moment of unproductive effort, she shook her head.

"No. Except for a chili lunch he ordered but didn't eat, Steeg didn't 'buy' anything."

Steeg was little more than an hour west on Interstate 90, the rain pelting his windshield with growing intensity when the laughing started. Everything seemed so silly, he had to laugh.

And, so, he did. He laughed longer and stronger with each rotation of the tires as his Buick sped along the rain soaked interstate. The more he thought about the events of the day, the more he recalled all he had ever felt for Gracie, the more he laughed. How could he be so incredibly stupid for all these years? What had she ever given him to justify such devotion?

He continued to laugh, laugh until his side started to hurt and tears rolled down his face so heavily he was having trouble seeing the road.

God, this is so funny!

And then, just as quickly, his hands shook the steering wheel, his chest heaved with heavy gasps and his laughter changed to weeping. Incredible, torturous pain came from somewhere deep inside and flooded over him. His entire body trembled so violently, it was all he could do to ease the car off the road and onto the shoulder. Hands quivering, he fumbled to turn on the emergency blinkers trying to collect himself at the same time. He failed. The deep sobs continued for several minutes.

The immediacy of the change scared him as suddenly more prolonged laughter was upon him, laughter he couldn't control.

Lord, what's wrong with me? What's happening?

The laughing fit continued, bringing more tears he wiped away, only to have them replaced by tears from another sudden surge of deep pain and something new: the real fear his sanity was slipping away and he was losing his mind.

"No, no, no," he kept repeating, gripping the steering wheel tightly, desperate to hold onto the very essence that made him whole, the very essence he now could feel slipping away. "Please, Lord, don't let this happen. Please! Please!"

Steeg pulled at his hair in desperation as he fell across the front bench seat and the car filled with terrible screams when yet another prayer went unanswered.

It was five hours past nightfall and still raining when Steeg turned into the thinly used roadside rest outside Tomah, Wisconsin. The car mirrored what was left of his sanity, almost limping into an isolated parking space deep in the shadows at the far end of the facility. He turned off the engine to sit in silence, numbed by hours of physically draining emotional torture that had both punished and cleansed him until he had nothing left to scream about. Exhausted now, he felt only defeat and so very tired of everything that was his life.

He needed sleep, but when he closed his eyes, the noises in his head kept sleep from coming. He reached down below his left side and pressed the button to lower the back of his seat. Nothing happened.

Cursing his stupidity, Steeg reached for the key still hanging from the ignition, turned it to the 'accessories' position and tried again. The back of his car seat eased into a lower more comfortable reclined position.

He cursed his stupidity again, reached behind and pulled the Smith and Wesson Model 60LS 357 magnum revolver from the belt clip holster at the small of his back. He held the pistol up and looked at it.

It was a beautiful handgun, really; finely crafted stainless steel with a polished narrow wood grip rounded at the bottom. Lightweight at a little less than a pound and a half and small with a two and one-eighth inch barrel, he remembered he hadn't liked the weapon when he first saw it. The 'LS' model designation was short for 'Lady's Special' and, as far as he was concerned, he deserved at least a man sized canon like a 1911-style 45 caliber automatic, the kind John Wayne had in "The Sands of Iwo Jima". The salesman talked him out of that idea when Steeg explained he intended to carry the gun concealed behind him in his lower back when he wore a suit coat or, like today, a light windbreaker for the damp weather. The Model 60 was a perfect choice.

He laid the handgun on the seat next to him and stared out the window to watch the rain as he tried to make sense of all that had, and hadn't, happened that day. Nothing made sense. The more he tried to reason away a lifelong succession of bad decisions made for what he considered to be at the time good and noble reasons, the more he knew he hurt more than helped those closest to him. This was especially true for Carol. She had married a man who was, at best, only half a husband to her. The half-husband she had put up with for nearly three decades had abused her in ways he only now could see. The weight of his shame was unbearable.

He had no other place to go and he knew he couldn't go home. Since his collapse outside Chicago, he had stopped at more gas stations and roadside cafés then he could remember. It bought him time to think: think poorly, he knew, but think nonetheless. He couldn't go home. Yet, he pressed onward across Illinois, then north into Wisconsin to the next exit and another stop, inevitably heading toward Minnesota.

Why? What's the point? To continue the lie? To put her through more hell? That's what it would be, hell, because if she knew the truth it would destroy her. Congratulations, Steeg, another life ruined.

More than two hours passed before the rain let up. The lack of patter on the windshield drew his attention to the outside where he could see the vacant open table shelters shrouded in darkness matched only by the darkness of his own soul. Morbidly Steeg reasoned a shelter would be a good place for what needed doing without soiling the car. He left the keys in the ignition and walked steadily to the second shelter, took a seat facing away from the table bench, his revolver in his hand.

The Model 60LS cylinder only held five rounds, but they were hollow points so they'd do the job well enough.

Besides, he thought dryly, oddly detached from what was about to happen. *I only need one of them.*

He pulled back on the hammer until it locked with a loud click. He brought the muzzle up tight under his chin, hooked his finger over the trigger, took a deep, cleansing breath and squeezed the trigger.

Steeg froze. A whisper, calm and disturbing, stopped him. He turned his good ear slightly to one side. A single word tumbled from his mouth.

"What?"

The whisper repeated, slightly more distinct this time but Steeg couldn't make it out. The voice came from all around him, but no one else was there.

"What you are saying?" Steeg asked, his hand shaking to hold a gun suddenly double in weight.

The whisper became such profound substance it sliced right through him.

"What you intend to do does not honor Me."

Steeg's mouth quivered as his eyes clouded over with tears. The reality of who he heard shook him to his core. All strength left him. The revolver was heavy beyond bearing, pulling his hands down between his knees, hanging momentarily before slipping from his fingers and sliding harmlessly to the pavement.

Steeg followed, rolling from the table bench to collapse in a heap. He hid his face in shame.

"I'm so sorry!" He cried. "I only want her to know how much I still love her but the pain is more than I can bear."

The voice touched him deeply with so much real love, Steeg's whole body quaked. "You are feeling what I feel for the whole world."

Prostrate on the ground, Steeg covered his head with his hands and wept bitterly. "Forgive me, Lord, forgive me. I did not know."

"Then know this," Steeg heard the love in the Voice say. "As my Father is in me, so I am in you, and you are in me, also. And I am with you always, even unto the end of time."

The truth of the revelation punched the air from his lungs and sliced deeply into his soul. Steeg couldn't resist raising his face to look up because he knew the Voice.

It was the bartender.

Chapter 37
Going Home

September 14, 2006
San Mateo, California

For the fourth straight day, breakfast in the hotel dining room reserved for the *Hornet* Reunion attendees was served buffet style, but it was just too excellent for Steeg and Carol Patterson, or Paul and Sue Muggins to complain: perfectly prepared hot scrambled eggs, cheesy hash brown potatoes, two types of breakfast sausage, bacon, Belgian style waffles, bagels, several types of breads freshly toasted while you wait, a variety of fruit, yogurt, several dry cereals, fruit juices, whole milk, incredible coffee and more accompaniments than any one person could possibly put on a single plate.

The dining room, with draping pulled back from the large, expansive windows, was bathed in bright morning sunlight. It was 7:30 and most of the four-place tables were filled with early rising Navy veterans of three different war eras joined by their spouses, children, grandchildren, even great grandchildren. The table Steeg, Paul and their wives shared was located just left of center in the middle of the floor.

"The second best scrambled eggs I've ever had," Steeg confessed, shoving a second forkful into his mouth, quickly following it with a bite of buttered rye toast.

"Oh, so you've had my scrambled eggs before, then?" Sue Muggins smiled.

"No, mine," Carol offered kindly.

Steeg agreed. "I'm sure your eggs are terrific, Sue, but Carol makes the best scrambled eggs anywhere… I have to say that, you know."

Both women shared a perceptive laugh as Paul shook his head in disagreement.

"I said it before, and I'll say it again: good scrambled eggs need to be runnier, more liquidity; more like what we use to eat on the ship!"

A confusion of banter, more laughter and guffaws rose between the four of them and then subsided. Reaching for Steeg's coffee cup, Carol left her chair for the coffee urn at the far end of buffet table, returning shortly with a full, steaming cup in each hand, a saucer balanced on the top of her cup holding a single Danish pastry.

"I have to try this," she said as she placed Steeg's cup to the right of his plate. "They look so good!"

"Thank you, Sweetie," Steeg said, taking a quick sip.

"So, you guys still leaving this morning?" Paul asked.

Steeg nodded. "Yeah, we're taking the hotel shuttle to the airport; probably around an hour from now."

Paul shook his head. "Too bad. You're going to miss the big feed tonight. They always have entertainment, too. You know, dancing girls with limited talent dressed in skimpy outfits, that kind of thing…"

Sue swatted at her husband's shoulder in a half-hearted rebuke and Paul chuckled.

"Well, it sure sounds like fun, Bear," Steeg replied with regret. "But, we've still got a business to take care of, not to mention a thirteen year-old daughter who thinks she's, oh, maybe, thirty-one? Bobbie's been subjected to a daisy-chain of rotating siblings every night since we came out here just to make sure she doesn't throw any wild parties for her hormone-infused friends or burn the house down."

"Ah, teenagers," Paul mused. "You remember teenagers, don't you, Honey?"

Sue nodded with a wry smile.

Paul continued. "Yeah, teenagers: Hell on Earth. I'm amazed you were able to break away for as long as you did."

"She's a good girl," Carol added softly in defense of her youngest child.

"Yes, she is," Steeg agreed, pushing his not-quite-finished plate away. "It's her friends I don't trust."

"Well, you'll be missed," Paul said sincerely, raising his orange juice in a salute. Steeg respectfully returned the toast by raising his own juice glass.

"Alcatraz was interesting," Carol noted, referring to the tour they had shared the previous day.

Sue somewhat agreed. "Kinda depressing, I thought."

Steeg was more reflective. "The *Hornet* was amazing. Everywhere I looked brought back memories so alive, so real, it was chilling. I have to go back there; maybe next year. We'll have to see if we can make another trip out here."

Bear's eyebrows arched in awareness. "It's haunted, you know – the ship. It's loaded with ghosts. People say they actually see them walking around, down the passageways, going through the bulkheads room-to-room."

Steeg and Carol shared a knowing glance. The corner of his mouth curled up with an understanding grin.

"It's true, Paul. I've seen ghosts there myself."

The hotel's airport shuttle was a comfortable conveyance with upholstered bench seats, tinted windows and air conditioning. Steeg and Carol settled themselves into a bench on the port side one row aft of the rear axle as more people continued to enter the bus. Individual seat backs reclined, so Steeg adjusted his slightly back for a more relaxing position. Carol adjusted her seat back to match his.

"How are you feeling?" She asked, visibly concerned.

He covered her hand with his to ease her concern. "I'm okay, Sweetie. It's a good day, today."

Since Chicago, Carol had been his rock. He had returned a changed man, emotionally drained yet spiritually supercharged, defenseless yet empowered knowing that there was no more time left for lies. The bartender had taught him that.

It was late when he entered his home the night following his roadside rest stop encounter. Bobbie was sleeping in her room and Carol was already in bed, as usual reading a book. He walked in, quietly sat on the edge of the bed and resisted the need to hold her hand until after he told her everything about Chicago and Gracie Ofterdahl. He knew chances were more than good she would leave him once she knew, and so telling everything was a struggle unlike anything he had experienced before. But, through frequent tearful starts and stops, tell it all he did.

"And, that's it," he finally concluded. For the entire time he talked Carol's eyes hadn't left him once. "I have no excuse, only that I met her years before I met you. I had hoped you'd be able to replace Gracie, but my own weakness wouldn't let that happen. I don't deserve it, but if you could forgive me, I promise I'll never intentionally lie to you again."

Carol hesitated and then asked just one simple, painfully difficult question.

"In all the time we've been together, Steeg, have you ever cheated on me?"

He caught only half of the painful laugh. *Have I ever cheated on her? More ways than I can count! Scripture says a man who simply lusts after another woman is an adulterer. I've cheated on Carol so many times and in so many ways, I can't possibly profess faithfulness now.*

Yet, when his eyes met hers, he knew what Carol meant by her question. Had he been fooling around behind her back with Gracie? Had he had sex with Gracie?

Steeg shook his head. "No, Carol. I never cheated on you; not in the way you mean."

It was Carol's hand that then reached for his. Their eyes met and he saw the miracle of all the love she still held for him.

"Steeg, it's okay," she squeezed his hand tightly. "You can love Gracie, too."

He fell into her arms. She embraced him, holding his head close to her chest, and that night the healing began.

For several weeks afterward, every day Carol and Steeg talked about all the things they had never before talked. In some way that surprised him, the talking nourished both of them. On a warm early June evening, they relaxed on the back deck with some iced tea, discussing matters even more.

"The bartender," she asked. "Are you certain he is who you think he is?"

Steeg was certain, but he acknowledged he may be wrong. "Well, if we accept what the neurologist Dr. Fong referred me to said, the bartender could be just another incredibly real hallucination. Doc says the damage from my brain injuries is permanent and I will probably have hallucinations for the rest of my life. But I don't believe the bartender was a hallucination. I believe He was real, perhaps more real than anyone else could ever be. That night at the roadside rest, I asked Him why I had held onto Gracie for so long to cause all of this to happen. It was amazing what He did. Somehow, He revealed to my mind something I had forgotten – He revealed Puerto Rico."

Carol shifted in her deck chair and leaned in closer. "What about Puerto Rico?"

"It's not pretty, the things he reminded me of," Steeg warned. Her slow nod indicated he should continue. "I was twelve. We lived in Puerto Rico for eight months while my dad worked on a hotel construction job in San Juan. That summer I fell in with a small group of teenaged Puerto Rican boys who were friendly at first. It didn't take long for that to change. You know little kids: curious, naughty, excited to explore the beginnings of their own underdeveloped, immature sexuality. That was me at the age of twelve. At the time, I thought the other boys were the same way – a little naughty but innocent. I was wrong. One day, we played 'Doctor' at the house of one of the boys. His parents worked, so there was no one else there. My new friends grabbed me, held me down and took turns raping me. I tried to fight them off, but they were fourteen, fifteen, even a sixteen year old and so much bigger and stronger than I was. After they were done, I felt so guilty and ashamed. Somehow, I knew I had brought it all onto myself. After all, I had been 'naughty' to begin with, encouraging them to do what they did. I was to blame. I couldn't tell anyone. The only thing I could do was stay away from the boys I had thought were my friends."

When Steeg looked at Carol he saw the pain in her eyes.

"I'm sorry," he apologized to her. "I don't mean to hurt you, but it's important you understand this. If it had ended there, maybe things would have been different. But it didn't end. They found me, threatened to harm my sisters and parents if I didn't go with them. So, I went. When the school year started, every day they waited for me at the bus stop. They would surround me and take me to the house where they did things, things that became increasingly more terrible. They called me their 'baño' or sometimes their 'lavado' or 'inodoro' – Spanish for bathroom or toilet. When they finished, they let me clean up in the 'baño'. They were very good at making sure I had no bruises and my clothing was undamaged. This went on more or less every school day the entire time we lived in Puerto Rico.

"It messed me up, big time. Confused, I didn't know what kind of person I was. I only knew I didn't want to be that kind of person. I didn't know how to behave, especially around other boys. Around girls I was completely lost, doing stupid things and getting in trouble because of it. As a teenager, the stupidity didn't stop, it only got worse. I did hurtful things with girls because I was so desperate to not be what the Puerto Ricans had shown me I was.

"It was all pretty hopeless. And then, I met Gracie and everything changed. More than loving her, I needed her. She was the one person who showed me I was a good person. She proved to me I was normal. She loved me and she had captured my heart so completely, I could see being only with her forever.

She was my salvation from the horror of what I thought I was. I couldn't let her go."

He felt Carol squeeze his hand again, compelled to reassure her husband. "You are a good man. Don't ever doubt it."

He laid his hand onto hers and smiled. "That's how I know who the bartender is. No one knew about Puerto Rico. I never told anyone. I had shoved it down so deep even I didn't remember. But the bartender did. In an instant He revealed it all to my mind at a deserted roadside rest stop. I know Him. I know who He is and I am blessed because of it."

She moved closer, feeling the warmth of his body against hers as she placed her head on his shoulder. "But a bartender? Why a bartender?"

"When you think about it, it was perfect. It was where He knew I would be."

They talked for several hours that night on the deck after the sun had set. Somehow the words they shared washed away all his pain.

The shuttle driver closed the door and shifted the bus into gear. The passengers jerked in their seats as the vehicle emerged from under the hotel front canopy to follow the sun drenched curving drive toward the frontage road.

He heard Carol's sniffle.

"And now, you're going to die on me?" It was more a statement than a question.

Steeg reached around her shoulders, pulled her close and made a poor joke.

"Well, at least the life insurance is paid up. You'll be almost wealthy."

She gently poked him in his side. "Not funny."

"You're right, it's not." He gave her a reassuring hug and kissed the top of her head. "I think it's His call, Carol. You know, it's funny when you think about it. The *Hornet* almost killed me before – three times and it failed each time. The darn boat's not going to succeed this time, either. Besides, He told me He has work for me to do."

The End

ABOUT THE AUTHOR

Frederick Loeb was born in 1948 in Houston, Texas. This is why Fred doesn't smile all that often. The person who took the photo you see to the left asked Fred to smile and this was as good as he could do at that time.

Fred earns his living by writing and producing business promotions. He enjoys the work and has been doing it since 1993. Should you be interested in hiring Fred for a business promotion project, you can contact him through Steve Culpepper at email address *writeright@earthlink.net*.

A father of four grown children, half of whom periodically attempt to move back home, Fred lives with Lynn his wife of 32 years in the small town of Jordan, Minnesota. Founded in 1853, Jordan is a very pleasant town of less than 6,000 inhabitants, although there are way too many antique shops.

Fred also likes to write stories. The Patterson Chronicles' *Gracie's Ghost* series, volumes 1, 2 & 3 are his latest efforts.

* * *

Want to read more Loeb stuff?

Check out the first two volumes of the *Gracie's Ghost* series!

Available for order at better bookstores everywhere.

NORMANDALE COMMUNITY COLLEGE
LIBRARY
9700 FRANCE AVENUE SOUTH
BLOOMINGTON, MN 55431-4399